Call
Me
Anorexic

THE

BALLAD

OF

A

THIN

MAN

For anyone who has ever struggled with an eating disorder.

Call Me Anorexic

THE BALLAD OF A THIN MAN

By Ken Capobianco

Part One

Everything is Broken

One

Call me anorexic.

No, don't worry, this won't be another I starved myself silly and returned from hell, so live in the moment and count your blessings adinfinauseum kind of book. Leave that for the self-help pseudo gurus. Let's get it out of the way, and state things upfront: I was hell-bent on self-destruction and completely batshit obsessed. I didn't try to take down a great white whale—I simply believed I was one.

I honestly don't think I'll ever fully know why I just couldn't eat like a normal person. I guess if you want to find out more about anorexia, go look it up under A on WEB MD—it'll give you the technical jargon, small details, and psychiatric diagnosis for people with the desperate need to starve themselves into oblivion. Maybe you can ask other survivors. They may be more reliable. You know, if you keep looking for answers, you'll probably find experts and doctors with great insights and useful, pertinent observations. And if you really get lucky, you just might come across grand revelations about why a waist is such a terrible thing to mind.

Me? I can only give you my story.

Sometimes, the past rushes in, and I remember everything as if it all happened yesterday, and sometimes the years seem to blur together. While the timelines often get confused, the one thing I know for sure is my entire existence was consumed with the desire to disappear. All the events and all the stories—everything that made up what I called a life—had one common denominator: loss.

I do recall the very first time I genuinely understood I had a problem, and how it was destroying my life. I was sitting in Dr. Rigatta's office at Massachusetts Central Hospital when she asked, "Did you ever hear of the word anorexia before?"

I nonchalantly said, "Sure," because I knew a lot about Karen Carpenter. She was a girl, though, so I never thought anorexia might apply to me or my inability to eat. I was dieting.

Just before I tried to run out of the office door, Dr. Rigatta dragged me back. Her fingernails dug into my frail upper arm as she led me to the scale next to a stool. I stood rocking back and forth on the scale floorboard, imagining myself out on the sunny California surf.

Dr. Rigatta gingerly lowered those block weights until she recognized that the smaller weights measuring pounds in two digits were necessary. Her office, down in the old building connector of Massachusetts Central, had a musty, claustrophobic feel. There were no windows, so all the germs, diseases, specimens, samples, and whatever the hell else they sucked out of the rotting bodies of the sick souls of Boston, created this hovering, mind-numbing cloud of illness.

You could smell the decay, even though they tried to mask it all with alcohol. I hated going there. It was for dying people.

"Michael, look at your weight."

I glanced at the scale before redirecting to Dr. Rigatta's eyes. She had these large blue pupils with wispy eyelashes that fluttered uncontrollably when she got confrontational. So pretty. Very simple, nothing much to her really. She was what she was, but there was something about her that made me go back to her office over and over again. I went once every two months for a year to monitor my weight. Each time I left her office, she gave me lollipops as if I was a child. I sucked on them, wracked with guilt over the terrifying uptick in my daily calorie count.

As I maintained balance on the springy scale that day, Dr. Rigatta rested her hand on my shoulder blade. "Can you feel how thin this is?" she said before pausing to let me think.

"Do you see what I see?"

"What?" I answered stupidly.

"Michael, look at the scale and not at me, alright?" I took a long scan around the yellowing wallpaper at all her diplomas mounted on the wall and focused on the weights.

It was the space between ninety-seven and ninety-eight pounds.

This was the first time in my life I had weighed less than one hundred pounds.

"Ninety-eight," I said.

"Less, Michael."

"What's a quarter pound?" I replied, smiling.

"For you, too much." She spoke sternly.

"I'll pick it up at McDonald's," I glibly added with a quivering stomach.

"Don't joke. It's not humorous. We're not talking about a quarter pound, are we? You know that."

"Yeah but..." I couldn't believe I weighed ninety-seven fucking pounds, but I didn't let on to my fear. I had left my apartment that morning feeling bloated, stabbing at imaginary loose flesh hanging over my jeans while standing on the trolley heading from Park Street Station to Mass. Central. I thought I was gaining weight, and there I was, weighing no more than a fat fifth grader.

I stepped off the scale and struggled to breathe.

"Next time you come back Michael, you are going to be at one hundred pounds. At least. Do you hear me? I'll check your pockets for large rocks and stones too. And don't bring much loose change." She wasn't smiling.

"Are you listening to me because I'm going to recommend hospitalization if this doesn't change?"

"I hear you I really do," I said. I heard her words but absorbed none of them.

That morning I had told Jessie I was tired of worrying about my weight and looking in mirrors. Jessie said, "Michael, I know you always say that. You can't do it alone, though. Just go see what the doctor has to say about it."

Ninety-seven pounds. What the doctor had to say was, "Michael, you are anorexic."

Dr. Rigatta wasn't going to let me out of her office without a lecture. "Listen, what you're looking at is something that kills women and men left and right, Michael. I'm not being dramatic, but of all the disorders we have, this is the one with the highest mortality rate. Now granted, it's considered rare for men, but with our culture there are no absolutes, and men are suffering from anorexia more and more.

"You are going to have to get on the stick. I can get you hooked up with a good therapist. You don't have to suffer in silence." She looked me in the eyes and said, "You have to understand the magnitude of what you're facing."

"But I'm not suffering," I quietly replied.

"You are in denial. What does your girlfriend say when she sees your skinny arms?" She grabbed my right forearm, tugging me closer.

"She just lets me be," I said because Jessie did just that.

"She won't for long. I know I wouldn't. Something is going to change. You know things can't remain the same. You are disappearing before her." Her eyes turned to slits.

Dr. Rigatta was certainly prescient, but very, very wrong. Yes, of course, Jessie disappeared first.

When I first met Jessie, she asked me why I was dieting. I told her I wanted to get down to my original weight…nine pounds, seven ounces. She laughed. She left.

It was the old BLT served up cold. Baby's left town. A blues lament performed around the world many times before. When I first heard it, though, everything changed irrevocably. In fact, how the song was played probably saved my life.

Jessie left a few years ago, months after that visit to Dr. Rigatta. Maybe, it was a bit longer. I don't know for sure—it's often easier to let time drift away. Memories fade in and out, the early years bump heads with the later ones, incidents repeat, they color other ones in, they evaporate. Like a dream or a nightmare, faces come and go in my head and remind me of an earlier time when things were very different.

You have to understand, it was just a few weeks before Christmas when Jessie walked out of my life, and I really didn't see it coming. I guess I was just too fucking dense to see that she had long checked out of our relationship, but I knew something was unusual because Jess hadn't sent out any invitations to our annual Christmas party.

That was not the girl I knew. She'd usually get out her address book during Thanksgiving week and make sure invites were in the mail by early December.

Something had changed—I figured it would pass. But I was always figuring. Problems always surfaced, and I just ignored them until they dissolved. I had other, more important things on my mind.

On December 7, yes, a calamitous day we all know too well, I asked Jessie to go to Lox-a-Luck, a deli putting on Sunday night concerts in the hopes of turning into a music venue. Bagels and blues. When your world is missing a center, the blues will set you free. Jessie told me she was too tired, so I decided to head into the bitter cold night anyway.

A group of local musicians were playing an acoustic tribute to Morphine in a benefit concert. It was something I couldn't miss because Morphine was my favorite band. I stood alone in the back of the crowded room listening to music amid the baked goods until around one in the morning.

When the show broke, I picked up a few bagels for Jess before making the short ride home through the frozen morning.

By the time I got the balky heater working in the car, I had already found a parking space on Commonwealth Avenue about five blocks from our apartment. The walk up the stairs winded me, and I paused before opening the door. When I entered, Jessie was sitting in the dark in the front room. I couldn't hear very well with the saxophone still ringing in my ear, but it sure sounded like she was crying as the door creaked behind me.

"Jess?" I whispered.

There was no answer, so I turned on the light. Sure enough, her eyes were red-rimmed as she snorted back tears. She nervously tapped the outer edges of the photo albums on her lap while steam blew from the old, upright radiator by the far wall. I dropped my coat behind me onto the floor. I was going to be the knight in shining armor and make up for all the fuck-ups she was probably crying about. Penitent for unknown crimes, I got on my knees to put the bagels down. The room was transformed by the smell of Lox-a-Luck—the bagels' aroma was powerful and intoxicating.

"Jessie, what's the matter? Please tell me." I hoped this could be resolved easily.

"Michael, sit down please."

Across the street, a college student was dancing naked while decorating his Christmas tree. He was setting the end of a string of popcorn on the lower branch near a green blinking light. On the wall behind him was a framed print of *Blue Velvet*. I watched him randomly toss tinsel up to the branches and winced when he came perilously close to the tree bristles.

"Look at me alright, I have something to tell you," Jessie said with a yank of my sleeve.

The blue, red, and green lights on the guy's tree flickered on and off. It was such a pretty scene.

Jessie sucked back tears. "Let me get you a Kleenex," I said magnanimously.

"You mean tissue," she replied. There was bitterness in her voice.

"It's all the same."

"No, they're not—you call tissues Kleenex. You always did. They're not all one brand. It's wrong."

"I'm sorry. I don't see why it matters," I said. Who cared what they were called?

"No, you're not, but get me the box anyway."

She blew her nose while asking, "How was the show?"

There was a short silence before Darlene Love's "Christmas (Baby Please Come Home)" exploded from the apartment below. People played music at all hours of the night in our neighborhood. It was all part of the nonstop Allston noise in our lives.

"Michael, I'm leaving," Jessie whispered.

It didn't register. "You want to go inside? Where you going? You mean for Christmas?"

She squinted at me. One tear popped out of her left eye as if squeezed from a Visine bottle.

"I'm leaving for good."

"For where?"

"For good."

"You mean for bad, for us it's bad," I said as it slowly kicked in. I could feel the rapid beats of my heart against my chest. It was the same feeling I had when I didn't eat during the day.

"Maybe, I don't know, but it's something we both know must be done," Jessie said.

"I don't know that. I really don't," the words just tumbled out of my mouth.

"You don't know anything these days, Michael. I just can't take this anymore. This may be a selfish move on my part at this point in your life, but I've got to do something for myself. To stay sane. I'm done. I'm leaving. And I'm just so, so sorry." Her eyes were glassy—tears dripped off her eyelashes.

I didn't react as I braced myself against the wall. Small trickles of sweat slowly fell down my chest. There are times in our lives when our bodies understand the true nature of a situation before the mind fully absorbs it.

"Can you just sit down? At least say something," Jessie said.

"What do you want me to say?"

Limp and dazed, I ended up collapsing on the couch. I wasn't angry because I didn't believe she was going to leave. And I certainly wasn't sad because, well, you don't get sad right away, do you?

"There's more," Jessie said as I rested my chin on the palms of my hands.

"What could be more?"

"I'm moving in with Les," she fired back.

The words must have come out of her mouth, but to this day I don't think I heard them. I was still working on the first part, the leaving.

I asked her to say it again. After she immediately obliged, the right side of the back of my neck stiffened. "Les?" I asked, barely able to say the name.

"Yes."

"No, no."

"Yeah, Michael, yeah."

"You're absolutely fucking kidding me," I laughed absurdly in a shrill tone, like a dolphin mocking tourists.

I stared back out the window toward the prancing, decorating neighbor, still stark naked and holding a beer. He was ungainly fat—like a mini Buddha. I unconsciously nodded as he raised the bottle in a toast towards me.

"You and Les, this is a fucking joke, right? You're trying to get a charge out of me," I yelled.

"Just sit down and absorb it because I can't live a life like we are living. It's not really a life at all. I'm tired of floundering. You've got to understand," Jessie said, reaching out her hand as if she was singing "Stop, in the Name of Love."

"Les?" I whispered to myself. We sat in silence for a few seconds before she put the photo albums in the few bags she had already packed.

"Where you going?" I said before finally standing up.

"I'm going to meet him at the Colony Motel. The number's on the bulletin board if you need me," she added dismissively.

"You are going to the No-Tell motel with him. You mean he told Patty?"

"He told Patty tonight," Jessie said with her back turned. Patty was Les's live-in girlfriend and Jessie's best friend. When Jessie and Les pulled the pin, they sure knew how to blow up shit up in a big way.

"Coincidental timing. Jessie c'mon, you can't be serious. I mean, are you sure about this?"

"No, but when are we ever sure of anything? If I did only things I was certain of, I don't think I would get out of bed," she said, shaking her head.

"So, you are going to walk out that door and move in with my best friend, our best friend?"

"Yes. You mean to tell me you didn't see this coming? It just confirms to me the kind of space you've been in, Michael. You are too busy looking in mirrors for imaginary fat to see what's in front of you." She dropped her bag on the floor and faced me.

"Michael, you know I've always really loved you, but it's time for you to understand what is happening, what has happened to you. There's a big world beyond your quest to out-Kafka Kafka. You need to find better heroes in a hurry. You want to be the perfect hunger artist, but you have to do it on your time from now on. I've had enough," she said before picking up the bag once again and walking away.

As Jess yanked the doorknob, I had this grand vision of her tossing the luggage and saying it was all a big mistake. She would act just like all winsome lovers do in those movies with the happy endings you can't resist even though you know they're all pure Hollywood bullshit.

The door closed behind her. Yes indeed, she was shacking up with Les.

I sat down in the still-warm chair Jessie had vacated. It was a small measure of comfort. I picked up the bag of bagels I had brought home, opened it and took a deep breath. The sweet onions and garlic smelled so good—my eyes began to water.

Two

Ah yes, Jess and Les, Les and Jess. Of course, I should have known, but let's face facts, it's often easy to overlook the things right in front of your eyes. That is if you are paying attention.

I met Les a few years before Jessie decided to move in with him. Both he and Patty were our best friends, comrades in arms, and confidantes. It took me a while to get used to Les's odd rhythms of speech and moody ways—sometimes he spoke as if he was constipated—but I genuinely came to like the guy despite his crusty ways. Patty forever remained a chilly enigma I never even attempted to figure out.

As a couple, they seemed to neuter each other's worst tendencies, which made it easier for all of us to go out as a foursome. Les was an obsessive retro folk music and Bob Dylan fanatic. We would spend afternoons together, analyzing music while shopping for books, going to movies, and aimlessly browsing through the Museum of Fine Arts.

From the very first time he walked through our apartment door, though, it was eminently apparent Les could be Jessie's guy in alternative universe. How could I tell? Well, some things you just feel it in your gut, and during those years, my gut never, ever lied.

It was a cold November evening when he first entered my life. Jessie and I were holding a Trivial Pursuit night at our place. It was just an excuse for Jessie to have friends over. We did dumb shit like that in our years living in Boston. She would invite a group of people, and we'd all sit together in our cramped apartment, pretending to have a good time. I was never comfortable with others, so I usually felt like an outsider looking in at the festivities.

Les and Patty were the last guests to show up at the party after all of the couples had already settled. Some friends had brought pages of poetry to read during breaks in the pursuit of the trivial. Les arrived wearing a long, black overcoat—the type Jessie had been badgering me to get—and a black beret. As he took off his coat, the many scarves he wore swayed from side to side. He stripped them off slowly while gently giving Jessie each one. A royal blue silk scarf remained swept over his shoulder.

"Damn, another freezing Boston night. Dressing in layers is the key to surviving in this city," he said.

"Never go out. That's the key, I'm convinced," Patty smirked before waiting for Les to remove the remaining winter gear. She handed him the homemade apple pie she was cradling. Patty was just as thin as I was at the time. Her arms looked like dry tree twigs, and her pants hung down low on her ass—everything just sort of fell off of her.

"Fresh apple pie, baked just for you," Les said.

He extended it to me, slurring, "Don't take offense, I know how you eat, or don't eat. Jessie told me all about that. I'm just joking. Hey, I would never bust the balls of a Dylan fan."

He nodded to the pie with a wink. "She takes just like a woman, but she bakes just like a little girl. I know that's awful, but what the hell, I've already been drinking."

Les thought I loved Dylan as much as he did because Jessie once told him I owned *Blood on the Tracks*, which my brother David gave me as part of my ongoing musical education. But I was never a Dylan-ologist like Les, who was prone to quoting lyrics at every opportunity.

Jessie rushed over to Les and Patty and gleefully hugged each one as I looked on. "I'm glad you guys are finally meeting. C'mon and join the party."

She abruptly pulled me aside by the arm. "Michael, your brother came in when you were talking with Les and Patty."

"David's here already?" I said aloud to no one.

"Unfortunately," Jess replied with a forced smile. "Did you tell him about the party? Why?"

"I told him that we were having people over, and…"

"He invited himself?" she snapped.

"No, he just said that Monique was going out, and he had nothing to do, so why not?" I immediately knew the night might go sideways, just as others had fallen apart when Jessie and David spent too much time in the same vicinity together. I guess it would be easy to say Jess always had David in her crosshairs, but that would be putting it much too politely. She just fucking hated him ever since the first day they met.

After slinking away, Jess went to work as the circulating, ingratiating host, passing around hors d'oeurves and bottles of wine, even though our budget demanded paint chips and Gatorade. We were barely getting by, struggling to stay afloat in the run-down part of Allston, where you could get a one-bedroom apartment if you didn't mind living with roaches, broken window casings, elongated, jagged cracks in the ceiling paint, and floorboards that spoke their own languages whenever you walked on them.

A group of people I didn't know—apparently, they were new friends of Les and Jessie—were sitting in a circle, organizing the game board and drinking.

"Are you reading poetry or playing?" Les said with a mischievous grin.

"I might play but no poetry, c'mon, that's pretty ridiculous, no?" I replied as he shrugged nonchalantly.

"Jessie always tells me you don't always like to participate," Patty said, leaning in.

"She didn't really, did she?" Even though it was true, it didn't sound like something Jessie would say behind my back.

Les opened a bottle of wine while standing next to me. "I won't ask you about the eating thing. I'm sure you get enough of that." Actually, I didn't. No one asked me about it because I usually avoided situations in which I had to eat with other people.

"It's okay, you can ask what you want. I just don't eat much," I replied.

David stepped in and reached his hand out to Patty and Les. "I'm David, brother of the thin man. I keep trying to make him write a mystery novel. No one's ever thought of it." Les and Patty offered polite hellos before backing away as if he had herpes lip. I was sure Jess had already debriefed them on her contempt for David.

Jess called us all together to announce that some cards in the game were missing, so it was pretty much going to be ad hoc pick a question without strict rules.

Patty walked away just as David grabbed me by the shoulder. "Is this really the kind of parties you have? Michael, seriously, I might have to disown you. Board games and poetry? Fucking awful. Is somebody going to knit a sweater? This is kind of like a circle jerk where no one comes."

"Leave it be, David. Jessie likes to get her friends together. She thinks if I meet a lot of new people, it will help me get out of my own head. I don't know, she believes I won't obsess, and eat more."

"Well, she may be right, but I think you need a real shock to the system instead of this bullshit. Mike, you better fucking eat because I don't like these skinny arms.

"I gotta tell you, Monique is always asking about you, but she says she doesn't want to intrude and, frankly, I try not to either. But if I have to kick your ass, I will." He tilted his head sideways to make sure his point came across. There was a faraway look in his glazed eyes.

"Are you high?'

He laughed dismissively. "Not right now, but I smell joints in that room, and it won't be long."

"You still don't smoke, do you?" he added while ripping open a bag of potato chips.

"No, I want to know what I'm doing or saying. When people get high, they say the stupidest things. I can't be that guy."

David held out one chip before my lips with his left hand. "Can I give you communion, my son?" he said, smiling slyly. "You know maybe getting high would help you eat. You could forget about things, and get happily, stupidly hungry."

"Stop, you know it's not gonna happen. I could not live with myself if I woke up after a binge."

"I'm not sure how you live with yourself now," David said. "There's more to life than controlling the fear to lose control."

I could smell the funky, skunky weed drifting throughout the apartment as my brother downed a Heineken.

"Not in my world."

"Michael, look around you. This small one-bedroom apartment in Allston is your world. You have a master's degree, goddammit.

You should be out dominating. You know you deserve better. Listen, I'm glad Monique and I moved closer to you, but I really still don't understand what's going on. How did you get so fucking crazy with this weight loss thing?"

David placed a potato chip in my hand. "You worry about getting fat when you are in your fifties, not your twenties. Eat and exercise. You are still running, right?"

I had cut down on my daily running because I was getting winded too quickly. After one mile, it felt like I was staggering through the streets of Allston.

"Yeah, I'm still running, no problem," I answered confidently.

He shook his head. "I'm not sure what to say. You want to worry about your body, then get strong. Get powerful. Get a body you can be proud of. Eat, and get ripped. Don't stop eating."

I tossed the potato chip I was holding on the table. David simply offered me another. "Now I know you can eat just one."

I crushed it in my palm.

"Okay, you know my motto has always been live and let live. But you realize I did move back here to keep an eye on you."

"Don't you dare fucking say that. You can go back to San Francisco. That's insulting. I can take care of myself." I didn't like the notion that I owed my brother something for coming to Boston.

David had moved cross-country with his wife, Monique, months earlier because he said he needed fresh ideas for the novel he was trying to finish. He got a teaching gig at Brandeis University and was invited to curate an exhibit on the history and artifacts of the blues at the Institute of Contemporary Art.

Boston also was also a short commute to Manhattan where Monique had a loft and an office for her burgeoning skin care company. She frequently traveled back and forth while transitioning out of modeling. So there was no doubt in my mind that there were many factors beyond my extreme weight loss motivating David's move from San Francisco, his home for many years.

My brother had been a music critic since he sold a piece to *Rolling Stone* when he was eighteen. Even though his great love since childhood was soul music, he was among the very first writers to bring rap to the attention of the mainstream. He constantly traveled around the country in search of the next great MC or DJ. His long profiles helped break a number of artists wide.

Once he started publishing, David's productivity often made me dizzy. There were two collections of criticism by the time he was twenty-eight, and he just kept turning books out. His exhaustively researched biography of Sam Cooke was a critical and popular success. The voice of that book was foreign to me, controlled and careful, and so unlike the sharp-tongued tone of his music criticism, which was closer to the boisterous David I had known and loved so dearly.

His biggest success, though, came with his first novel about a famous rock star who descends into madness right after recording his masterpiece. It was optioned by Hollywood and turned into a slick film featuring a bogus love story and a sentimental ending. David was so nauseated by the changes that he asked the producers to come up with a new title and change the characters' names.

They just told him to go fuck himself and, of course, the movie became one of the year's highest grossing films—he ended up cashing out with a huge payday.

After his experimental novella about a glammed-out pop starlet's sexual obsession with her boyfriend's Great Dane flopped, he and Monique relocated to Boston. The move came as such a surprise—it immediately created a fissure in my relationship with Jessie. The change disoriented me because I found it extraordinarily difficult readjusting to David's presence in my life again. Unfortunately, he reminded me of everything I wasn't, and probably never would become. He'd married a model, won a National Book Award, and was now living in a beautiful condo in Beacon Hill.

I had dandruff.

But David was always my best friend despite the nine-year age difference. He was a father figure when I was a kid—telling me what to do, and how to do it. When he left home to go to college, I felt abandoned and thought he had disappeared for good. It was irrational, but we believe what we believe. And at that time, that was my truth.

Life has a very odd way of circling back on you, though, and the truth seems to change every day. Once he arrived in Boston, we immediately became inseparable again in an attempt to repair the sacred bond I thought was broken.

"I guess we better get in there," I said to David as he dipped five potato chips into a bowl of sour cream set out on the table.

"I bet one of these trivia geniuses is going to ask why sour cream has an expiration date," he said with a grin.

"Just come in and sit with me, it'll make Jessie happy," I was almost pleading.

"Oh, bullshit. I think Les makes Jessie happy. You see the way she looks at him?" he whispered.

"I didn't notice."

"That's because you have your head up your ass half the time." We walked into the main room with everyone gathered. "You know Monique really wanted to be here because she loves nonsense like this sometimes, but she wanted to see The Pogues more. They're playing Avalon tonight."

"And you didn't want to go with her?"

"Who needs to see a bunch of drunk Irish assholes with no teeth in Boston? I mean, I'm surrounded by them all day now," he said before stuffing his mouth with more chips.

"And you let your wife go alone?" It seemed absurd to me.

"She wanted to go, and I didn't. When you are married, you make choices to stay sane."

"I don't know about having someone like Monique alone at Avalon."

"Michael, I'm not worried. We've been together long enough. She'll always be beautiful. I can't follow her around. And for fuck's sake, she certainly doesn't want me to. She's a big girl."

"And big girls meet big guys," I answered with what seemed like perfect logic.

"Says the little, vanishing man as if he knows. Listen, if she's really going to cheat, it's going to be at a Wu-Tang show with three thousand black guys with horse cocks instead of with pale muthafuckers who make Joe Strummer look like Chris Isaak. Be serious."

"I admire your confidence," I said warily.

"No, you admire my trust. Different thing," he added with a flick of his hand. "Okay, when does this stupid game start?"

"I think now. I hope now. I beg now," I said. We both laughed.

Jessie had set up the game in the middle of the room. Les took a card and prepared to ask the first question to a disheveled guy in a Mao t-shirt. He had a paunch and thick oval glasses like Bill Gates if he got lost in a Twinkie factory.

I leaned over to Les, "Who's this?"

"Joseph, he's a flake. It's Jessie's old reading group leader." Jessie bounced from reading group to reading group after quitting her job at an art gallery on Newbury Street. I couldn't keep up.

"How do you know that?" She had never mentioned him to me.

"I asked. It's simple enough. You want some?" he replied, waving a joint in my face. When I declined, David took a hit.

Les looked at the card and pointed at Joseph, who put his hand up in protest. "I just want to say that since the cards are not complete, and we are doing this randomly, I don't think this is quite fair."

David broke into ostentatious laughter. "What in the world is fair? It's a silly trivia game. Can we just please play for Christ's sake?"

"Category is 'brothers,'" Les announced in a deep bass voice. I grinned towards Jessie, hoping she would appreciate the irony. She stared back grimly.

Les continued, "Name the only three brothers to play together in the same outfield during a baseball game." Everyone shuffled chips on the board with audible sighs. Of course, no one knew.

"The same outfield? See, this isn't quite fair. Outfield?" Joseph mumbled at David.

"Baseball, man. See the ball. Hit the ball. And the ball sometimes goes foul. Sometimes it goes...fair," David said without missing a beat.

"Oh, I know nothing about baseball," Joseph whispered with a joint between his lips.

David let out a long honk, imitating an air horn. It startled everyone in the room.

"That's a ridiculous question. Who would know that? Move on," Jess laughed while blowing an umbrella of smoke.

"I bet I know someone who has the answer," David shouted with hand raised.

"David, nobody cares if you know," Jessie barked.

"I don't have a fucking clue Jessie, but I bet your boyfriend does." All eyes focused my way.

"Michael doesn't know," Jessie waved dismissively at David.

"Five bucks, Jess. Michael, don't say a thing. Stare out the window and keep a poker face. My money is on you," David replied.

Jessie looked wounded, "Michael you know?" I couldn't believe she would have to ask. She knew baseball was one of the most important things in my life, but I also realized Jess didn't want David to be right. My brother threw a five-dollar bill at her as she smiled with a mix of stoned amusement and defiance in her eyes.

"You've been challenged, Jessie. Play or pay," Les said in his best mock game show host voice.

"I say nobody knows that. You're on." Jessie tossed a five on the floor. I was disappointed she bet against me.

Patty tapped me on the shoulder. "You don't know that, do you?"

David reached out to Les with an open palm, "Les, please hand over the money. Michael, the answer is…"

My stomach convulsed. "The Alou brothers: Matty, Felipe, and Jesus." The room turned quiet as Jessie asked desperately, "Is that right?" Les gave David the money, applauded and raised his hand to offer me a high five.

"Jessie, Jessie, Jessie," David teased. "Betting against your boyfriend. Sooo bad."

"Michael, why didn't you?" Jessie's plea made me wince.

"Why didn't he play dumb?" David interjected. "He may look like the scarecrow these days, but when it comes to baseball, I know he's the wizard, baby. And you know that too, Jessie. I win. I'll buy Monique a pint of chocolate Haagen Dazs, which she will eat in Michael's honor. Life's small pleasures."

"I'm impressed," Les mouthed to me. It was a hollow victory and self-defeating.

Patty picked up another card, looked around the room and told Jessie she was up to answer.

"Okay, okay, okay, I'm ready for this one," Jess stood, pulling off her sweater to reveal an old, faded black Bon Jovi t-shirt, falling past her slim waist. David laughed mockingly.

"Yes David, I still love him, sorry," Jessie teetered on her bare feet with joint in hand.

"No comment, but apology accepted by all rock music fans," David nodded. I considered putting a stop to the game once Patty announced the category. "I took rap music for Jessie. I don't like the others." Of course, Patty was clearly testing Jessie—they were always so competitive.

After taking a deep breath and stuffing a few Fritos into her mouth, Jess dramatically pulled her long blonde hair back while glaring at David. "You don't think I can get this, I know, but I can. I can. I'm a rap person. I know."

This was Titanic territory—Jessie hated hip-hop. "You get 'em, Jess," I shouted with half-hearted encouragement because I knew things were about to go from bad to much, much worse.

"Can't wait to see this," my brother said, grinning at me. Patty paused over the card. She spoke deliberately, stumbling on the name Tupac Shakur pronouncing it "Two-pack Shewker."

"Iconic west-coast rapper Two-pack Shewker had what phrase tattooed on his chest?" There was a small murmur in the room as a car alarm went off outside on the street. David stood to look out the window.

"Why don't we go onto the next question," he said before asking if anyone owned a black Volvo.

"Jessie, it's gotta be something with a muthafucker or fuck in it," Les hinted while smiling playfully and lighting a cigarette. "Something with fuck in it." He began laughing uproariously.

"Fuck something—it's rap and Tupac." He pronounced the name properly. "Gotta be."

Jess looked at him innocently. "You think so?"

"No, of course not, I'm just joking," he replied.

"Yeah, has to be fuck," David mumbled.

"Well, Jess?" Patty whispered.

Jessie looked to me, standing by the wall, before staring down Les. "I have to get this right." She talked to herself like a little girl trying to figure out what dress to put on Barbie.

Finally, Jessie shouted as if she had Tourette's Syndrome. "Fuck you. He had fuck you tattooed. It said fuck you! Tupac had fuck you on his chest. I will repeat. It was fuck you." Les offered her the end of the blunt from which she inhaled deeply. I couldn't watch her yelling anymore and retreated towards the doorway. I'd never seen her quite this stoned.

Patty arched her eyebrows. "That's your answer?"

Les turned to me with a shake of his head. "She's hardcore."

Jessie stood erect, small shoulders at attention. While intensely focused on David, she seethed, "Yeah, yeah, yeah, David I bet you know, but I bet I'm right, too. It's fuck you."

David edged away from the window to join the group again. "Jessie, tell everyone your answer instead of me. It's a good guess if it was Joe Pesci, but I think you know that's not right."

"And I bet you know Mr. fucking genius," Jessie said with crimson cheeks to David.

"You don't want to bet me. I know that's just a phrase. I can't take all your money," he replied with too much satisfaction.

Jessie spun towards me with broken eyes.

"So David, show everyone you know everything. Go ahead. Patty let him answer before telling us." The words just poured out of Jessie's mouth.

I squinted at David. I couldn't watch him rub it in, but he just shrugged, laughed and said, "Thug life."

With a nod, Patty slapped Jess's leg, "That's it, wow"

"Fuck you, David," Jessie yelled. "Fuck you, fuck you, and fuck fucking dead Tupac." Veins popped out of her temples, and her eyes were red and watery. It appeared as if Jessie was about to have a hemorrhage, but when I looked more closely, she looked truly exhilarated.

Three

I t took a good five minutes for Jessie to calm down after talking to Les and Patty and taking a few more hits of a new joint. David casually blended in with a few of the women who had arrived with Joseph. He was sitting quietly while shuffling the question cards next to a blonde sporting a k.d. laing-like pompadour and horn-rimmed glasses. She seemed amused by the night's theatrics, laughing and affectionately tapping David on the shoulder.

I disappeared into the kitchen to wipe down my sweaty arms with a paper towel. Jessie's yelling and stoned fury had exhausted me. My legs were giving way when David placed his hand on my back.

"Listen Mike, I think I'm going to leave. This is just not good," he said, dragging me to the table crowded with trays of food.

"No, don't bail on me now. I know this sucks."

"Brother, you have your friends and girlfriend, although I think she's on planet Claire right now. She is one royally pissed off woman. When is the last time you guys fucked? There must be a reason she's that irritating." His slight smile betrayed the anger in his eyes.

"She's just stoned and mad at you."

"You think? I'm telling you she's always angry at me as if I'm the orchestrator of her sadness," he said.

"I'll deal with Jessie, so just stay, please. Are you okay?" I asked.

"Me?" David looked startled. "Yeah, I'm fine, but I think you are filling your life with nights like this while ignoring much bigger issues. I'm really more distressed at how you look tonight. You look thin, I mean really thin. I'm hiding it really well, Michael, but I'm upset right now. Slightly stoned and upset. Not at Jessie. Fuck Jessie and her 'fuck you.' I'm upset at you. What have you eaten today?"

"I'm not going to give you an inventory. Let's not go there."

"I don't want one. Just answer me," he stared without blinking.

"Things," I said.

"Like? Just mention off the top of your head. Chicken? Yogurt? Soup?"

"Yeah soup?"

"What kind? Don't fuck with me."

"Listen, today was a tough day. I haven't had anything. I'll eat when everyone is gone." I just needed to placate him until he inevitably forgot about it all and changed the subject. We'd been through this routine before.

"That is not normal, man. No, it's just wrong—I mean how can you survive this way? Have you been going to your doctor?"

"All the time," I said. I wasn't seeing anyone.

"And what does she say?"

"She says eat."

"And you do this? I don't get it. You know I'm worried, but I'm lost. I keep waiting for that phone call from emergency saying, 'Come get your brother.' Every time the phone rings at night, I jump. Monique feels the same way. I'm worried, really worried. What will it take for you to get with the program of normal life?" He sat in a chair by the table only to stand again as if disoriented.

"I don't know," I said.

"Not a valid answer. That's for stupid people. You are not stupid, Michael, I know that."

"Let's leave it behind, David."

"You can't leave life behind. I want you to sit here and think of an answer because this is getting alarming." He stormed back into the main room. I struggled to maintain my balance as the walls spun before my eyes. Steam rushed out of the radiator, sounding like a sigh.

I stumbled into the bathroom to sit on the edge of the bathtub and hopefully regain my bearings. My arms were numb, and I was seeing double. Sweat streamed off my neck. These kinds of attacks had become a regular thing, but I refused to tell anyone—including, and especially, Jessie.

The muscles in my chest constricted—it felt like someone had placed an anvil on my breast. I tried to wait out the pain with my head buried into a towel between my knees. After a few minutes, the involuntary motions and quivering slowly eased. David's voice was audible above the music and collective laughter.

I stared into the mirror—my shirt was soaked through with sweat—while repeating, "Focus, focus…"

All I needed was to see straight, and somehow make it through the night. I crumbled onto the bath mat to sit in silence for twenty minutes until my vision and hearing completely returned. When I was finally strong enough to make my way back to the party, I casually sat behind Jessie to make it seem like I'd just slipped away for a satisfying piss. She leaned her elbows into my thighs for support.

"What did I miss?" I whispered.

"Les put on some music. You know the game was a disaster," Jessie's said, facing me. "Michael, your brother ruined this night." She grabbed my biceps after doing a double take. "Wait, you look terrible. Are you alright?"

I nodded repeatedly. Feeling slowly returned to my arms.

"Will you answer me?" she demanded. I watched David laughing with Les by the window.

"Feel your pants. Michael, what the?" Jessie squeezed my hand.

"I'm hot, alright," I could not let her know.

"No, not alright." She marched to the kitchen. "Michael!"

I jumped up, suddenly feeling renewed, and ran to her.

Everyone at the party was watching us as we stood together in the kitchen doorway. "You're sweating like a pig. You expect me to believe that nothing is wrong? The person whose body temperature is three degrees below normal? Who is cold in Provincetown in August? You are going to tell me you are hot? What the heck happened in the bathroom? You are sick, right? And you didn't eat." She wiped my face with a dish towel. "I'm going to get you another shirt."

"Jessie, let it be."

"No, no, no, this is not The Beatles. I'm seriously scared and frustrated. Is this what you want our life to be like?"

I waited patiently, listening to David laugh over the din of conversation. He always had the loudest voice.

Jessie returned with a U2 *Unforgettable Fire* t-shirt.

"I'm going inside with everyone, but I simply can't let this ride and watch you fade out on me. I don't think you recognize that." She paused before walking away, "You also don't realize your brother's an asshole. I told you he was coming to cause problems."

I sat by myself before the entire spread of cold cuts and salads. There were slices of ham and salami left over. No one had touched the bologna, which had turned splotchy gray. I fingered a few poppy seeds scattered on the table, placed them in my mouth, and immediately wondered how many calories I'd ingested.

"Hey Michael, get in here with us. Brother, don't get stuck by yourself. Be part of the party, right folks?" David boomed from the couch. When I entered the room, the small group was laughing while huddling around him. This was David, right in his element as the ringleader of the circus he somehow always managed to make his own.

"We've concluded after much bullshitting that nothing matters."

Les looked at him delighted. "And what if it did? Who was that in the '80's, David? You'd know?"

"It's John Mellencamp's line, but who cares? Nothing matters," David replied with a laugh.

Jessie rifled through the CDs and popped Nirvana's *In Utero* in the player at a low volume. It cast just the right mood for the acidic night filled with heavy eyelids.

David sighed. "I miss Kurt Cobain. I'll never understand that. Such a fucking waste."

Years before, he'd written a long, angry essay about the failed promise of rock stars who died young and the dangers of deifying broken pop culture idols. He'd always told me he'd become numb to so many senseless deaths, but I knew just how much Cobain's suicide had affected him. On the night it happened, David seemed to be in tears when he called me at one a.m. Soon after his appreciation appeared in *The New Yorker*, he told me it was the most difficult thing he'd ever written.

Suddenly pensive, he said, "Michael, this night demands a stiff coffee. Where's the coffee maker?" David quickly looked to the kitchen before shouting, "Anyone else for coffee?"

"I'm good with that and some of Jessie's crumb cake," Les said as Patty leaped out of the room. Les quickly moved on the floor next to Jessie. I watched them whispering and giggling like kindergarten Brutus and Cassius. There they were, conspiring right in front of me. You may be wondering how I failed to see my forsaken future. The answer is well, okay, yes, yes, of course, I saw it, but I just looked away. I mean really, what was I going to do?

I think everyone who loses something important knows quite precisely when and how it got away. We always see the loss coming. Somewhere down deep, it's there. All those years ago Ralph Branca must have known he was going to serve up that pitch to Bobby Thompson. Look at that grainy videotape. The guy walks off the field like a trooper. Not because he had dignity, but because he must have envisioned it. Dennis Eckersley too. Stare into Eck's eyes as he serves up the backdoor slider to Kirk Gibson, and you'll see total recognition.

Let's face it, Napoleon must have realized there was oncoming doom before Waterloo, and Dewey understood his fate the night before election day. And sure, MacArthur knew what would happen before he was stripped of his ego. That's why he could say he would return. Hell, we all return, only changed.

Cobain's pained voice drifted through the room as David fielded orders for coffee and dessert.

"Folks, we've got some homemade apple pie that looks killer, and there are sinful pastries from the North End. Man, I got to say, part of the joy of living in Boston is being able to get a North End cannoli," he said.

A smattering of those who remained straggled into the kitchen. As everyone ate, I snuck out the door and down the stairs into the night. I walked slowly up the hill in a t-shirt and jeans through the arctic cold towards the 7-Eleven a few blocks from our apartment. When I finally found refuge near the Big Gulp dispenser, the sweat on my legs had frozen. The Indian clerk, who had come to know me from my frequent visits, looked on sadly as I held a Diet Coke.

"No one drinks as much soda as you, my friend. Someday I want to see you buy food. Women like men with meat. My brother has a restaurant less than a mile away. You come to see him. We'll feed you for sure." He smiled politely before handing me my change.

I never remembered so many people telling me the same thing on the same night. I wondered if indeed there was some larger, grand, dark conspiracy.

Fuck them all. I knew what I was doing with my eating. No, I truly believed in what I was doing. And it was pure.

"Someday, someday, you hold that reservation for me. I'll see ya tomorrow," I said, heading back into the frozen evening.

"Fucking Boston, fucking Boston," I whispered aloud while imagining what it would take to simply get in a car and hit the open road without looking back to find a place where no one knew me. I'd never hear advice on what to eat and how to eat it.

Upon returning to our building, I realized my keys were still in the apartment. Luckily, our downstairs neighbor opened the main door, allowing me to slip in. As I staggered up the steps, I heard voices yelling from the stairwell. At first, I thought the party was still humming, but then I realized it was Jessie and David alternately railing at each other. In no shape to get into the middle of the fight, I sat next to the door to catch my breath.

Jessie's voice echoed through the hallway. "I don't know why you have to come here, and try to be the star. It's your brother's party, they're my friends, and you have to insert your opinion into everything. You know all I wish is that you go back to the west coast. You do whatever it is you do that people seem to love, and get the hell out of Michael's life.

"You are a bad influence. At first, I thought your moving here would be good because Michael could see who you really are now. You realize he has this crazy, outsized view of view of you. It's ridiculous. He even talks like you now, and he's gotten worse since you've been back. Your poison and negativity are seeping into his system."

David's voice was already hoarse. "Jessie, I'm not going anywhere. I know what the problem with Michael is. It isn't me or anything else that you and your pop-psychology-weaned-on-Oprah mind wants to believe."

"Just get out of here, I wish I didn't have to see you tonight at all. You manage to ruin everything and you, you…"

There was a long pause before David spoke again. "Stop. You are stoned, and like I said, I'm going to be right here and help my brother."

"Help? Help? Just get on the next plane and get out. I don't care if you live here now. You don't belong here. Michael doesn't need you."

"Oh, he needs you? You know what you are Jess?"

"Go ahead and say it. Say it. I know you've wanted to say it for a while. I'm a cunt, right? That's your big insult."

"Don't flatter yourself. I've known a lot of glorious, ranting cunts in my life, and you don't measure up. You are just what he doesn't need now. He doesn't need a crutch. And he certainly doesn't need the perky cheerleader with flower petals up her ass, making him think if he continues on this path everything will be alright. You are his grand illusion. He has you, but he's lost sight of himself." David's words could probably have been heard in the street.

"I guarantee if you walked out that door, he'd be a different person. He'd be forced to see his disappearing act won't play outside of the confines of this little warm cocoon you two have set up for yourselves."

Our neighbor, an elderly man with a long gray beard, stuck his head out from behind the door. I waved him off. He looked panicked but quietly disappeared without a word.

"You want me to leave him? Go to hell."

"Yes, that's what I want, and what he needs. Don't you see how wrong all of this is? What is the matter with you?"

"You know I can see through you. You just want me out of your life," Jessie yelled, her voice nearly shot.

"My life? My life? Jessica, my dear, you are a footnote to the footnote in the index of my life, but you are the spine to the fiction Michael calls his life. You are the thing holding his imaginary world together. You and I both know it's a fucked up, magical world divorced from reality. He's not fucking eating. You must see this. That's not normal. With you here with him, he thinks it's fine. He's never going to change.

"What I see is a guy who is working in a music store while pursuing a trivial life with you after he burned through his master's degree like a man possessed. This can't be the end result of his obsessive quest at school. Tell me, is this what he's supposed to be doing? I'd be so fucking depressed too if my only ambition was to play house with you. It's so sad, I…"

Jessie wouldn't let him finish. "I'm going to ignore you because you know so little about us. That doesn't ever prevent you from talking, though. You want me to leave your brother? To hell with you. He'd say the same thing. We've been together long enough to know he can get better. I know he will come around. He has been eating a bit more."

"A bit more? He doesn't eat at all. Jessie, I just want my brother back. That's all I want. Is it that difficult to figure out? This is not him. I'm not sure what to do anymore. You know, I'm going to lay it on the table. Michael may care about you, and he may even love you, but I really think he's in love with the idea of you and being in love. Michael's like a punch-drunk boxer who can't see straight. You can. You fucking can, and that's what kills me."

With that, David pulled open the door, threw it closed and blew down the hall without even seeing me sitting in the hallway.

I sat paralyzed for an hour with my knees by my chest and eyes welling up. No tears would fall, though.

Finally, I knocked on the door. It took Jess close to ten minutes to answer.

"I left my keys on the table," I said sheepishly.

"I know I saw them, but I went to sleep. You were gone so long."

"I went for a walk."

"I was really worried," Jessie said with clouds in her eyes.

"I needed some space."

"From me?"

"No, of course not. It was a long night, and just so much noise in my head. Anything happen while I was gone?" I said.

Jess seemingly had already buried everything I'd heard. "No, everyone just left soon after you went out. It went well tonight, it really did. I think everyone had a good time. You know all that anger and cursing I did before, that's not me. You know that, but sometimes..."

She rubbed her eyes with the back of her wrists. "Your brother, well, he said he'll call you in the morning. You know he, well, no, nothing. He'll call you. Hey, I'm going to sleep. I made you a sandwich. Michael, please promise me you will eat something tonight. I don't want to see you getting the sweats anymore. Okay?"

"Yeah, I will." I was still holding the Big Gulp in my trembling hand.

"Can I ask you a question?" she whispered. I thought she was going to talk about David.

"Of course, is there something wrong?"

"No, just, why couldn't you just have missed that baseball trivia question? Was it that important to get it right?"

I didn't know what to say, so I just told her the truth. "Well, yes. I didn't get it right for David. I got it right because I knew it. Why did you doubt me?"

Her face went slack. "I don't know. Something, something...I guess I can't explain it. I'm sorry. I was stoned. I am stoned. I'm not sure why it mattered. I'm sorry." She wrapped her hair up with a rubber band and put her bathrobe over the chair in the main room before quietly walking towards the bed.

The crusts of the ham and cheese sandwich were neatly trimmed and little smears of yellow mustard peeked out of the sides where Jess had sliced it in half. I sat quietly, completely depleted, next to two Hefty bags jammed with empty beer bottles—the stale stench of smoke still lingering like a bad dream.

As I raised the smaller half of the sandwich to my mouth, I thought for sure I was going to throw up.

Four

I repeatedly recounted everything that transpired during the night of blunts and bile while sitting alone in the apartment for the first time. It was the initial thing that entered my mind after Jessie walked out. Was my own brother the mastermind behind her great escape? Maybe he planted the seed or maybe he just greased the wheels for plans already in motion. Exhausted and in denial, I swallowed two orphan Sleep-eze tablets sitting on the medicine cabinet shelf and waited to go into a quiet, comfortable coma.

I fell off and dreamt of the party. In a nightmare, I wandered throughout the crowded living room with boxes of pizza as Jessie smoked a joint and ate chocolate ice cream with Les and David. She looked very different. Her tight jawline, fine cheekbones, and sharp nose were replaced by grotesquely puffy features. It seemed as if she'd suffered a horrible reaction from a Novocain injection.

When Jess spoke, I heard nothing but odd squeaks and gibberish. Her friends listened intently to the strange, incomprehensible utterances. Subtitles scrolled just beneath her chin. After David opened two of the pizza boxes, everyone broke into loud, hysterical laughter. As blood tears fell from my eyes, I looked down to find the boxes empty.

I woke up sweating in the middle of the night while reaching for Jess across the empty bed. Somewhere she was next to Les, fucking him and taking his cock deep into her mouth.

Startled by visions of Jessie's face flushed with sexual pleasure, I ended up watching consecutive reruns of *Three's Company* before switching to one infomercial after another. Finally, I settled for the toothy grin and bouncing breasts of the now middle-aged Suzanne Somers doing kegels with the Thighmaster. Legs spread, legs closed, legs spread, legs closed, repeat until satisfied.

The older Chrissy Snow still had the same irresistible cartoon sexuality that always turned me on. I was getting hard and feeling angrier as I watched with rapt attention. Just how the fuck did I let Les become Jessie's thighmaster while obsessing over wanton wontons and forbidden fruits? With a sad, desperate hard-on, I tried to remember the last time I was inside Jessie. It had been months. Her taste, smell, and the way the curve of upper thighs quivered as she came all rushed back to me.

After washing my face to scrub the memories away, I turned on CNN to see some flirtatious anchor with a suck-you mouth and Jennifer Aniston hair. Another massacre in the West Bank and a shelling in Pakistan. The images were horrifying, the carnage unimaginable. People were dropping bombs on each other all around the world, yet the only thing that mattered was Jessie detonating our life.

I felt like a victim, but I also couldn't shake the fear that maybe, just maybe, Jessie was right: She was the collateral damage of my own unwinnable war—a crazy, private Vietnam in imaginary rice paddies.

It was all too much to absorb, so when my search for more Sleepeze came up empty, I knew the only answer was to drink the whole fucking night away. I scoured the kitchen cabinets to find an old, dusty bottle of Blackberry Brandy above the refrigerator. The sweet liqueur tasted like cough medicine, burning the back of my throat. For that one brief moment, the calories didn't matter. After all, I was home, sitting in my underwear on the floor of the kitchen while Jessie was blowing Les in a shitty motel, ten minutes away.

When you weigh ninety-eight pounds, one drink is like a Mike Tyson right hand, so I ended up slightly stunned on the bed with just the bottle and the television remote. Boobs, booty, and beats on BET hypnotized me into a stupor before I stumbled upon a documentary about great New York Mets players on ESPN Classic. Daryl Strawberry sadly reminisced about his drug fueled years, culminating in a squandered career. His name at the bottom of the screen was transfixing.

I leaped off the bed like Peter Pan and grabbed a pad and pen from the bookshelves. On the top page, I wrote All Food Baseball All-Stars. Beneath the header, I scribbled:

Daryl Strawberry: Right Field

It was a good start. I created food lists for everything to fill in the dead spots of my life. The All Food Film Blockbuster was my favorite. Of course, it was toplined by Halle Berry. She could play any role, and direct. Her co-stars were Kevin Bacon, Tim Curry, John Candy, and Christina Applegate. This kind of nonsense kept me busy throughout each day—I even daydreamed of Carrie Fisher in her Princess Leia bikini.

As I ate less and less over the years, I found myself thinking more and more about food. My life was consumed with the one thing I could not, would not have.

Now with the list as my new mission, I pulled *The Baseball Encyclopedia* from the shelf while drinking the Blackberry Brandy like I was sitting on a stool in *Cheers*. I shuffled through the pages at the dining room table. After racing through the thirty major league teams in my head, I had a list in moments:

Jim Rice: Left Field
Bob Veale: Pitcher
Cookie Lavagetto: Third Base
Peanuts Lowrey: Right Field
Bobby Wine: Utility
Bobby Sturgeon: Shortstop

The slow rising, warming effects of the liqueur were liberating. There's an undeniably delirious freedom in the complete loss of all feeling. At that moment, I knew I would make it through the night.

While slumping on the floor, I somehow managed to write Herman Franks: Manager, punctuated by double exclamation points. Suddenly, the label on the Blackberry Brandy bottle turned into a glowing, flying hologram. It hovered throughout the room and fluttered in front of my face before escaping into the bedroom as I lay on the floor with the pad at my side and *The Baseball Encyclopedia* on my chest.

. . . .

I had no idea how long I'd been out, but I awoke with my head in the middle of the bed and my feet propped up on a folding chair next to the bureau. The room was black except for the flood of light from the muted television. The phone rang twice before our old answering machine picked up the call. I glanced at the digital clock to see it was just past eight o'clock.

I missed work. I missed the day. I missed waking up next to Jessie.

"Hello, Michael. Michael, I know you are there. Please pick up the damn phone. I know you have to be home. Will you please pick up?"

It was Patty. I hid timidly under the blanket and comforter.

"Don't let this machine cut me off, pick up...Michael, c'mon."

I just couldn't leave her hanging. "Patty I'm sorry..." I said, cradling the receiver against my shoulder.

"No need to explain, I didn't want to talk to anyone either all day, but I'm over that phase now. Do you believe those two motherfuckers? I mean do they have balls the size of King Kong or what?" Patty was a quiet, controlled, surly girl who hardly ever cursed. In fact, she once chastised me for cursing too much, but I understood that this was Patty uncut—the Patty she kept hidden away. You usually have to be in a relationship with a girl to hear her like that.

"You know fuck them, Michael. I've cried all day, but now I'm angry. I'm so goddamn angry, I'm throwing shit out."

I slipped into the bathroom, took five aspirin, put the toilet seat cover down and sat limply. There was nothing to say.

"Michael, where's your head at? Has the numbness worn off?"

Sadly, it had.

"Are you angry, Michael? Are you as angry as me right now? Motherfuckers. Are you at that stage yet?"

I wasn't sure if I was talking to Patty or Elizabeth Kubler-Ross.

"Patty, honestly, I just woke up."

"Hey, I'm sorry, naps are important. I didn't get much sleep last night either. I guess I just want to check in with you to make sure everything's alright. Is it?"

"Well, no it's not. I mean I don't know. I really haven't done anything today for it to go wrong."

"You mean you just woke up for real?" she said.

"Well yeah, am I supposed to feel guilty?"

"I'm sorry, but Michael do you realize that it's after eight in the evening? How could you sleep so soundly?"

I looked at the bottle on the floor across the room. "Brandy."

There was a long silence. I used it to grab a fresh t-shirt. "Hello Patty, you still there?"

"Brandy? Who's that?"

"What's that, Patty. I drank it. I didn't fuck it."

"Oh man, okay, I'm so confused. Well, I get that. You know I don't know what to think anymore. When did she tell you?"

"She told me last night when I came home from the show. After midnight."

"You were lucky. Les told me around seven. It was slow, and he made sure I had the entire night to think about it. I haven't stopped either. He's a cocksucker, alright. I hate the sonofabitch, and I hate Jessie, too. I mean for them to screw around and plan this behind our backs while we were going out together. I can't believe it. I mean when we went to see the Dave Matthews show, they were planning it then. In fact, Les said they made the commitment the night of the show."

The night of Dave Matthews? I hated Dave fucking Matthews and his unwashed, white dreadlocked hordes. I went to the show because Les convinced Jessie he worth seeing. That's what Jessie told me. Apparently, what was worth seeing was each other.

"That was well over a month ago. Are you sure?"

"You mean you don't know?" I really didn't want more information but listened anyway. "Oh yeah, it's been a while. This was planned. I absolutely can't believe Jessie didn't tell you any of this. You deserve that much. Did she call or stop by today?"

I couldn't remember the phone ringing or hearing the door unlock, but I wouldn't have heard a work crew trying to build a freeway through the apartment.

"No, I don't think she did. Did Les stop by your place?"

"He sure did cause he needed to get his shit, but it was already in his bags and out on the lawn. I threw them out the window last night." The image of bony Patty tossing luggage off the balcony amused me.

"You threw them off four flights?" I said "You know I did, and it felt good. Why are you laughing? You need to get angry. Don't keep it in, it'll kill ya. Don't swallow the pain.

"I mean they were, well, this is…sick, we were all friends," She broke down, crying. "I don't think I have to tell you, you must feel the same way, right?" She was looking for an affirmation, but I wasn't sure what I was supposed to be feeling.

"You don't know how hurt I am. I spent five years with Les, and he walks out on me because he says they would be good for each other. What about me? What about you?"

I knew if I waited a few minutes she might have channeled Ann Wilson and asked, "What about love?"

I leaned unsteadily against the wall to think about her questions. My arms ached nearly as much as my stomach. I hadn't eaten all day. Again. The television images flashing against the wall illuminated the room. I was talking into a void.

"Michael listen, I asked Les almost everything I could think of, but some things I don't want to know. Did you know they slept together on your bed the night after my birthday party? Do you believe that? In your bed?"

I yanked the comforter off the mattress and saw wet spots and come stains on the sheets. Now completely paranoid, I clumsily felt my way to the dinner table in the dark apartment.

"Uh Patty, I think I need to go. Right now, I'm still in my underwear. I have morning breath in the evening. I feel like a bad country song, and I gotta get something to eat real quick."

"Hey, I'm going to tell you one more thing okay? I'm not sure you'll want to hear it, but you should."

"Is this necessary or is it one of those things for my own good everyone needs to tell their friends for some reason? If it is Patty, I can do without honesty in the name of friendship. Frankly, I don't want to hear another fucking thing about how Les and Jess fucked here because I swear I'll...I'll..." I wanted to throw the phone against the wall, but remained calm as ever.

"Michael, you'll what? Don't say kill yourself. Please. Please, calm down."

"Patty, I'm not going to kill myself." The thought never entered my mind. "I'm going to go and get Jessie back."

She fell silent for minutes.

"You want to know what else Les told me?" Patty finally asked without prompting. "Michael, Les told me that the reason Jessie left you is she's tired of living with someone beyond help. That you are going to die at the rate you are going."

I had to catch my breath as my knees faltered. "I don't believe she said that." I really didn't.

"Maybe not in so many words, but she said that you just don't take care of yourself anymore by doing such a simple thing like eating."

"You don't know she said that. Did she tell you that?" Now I was angry.

"No, Les did."

"And he's not going to lie to you now, is he?"

The phone nearly slipped out of my fingers. The phrases "beyond help" and "going to die" just kept buzzing through my head. "A simple thing like eating."

Simple. Eat. It just wasn't.

"Listen Michael, I don't know if what Les said is true, but just take care of yourself, alright?"

The phone clicked.

As I turned on the lights in the apartment to search out the bag of bagels I'd left in the main room the previous night, the phone immediately rang again. I desperately needed to take a shower, but I hoped it might be Jessie.

"Hello." I juggled the bag in one hand with the phone receiver buried in my ear. The bagels were like iced hockey pucks, yet I managed to chip a bit off the crust of one with a fork sitting on the table as Monique's voice settled in.

"Babe, is that you?" Mon always called me Babe because she said I had the smoothest skin of anyone she'd ever known. I barely had to shave—most people said I still looked like a teenager.

The first time I met Monique was at the Bowery Ballroom in New York. This was before Jessie and I got together. I knew Mon's face from pictures David had sent. She was a model for years at that point, and familiar to me from magazines. After David got married, I began clipping her advertisements from *Rolling Stone, Sports Illustrated,* and *People*. I couldn't believe he would ever be with someone like her. She was way, way out of his league. She was out of every fucking guy's league.

We'd talked on the phone for years, but we finally connected when she and David flew into New York from San Francisco. They took me to see a special one-off club show by U2.

The bouncer refused to believe I was over the drinking age limit, even after I flashed my license. He wrapped his thick fingers around my arm and said, "You're kidding me. No way. You're just a kid."

With a broad smile, Monique gave him a quick kiss on the cheek. "Let's just say he's my baby." He, of course, let me in without hesitation. After that, she ended up calling me Babe all the time.

I was thrilled to hear from her while still forking the skin of the bagel. "Monique, hey, I've got so much to tell you, if you got the time."

"I heard, Babe, that's what I'm calling for. I'm really sorry about what happened. I don't know what to say. But I'm here for you."

"You heard? How? Does David know?" I was fuming. I, at least, wanted to tell the two people who now mattered most to me that the one person who used to matter most, didn't matter anymore. I wanted to be the courier of bad news and hear the hushed silence on the other side of the phone. You don't want friends or family to learn about bad shit second hand. By then, they've absorbed it and formed a reaction. They are ready to give you some kind of rational advice. I wanted to hear primal feelings—all the things I just could not express.

"Naomi told me." Naomi was Monique's assistant and a friend of Jessie's from college. Jessie had asked me to recommend her.

"From Naomi? How did she find out?" I laughed at the thought of Jessie's leaving becoming word-of-mouth news. While waiting for

Mon's explanation, I had created a mini sculpture out of the bagel with each fork stab.

"C'mon Michael. She's Jessie's friend," Mon said. "Michael, are you okay? I called to tell you I will do whatever it is you need me to do. I'll stay with you for a night or two so we can talk. You can fill me in what happened. I think David is going to New York overnight. You will be fine, trust me. Try and relax. You have people in your corner."

Monique was much older than me, and her steady, cool demeanor was often unnerving. Nothing rattled her. She was always so meticulous, composed and put together.

After a deep breath, I finally gave up on the stupid, useless fork and opted for the scissors I had left on the table while wrapping gifts the previous day. Darting specks blurred my vision.

"Michael, you there?" Mon's voice was faint.

"Yeah, I'm sorry. I'm just cleaning up the place a bit. Where were we?" My chest muscles constricted again as I hacked at the bagel.

"I want to know you are alright and not going to do something stupid. I know better, but things like these trigger extreme emotions in us all."

Raising my hand up like Anthony Perkins in *Psycho*, I wildly stabbed the edge of bagel one more time. The scissors deflected off the crust and jutted into my left forearm.

I let out a low grunt while dropping the telephone receiver to the floor. The blood flow was the darkest red I had ever seen. After pulling the scissors out of my arm, I scrambled into the bathroom to snatch a towel from the rack. The white fabric immediately went crimson as I frantically reached for one of my beach towels. Blood made plopping sounds on the tile and splattered near my feet.

With the floor giving way, I wrapped my forearm with the beach towel and pulled it as taut as I could with one hand and my teeth. There were slow rhythmic throbs—the blood was oozing to a slow blues beat. The arm quickly went numb. Pain shocked the right side of my neck as if shards of hot metal were shooting through the skin. My head fell between my knees when I realized I had to rush to the emergency room.

I hated hospitals because I'd been in so many, so often, but there was no other option—the return customer was going back. Step right up and take a ticket. I knew if I hurried, the interns would still be running on caffeine, and we could get the circus started.

I staggered to my feet, shoving the arm and towel into the sleeve of my coat. The phone was still on the floor, but Monique was long gone. She must have realized something serious had happened.

But really, what could be all that serious?

I hadn't eaten in nearly two days, I'd watched my girlfriend walk out the door, and now I was bleeding to death.

Teetering and about to collapse, I somehow scratched Boston Mercy on an old post-it note from the trash and stuck it on the door with scotch tape as the blood dripped onto the hallway carpet. Mon would understand the message. My legs wobbled while I stumbled forward on the way towards the stairwell.

Halfway down the hall, though, I toughened the fuck up and headed back into the apartment to get what remained of that goddamn bagel.

Five

When I got to the ER, the doctor on call calmly stitched my arm before the pensive, concerned nurses hooked me up to units of blood and bags of fluids. I must have looked like the Scarecrow in *The Wizard of Oz* carefully being repaired by the munchkins. I was hoping that whatever was pumping through my veins had enough nutrients and a Red Bull kicker to keep me going. Just maintaining the ability to sit up and talk seemed like a major triumph after I nearly passed out in the car.

I was seeing double and struggling to focus on the road when I made the five-minute drive to the hospital. I'd parked on the far side of the building and somehow found the energy and balance to rush from the car to the reception desk. I'd always heard stories of people doing extraordinary things while under extreme duress, so the very ordinary dash in a frenzied moment of panic made me wonder what could be possible if I lived my life with even a modicum of the same determination I showed during the sprint.

After an uneasy nap on the creaky bed, I was happy to still be among the living, but I knew my real trial was coming up. Somehow, I'd have to explain myself to disbelieving doctors. A tall, athletic Latina nurse emerged from behind the curtain with a clipboard and papers. She looked at me skeptically when I told her about the scissors and immediately summoned the doctor who had stitched me up. I recreated the story down to the most minute detail, emphasizing it was all accidental.

The slim Indian doctor with a pimple on his chin took extensive notes before leaving me with the nurse. "I will talk to the attending. You do the paperwork with Nurse Roncal. Doctor Graynor will be with you in a while."

The painkillers began to kick in as the hovering nurse asked about insurance and emergency contacts. I stared into the fluorescent lights drawing me into another dimension. I was hoping the whole episode was all just a moment of hysterical delirium, and I would soon wake up to the sight of Suzanne Somers' mighty thighs.

"Okay, Michael I need to know when your last meal was?" she asked. Now we were heading down into the black hole. I let the question echo in my head while pleasantly floating through a wonderland of drugged indifference. Meal? Steak and potatoes? Veal cutlet parmigiana? Sweet and sour pork with a side of fried rice? That kind of meal? Oh, about three years ago, give or take a couple of months.

"Ten hours ago." It seemed plausible.

"Have you had anything since then? Anything?" I didn't have the wherewithal to stack lie upon lie and simply wanted to quietly fade into oblivion while on the bed. "I had Diet Coke."

"That's all?" she asked, alarmed.

"That's all, folks."

"You are extremely thin. I need to know what you've eaten today."

"Tonight, today, whatever. You can ask me that again. The answer won't change. Nothing."

"May I ask why?" she fired back. I hesitated for almost a minute as she tapped the clipboard with the pen. "You are very quiet. You don't want to talk?"

"Can you give me a few seconds to return to planet earth? Then I'll gladly answer all your questions."

Her sigh was so emphatic I could feel her breath on my chin. "Michael, I don't need attitude. I need answers. You are in no shape to be smart here. This demands a doctor's attention. I'll be right back."

When she returned five minutes later to sit on the edge of the bed, the emergency room was surprisingly quiet. I could hear a patient snoring across from me.

"Miss nurse, you gotta understand. I can tell you what you want to hear, but the truth is I just don't know what to say anymore." I was completely out of answers.

"You had to have eaten something? What can I write here? Give me something."

"Nada, zero, nothing, zilch."

She just shook her head and stared at the curtain. "So, you are telling me you have eaten nothing at all today?"

"Yup. I explained my problem to that doctor, and now he's playing doctor with the other doctor. So why don't I wait until she gets here and save a lot of time. I'm not being rude to you, really. Honestly, I'm just really fucked up right now. My arm is the absolute least of my problems."

She squeezed my toe. "Alright, I hear you. Relax. You'll be fine. Let's wait for Doctor Graynor. I'll leave you be."

After forty minutes of falling in and out of sleep, I finally got to see the taciturn, slightly morose Doctor Graynor. "The wound was pretty deep and since the circumference of your arm is quite small. It may take some time to heal," she said upon arrival. Circumference. It was a word I'd never actually heard in a conversation. Diameter, 3.14. Somehow, I smiled while recalling my All Food Baseball All-Stars list. Pie Traynor would be perfect.

"Michael, please listen to me because you really have to keep the dressing clean here. You need to follow what I tell you or else you will have complications."

Dr. Graynor spent the next half hour asking about my weight and food intake. I had heard the same questions in different variations a thousand times before from every doctor I had encountered since I'd been in Boston.

I told her about what had happened with Jessie after explaining my long struggle to put food in my mouth. I could have told her a creative story or evaded the questions, but the truth would inevitably come out. I was tired of lying to doctors and my family.

And yes, I guess, I was simply exhausted by lying to myself.

Dr. Graynor basically repeated the same things Dr. Rigatta had told me, and she ended up detouring into a long speech about change. I had already resisted everything I had been advised to do, so it seemed like a waste of time. Even though I listened carefully, I knew damn well I'd just go right back to living the same way. I really didn't want to live that way, but it wasn't about what I wanted. I was compelled to resist food. It had become my way of life.

Finally, she asked me to rest just before Monique entered the room. Of course, Mon tracked me down after finding the bloody post-it note. She hugged me after running to the bed. I quickly explained all about the accident. "I was told by the doctors," she replied quietly.

This was the second time in just over twenty-four hours Monique heard about my life unraveling from a second-hand source. I needed to gain control of my life's narrative again.

Dr. Graynor touched Mon on the shoulder while asking her to step away from the bed. She detailed what I needed to do for my future as if I was not in the room. Her directions were clinical, emotionless and sharp. "You need to get Michael help. Not next week, not next month. Now." Monique intently studied the doctor's face.

Dr. Graynor turned to me and added, "Am I right? There has to be a course correction."

I wiggled off the portable bed, but she placed her hand on my arm. "Not yet, Michael, there are still some things I have to check before I release you. If I decide to release you."

"What do you mean if?" I was afraid I was being condemned to spend the night in the hospital.

"Just rest for a while. You lost a lot of blood. Even though we gave you blood, nutrients, and fluids, this was a traumatic event for someone in your condition. Do you realize how dehydrated you were? My friend, that wound was not a pinprick. This is more complicated than you think. To state the obvious, you are much too thin."

Monique was holding her head in her hands as she stared at the curtain. Nurse Roncal slowly sidled up next to Dr. Graynor with a container of orange juice and a wrapped sandwich. Both were placed perilously close to me. "I want you to drink and eat these. You need to if you want to get out of here," Dr. Graynor said with a frozen smile.

As I nodded politely while ignoring the sandwich, David rushed towards the bed. He must have been running to get to the hospital because his face was splotchy red. Strands of hair were matted to his temples.

"I'm sorry I'm so late. I got here as quickly as I could." He kissed Monique before tapping me on the foot. "What the hell were you trying to do?" He introduced himself to the doctor with one eye on my bandaged arm. "You going to be alright?" His eyes were popping out of his head in a cartoon, Wile E. Coyote way. Monique, Dr. Graynor, and I all nodded in unison.

The doctor asked David to step out of the room with her, leaving Monique and me in silence. "Babe, I don't want to get into an emotional scene here, but I hope the bagel story is true. I mean, David doesn't know about Jessie yet, but I do. You didn't…"

"Monique, I swear." Prepared for questions, I reached into the pocket of my jacket spread out on the chair. "Here's the bagel." I was proud to have proof.

"You saved the bagel? Really? While you were bleeding?" Mon delicately fingered the hard, gashed bagel.

"I knew you and the doctors, or anyone else, would never believe me and think I slit my wrists. I'm not about to kill myself. Especially not that way."

This is beyond me." Mon's chin fell to her chest after she tossed the remains of the bagel in the garbage.

"Mon, you know me. Would I ever be near a bagel if I didn't have to?"

She sat down next to the bed. "Michael, you have to understand where I'm coming from here. I'm talking to you on the phone about Jessie leaving and, well, people just don't stick scissors in their arms every day. People don't do that any day. I was yelling into the phone, and I got no answer. What am I supposed to think when I get to your door and see blood?" she said with tears forming.

"In a court of law, I'd be strung up. I admit things lead to one conclusion, but I'm not lying. Sometimes, we do stupid things."

"Drink this," She demanded while opening the container of orange juice.

"Mon, I…"

"Shut up, and drink it now." Her eyes were on fire. "I don't know what's happening with you. You know they say when life gives you lemons, you make lemonade? Well, from my viewpoint, life has given you salmon, and you are doing nothing but making salmonella. You have everything to live for, but you are throwing it away. For what?"

I knocked the juice container back with my eyes closed.

My arm was as numb as my brain. I was simply worn out by trying explaining myself. Monique spoke blankly to the window. "People care about you. Can't you hear what people who love you are saying? We are in the hospital in the middle of the night. Look at me." She moved to the bed and held the sides of my face in her hands.

That was one of the first times I had seen Mon without makeup. "I can't say anything here because you are David's brother, but I am very much invested in you, too. You are not some stranger to me. You need to understand people eat, and do not stab themselves with scissors. You've done it and it's just..."

"What Mon? Crazy? I'm not crazy."

"Babe, I know you are not crazy, that's the problem. This is just not good. We've got to get you to good somehow."

"Please don't get angry." I didn't know what else to say as Monique glared into the empty hallway. I watched the small of her back rise and fall with each breath. She was thin, but not frail. Her tall, lanky frame just made her look skinny. Holding her leather bomber jacket in her clasped hands, she seemed to be wilting in the late-night hour. I could hear Dr. Graynor talking to David near the main desk. The conversation was muffled by the shuffling of nurses' feet and the buzzing of the old intercom system.

"Babe, I guess you don't see, do you?" Mon said, ambling back to the bed. "You don't see you...Forget it. I'm not angry. I'm tired. We're all tired." She placed her hand on my thigh with a weak smile.

When she was a child, Monique cut the right corner of her mouth after a boy pushed her to the ground while she was drinking from a glass. That side of her lips involuntarily pointed down every time she smiled. It was as if she was frowning and smiling simultaneously—such a distinct, oddly alluring imperfection. An aesthetic contradiction so rare for a model. But it made her seem eminently human. She had familiar diamond cutting cheekbones and soft, oval eyes, but it was that smile that separated her from the phalanx of Barbie clones destined to appear in Sears catalogs and commercials for Billy Bob's Beer Emporium.

Mon held my hand while sitting next to me on the hard bed. I searched for words to change the subject. "I thought David was going to New York for an interview."

"He cancelled once I called him."

"Who was he supposed to talk to?" The orange juice was burning my stomach.

"Madonna," Mon said softly.

I looked at her with owl eyes. "He cancelled an interview with Madonna to come back for me?"

"No, of course not. He would have told me to put a pillow over your face if it was Madonna." We both laughed as she placed her feet up on the chair. "It was just one of those dopey, poppy hip-hop MCs. He'll reschedule it."

I was glad to see the tension drain out of Mon, but I was also still unsure if she believed the scissor stabbing was an accident. My brother once told me there are no accidents in life. I knew that's what he was probably telling Dr. Graynor.

Mon drifted with dazed eyes. "Babe are you alright? I mean really alright?"

"Monique, I'm sorry for everything. Sometimes things just get beyond me."

She embraced me, once again carefully maneuvering around my limp arm. I held her at a distance. "Michael, you need help, and we will get it for you. I'm here for you."

I knew she was right, and it was also eminently clear she didn't deserve what I was putting her through.

"You have to do something for me now, though. Eat this." She unwrapped the plastic off the sandwich. My stomach contracted when she pulled off the top slice of bread to inspect the meat. "Ham and cheese, not bad. You have to have this."

"Mon…" I said, raising my arm.

"Half. Go half with me," she conceded. "Please. I won't push you for the whole thing tonight after all that's happened, but if you don't do half I'm gonna be disappointed."

"You are going to go guilt on me?" I was hoping she would smile again.

"Fuck, yes, you better believe I'm going guilt on you tonight. By any means necessary," she snapped. "Here, I'll put mustard on just a bit, and we'll eat it." When she carefully ripped the mustard packet and neatly covered the cheese in French's, I felt like I was in kindergarten.

She handed me half the sandwich with a command to eat. There was no choice. I was so weak and afraid that if I didn't eat something, I'd pass out. Angrily, I bit into the bread.

Mon finished her half in less than a minute. "Jesus, I was starving. I might ask the nurse for another. Now you finish it, so we'll get out of here, hopefully." The first lump of ham and cheese was still negotiating its way through my intestines, but I stuffed the remaining piece into my mouth anyway.

"Chew and swallow, Babe. I don't want them to have to do a Heimlich maneuver on you." My hand shook uncontrollably. Where the hell were those calories going to show up?

"Breathe, will ya?" Mon brought us both cups from the water cooler. "Was that so hard?"

She had no idea. I would be thinking about that half sandwich for days. Dr. Graynor mournfully walked into the room with David. My brother moved to Mon's side after placing a piece of paper in his wallet.

"Okay, I'm going to release you," Dr. Graynor said sharply. "I don't think we can help you very much more tonight. I wrote a prescription for pain. You are going to need it, but be very careful. It's powerful." She pulled the sheet off of me. "I want to weigh you again. Mind getting on the scale for a second? I will say I'm impressed to see you eat the sandwich."

She couldn't think I finished the whole thing. "I only ate part. She ate the other half," I pointed to Mon.

"At least you ate something. A start. Now can you get on the scale?" Her eyes never left the charts nestled in her arm.

"Is that a question because I really do mind and would rather…"

David interrupted with face flushed. "Michael, get on the goddamn scale for a second. C'mon, then you'll be free. Don't make a big deal out it. Shut your eyes if you want to." He waited impatiently next to the doctor as I made my way to judgment. The springs on the scale must have been loose beneath the platform because I quickly lost my balance. Dr. Graynor placed her hands on my spine.

"You steady?"

"I'm fine, of course." As she played with the weights, I kept my eyes closed just as David had suggested. When I heard the metal fall into place, I immediately scurried into the hallway. Dr. Graynor called me back.

"Michael, pay attention. I know you think a lot and have a good education, but this isn't a matter of smarts and ignorance. As I was telling your brother, some of the smartest women go through what you are right now. This is not an intellectual challenge—it's an emotional one. The thing you have to remember is, it's not really about food. I gave your brother names of doctors who can help you recognize this.

"You say you saw Dr. Rigatta at Mass. Central for a while, so I'm referring you to her. If you don't want to go back, I can set you up with someone here to monitor the wound and work with you."

"I liked Dr. Rigatta. I just drifted." I was whipped and willing. "Thanks Doc, you know, I'm not sure a pill's going to help me with the pain here."

"You are probably right, but for tonight and tomorrow, they sure will make a difference. You obviously realize it's about something bigger than pills can fix. You have a lot of things you have to think about. Your brother knows the urgency. The one thing you always have to understand is that you will encounter many enemies in this life, but food is not among them. Please trust me."

Six

The sun filled my bedroom as I awoke to the voice of Marvin Gaye outside the door. It was 1:15 p.m. My forearm was so numb, turning on the radio seemed like an arduous achievement.

The newscaster with an authoritative, soothing bass voice analyzed the "deteriorating relations in the Middle East" and broke down the difference between the Kurds, Sunnis, and Shiites, but very little registered. The Dow dumped 220 points and Barry Bonds hit another home run. My filter system only retained curd, deteriorating, and dumped. I considered shutting the radio off, but it was important to hear some other voice beyond the static in my own head. All I could think about was Jessie and Les.

My life was Jessie-less for the first time in years, and the empty feeling in my stomach, usually the first stirring of a long-forgotten hunger, was now loneliness. I breezed through the radio dial as Monique sang "Got to Give It Up" in the other room. An obnoxious know-it-all was bloviating about the Red Sox on an all-sports talk station.

"The Sox are in no shape to contend, so let's face it, we're going to have to get used to losing until they make some drastic changes." I rested against the headboard to let the thought marinate for a few minutes while watching a spider crawl across the ceiling before ultimately finding a home in the light fixture.

"Michael, are you going to get your ass out of bed today?" Monique knocked before blowing through the door.

"I'm up, I'm up. I'm not sure I want to be," I mumbled.

"One thing you are not going to do is feel sorry for yourself. Get in the bathroom and take a shower. You'll feel better. I called your work and told them you won't be in for a while. David and I think you should quit that stupid job anyway. Just take a shower or you are going to grow crust." Mon looked casually resplendent in jeans and a powder blue *London Calling* t-shirt. Her hair was pulled back and clipped on the top of her head, highlighting her delicate features.

"Mon, today is…humor me, is it Sunday?" All I wanted to do was fall into an anesthetized dreamland.

"Yeah, and a terrific one at that. Now, get your bearings and let's get on with things. Only grandparents and tweakers don't know what day is," she said, picking up an array of socks off the floor. "Stop with the nonsense. I'll make you some kind of breakfast. You tell me what, but you will eat something while I'm here." Her voice was stern despite the relaxed smile.

I flipped the television on to an E! news report about Britney Spears celebrating a birthday and possibly being pregnant from a mystery guy. It was no doubt bullshit, but I just wanted to watch a little bit of Brit to keep the blood flowing.

"They will do anything for viewers. You know she's not pregnant at what, twenty? I can't imagine Britney pregnant and fat. Jesus, that would ruin things completely." The afternoon morning wood I was trying to hide from Mon slowly descended.

"There's something about Britney Spears. She gets to me. I actually jerked off to her wearing those polka dot shorts on the *Rolling Stone* cover." My words were just stupidly spilling out like I had no filter. Maybe it was the painkillers or maybe it was just Post-Traumatic Scissors Disorder.

Mon threw a towel at my head. "Thanks for sharing. I didn't need that image in my head. If Britney's pregnant, which I doubt because the record is way too successful, she'll happily have an excuse to eat all that Ben and Jerry's her mom probably doesn't allow."

"She'll look like she ate Ben and Jerry. I'm sorry, it would be over for her. She would never have that body again." I turned back to the television only to be mesmerized by Britney's image with the pearl white smile and bare midriff.

"That's an asshole thing to say, Michael, you know that. I think someday Britney will be a very beautiful pregnant woman, but now is not the time," Mon said while aggressively wiping down the bookcases.

She tossed me a rag and said, "Clean. How do you live like this?"

"I don't know how pregnant women watch their bodies get distorted like that. I can't gain a half a pound without feeling like I'm going to float away. Imagine gaining fifty?" I said.

A rush of cold air flooded the room after Mon opened the windows wide. "I think you just avoid real life actualities. A pregnant woman disgusts you. That's sad, if you ask me. You know you won't stay this age forever. You can't hide from the inevitable. You can't prevent weight gain if you don't exercise as you get older." As Mon rummaged for a folding chair from behind the bookcases, she pulled the clip from her hair and let it tumble to her shoulders.

"Yes, you can," I maintained.

"Not your way. You know that now. You do things your way you don't get old, you..." She trailed off. "I'm not going to say anymore. You know the distortion. If you don't, we're going to make sure you do. C'mon now, can I ask you a serious question, Babe?"

"They seem like all serious questions these days."

"This is just the beginning, so get used to them. Maybe it's practice for therapy. You have to tell me, where did the mania come from? You were never that heavy, were you?" Mon sat with feet on the bed while stretching her arms over her head.

"Depends on what you consider heavy. The most I weighed was 171, and that was when I was fifteen," I quickly replied. The truth was I made up a number every time someone asked me. I never knew just how fat I was because I always refused to get on scales.

"One-seventy-one is the most you ever weighed? You make it sound like you were obese. Hold that thought," she whispered on her way into the kitchen. Moments later, she returned, sipping from a can of Diet Coke.

"It might not sound like a lot, but that was a lot of weight on me when I was young, so I never felt comfortable. But Mon, you know this stuff already because you've seen my pictures." I was now caressing a pillow on the bed.

"Get out of that bed, Babe," Mon snapped. "I wish I understood your...your, I don't know, this obsession, your guilt trip whatever it is.

You know, I've seen many a girl with anorexia and understood their pressures, but I still wanted to shake them awake. They didn't know the danger they were in, or at least, they didn't want to acknowledge it.

"I knew what those girls were dealing with, but I don't understand you. Maybe, that's my block. Both David and I don't get it. We wish we did. I've talked to friends about you and other men with anorexia. They know little about it. That's what worries me. Everyone seems to have so little information about men. That's why it's going to be so important for you to see a good therapist."

I drifted in and out of consciousness, but tried to appear wide awake for Mon as she began to straighten books. She tossed a stray sock off the floor at me. "With the girls, there was only so much I could do. You, we can get help. This has always been an issue we never talked about. When we've spent time together, it's just been like some dirty little secret. I didn't know if it was my place. I left it to David, but I found him leaving it to you."

"We can talk about it. It's fine. There's nothing to hide. Whatever you want, I'm okay with." I was simply pacifying her, as I did everyone else. Talking usually made me want to bury what Mon called the "dirty little secret" even deeper. I did feel comfortable enough around Monique, though, to explain all the things she could not possibly understand.

"Can you tell me, is there a moment during the day when you are not actually thinking about fat or food?" she said with the can of Diet Coke extended to me.

"Mon, without getting too weird here, I'll just say there's really only one moment in life when we're not thinking, and that's when we, well, how do I say this? Honestly, it's when we come. Seriously, that's the only time I'm not thinking about fat, food, or how much I've eaten. And we know how long does that lasts. Never long enough, right?"

"Jesus, stop. This is a bit beyond me. You are way out there today," she replied, seemingly embarrassed. "You and Britney was plenty enough information, thank you. C'mon, you gotta get your ass in motion. You have to eat, and we're going to figure out which doctor to see. David got names from Dr. Graynor."

She inspected my old clothes in the bureau and raised her hand in disgust. "Throw these old shirts out, will ya? I'm not going to dwell here, but I have to ask you one more thing, and then I'll leave the rest for the doctors to explain to me. Let's say for the hell of it, what if Jessie was fat? Would you still feel the same way about her?"

"That's impossible." It was a ridiculous question I didn't even have to consider. "I never would have dated her. She would just have been another girl."

"And knowing who Jessie is, and how much you say you love her, well, you got me questioning. You would never have known her because you would have passed on by because she wasn't, wasn't…"

"Like Halle Berry," I fired back.

"Babe, now really stop. Are you kidding me?"

"No, who can kid about Halle Berry? I don't mean the person, I mean all that she represents. It's close to perfection."

"And now is where we begin to lose touch with reality, right? You understand that." Monique asked me to sit in the chair, directing her index finger like a schoolmarm. "What you say Halle Berry represents is a fantasy. You see the Halle Berry without flaws. Michael, look at my face now and compare it to how I appeared in magazines with makeup, tricks, and lighting. Halle Berry works in the world of unreality and fantasy. She's not real to you or anyone who sees her films."

I knew Mon could never understand my point of view. "But you are really beautiful—you know that. There are people like you, Mon, and there are people like me."

What she didn't understand was that there are standards of beauty some of us aspire towards and fail to achieve. It seemed so basic. I would always come up short of the body image I wanted to have. That was my reality. If I couldn't approach the ripped male body of the models with the ridiculously taut abs and broad chests on the boxes of Calvin Klein underwear, what was the point in trying? Futility led to despair, which led to a desire to disappear altogether. It all added up to starving. That was my precise, scientifically quantifiable equation I understood and felt completely comfortable with. It made sense to me.

"Babe, I'm sure you think Jessie is beautiful," Mon said, ignoring my reply.

"True, true there."

"So, you mean if Jessie was still as beautiful as you think and really overweight, you couldn't fall in love with her?"

"I don't know. It's not about the girl. It's more about me. I can't stomach flesh, fat, imperfection. I can't deal with…"

"Being human? That's what you are saying." Mon glared at me. "I think I get it." She underhanded a button-down shirt to me from the closet. "Time to shower. You realize we're humans. We struggle with our weight, we eat, we gain weight, and lose it."

It sounded silly coming from Monique, who was still liquorice stick slim and so put together. "Oh please, Mon, you are different."

She snapped to attention. "The difference is you gave up. Yes, I work hard at staying healthy and yes, it's been my job to look a certain way, but I have struggled with a lot of the issues you have. I chose to fight to live a normal life, eat right, exercise and take care of myself.

"You don't want to live in the real world, and face tough choices." Her face had gone crimson. "We all struggle with our bodies—we do. It comes down to finding balance. Balance is the word missing from your vocabulary. There's a reason they call it the happy medium. You need to find that or you will forever be stuck in the miserable. And I don't want to see that, Babe. I don't."

"Mon, I can rationally understand your point of view and everything you tell me, but I feel something else. I truly believe if I ate like normal people, I would just keep eating and have man boobs, and be embarrassed to be alive," I said, gathering my shoes and underwear.

Pulling her hair back with both hands as if she wanted to rip every strand out of her head, Mon snarled. "No, you wouldn't. You'd be normal. You'd be like everyone else. If you'd just lived your life, you might still be with Jessie. But look what your obsession has gotten you. Is this what you are starving for?"

"She wouldn't love me if I was fat." I was adamant—it was undeniable.

"That's ridiculous. Part of me thinks you really don't know how you actually sound. I honestly have to say, I really didn't understand this, the severity. I know David didn't."

"Mon, c'mon, there's nothing you really can do." I began to feel guilty for her helplessness.

"Oh, yes there is. There is. I'm so glad we talked. Now shower," she said, pointing to the bathroom door. "We are not sitting here all day."

"Okay, I will, but first listen, please. Let me try and make some kind of sense to you. "When I was nineteen, I went out with this fat… wait, wait, you're going to get angry, so let's say kinda overweight girl because she really liked me. No one had really ever responded to me very much in high school, so I went out with her. After a few weeks, it was kind of intense. We ended up having sex. I mean sex was sex. I was just happy to get laid, but down deep I hated myself afterward. Not her. I didn't hate her—she had nothing to do with it. I knew it was all about me.

"I know you don't want to hear this, but I'm confessing. And I got to tell you, these painkillers are fucking amazing. I can't feel my body. If I had these every day, I'd have no problems with food. Everybody should have them." I laughed at Mon shaking her head. "So, what was I telling you?"

"Some girl, probably imaginary."

The haze gave way to a moment of clarity. "Okay, well, just before I met that girl, I lost my virginity to an older girl. Bear with me here because it doesn't get gross. I worked with her for a few years at Marshalls. She would always innocently flirt with me in the break room. Each night I'd drive her home, so we used to talk shit and have a lot of laughs.

"Believe it or not, and I still don't, but one night I told her I was a virgin for some reason. A few weeks later, she directed me to a lot behind a deli and put her hand in my pants. She was amazingly hot. I mean a really hot Cuban girl, probably the only Cuban I ever saw on Long Island—they don't grow Cubans on the Island. I couldn't believe I was touching her perfect, naked body. I was just thrilled just to look at it. That was enough, but we did it a couple of times, and I knew those were no doubt pity fucks for her."

"And you're going to tell me the other girl then didn't compare to her." Mon sliced an apple and ate it one piece at a time at the table. "That girl was going to be your standard?"

"No, Mon, no, no, the point is when I saw the other girl without clothes, it just fucked me up," I said while trying to prevent my jeans from falling off my hips. "She took off these panties the size of a tent. Grandmother underwear."

"Babe, no, please. What is with you?"

"I should be telling a shrink this then. You want the truth? Here's the truth. I can tell you bullshit if you want. People say talk, then they don't want to hear it raw."

She carefully placed the last slice of apple in her mouth. "Go ahead, go ahead, but know this is some ugly stuff."

"Okay, yes, ugly, cruel, sexist, whatever, but it's the fucking truth. So, there she was, reclining naked, and I saw the elastic of her underwear had made a deep, pinkish crease in her flesh. I freaked out—I once had those same creases. I actually couldn't get it up after I saw that. I mean not at all. I felt dead. There I was with a girl who reflected everything I hated in myself. I realized the way I saw that girl's body must have been exactly how the Cuban girl saw me. I knew she had to be grossed out, too. She was telling all her girlfriends I was a fat fuck. I couldn't live with myself knowing that. It just killed me. Like literally. I couldn't get out of bed for a week."

"Oh please." Monique's face was all twisted up as she hung her head. "You said the most you weighed was 171. For a nineteen-year old boy, that is not fat."

"I wasn't 171 at the time. I was much less," I said defensively.

"I believe you were. You are undermining your own story. I don't even know if you can be trusted as the narrator of your own crazy stories." She pointed again to the shower as David finally arrived.

"Fat, all this fat talk. I don't want to hear anymore. Enough," he shouted. "Mike, I've been listening to you. Do you two realize the door is wide open? The whole building can hear you talking about fucking fat girls and creases of flesh. It's like listening to some weird fetish diary. I was standing outside just taking it all in. A little voyeuristic I know, but there was little I could add. I think one of your neighbors was taking notes for a book on mental illness."

I peeled my shirt off and looked in the mirror. My long hair was straggling around the beginnings of a sad, wispy beard.

"You know that story about the girl with the stomach? Wanna know why that's still in your head? I'll tell you why. You want to hold onto it, somehow." David's voice echoed throughout the apartment.

Through a crack in the door, I saw Monique light up a cigarette. "And I bet that girl wasn't even fat," she said.

"Who the fuck knows? He's probably high as a kite on painkillers," David replied, laughing. "Thing is, he's told me this stupid story before. I actually think his freak-out was some kind of sexual panic. But that's a whole different issue we can't even begin to deal with. I really don't think this is all about fat. It's got to be something bigger. Only you know what it is, Michael. You hear me? Everybody has their own version of fat, but your anxiety is manifested in a very bad way here. I went to therapy for my issues. Everyone in the world goes to therapy for their fat." He yanked the bathroom door shut with force.

"But I've been to see therapists," I said while brushing my teeth.

"The wrong ones. We'll find you the right one. We're going to go to the therapist the doctor recommended. I'm making an appointment as soon as possible.

"We'll let the doctor figure out what the fat is. It isn't about diets, losing weight, and fat girls who love fucked-up fat boys." As I took another pain killer and fixed the bandage on my arm, he banged on the door. "I hope you are listening, Michael. Monique is right. You're living in a crazy world of perfection. People aren't Platonic ideals. Your visions of perfection, well, they don't exist. You know that.

"Once you realize this and get down to the business of living in the world that Jessie and Les are living in now you will be out of your Peter Pan fantasies of childlike never, neverfat." The doorknob rattled. "I don't hear the water running."

From the shower, I heard Monique say to David, "Did you hear what he was telling me?"

"Yeah, but we'll figure it out. We'll get him help."

David suddenly lowered his voice. "You know if I'm being honest, you have to know the truth. If Halle Berry is fantasyland, why would anyone want to live in reality?"

"Fuck you," she said. Their playful laughter was somehow oddly comforting. The stream from the showerhead pulsed through my hair and down my body. I watched all the sweat and grime, which felt like a suffocating sweater, slide off my ankles and circle the drain. Even though I was struggling to breathe and feeling faint, the rush of water was renewing.

Seven

After finally emerging from the shower with wet hair, I had dull chest pains and severe cramps in my legs. This usually happened at night when the day's fasting began to take its toll, but it rarely occurred in mid-afternoon. David and Monique were sitting across from each other and eating a microwaved frozen pizza.

"What were you doing in there so long? I thought you might have slithered down the drain and was coming in to get you." David's collar was amiss. More than a few strands of Mon's hair were falling in her eyes. I realized that they might have gotten in a quickie while I was playing with my luffa and checking for stomach fat. Jessie and Les, David and Mon—apparently, the apartment had become a fuck palace in my absence.

David was slowly peeling slices of pepperoni off the cheese when the phone rang. "Answer that, Bobby Sands," he said while licking his fingers. I let the machine take the call.

"What are you doing with an ancient answering machine from Fred Flinstone's garage sale?" David said over my greeting message. "I will give you the goddamn money to buy a cell phone. Tomorrow, we'll go to Best Buy."

"I don't want your money," I snapped.

"I'm your brother. You are supposed to take my money, but you never ask for anything."

"I don't want or need your money."

"Mike, I see the way you live, and I'm confused. I mean you are too old, too poor, and too male to be anorexic. I always thought it was for spoiled rich, teenage girls angry at mommy and daddy or really old rich women with nothing left to do but stave off the inevitable spread. You have everything to live for." He devoured the last two crusts of his slice.

"I don't want to sound like a beer commercial, but it's time to fuck crazy women, do drugs, be creative, go for that gusto," he laughed, no doubt recognizing how ludicrous the word gusto sounded. "You want to live like a monk, make it Thelonious."

I played back the message—it was Patty's pained voice again. "Michael, please if you're there, answer. I'm going to wait a few seconds, and if you don't pick up...." She sighed slightly. "I'm really vulnerable right now. You know I don't like talking into these machines. Why do you even still have one anymore?"

David laughed even more heartily. "We're definitely going shopping tomorrow."

"I'm done with this shit and this city. I'm going to change my life. It's time. This was a signal. You too, you need to move on now." The message cut off.

Monique looked at me. "She doesn't sound good. You should call her back."

I realized she was right, but I couldn't muster the energy to get out of the chair. "I don't know, that's kind of the way she always sounds."

"Don't be cruel. Just imagine how you feel now. She is going through the same thing, probably worse. She was with Les a long time." Mon pointed to a button-down shirt laid out over the back of a chair. "Wear that. You need to a whole new wardrobe. When was the last time you bought clothes, Babe?" I really couldn't recall. It might have been when Jessie first moved in.

"You really don't know how much she loved Les," Monique added before pushing the plate with her slice of pizza to the center of the table. "Besides, I thought she was your best friend."

"Les was my best friend. She just came along with the package." I went to the mirror to check just how sadly the shirt sagged off my shoulders.

"You're speaking out of anger towards Les. There's nastiness to your tone, and that's not you. I don't like it," Mon said, her voice straining.

The phone rang again, cutting her off. "I'm going to answer it" She rushed to pick up the receiver.

"Don't unless you want to talk," I said.

"I do," Mon fired back. It was indeed Patty again. I tuned out the chatter and went back into the bathroom. A brilliant sunbeam penetrated the window beneath the half-drawn shade, but I turned on the fluorescent light anyway. I could see better under the bright light—it exposed things in the mirror that would otherwise remain hidden. My skin was pale, sort of a milky white. The rings around my eyes were big enough to hold a championship fight.

The pathetic, wispy beard I'd grown only made my eyes appear to sink deeper into my bony face. I unbuttoned the shirt to see red blotches on my chest—they may have been a result of the shower scrub or maybe too many nights sleeping on our shitty, lumpy mattress.

My Adam's apple was sticking out of my neck, seemingly ready to puncture the skin. I stared at my reflection while wondering why Adam had to eat that apple. Where was his willpower? Where was the denial? If he only had the wherewithal to say no to Eve, our bodies would never wither or fall apart. I could have fasted forever without consequences. All it took was a simple no.

I spread my ribs apart and carefully focused on the contours of my body while standing naked before the dirty mirror. I did this sometimes to make sure there were no new pockets of flesh, and to confirm the visibility of my bones. I truly admired what I saw—I had graduated from thin to thinner to thinnest. How rare it was to be so skinny. It was truly thrilling. Of course, it wasn't what I planned when I started dieting, but there seemed to be a kind of nobility in my frailty. No one else could achieve what I had done.

Carefully, I examined my numb forearm, which felt like a dead weight. Oh, how wonderful it felt to be free from the pain. I proceeded to wrap my fingers around my right bicep to see the thumb meet the forefinger in a perfect little circle. Such a thing of beauty. With a sigh of relief, I yanked the door open while wearing nothing but a towel tied loosely around my waist.

Jessie was standing before me.

"Jessie. Shit. What the…Hey, just wait a few seconds, and let me get some clothes. We can talk about things. I'm so happy to see you." She had to know I was lying. There was no place to hide, though. "You want something to eat? There's food in the cabinet and refrigerator." I was babbling in the cool hallway as my heart raced. Suddenly feeling completely exposed, I headed back into the bathroom to cover my chest my chest with a towel. "Where's David and Monique?"

"They left for a bit and will be back soon. What happened to your arm?" Jess spoke serenely.

I didn't want to tell her about the accident or the hospital. She'd been there too many times to help me after my emergency visits. The truth would only bring back the kind of memories I needed to blot from her mind. "Don't ask. A long story."

"Michael, why don't you get dressed? I only came to pick up a few things, so there's no reason for you to stand around with towels. I'm going to get something to drink. I'll wait for you."

"There is plenty of bread and cold cuts if you want them." The words just tumbled out. I was hell-bent on feeding her.

"I'll just have a piece of fruit," she said.

I was hoping she would not reappear with an apple. I just couldn't bear that. I had never cared about being half-naked in the hallway in front of Jessie, but at that moment I felt stripped of everything and so fragile—sculpted by Giacometti.

A good, long nap was in order.

"Michael, are you getting dressed or sleeping?"

I sat on the bed with my pants around my knees, convinced Jess was there for a purpose. She was coming back. One night with Les had made her realize her folly. After clumsily tying my sneakers with my one good arm, I made my way out of the bedroom, determined to get her back.

"Jess, listen, hey you know things haven't been great…"

"Don't start. Don't even think about it." Jessie emerged from the kitchen with Scott towels in her hands. She was dressed in a gray vest over a black turtleneck with her hair tucked beneath a weathered Red Sox cap. It was Les's fucking hat.

"It's too complicated, and I'm much too worn out by what's gone down to really talk about it. You wore me down, Michael. You know that. You sucked the life out of me. We will discuss it at the right time when our heads are clear. For now, I just came for clothes, not to argue."

"Who wants to argue? I want to tell you I love you. I do love you for Christ's sake, and you love me. You will admit that, won't you?" She didn't reply. "Won't you?"

More silence. "Won't you?"

"Three strikes, Michael. You know I loved you. I wanted to help you and live with you and have a future together…listen, I came to get my clothes. I can't do this." She returned to the refrigerator. I watched her bend and wipe the bottom shelf.

"What are you cleaning? Let the food rot. Let the crumbs fall. Why are you always cleaning? So what if I like things a little messy."

"It's all too messy, Michael. Let me clean if I feel like it. Take a step back from everything. You need space and time. Then you will understand that what I did was for the best for us. It was the right move. We weren't going anywhere anymore so…"

"So, you decided to go nowhere with Les? Is that the space you need? I understand you wanting to separate but to move in with someone immediately. Let alone Les."

"Michael, don't you dare. Don't say anything about Les. I love him."

"Oh please. Jess, you fucked him, so you love him."

"I'm going to ignore your silly boyish anger, but you know nothing about me and Les right now. You know nothing, you…" She paused for a breath. "You just really know nothing. I'm just going to tell you, and I want it to sink in. I love Les. If you want to substitute your word go ahead, but that's you. It makes no difference because I know what word you hear."

"You don't love me anymore? Is that what you're saying?" My voice cracked.

"I loved you—I know that. It's just that I think we were more in love with love, with the idea of it. You and me, we never loved anyone before we met each other, and we fit so well together. Things happened. All we had was this concept of love." She was perched where David was previously sitting. Her words sounded eerily familiar.

"It's not a concept. It's a feeling." I sounded desperate and knew it.

"I don't know. We didn't let other people into our lives. We didn't strive to be better, to get better jobs, to be more. We loved being who we were."

"You're telling me you left because..."

"Because Les lets me see who I can be."

"And that is what precisely, Jess?"

"I don't know. That's the real beauty of it." She smiled radiantly. "And you must realize I left for other reasons. Ones you don't want to hear."

"Try me."

She walked briskly into the kitchen again, reached into the refrigerator and pulled out an old potato that must have been sitting in the vegetable tray for months.

"I left you because of this."

"Because of a moldy potato? What are you talking about?"

"Because you can't eat this. You remember when I bought this? I bought it one night, months ago, because you randomly said you once liked mashed potatoes. You know I hardly ever cook, but the next day I went out to Stop and Shop and bought a bag of potatoes. It was so damn heavy."

She stopped to slam her fist against the refrigerator. After opening the door again, she pulled out the bag. A few potatoes spilled on the floor. "I swore I wasn't going to get upset, and I'm not going to, Michael. I'm really not.

"Remember the next night I made some mashed potatoes, no meat and nothing else, because I knew you wouldn't eat anything more. But I figured you'd eat some mashed potatoes if I made them. I boiled the damn things. Instead of doing all the other crap I had to do, I sat here and mashed and mashed and mashed like a crazy slave working in a Chinese sweatshop. Remember that?"

I said nothing because I quickly recalled what happened when I came home from work. Jessie was waiting for me on a stool in the kitchen. After I walked in, she said she had a surprise.

I thought box seats to a Red Sox game—something I would never buy or indulge in. I opened my eyes to a large pot of paste. Maybe it was mashed potatoes. Who knows? I couldn't tell the difference. With a broad smile, Jess told me they were homemade mashed potatoes with garlic and basil.

"You said you didn't remember when you last had mashed potatoes, so I thought you might want to try some I made," she said sweetly. "I made them just for you, Michael. I want you to eat them."

I was completely silent and stupefied. What the hell was I going to do with a pot of mashed potatoes? I stammered for five minutes, shrugged and told her my stomach hurt too much to eat anything. Eating from that vat of white mush with garlic and basil was unimaginable—even nauseating. After putting Saran Wrap around the top of the pot, I placed it on the top shelf of the refrigerator.

The terrible memory made me squeamish as I stared at Jessie. She was now going to be making mashed potatoes for Les.

"Remember that awful night, Michael? Remember how those mashed potatoes sat on the shelf for a week until I threw them out?" She slapped the wall, rattling the picture frames, and kicked a potato that had landed near her foot.

"Well, I sure remember it and don't want to think about it again. Past tense. I'm putting that, and all that came with it, behind me. So why are we over, Michael? Why did I leave? Mashed potatoes, and all they represent." She was yelling while walking towards the door.

"This is absurd, Jess. Something out of the *Twilight Zone*." Of course, I knew it was very real while finally understanding how fucking wrong I had been.

There were tears in Jessie's eyes as she looked blankly towards the door. "Our whole life revolved around what that potato stood for."

I touched her arm, but she pushed back with enough anger to force me to step away.

"I tried. I mean I really did, Michael, but you don't want help anymore. We lived like this for a long time. And each time you got ill or went to the hospital, you said you'd change. You've been through how many psychiatrists already, and nothing's worked. You don't care anymore. Maybe you don't want things to work out. You're as thin as ever—you don't look good at all— it kills me to see you this way. When we first met, you were so different. Despite what you thought, I loved your body. But now you scare me. Have you looked at yourself? I mean really look?"

If she only knew. Jess blew her nose into a sheet of Scott toweling sitting on the table while shuffling towards the door. The breeze outside had kicked up enough to rattle the shades.

After I slammed all the windows shut and returned, Jessie placed her hand on my shoulder. It barely made an impression. What once seemed so casual and intimate—her touching me—now seemed so special and so final. I was so overwhelmed, I had to sit down. Jessie moved into the seat directly across from me. When I looked up to her, I realized we had never shared a full meal at the table.

"Listen, please listen to me, Michael. What I understood is, I will never make a difference in your life," she said with a wavering voice.

"That's ridiculous," I interrupted.

"Will you let me finish? I know you want something different, but we have to live in reality." We stared at each other, frozen in time, as she gathered her thoughts. At that moment, I knew Jess was indeed already finished and long, long gone.

"When we first started out and this food business seemed as if it might turn into a major problem, I figured I could change you. I figured you'd want to enjoy our life together. If we worked out and found some people to help you, things would change. We would change together. I always held out hope you would get better. You know that.

"I believed you would come around. I wanted to fight it with you. I thought you would be able to enjoy the small things in life—things like mashed potatoes. I tried to make the other parts of your life less difficult so you could somehow come to grips with the demons keeping you from eating and living a normal life.

"I gave ground and gave ground until I found there was nothing left to stand on anymore. I...me...Jessie was not going to make a difference in any of this. And I lost sight of what I needed. What I need, and who I was. I know now you have to deal with your stuff whatever way you can. You need to find the answers. And you'll do it without me, and be better off. And so will I."

I stared at the framed print of *La Dolce Vita* on the wall as my

creaking chair punctuated the symphony of late afternoon noises—
the trolley running down Commonwealth Avenue, students yelling
at each other on the street, and the wind rattling through the cracks
in the broken windows.

"I'm going to get going. Forget my clothes," Jessie said while putting
her coat on. "I'll set up a time to pick them up when you're gone. That's
all I'm taking. You can have everything. I'm sorry. It can't replace
what I'm taking with me but…"

"Jessie, wait." There was little to add.

"No, I better leave. There's nothing that will make sense anymore."
She opened the door and walked out.

I watched her hurry down the hallway and gingerly pass David and
Monique, who was sitting on the staircase with a bottle of Coke and
a plastic bag of food by her feet.

I gazed incredulously at them. "You've been out here the whole time?"

"We'd only be in the way, so we disappeared for a while," David said.
"We went for a long walk. Got some sustenance the Allston way at
Store 24. Where would the world be without the inconvenient prices
of convenience stores?" Monique fingered her hair behind her ears
before making her way into the apartment as David did deep knee
bends in the hallway.

"You alright?" Mon said.

"I'll be okay. I'm just spacing out. I'm sorry, I just…"

"No need for explanations, Babe. Sometimes we spend half our lives
living and the other half explaining why. You've got a lot of absorbing
to do. Just try to relax. We're going to hang out. David bought the
Times and the *Globe*. They make sitting on stairs a bit more comfortable. My ass was killing me."

David quickly went back to the stairwell again to grab a bag of Fritos.
"I'm going to eat this whole bag. These are like virgins—nobody can
eat just one."

Mon rolled her eyes after a sigh "Ignore him when he's hungry.
He's a complete idiot."

David emptied the bag onto a plate before dragging me, along with
the bottle of Coke, into the front room by the television.

"I love this stuff. A Coke and a smile, right?" David said, punching my arm. "The greatest business blunder of all time was to change this. You have to wonder why someone ever thought that we needed a New Coke. Who could be so stupid to change this formula? Nobody wanted the change. Sometimes you just can't change certain things."

"Change for change's sake doesn't work," Mon said before placing a sandwich in front of David. "That's why New Coke didn't fly. There was no reason to change it, but sometimes, you just have to do it because it makes things better. Imagine if they didn't change Tab into Diet Coke all those years ago?" Finally, she carefully wiped off the couch with a napkin and sat next to my brother.

"That was not change, that was reinvention. Complete reinvention," David said, drinking out of the bottle. "Sometimes, that what's needed, and that's why we need bold people to re-imagine things. What do you think, Michael? You are too silent for me right now."

I knew what they were really talking about. Neither gave a fuck about New Coke and the business ramifications of change.

"Hey, Mike, I know this sucks now, but you're looking at it as an end. You need to rethink it. See it as a beginning. The real work begins now. We'll be there for you. We're going to get you to a doctor, you'll eventually meet someone and the wheels on the bus go 'round and 'round. Right?" David smiled with his arm around me.

He pulled me much too close—I could smell the sweat of his day. "Guess so," I replied while still thinking about potatoes. I realized my brother might have taken great satisfaction at seeing Jessie walk past him down the stairs.

With his sandwich in hand, David pushed the dish of Fritos before me.

"So, for now, put all this out of your mind, and have a Frito. One or two, maybe three. If you don't, I will." He scooped up a few, took the bread off the top of the sandwich, dropped the chips on the cheese, put the bread back on, and pressed his hand down to crunch it all together. "Did I say I love these things?"

The dish of Fritos remained untouched as David ate with pleasure. Monique slipped into the kitchen only to return moments later with an apple. She dropped it in my lap. "Forget the chips—eat that. I'll trade with you. I'll eat a few of your Fritos if you eat the apple. I'll make you something in a few minutes."

Mon held a Frito in front of her face while smiling at me. "You know these are going straight to my ass today, but I'll work it off tomorrow. That's when we all start anew."

Part Two

My Back Pages

Eight

What Jessie called the "food business" began slipping into the red just around the time I met her. That's when the real darkness set in. The roots, though, probably could be traced all the way back to my childhood years when I was eating bagels slathered in butter during the day and crying in front of the bathroom mirror at night. I was lulled into false hope by my mother's encouraging, "It's just baby fat." Of course, it wasn't. It was good old fat fat I just couldn't seem to shake.

I completely accepted and embraced my fate as the fat boy throughout my teenage and college years. I thought that's who I was destined to be. I never felt the obsessive desire to completely transform my body—and everything it represented—until I got out of college on Long Island.

During my four years studying literature and writing at Adelphi University in Garden City, I did little more than play baseball or lose myself in the far recesses of the library. Each day, I would confiscate a cubicle in the corner of the library's literature section and read novels until well after midnight. My focus never wavered, but on days after paper were due, I enjoyed thumbing through cheap porn magazines while hiding between the stacks and eyeing the pretty girls with skinny asses.

David had already set a successful path out of the Island by doing nothing but listening to music and locking himself away in his room and libraries, so I thought what he achieved couldn't be that hard to emulate.

If David's blinders on, no-look-back determination was necessary to escape the suburbs, then I was going throw all my chips in. And once I committed, there was no going back. I plowed my way through school without distractions or detours. Ultimately, that intense form of tunnel vision became the blueprint for how I would lose weight. If you completely give your life over to something, it's pretty difficult to fail.

I first started dieting in an attempt to make a semi-pro baseball team in Smithtown during the first spring after I graduated from college. Even though I was nothing more than a marginal pitcher in college, I felt compelled to continue playing ball. An electric arm, though, only gets you so far when you have a marshmallow body. While in school, I was nothing more than a middle innings relief and mop-up pitcher, but I always enjoyed being on a team.

It made me feel a part of something and alleviated all the lonely hours spent reading and researching. I also found kindred spirits in the coaches, who constantly engaged me in discussions about baseball strategy, trivia, and history. I had fun talking with them during and after games about the art of sacrificing, hit and runs, split seam fastballs, and forkballs. They became my short-lived family, which I knew would eventually abandon me once I graduated.

The yearning to feel that kind of connection and camaraderie again was what drove me to try out for the semi-pro team. As I prepared to make the squad, I decided to change some of my life routines in order to reshape my body and turn the fluff to buff. I remember talking to David and neatly detailing the workout program I had designed after reading books about running and exercise.

He seemed bored by my ten-point program and constant yabbering about the kind of work required to make all the years of life in the chubby section of the department store disappear.

"Michael, you need to stop talking about this and just fucking tell yourself that you can do it. You have been going on about losing weight for years. Prove to yourself that you can get to where you want to be. Get in shape and make the fucking team. Even if you're not good enough, you will finally put all this talk of losing weight behind you. I'm daring you. Lose the weight, goddammit, and move on."

That was all I needed to hear. His dare became my quest. I set out a precise plan of eating in a spiral notebook. It outlined what was verboten in minute detail. I wrote "Food" in thick black magic marker on the cover and split the pages into two sections: Ride or Die. It sounded cool to me somehow. Like a life and death matter.

Thanks to hours of exhaustive research in food journals and diet books, I discovered that bad foods far outweighed the good. I realized I had lived my whole life indulging in what could be called the angioplasty diet. And that's when the food I'd relied on became the enemy to be conquered.

When I was growing up, our refrigerator and cabinets were always stuffed with junk food. My family wasn't about tasting. We consumed. My mother loved to fry everything, and there was a heavy emphasis on pasta, especially on Sunday afternoons.

Both my mother and father devoured their meals without ever savoring taste or smells. When I wasn't sharing dinner with my family during my childhood years, I was snacking on Twinkies, Cool Whip, Ho-Hos, Pop Tarts, Devil Dogs, Yodels, and Oreos, all of which I found totally, completely, and utterly irresistible.

And no one ever told me this behavior was wrong. Whoever thought you could actually resist the things you wanted most? I never received any real guidance during those years because my parents seemed to give up on life after David left for college. It was as if he had abandoned the fortress, and went to fight for the other side. I felt his absence the most, though. He was the only person I could talk to, and he always took the time to listen. Damn, it's tough to explain—some of you must understand that connection with a brother. Let's just say, I just always felt safe around him.

Right after David moved away with a motherload of scholarships and awards, our whole family changed. My father retreated further and further into his own world. The air went out of my mom's balloon as if my father's deep despair had sapped all of her energy.

Dad had slowly drifted away from us after he lost his job as an executive for a limousine service in Garden City. He was downsized in every sense of the word. The tall man, who once walked so proudly, was transformed into a stooped shouldered, sad, directionless survivor with a perpetual scowl on his face. To help keep the roof over our heads, he took a job as a taxi dispatcher while working part-time for a friend in a small antique store in Manhasset.

He was always exhausted, and I barely saw him when he finally got home from work. The emotional and physical fatigue—his steps became slower and his words barely audible— took its toll on my mother, who clearly wanted to help shoulder his pain and draw the man back into her orbit.

As a couple, they had always kept to themselves without making many friends. No one ever entered our house, and we never made family visits. They pretty much withdrew from the world, and my mother stopped cooking. We essentially evolved into a ready-to-make, microwave family. Our relatives and friends became Mama Celeste, Uncle Ben, Sara Lee, Mrs. Paul, and Aunt Jemima.

By the time I hit my teens, my mother had become a culinary midwife. Every night, she did little more than set the timer and wait patiently next to the countertop with a blank stare on her face and plates in hand. Her speech patterns were reduced to monosyllables. I would watch her as I sat in the corner of the kitchen by myself, desperately hoping the color would return to her eyes.

I'll never forget the sight of her standing alone and glaring at the time running down on the microwave clock as my father silently read his newspaper. Every so often, my mom would smile limply at me and say without prompting, "It's going to be alright, Michael." We would end up quietly sitting over the steaming plates of wilted lasagna or pallid macaroni and cheese before getting on with our evenings.

This pre-packaged, processed world became my way of life. I never thought twice about it or even considered an alternative. I came to believe everyone ate that way. Unfortunately, I was the only one in the family to gain weight. My mom and dad could eat, and eat, and eat cholesterol-choked meals and gallons of Sealtest ice cream, and somehow remain slim. David seemed to live at the Carvel ice cream store after going to White Castle or Burger King, but he never gained an ounce. I seemed to absorb every calorie they swallowed and ended up carrying their weight around.

It took years after they were gone, but something kicked in for me right after college. I understood I couldn't blame my family for what I ate and how I looked anymore. I re-evaluated everything so I could move beyond my Puffinstuff life and grab the wheel of my own out-of-control clown car.

David's challenge to lose weight helped reinforce my new mission. I knew there could be no compromise or margin of error. I had to prove I could finally transform myself, and go beyond his minimal expectations.

I need to clear something up, though, and be very honest with you. David's tough love and the way he egged me on was completely justifiable because he had every right to doubt my willpower and strength. Over the previous years, there were so many false starts at weight loss. Throughout high school, I repeatedly called him to complain about being fat and unattractive. Time and again, I would hastily commit to a diet and fail miserably.

I'd say to myself before sleeping, "Tomorrow, you must stop eating junk food." The next day, I would try to eat just one Twinkie instead of two with my breakfast, and then skip an extra fruit pie for lunch. By nightfall, my mom would eventually ask me if I was hungry. I'd eat some kind of sodium soaked, artery-busting meal but opt for just a small snack for dessert. I thought that's what it took. At bedtime, my long, grueling day of dieting would end.

This silly charade would recur at least once every month or so. With each stumble, I'd hate myself more and more. It was an endless loop of fierce commitment, abject failure, and rabid self-hatred. My own private, imperfect circle of hell.

I continued the same routines and patterns throughout my college days, even though I was on my own. It all seemed so familiar and so easy. While I tentatively changed things with my pre-tryout food plan, my life was irrevocably altered after the first few fiasco practices for the semi-pro team, which truly motivated me to finally break the vicious cycle that had lingered long after high school. I just wasn't prepared for what I encountered and found myself among the first cuts. All the players I was vying against had taut musculature and looked sleekly fit in a uniform. I was the odd man out as I waddled through the running drills with my button down uniform top sagging over my belt.

After feeling completely inadequate after my second practice, I called my high school coach, Mr. Stacatella. He advised me to start running. "Running is the quickest and most effective way to keep the weight off," he said. "You will literally see yourself running into a new you.

"Michael, you also need to begin to consider what you put in your mouth. You can't eat the kind of food you eat and be who you want to be. Changing your body is a change of lifestyle. Set goals and forget who you were. Imagine what you want to be. If you can imagine it, you can do it."

I had no idea that I would eventually hear the same words from Monique only months later. Imagine. It sounded overly romantic and more than a little bit corny to me, but I bought in without hesitation.

I'd been challenged by my coach and my brother, so I narrowed the Ride or Die food plan even more, and knew there would be no going back. It was time to chase down the thin Michael who had always eluded me.

One night, I cut out pictures of sprinter Ben Johnson and taped them to the back of the door in my room next to dizzying shots of Kim Basinger from 9 ½ Weeks. Before heading out for a run each day, I stared at the images of how I wanted to look and the reason I needed to get that way.

I read dozens of men's health magazines. Even though the pictures of all the ripped gym rats made me feel feeble and impotent, they gave me incentive and hope. If I couldn't get their bodies, maybe I could at least develop a bit of self-confidence. After I had tossed out all the food in my refrigerator and spent a few weeks developing strict mind control, I was convinced that my reinvention would eventually come to fruition. It wasn't a matter of if it was going to happen—the question became just how quickly the transformation could take place.

Each morning I ran through the streets of my tree-lined neighborhood at six like a suburban Rocky, counting parked cars and inhaling the dew of a new day. I loved hearing the thwack of my feet hitting the pavement. It was the sound of progress. Slowly, the lights in each house of the residential community would flicker on and cars coughing up exhaust fumes emerged one by one from different garages.

I dashed past men in ill-fitting suits as they placed the trash cans on the sidewalk and waved at women gingerly walking their scruffy dogs down driveways.

At first, the short, two-mile run was brutally difficult—often painful. Frequently, I was forced to stop while gasping for breaths of air. But I pushed on because I simply refused to be denied. My breathing became easier as my strides got longer. I felt alive—like a superhero. Fuck Ben Johnson and yes, fuck Kim Basinger. Why not? I suddenly thought I could do it all.

There were sacrifice and denial, but I knew I could get to the point where all of the days of going without and saying no would just become a regular part of my life.

Pounding the pavement got easier with repetition. I'd get lost inside my own head while listening to the birds chirping, my heart beating, and the early morning cicadas' shrill songs. This was my new reality. There was great comfort in the isolation—a special kind of solitude, unlike anything I'd ever felt. It was like meditation or finding an inner stillness while moving towards something.

Something different, something real, and something surprising. A new me.

Even though my life had become one of complete isolation, running every day connected me to something bigger—I couldn't identify what it was. I just felt it.

I made my way through the streets and jogged along the bike paths next to Long Island Expressway. I was recklessly sucking in fogs of blue exhaust fumes, but watching the blur of cars streaming past the extended running lanes through the woods exhilarated me. When my speed picked up, I tried to outrace the traffic. It seemed like I was turning into an overly determined machine that would someday rush past the whir of cars.

Throughout my long jaunts down the paths each day, I tried to remember a time when I actually felt moments of happiness. A single memory, any memory, always proved elusive. I knew it was never about my parents or David, though. At least, it didn't seem so. I thought it was always about me: my problem, my deal, my sadness. No matter how hard I tried, I just couldn't recall a time when I wasn't a disconsolate, restless child who wanted to break out of his own skin.

Jogging never made the despair and self-hatred disappear. You just can't out-run all of that. With every mile, though, the intensity seemed to diminish. Running helped transform life into something I could manage. Maybe even something I would like.

Running seven to ten miles each day for weeks, finally produced results. I could see the pounds slowly coming off and my face becoming thinner. All of my pants fell far below my hips. One night after a midnight run, I gathered up my old jeans and tossed them in a garbage can for a brilliant bonfire in the driveway. I rejoiced at the sight of my forlorn past forming billows of smoke before evaporating into the humid summer breeze.

You have to understand that losing weight rapidly is a very strange thing. Each day I'd look into the bedroom mirror and wonder, "Where did all the fat go?" I mean, did it disappear? Could I have possibly eradicated a vital part of my essence during all that dieting and exercise? How did the body know what to retain? Did the good, fundamentally sound elements of my former self dissolve in the process? Could I trust what remained?

The questions haunted me.

At times, I would sit alone at night, feeling strangely sad, as if I had lost something I could never regain. The wonderful euphoria of slimming down was undermined by a fear that I was moving from being to non-being, existing to nonexistence. I seemed to be slowly disappearing. My face became angular and a bit demonic, especially when I didn't shave. I saw a new Michael every morning. My face and body looked foreign—even a bit frightening. I didn't recognize myself.

Annihilating the young Michael was what I had always wanted, though. Finally achieving such a small goal in life's big scheme became such a liberating thing. The failure of the past was indeed history. I did more than meet David's challenge—I far surpassed whatever he possibly could have expected.

It felt like a mere beginning—I wondered what else was possible. In fact, I was losing pounds at such a wonderfully fast clip, I saw no reason to stop. The idea of merely maintaining my weight or slipping backward was unfathomable.

Every so often, I had a recurring dream about waking up again as the bloated, chubby, and dazed boy gazing at the ice cream in our family's refrigerator. Sweating profusely and trembling, I'd run to the mirror to happily reassure myself that the nightmare was over.

Who could have known it was just beginning?

Nine

As life would have it, I met Jessie at the Original Ray's Pizzeria in Greenwich Village. Yes, the corner, hole-in-the-wall home of the greasy, over-cheesed belly-bomber slices. Despite my commitment to eating nothing but foods that fell in the Ride side of my ledger, I still believed getting stressed out about eating pizza was a bit like worrying about maintaining a hard-on when you are drunk: If it feels great going in, don't worry about it going down. I would allow myself a small indulgence every so often but pay for it with extra roadwork the next day.

I was tired from my weekly walking excursion through Greenwich Village to visit favorite record stores like Bleeker Bob's and Generation Records, so after all the exercise, I decided to treat myself to Ray's. One slice, no topping. That would be my dinner caloric budget for the day. Earlier, I'd bought *The Art of Eating* by M.F.K. Fischer and Calvin Trillin's *American Fried: Adventures of a Happy Eater* in the Strand bookstore. Both books were highly recommended by an old English teacher from Adelphi after I told her about my curiosity with the literature of food.

I stood by myself at a circular counter near an old man reading *The Daily News.* Weary, perspiring people shuffled around me while I gazed through the big glass windows onto Sixth Avenue. Police cars sped through the night, and a group of kids was arguing about whether Giants' quarterback Danny Kanell could throw a deep ball. Clumsily holding the large slice—overflowing with cheese—in two hands, I carefully examined the oil slowly drip off the tip, and onto the paper plate, creating a small yellow pool with a gray stain. After just one bite, the heavy dough and mozzarella cheese descended into my stomach as if I had swallowed an anchor.

I had been living on cottage cheese, yogurt and salads for weeks, so something so leaden begging for digestion felt like a foreign invasion. I breathed laboriously while playing with the cheese oozing off the slice.

"I hate when that happens." Her voice was barely audible. "You lose so much of the good stuff." I looked up to search the small room and connect the words to a face. Jessie was pointing to the lump of melted mozzarella.

"It happens to me all the time. That's why when he serves it, I get a fork and knife and scoop all the cheese that spills over. All you gotta do is pile it up at the end of the slice." I nodded idiotically like a bobblehead without saying a word.

We were surrounded by men in their late twenties or early thirties. The guy to the left of Jess wore a tight mesh muscle shirt exposing sculpted arms and a thick neck of a linebacker. She ignored him, even as he kept inching closer to her.

"Isn't this place great? The best. I come here as often as possible, but I don't get into the city that frequently. Do you live in the city?" Jess spun her plate in circles while talking.

"Me? Do I look like I'm from the city? I'm from Long Island. No, I just take the train in every so often to walk around and buy books and music." This was the first time anyone had talked to me at Ray's. I was usually comforted by the anonymity and lack of conversation. Talking to strangers just wasn't something a Long Island kid did in Manhattan.

Jessie smiled ostentatiously—she had such thin lips and large, white teeth. I stared much too long. "You are from the Island? Get out of here," she said. "So am I. I'm from Oyster Bay. You believe that?" At first, I didn't. "I'm Jessie, that's with an e. Jessica, actually, but no one calls me that, so you shouldn't."

I paused long enough for her to add, "And you are? Besides kind of quiet."

I almost replied, "Are you talking to me?" but realized it would instantly translate into sociopath.

"Let me rephrase, what's your name?" she said slowly as if talking to a third grader.

"Michael."

"Okay, Michael talks," Jess squinted to gauge my reaction. I quickly thought about all the hackneyed B-movies I'd watched in which the guy meets a girl in a pizza parlor, and they end the night with the munchies only to discover that the hot dog does indeed fit right inside the donut.

This was Adam Sandler territory. I wasn't sure I wanted a part in a bad meet-cute rom-com, so I studied Jessie skeptically. She had a small scar just to the left of her right eye and lightly dusted cheekbones. She wore minimal makeup, no doubt because such attentive green eyes and etched features didn't require any embellishment.

I was always undeniably uncomfortable when I first met women because I was afraid my breasts were bigger than theirs, so I ended up talking nervously about why I was eating pizza—it seemed like such embarrassing behavior.

"I don't come here often, but my brother is a big fan of this place. He takes me here when he visits. He's a music critic," I said.

She looked at me quizzically. "That's great, good for your brother—he writes about music. Nice. But you must do something too, right?"

I tried to think of an appropriate answer besides, "Not really."

Jessie delicately picked up the books next to my plate. "Sorry, hope you don't mind, but I love to see what people read. I love books." She scanned the titles before turning each book over to inspect the back cover.

"These are books on food. I haven't met many guys who read about food. In fact, I haven't met many guys who read, which kind of tells you a little bit about my life." She laughed quietly to herself. "So, are you a chef or something?"

The suggestion seemed ridiculous. "I really don't know how to cook."

"And you are reading food books? Interesting. Now, c'mon, I am not a good cook, but I can make myself things for dinner. You have to be able to cook something. What can you make?" Her thin eyebrows ascended her forehead.

"If this was a movie, I guess I would answer 'reservations.'" I flinched. It was much too lame—I fell right into the Happy Madison trap. No doubt, somewhere deep inside, I was hoping she'd be irked enough to move on to the next table and talk to another guy. Instead, she answered instantaneously.

"And that would be a movie I wouldn't want to see." She pushed the books back to me. "Just tell me what you do, and we'll forget about the movies."

"Well, I recently graduated from college. I work in a department store on the Island until I go to grad school. I think I'm going. I really don't know." Of course, I knew I was headed back to school in September, but I didn't want to reveal myself too quickly. My right hand was shaking so visibly that I stuffed it in my pocket only to feel my erection involuntarily poke my upper thigh. There I was in sixth grade all over again, staring at little Nancy Palmisano's plaid skirt hiked up as she picked up a pen cap.

Jess rubbed her sharp chin deliberately after I rushed through my brief life synopsis. "Grad school for what?" she said with wide eyes.

I tried to think of some exotic or grandiose story while finally taking a bite of my slice. She'd never know the truth because I'd simply disappear into the ether, and my lie would never be exposed. Of course, I came up empty and settled for the truth. "Well, literature. Not sure what I'm going to do with it. Very few job prospects."

"Aha, so you are the kind of brainy type. Likes to read. Novels and books on food. Odd combination. I bet you read *Green Eggs and Ham* as a kid."

I refrained from smiling.

"It's really okay to laugh, you know. The mouth doesn't break. At least, I don't think." Her eyes darted back and forth before I reluctantly grinned.

"I'm not really brainy. I just read and think a lot," I said, relaxing.

She picked a piece of cheese off her slice and dropped it in her mouth. "Thinking a lot is good, especially in our world."

We had two different definitions of 'thinking a lot.' To her, it seemed to mean pondering the universe. To me, it meant wondering 'Why the fuck is this girl flirting with me?'

"I'm not so sure, I probably think too much," I said as a teenager with a Metallica t-shirt and skull earrings moved into the space vacated by the jock with the muscle shirt.

Jessie paid no attention to him. "I don't think it's possible to think too much, I really don't. I do think you better eat a bit. I actually might be talking too much."

I eyed the way she gesticulated with her small, tan hands. "I like to listen," I mumbled.

"Good, even better then. Mind if I tell you about my night. I don't usually hang here by myself. In fact, it's a bit embarrassing."

As Jessie explained the way her night began over drinks with a group of girls at The Mercury Lounge, she spoke rapidly as if pitching a used car. She precisely detailed how they split up when one friend became violently sick in the bathroom and went home early. Her best friend disappeared with some hot guy she met at the bar during the hair metal concert.

When Jess smiled at me with her eyes, I was quietly pleased that my weight loss seemed to be paying off. Finally, I wasn't invisible. I stood straight and tall with my stomach sucked in tight.

"I can't believe I'm way ahead of you here," she said, wiping her mouth. "I guess you eat pretty slow. You really didn't eat that much. I kind of eat fast, though. I like food. And that's probably why they write books about it."

I wasn't finished eating, but I didn't want her to just stand there and watch me chew alone. That would be embarrassing. I liked to eat by myself—hidden and incognito. Once I started running, I could never let people think I ate more than they did, so my eating habits changed. I usually ate at home as often as possible.

"I'm not even sure if I'll finish this," I said.

"Really? The cheese is so good here. I admire your willpower," she laughed.

Ah, indeed, thank you, I thought. Yes, yes, less was indeed more. Jessie was admiring my denial and paying full attention. I knew I had to be doing something right.

Jess carefully dabbed her mouth with a napkin—the ones she'd already used remained crumpled in a little pile on the plate before her. A man in a three-piece suit snuck in next to her right arm, so she immediately shifted to my side of the table.

"You want the rest of my slice? I don't think I'll finish it," I said.

"Uh, well, you realize that's kind of gross, right? But I might buy another." She marched to the counter and quickly turned back to me. "You want anything else? Soda?"

I shook my head. More denial.

As she waited for the sweating Hispanic teenager with a wispy mustache to throw the slice in the oven, a teenage couple took her spot. Before I tried to reclaim Jessie's place, she bounced back next to me. "Hope you don't mind, but for some reason, I'm really hungry. Let them stay there—we'll just move over to the corner."

She pointed to an angular table in the back of the restaurant. Her hyper-alert attentiveness and voraciousness seemed so sexy. After a small tap on my arm, she added, "I run a lot. You know I will work this next slice off tomorrow. No big deal."

Her words instantly paralyzed me. She was a runner. Jesusfuckingchrist, no. I realized she probably could leave me in the dust. "Er, how long you have you been..." As I spoke, she briskly walked back to the counter near the register.

I watched her maneuver through the crowd. She stood next to a heavyset, bald man in a *Lust for Life* t-shirt that barely covered his hairy belly. I gazed at her small, taut body. Her back arched slightly as she leaned forward against the old wooden counter. She was obviously an athlete with thin, muscular arms and short, toned legs in faded jeans.

She craned back and caught me staring. It suddenly dawned on me that there was no way it was going to work out the way I'd hoped. Girls like Jessie just did not go out with guys like me.

I figured something would soon go wrong. Jess would turn out to be gay or have a brain tumor. Maybe she was on parole. No doubt, she'd reveal that she was a dying gay parolee with an oozing mozzarella fetish.

I was never going to see her naked.

She eventually huddled next to me with her slice at our new table.

I finished my Diet Coke before she blew on the bubbling cheese and some sprinkled Parmesan on it.

"You were checking out my ass when I was standing up there. I saw you," she said with a mischievous grin.

I winced and went flush. "No, I definitely was not. I was…"

"It's okay. Yes, you did. That's cool. Don't lie, M.L.K. Fisher King." She took a quick bite, stepped back and dramatically stared at my body.

"No, no, no, don't do that." I picked up the paper plate to block her vision, waving it uncontrollably. Obviously, I looked like a ten-year-old boy being taunted by a girl on the playground.

"What's with this, Captain America? Is this your shield?" She snatched the plate from my hand. Her laughter rose above the muted talk from the tables around us. "Stop, will ya? I'm just having fun. Bit of an overreaction, no? Okay, I won't check you out. Relax."

"Jesus, I'm sorry." I wasn't sure what I was more ashamed of—my reaction or my body.

"Even though I just did." Jess smiled knowingly while steadying herself against the empty stool next to her. "What are you so paranoid about? You growing something no one has? I think I get where you are coming from." Lowering her voice, she added, "A man who refuses to be objectified. He is a twenty-first century man." She ripped her slice in half with a giggle.

I knew I'd blown it with her by acting like a scared, naked fat boy in a locker room with the football team. "I'm sorry. You can look if you want. I'm an idiot."

What man covers up his body?

"No worries, how do you know I didn't already check you out when I first walked in?"

I froze at her words, now even more embarrassed.

She pounded on the table in front of me. "Hey, you awake or am I making you fall asleep? You want half of this pizza? I can't finish it. Sometimes, I eat with my eyes."

"Not really. I'm sorry, you know. I didn't mean to wave the plate at you."

"It's alright, Michael. Friends." She put her hand out to shake. It was extremely warm. I hadn't touched a woman in months, but all the tension inside seemed to evaporate.

"I kind of like your modesty," Jessie said, her chin high. "Most guys ask you to feel their muscles, but they're mostly Play-Doh. Hey man, last call for this half of the slice. Want it?"

"Pass."

"Gone, sold to the garbage bin," she said before quickly tossing it in the trash can by the window on Eleventh Street. "So, are you headed back to the Island or are you staying in New York to see a show or something?"

"I'm going straight back." I was hoping we would share a cab.

"Excellent. Do you mind walking back to Penn Station with me? You know I would like to get some exercise, but I definitely don't want to walk alone."

"I've walked all day," I replied immediately. "A bit more never can hurt. I can walk off the pizza."

Jessie peered at me out of the corner of her eyes as we dodged couples on the sidewalk. "You barely had one slice of pizza, for God's sakes. You can work that off by blinking."

"So, you are a runner?" I said. It was a necessary misdirection.

She seemed delighted by the question and proceeded to tell me about her prolific running life as a member of the track team since her freshman year in high school. Jess walked as if her car was double parked next to a hydrant outside of Madison Square Garden. I had little trouble keeping up with her, though. A year before I would have needed an oxygen mask.

When I offered to drive her over to her car in Oyster Bay after the ride to my station on the Long Island Rail Road, she accepted without hesitation. I thought maybe, just maybe, she liked me.

I could feel the blood coursing through my body and the adrenalin flowing. My hands were stuffed in my pockets again, just in case I got another unwelcome hard-on when she bumped into me. For the first time in my life, I didn't feel inadequate or think about my weight. I wasn't thinking at all. I just reacted. It seemed like everything I did and said was right.

On the train ride back, Jessie fell asleep against my shoulder. I studied my face in the window as the cars rushed past the black night. The lights of the stations and the blur of the passing houses just outside of Jamaica transported me. My reflection flickered, disappeared and re-emerged as the train sped through the evening.

We were moving so rapidly, almost hurtling along, as Jessie slept. I carefully listened to the only noises in the empty car—train wheels squealing against the tracks and the whoosh of air outside the windows. Quiet, unsettling screams. When the train began crawling to a stop, my reflection in the window vanished amidst the bright floodlights of the station.

I offered the conductor our tickets. She politely held both in the space before us. After I mindlessly retrieved them, Jessie's hand was holding mine. My first instinct was to silently untangle them, but it felt so, so right. When she finally opened her eyes, Jess offered a dazed smile while squeezing my hand.

The hushed walk through the parking lot was a long one with our footsteps softly echoing throughout the station platform. The cool evening breeze awkwardly pushed our bodies together until we arrived at my car.

We didn't kiss outside her apartment after the forty-minute drive on the empty Long Island Expressway. Somehow, it seemed redundant.

"My last name's Benjamin, like in *The Graduate*. Look me up and give me a call. I'm going to expect it, Michael." She gently embraced me before waving an imaginary plate while walking away.

I waited until she disappeared into the darkness. On my long, silent trip home, I could still feel the warm impression of Jessie's hand. When I finally pulled into my apartment complex's parking lot, the night felt electric, like a switch in my life had been flipped.

For some reason, I impulsively called David immediately after settling in.

"Brother, you alright?" his voice was animated.

"Yes, uh-huh, David hey, you got a minute?"

"Yeah sure. I'm just transcribing this interview I did with these illiterate douchebags from Great Britain. Terrible band, but the record is going to be huge. People can't get enough of generic fake funk shit."

I didn't want to hear about music or writing. I needed something else.

"David, you remember when you first met Monique? Did you know from the start?"

"I did, yes, absolutely, but she hated me. Thought I was an arrogant asshole, which I might have been."

I had heard him tell me this before—it was a story my brother enjoyed perpetuating.

"Why? You meet someone?"

"I don't know. Maybe. It was just kind of a nice night. Accidental, you know? I wasn't looking."

"That's the best, and the kind that matter. It's all random. You know that."

"David, I have to tell you, sometimes I'm just not sure..."

"About?"

"Myself." I cringed at the thought of waving the plate at Jessie.

"No one is sure about anything. It's just a lot of us know how to fake it. You'll figure it out. Just trust your instincts. When you over-think things, that's when they go wrong."

"But what if I'm not good enough?"

"Good enough for what?"

"For a smart, good-looking girl."

"Michael, remember one thing. No man is good enough for a great woman. Treat her right, be yourself and you are good enough."

"But what if she's out of my league? You know, physically."

"This is silly. We're really not going to talk about this, are we? Listen, if she's going to like you, she's going to like you. Michael, you told me last week you lost a lot of weight, and you are running. Monique said you must look hot. That's weird for me to hear, but that's what she told me. So, what does that say?

"Keep yourself healthy, and just make sure there's no broccoli in your teeth." He laughed into the phone. "I get you, Michael. You are working hard on getting rid of that weight from the past. Keep doing it, but say to yourself, 'You are not the past. You are becoming.' One thing I do know is that women love confident men. A confident fat fuck gets more pussy than the insecure skinny guy every time."

"I don't know. I really don't think that's true."

"Think what you want. It just is the way it is."

"Easy to say." I was sitting at my kitchen table, looking at the bowl of apples perilously close to the edge.

"No, Mike, it's easy to do too. And what's her name?"

I wasn't going to tell him.

"Does she have a name?"

"Jessie." I turned out the lights.

"Great. Like I said, trust your instincts Mike, and Jessie will follow. It's really basic advice, but all of this is not complicated. We are taught it is somehow complicated. It's not, brother. You have to trust me here."

My instincts, though, were what I feared most. I hung up to sit in silence with my eyes closed and head on the table. All I heard was David saying, "You are becoming." Exactly what I was becoming, I did not know.

Ten

I called Jessie two days later. "I actually wasn't sure I'd hear from you," she said. "You didn't seem like the most confident guy I'd ever met. Part of me wondered if I was going to have to call you."

"Can we put the paper plate part of the other night behind us. I know that was embarrassing. I'm just not sure what got into me," I said, still haunted after replaying the evening in an endless loop in my head.

"Maybe," she replied with a small laugh. "There's nothing wrong with a little Captain America in every guy."

"Okay, I'll remember that." I was desperately hoping she was not a comic book geek.

"Hey, I was wondering if you'd like to get together. Maybe go to a movie," I suggested without any actual desire to stare at a screen displaying impossibly beautiful people with impossibly straight teeth living out screenwriters' fantasies with impossible endings. I wanted to remain in the possible.

"Michael, you like to run, right? Why don't we get together, and I'll put you to the test? There's a long bike trail by my place I run all the time. It's quite beautiful, especially in the summertime. It leads a lot of different ways. I think you might love it. You game?"

And, indeed, it was game on. I had never run with anyone because jogging was a refuge to get away from things. The hours of silence allowed me to be one with my thoughts. The idea of talking while running seemed counterproductive. There was no way I was going to turn Jessie down, though.

So, we ran and ran. The first few treks of the day were leisurely and ambling as we made our way over the dirt paths nestled between lush, green fields. Jessie was mostly quiet, only asking random questions about why I liked to read and how I got into running. I told her about the baseball tryouts and only hinted at the story about the fat little boy I was running away from. After the relatively short two or three-mile runs, we found a place to unwind near a spacious area filled with trees.

I remember staring straight into the sun while reclining on my back. Jess sat with legs crossed in a pretzel-like yoga position. "You really don't talk much about your family besides your brother," she said.

"I don't really have any other family besides my brother. He lives in San Francisco, but we were close as kids. I miss him. My parents are gone." I saw no reason to elaborate. Jessie's eyes mirrored the bright, verdant landscape surrounding us.

"I'm sorry, that's really hard, and I definitely understand. At least you have your brother. I know he must mean a lot to you because you mention him a lot. David, right?"

"Yeah, yeah, David. And hey, don't be sorry about my parents. It's part of life." I replied, exactly as I did to everyone else who offered the same condolences. Jessie tossed random pebbles aside without making eye contact.

"I guess it is part of life, but I don't know. It's really not easy. You know, Michael, I was raised by my aunt. My parents were killed on the Wantagh Parkway when I was five. I barely remember them. I do remember that night with my babysitter. Waiting and waiting for them only to wake up to find out they were not coming home. That night is never going to leave me. It feels like it never ended."

She began throwing rocks and sticks with force while peering into the sky and taking long pauses between words. "A drunk driver in the oncoming lane lost control. The car hopped the divider straight into my parents' windshield. It was bad. I didn't see the pictures of the scene until years later. The first time I saw them was when I was fourteen—I actually was never supposed to be exposed to them. But you know I just had to understand what happened. I ended up climbing up into my aunt's attic where I knew they were stored.

"Those images will never disappear from my head. It had to be beyond awful. I still can't imagine it. I do feel at peace knowing they must have died instantly. No pain, you know?"

Jess seemed to be talking to herself as she tossed grass blades into the wind. "I kinda have been on my own ever since. I love my aunt very much, but when I graduated high school and went to college up in Syracuse, she moved to Virginia. It's just been me ever since. I sold my parents' house, but I didn't want to leave Oyster Bay. I really like it here.

"My apartment is just a mile or so from where I grew up. I'm honestly not sure when I'm going to leave. I'm kind of bored now, but I hope to figure my way out of the Island."

Her story was a lot to absorb for a first date, and I was genuinely surprised by her opening up so quickly. It was quite obvious, though, that telling me the story was her way of making sense of things.

"I'm really...Well, I'm..." There was so little for me to say.

"It's okay to say you're sorry. I know it's not phony or something. We don't want to be trading sorrys, but it's cool. I get you understand. You know, 'I'm sorry' obviously is inadequate, but it's really the only response we have. I've heard it practically my whole life. It happened so long ago."

She inched nearer to me. "I have to tell you, it's funny. I dated this guy a few months ago." A smile emerged as she tapped the toe of my right running shoe. "I told him about my parents while we were at a diner in Syosset, and he said to me, 'You were probably better off.'" Jessie clapped her hands together as if applauding a punchline.

"It's weird, he went on to recount this terrible life he had with his shitty father. In my head I was like, 'Whoa, okay, you had it hard,' as he just kept talking. His mother was an alcoholic. I kind of felt sorry for him because he thought I was better off alone. I think there were things he didn't calculate into the equation, but I let it slide. People sometimes..." After a shake of her head and a wan, resigned smile, Jess casually rubbed her sunburned cheeks.

"It's kind of good to know we have something more in common. Losing parents sucks, but it's kind of easier to talk to someone who understands," she said, now leaning against me. "Okay, enough of our parentless pity party. Let's race back to the car. Loser pays for lunch."

Thinking she was joking, I waved her off, but she just stared back, dead-eyed. "You have money to pay for lunch, right?"

"Yeah, I got money. Do you? I'm just trying to figure out how fast you might be. You might be hustling me." I gauged her warily.

"It's no hustle. Just you and me. I'm fast—I'll tell you that upfront. It's up to you to find out how fast. And yes, I have money, but you better prepare to open your wallet. Bet?"

"Sounds good," I said. "On three." After I counted down, she sped off into the afternoon, her feet barely touching the ground. At a half-mile, she was nothing more than a blur in the distance. I was forced to trot slack shouldered the rest of the way. I got played.

"Lunch is gonna taste good today." Jessie was breathing easily against the car when I arrived. The back of her wet, dark-blue New York Giants t-shirt was sticking to her ribs.

"That wasn't fair. You knew you were going to beat me. What do you do, run from drug dealers or something?" I leaned over with both hands on my knees and sweat dripping off the tip of my nose.

She smiled knowingly while reaching into the window to grab the towels. "I like to compete, Michael. It's fun. Running aimlessly is okay, but running as if something is on the line is better. Hope you are good with that."

And, of course, almost all of our subsequent running excursions felt like training sessions for the track team. Time and speed were never important to me, but Jessie sprinted with brisk, energetic strides. She darted effortlessly through the woods and up the rolling hills like Wile E. Coyote was chasing her.

We ran every day throughout our first month together. There were times when I would ask her to take the loop a bit more slowly so we could enjoy the long workouts, but she just kept pushing through as though possessed.

Initially, her remarkable endurance and competitive nature definitely were intimidating. I was embarrassed by losing so often, but she'd just shrug and say, "Don't worry. You'll catch up. I'm really enjoying this. I haven't had a running partner in months." I couldn't help but wonder why the hell we weren't simply fucking jogging. All I wanted to do was run and lose weight and forget about my life while having imaginary discussions with the birds.

Ultimately, when all of our treks felt like I was running long distances with Carl Lewis, I gave up pretending things were going to change. Acquiescing was easier—it was better to let things be.

I guess I just wanted to spend time with her. Simply being around Jessie made me feel better about myself. I was also very tired of being alone, so if I had to play on her terms, I'd learn to accept her rules.

We made our bet stick. The loser bought dinner each time out, which meant I ended up paying most of the checks. We went to every cheesy chain restaurant—Olive Garden, Red Lobster, Applebee's, Chili's, and T.G.I Friday's—all featuring a variation of the same faux décor. We became familiar with all the numbingly cheery waiters and waitresses, who were probably spitting in every dish they served. I knew that no one could be that happy on Long Island.

The nature of our runs finally changed in our second month of dating. I never cared about the money flying out of my wallet, but the losing gnawed at me, so I turned my training up to the maximum effort.

No, no, wait…it's time for another honesty check here. What really happened was I decided to start race training like a crazy, fucking madman with only one goal—winning. I spent my late nights reading books about running and how to better control my body. I learned breathing techniques, bought better running shoes, and stretched incessantly in my spare time.

Jessie's focused aggressiveness was wildly inspiring. It forced me to ramp up the speed during my numerous extra running sessions on weekend nights. I darted down Jericho Turnpike, counting each streetlight while waving to the shop owners locking up for the evening. The latter half of all my practice runs were liberating full sprints.

I got to the point where my breathing was mechanically steady—each leg muscle became taut and flexible. Incredibly, my abdomen flattened out completely. My waist size diminished to a thirty.

One afternoon, after successfully dashing through the back leg of a five-mile run, I met Jessie by the edge of the pond. "Men always love to finish first," she said with a smile.

"Well, it feels good," I replied, totally consumed with elation and completely oblivious to her innuendo.

"It does feel really good, but you don't have to finish first," Jess laughed.

"I honestly never ran for speed until we started together," I answered. "I always just ran to escape and get away, but you've kind of made it a competition."

"Alright, Michael, I get it. You're still happy about winning. Maybe I'll try that again later."

As I toweled off, I absorbed her words. Sex never seemed to be a choice on the menu for us. Most of our time together had been spent by bantering intellectually over food or sweating through the fields. We were kind of like the cross-country Bert and Ernie—playful and affectionate in a strangely polite way.

You must know by now that I thought Jessie was stunningly pretty. She had the kind of petite body I always found attractive, but she never seemed very sexual to me. I'm not sure, maybe I began ignoring all the desire I felt on the night we met because I was so focused on developing an edge in our competition

I was getting more hard-ons from racing past cars on the street than from watching Jessie's ass in a black bikini on the sands of Jones Beach. I became more obsessed with outracing Jess than fucking her. It never seemed like a cause for concern. I figured the sex would eventually happen. Becoming a faster runner than Jessie? Now that was something I was never sure would come to pass.

When I'd drop Jess off after our dinners, we'd kiss and maybe fumble at each other, but we never bothered to venture into each other's apartments at the end of the evenings.

Most nights, I'd sit in in the darkness of my apartment and listen to music with headphones until 2 a.m. Sometimes, I'd conjure up an image of what Jessie looked like naked—beautiful, peach-sized breasts and a small patch of blonde pubic hair. I could still smell notes of her Chypre perfume. These visions would spur immediate erections. Instead of jerking off, though, I'd quickly throw on my shorts, shirt, and sneakers and head out for a run through the silent neighborhood.

When we got together each day, I wasn't quite sure how to take our relationship—if that's what it was—to the next level. I knew I had to change the dynamic to keep her interested, though. If I didn't, she would probably look for a genuinely fuckable Captain America.

A few days after Jessie made her joke about finishing, I tried to renew the conversation. "You know I don't like finishing first. That's not what I do." It was idiotic, juvenile, and random. The truth was I was usually so relieved that someone actually wanted to fuck me, I ended up going off like a Fourth of July firework display.

Jessie looked at me quizzically after my absurd sexual non-sequitur. "Michael, no worries, I was just kidding. Relax. You seem really tense these days. I kind of think I created a monster with all this running and betting. I think I want to stop that, okay?

"It's just I don't mind you winning the competitions. I really don't," I said.

Jess slowly walked away, her hands tracing the hair around her ears. "It's not a competition," she said. "I hope you don't see it that way. That's not what I want this to be. I really just wanted to have fun. This is fun for me.

"You do enjoy this, don't you? If not, why are we doing it? I'm not trying to compete with you. Do you think I'm setting out to beat you? The first few times, I'll admit I ran really hard, and I'm sorry about that. But that's who I am. It's crazy I know, but I've just been running for fun since then. I wanted to impress you at first. I really did. It might have been silly. You think I'm competing against you, don't you?"

She grabbed my hand. "I'm not, Michael. I'm not competing."

"I don't think you are competing." Of course, that was total bullshit, but how could I have told her the truth? I would have sounded so weak.

"If you don't want to run every day, we can stop and just hang out at the park or go to the mall by you," she demanded.

"Jess, don't stop. "You made me realize a few things about myself."

"Well, I don't know if that's good or bad," she said. "Do you want to run today? Maybe try a different pace?"

"It's fine Jess, we go as we were. We're good, let's go. I want to talk to you about something afterwards, okay?" I wasn't sure what I was going to say but knew I had to do something. I didn't want to be Ken and Barbie much longer.

Ultimately, I didn't need to say anything at all. Things just seemed to erupt when I invited Jessie back to my apartment. We were both still perspiring from the workout and afternoon drive. "Michael, do you mind if I take a shower at your place?" she quietly said as I parked on the street. While we tentatively walked through the gate and up the path, Jess squeezed my index finger.

After bungling with the keys and entering, I closed the door before kissing her awkwardly. She pushed me hard towards the couch where our bodies collided in a clumsy act of desperation.

She pulled off her shirt and bra and forced my hand into her shorts. Her underwear was soaked with sweat as my fingers brushed through matted hair and skimmed over her warm, slick pussy before I cupped her ass. We were writhing like two animals let out of a kennel. There were no words, just the clap of the sweat surrounding her breasts against my chest. This was the moment I had imagined since I first watched her lean against the counter to wait for a slice at Ray's.

As I flailed against her damp body, I reached for the condom in my wallet.

"Michael, I have a rubber in my purse," she said.

"I have one," I said, throwing my wallet like a Frisbee to the far side of the room.

She guided me inside of her and bit my nipple. "Michael, please, I really want this."

. . . .

"Commercials last longer." I sighed. "That was really, really embarrassing."

Jessie's head rested on my thigh as her hand traced my lower ribs.

She laughed and wiped a stream of sweat from her under her eyes. "It was fine, Michael, trust me. I'm just happy something finally happened." Jessie took my cock in her hands. "Why did it take us this long? It's crazy. I've been waiting. Now you got that one out of your system, you have at least three more chances today to take your time and get it right."

I circled two fingers around her right breast while quickly getting hard again. Her tan skin was so soft, but her abdomen, leading down to her bikini bridge, was even more muscular than I possibly could have imagined. I felt a twinge of jealousy.

"I have a three pack of condoms in my bag. We're going to use them." She kissed me, her hand brushing the side of my face.

"You always carry around a pack of condoms?" I asked.

"Sometimes yes, but I bought them over a month ago. For God's sake, I thought I was going to have to rape you. We've been seeing each other so much, Jesus. Sometimes you barely kiss me at night. I thought you were not attracted to me or something."

I couldn't believe what I was hearing—those were supposed to be my words. "I'm very, very attracted to you. Did you hear the very? I just don't know. I'm not that experienced in getting close to anyone. I think, I don't know, that you might…I can't explain it."

"What? Might what? What are you talking about?"

I paused for nearly five minutes.

"Michael, talk to me." She fingered a ring of hair behind my ear.

"You might reject me or not want me once you saw me."

"I do see you, always have. This is about the fat boy you used to be—everything you've told me, isn't it? Look at yourself. Now. Here." She pulled back the blanket I had placed over us. "There's no fat here, Michael. You are not that boy. Please."

She slid her palm over my stomach down to my pelvis and pounded with the side of her fist. "That's solid rock. Michael, I've wanted to fuck you for so long, and you were worried about yourself? Your body? Are you crazy? That's so sick. We have so much catching up to do."

With her index finger to my forehead, Jess said, "Get it in your brain. Start focusing on my body instead of yours." She placed my hand between her legs. "That better get you really hard because I'm ready to go again."

"Me too." I said, her words "Are you crazy?" still echoing in my head.

"One thing, Michael—do you jerk off or are you a monk or something? It was really weird—there was like ten years of come in that condom. Like a damn milkshake. Were you saving that up since kindergarten?" She pushed me hard onto my back before slipping on top of me.

"I don't know what it was. I was actually afraid I shot out your eye," I laughed.

"Oh, my God, I would welcome it. I'm so glad this finally happened so we got it out of the way. I've been waiting. These past months of nothing have been surreal. And not in a good way."

Jessie grabbed my wrists to pull my arms taut. She hovered slightly just before sliding me inside her. Assertively holding me down, she shifted her hips while quietly grunting. I tried to move so I could get on top, but she resisted.

"No please, I like it better this way."

I watched her close her eyes to get lost in a rhythm I could not hear. While pinning me to the couch by my shoulders, Jess arched her back—her strength surprising me. Jessie's body twitched so violently—I thought my cock was going to snap off inside her. I quickly found out that pain was the absolute best thing to help prevent coming. When I accidentally slipped out of her after one of her wild gyrations, she firmly remounted to grip my shaft until it went completely numb.

"Yes this, Michael." Jess jumped up to squat while on her toes and bounce as she angled side to side. She was completely out of control. I'd never seen anything like it—those quivering concave upper thighs mesmerized me. Jessie's ass just kept pile driving my hips into submission. Her torso convulsed as she fingered herself and let out noises I didn't recognize. I winced while watching Jess's waist rock through my hands and her hair toss in my face. Finally, I just relaxed enough to let go.

After my eyes stopped rolling in my head, I had to make sure the upper half of my cock wasn't hanging out of her pussy. I'd never felt such intense pleasure and pain simultaneously. It was deliriously wonderful. Jessie collapsed on top of me, her breasts slapping against my chest.

"There. How was that? Little fat boys don't do that, do they? I just love it that way. It feels so good. I don't know about you, but I need water. Then we're gonna do this again." She tossed the sloppy condom over her shoulder before squeezing the remaining come right out of me. "I really hope you are ready. This is the beginning, Michael. It took a while, but now it's gonna be so great."

Eleven

David called me the next day to ask if I wanted to meet Monique in Manhattan for coffee or lunch. I was still riding the buzz of getting to "great" with Jess, who was even more aggressive than I could have ever imagined. So much for not being sexual. Somewhere deep inside, I needed to tell David something, anything, about the experience, but I knew that would make me look like a complete fucking amateur. So, like everything else in my life, I just kept it all to myself.

Jess had just left when the phone rang. She took my car home to retrieve some clothes and a toothbrush for the weekend. I wanted to go for a run with her, but she begged me to take a few days off. "We'll get plenty of exercise," she said.

While she was gone, my balls ached like never before. I felt an urgent need to be inside her again. I quickly discovered that sex is indeed a lot of like eating. If you go without it for a long while, once it becomes a part of your life again, it's mighty tough to turn off the hunger.

During my college years, sex was pure stress relief for me. After each lame fuck, I would quickly shut down my desire, so I could get back to work. The drunk girls I picked up in Long Island rock dives near school never mattered. I was never attracted to any of them, and I knew damn well knew they didn't find me desirable. They were just lonely and horny too.

The robotic sex was mostly just a notch above jerking off—more than a few girls ended up leaving jagged teeth marks on my cock. Of course, I usually thought they were well deserved painful souvenirs from my nights of sad, desperate need. Frequently, I felt worse about myself during the mornings after, but the idea of being celibate was unimaginable. So I fucked when I got tired of sticking my cock between couch cushions or when I ran out of peanut butter to put in a plastic bag.

All the sex with Jess wildly different, though. I didn't recognize those impulses. I thoroughly embraced them as I surrendered to her. She was voracious, experienced and demanding. I admired the way she went after exactly what she wanted and proceeded to take it. Jess often begged me to tell her what I needed.

Needed? If you don't think you deserve anything, the idea of need becomes a pure abstraction. What could I possibly need after watching her blow me?

"Michael, we all have something we need besides simply coming," she'd say when I'd look at her quizzically. "I've never met anyone who doesn't need something more."

I didn't—at least I didn't think so.

When David called, I was lost in thought throughout the conversation.

"Mon is flying in from London. She will probably only be in the city for a day, but she told me to tell you she'd love to see you if you can make it. I had her assistant get you something. I also forwarded her a list of contacts for you once you get to Boston. I made some calls to my friends. I hope you realize I'm glad you are going there. Columbia would have been nice, but you didn't want to stay in New York, did you?"

That was David's way of saying, "You have to get out the fuck out of New York, and see another city."

I was tired of talking to my brother on the phone all the time. After a half hour of going back and forth, I ended up prodding him into visiting Manhattan, so we could spend some time together and reconnect.

More importantly, I wanted him to see the change. I'd lost nearly forty pounds. He needed to see Michael 2.0.

"It's a maybe, who knows? I've been trying to set something up with the Wu-Tang Clan, but that's fucking impossible. Kind of like getting a reunion of the Last Supper. Each one those guys has his own schedule and agenda. Their publicist says the same bullshit to cover up their bullshit. Mike, I will let you know if I do come your way, but don't hold your breath."

As if on cue, he inhaled deeply into the phone.

"Hey, I realize you don't give a shit about what I'm doing, so tell me what's going on with you? How are things going with the girl? You're Jessie's guy, correct?"

I was surprised he still remembered her name. "It's good yeah, real good. We have fun times. She's really nice." I wasn't going to say anything more.

"Well, that doesn't tell me much, but my sense is Mon can get more out of you. Get that list of people, and start making calls. Set the wheels in motion. You want to be prepared when you get to Boston. You can't spend all of your summer spanking the tiny monkey. Better to do that while exploring a new city. I'll tell Mon you are good to meet her. I'm sure you'll hear from her to set things up. Give me a ring when you get the stuff from her."

I was about to hang up when he said, "And Michael, she's a runner, eh? You can keep up these days? She's not running way ahead of you?"

How the fuck did he know?

"The only advantage of that is you get to watch her ass."

I laughed suspiciously. "I can keep up, even though it didn't start out that way. I'm a machine now, David. You wouldn't recognize me."

"Now, that sounds ominous. If you really need to be a machine for some reason, then rage on. Well, I'll find out the details from Monique."

. . . .

Monique was wearing a light blue summer dress and heels as she approached the café just outside of Lincoln Center. She confidently walked down the sidewalk with sunglasses on the top of her head and a clutch and a small, thick bag in hand. Smiling to a balding pedestrian, she was still as beautiful as I had remembered.

Upon finally seeing me sitting at the table, she quickened her pace.

"Babe, I'm so sorry. Have you been waiting long? I got caught up." She hugged me tightly before grabbing my shoulders. "Let me look at you. I knew you lost weight but, my God. You look so good. It's so different, like a brand new you." It was just the reaction I was looking for.

She corrected herself while sitting, "Not that you didn't look good before—you did, but now you just look…Well, I don't know, vibrant."

She waved a hand in front of her face. "You know what I mean. I can tell from your glow that Jessie has made a difference. She touched the bottom of my chin to tilt my head back.

"Look at those smiling eyes. Wait until I tell your brother. He's going to be happy—as happy as David can possibly be. You know him." Mon's skin was tan and luminous. Her large, piercing eyes barely blinked as she sat with shoulders back.

"So how 'bout you? You happy? David and I have really wanted you to find someone, and be happy. There were times when you were in school the last year or so, I worried after talking to you on the phone. You know, your brother cares about you, and he talks about you a lot. I know he doesn't often show it, but that's David.

"I bet you know that probably better than I do. He's always preoccupied. Still, that's just to keep his mind off of the other things going on in the back of his head. He thinks in order not to think—if you know what I mean."

I knew exactly what she was talking about.

She stood up quickly to straighten out her dress before settling comfortably into the chair and continuing. "He writes about so many shitty bands I'm not sure he cares about at all. At least, I don't think so. I mean who really cares about Green Day? Between you and me, I hate them. People call them punk. Punk my ass. X was punk. The Minutemen and Bad Brains were punk. Guns N' Roses had more punk spirit than Green Day on their best day." She smiled before tapping my hand. "Why am I talking about this?"

I laughed, shrugged my shoulders and spied the bag she had placed on the table. A waiter in his early twenties stared at her momentarily.

"Do you know what you want?" he asked politely.

"Babe, do you need a menu?"

The waiter apologized for failing to bring menus.

"Actually, that was not a suggestion, but thank you anyway." The waiter never even glanced my way before scurrying off and returning with water and thin menus.

"I just want a tea right now, Mon said while scanning the pages. "Babe, what are you having?"

I ordered a Diet Coke.

"I bet that's not going to make you all that happy," Mon replied, looking towards the waiter, who scratched his head with the back of his pen.

"I think we just made an enemy out of…" she waited for the waiter to say his name.

"Alex."

"Alex, are you going to mind if we drink tea and Diet Coke at an outdoor table?"

"I absolutely don't mind at all." He shuffled away nervously while glancing at Mon's sky- colored shoe peeking out from under the table.

"Bring me a scone please, if that's okay." Mon smiled broadly at Alex.

"I'm sure you don't eat scones, and I really don't either. Between us, we can finish one. I just don't like annoying waiters by doing nothing but drinking tea. Too diva-ish for me. Here, my assistant, Emily, gave me this to give to you," she said after passing the bag across the table. "David told her to get it. Inside is the list of people to contact. It's long.

"Your brother knows most of those people really well, so it will help. Some are in academia and a lot are in the rock scene, like bookers and promoters. A few he went to school with. Maybe you can see some free shows or make some friends when you get up there."

I opened the bag to find new copies of *Ulysses* and *Moby Dick*.

"That bag was so heavy to carry," Monique laughed. "I guess he wants you to read them before you go to school or something. I looked over the first few pages of the Joyce before I got here. Good luck with that, Babe. You can tell him you read it, even if you don't. I don't know anyone who actually made it through that book. Your brother yes, but, c'mon, none of it seems to make sense."

"Maybe that's the point," I said.

"I have no idea what that means," she said with a wink. "*Moby Dick*, he swears by. I think your brother has read it about ten times. He either identifies with Ahab or the whale or both. Part of me thinks he believes if he keeps reading it, things will change, and Ahab is going to live." Mon squeezed my arm before laughing to herself.

"Silly, really. I just got off the phone with him. I told him tickets to the Mets game would have been better. He said the books are good for you, so eat your vegetables." She continued to smile while straightening her dress again and re-crossing her legs. "Only your brother would give *Ulysses* and *Moby Dick*, but it's done with love."

I fingered through the Melville to find the extensive three-page list of contact names. Alex arrived with a teacup and a small pot, from which he poured. He placed both in front of Mon before putting a glass filled with ice next to my arm on the table. Carefully, he emptied a quarter of the soda can into the glass and neatly arranged the plate with the scone in the middle of the tablecloth.

"Thank you so much, Alex, very kind," Monique said, apparently impressed by the waiter's thoroughness. He took another long look at Mon before walking away.

"I think he might butter your scone," Mon said, smiling.

"I'm totally invisible to Alex right now."

She meticulously picked up the cup with both hands. "Babe, you haven't said much. Tell me what's going on. You obviously look so different. What are you eating?"

"I've been eating less. I run a lot. I mean a lot. Jessie runs, too. That helps.

"You are eating less, but are you eating smarter? Where are you getting your energy from if you are cutting things out? You cut the crap out of your diet. That's good. But what are you actually eating?" Mon cut the scone in half. She placed one half on a napkin after pushing the plate in front of me.

"I really don't think about what I'm eating. I think about what I'm not eating. I just make sure to eat a lot less."

She gazed at me while dropping a small piece of scone in her mouth.

"I should have asked you these questions a while ago. You need to feed your body well. I know a good nutritionist and trainer you can call. I've worked with him. He's wonderful. There are a lot of books that give you a good idea what to eat, too."

"I have a book now," I said reaching for *Ulysses*.

"Yeah, Joyce got his nutrition from a bottle, didn't he? I'm sure he was a health nut. Are you going to make me eat this scone by myself?"

She'd eaten less than half of the half.

"Babe, I'm just recommending that you look into all the things food can do for you. You need to eat right." Mon paused and added, "I say as I eat a scone." Her eyes expanded as she ran both hands through her long, flowing hair. The sun had shifted from the east—her angular face had been bathed in a magnificent light for over twenty minutes. She took the sunglasses off of her head and held them in front of her nose.

"You mind if I put these on? We can live in a Bond film for a few minutes. Now Michael, tell me about Jessie. What's really going on? It has to be something positive."

"I don't know, Mon, things just feel right. I haven't felt this way about anyone ever. Do you remember when you first met David? How did you feel? I mean did you know?"

"I don't know if you ever know." Her voice deepened. "I've never believed in all that soulmate shite—that's my Joe Strummer impression. Of course, I knew I wanted to be with David. Your brother puts up this facade of indifference and arrogance sometimes, but when I met him—and it was me who tracked him down after reading the Sam Cooke book—he was actually quite charming." A smile creased her face. "That sounded funny, 'cookbook.'"

She fingered her sunglasses while staring off to the passing cars. "My parents loved Sam Cooke. I grew up on his music. All the great soul singers like Solomon Burke and Jackie Wilson were playing in our house. That stuff is so, I don't know, so sexy. I saw the review of David's book in *The New York Times,* and read the thing in about two nights. I just knew I needed to meet him. For some reason, his words had this pull on me.

"After a David Bowie show in Los Angeles—you ever see Bowie? He's so, oh, he's just so." She blushed. "Well, I was talking to Bowie's publicist. For some reason, the book came up during the conversation. He told me that David was backstage also. I had him introduce us. Jesus, it was kind of like an impulsive thing to do, but I did it."

She took a slow sip of her tea. "The rest is, as they say, history. I guess we were brought together by David Bowie and Sam Cooke. One hell of a combination. But it was not fate. I was smitten when I talked to him. And you know we went out on real dates. I actually flew up to San Francisco a lot when I was in Los Angeles just to spend time with him."

Mon waved to Alex in the distance. "Michael, I'm going to get you your own scone. I'm going to finish this one. For some reason, I'm hungry. Maybe because this is basically all I've had to eat today."

I examined her thin arms and the soft curve of her neck. "I thought you said I need to eat right to feed my body properly," I said, smiling.

"I know mixed signals. I'm not setting the right example for you. I'm not sure what it is today. I have some crazy days when I barely have time to eat." Alex almost bowed to Mon when she asked for the scone I didn't want. "We'll make a pact to both eat right from here on in okay, Babe?" She reached her hand out for me to grasp.

"You know what's funny, Mon? David always tells me that you didn't like him at first."

She offered a dismissive wave after swallowing the last piece of scone. A heavy wind blew down the sidewalk, forcing Mon to gather her hair. "Your brother. Typical. Bullshit. Shite, shite. That's my Johnny Rotten." She chuckled at her own silly British accent.

"By now, you can only believe half of what your brother says. He's a storyteller, and he's telling you and who knows who else, how he thinks how things should—emphasis on should—have unfolded in his neurotic head. That can't be further from the truth. Remember, take his stories with a grain of salt. If you want to know the truth about things, come to me."

Alex brought a small plate with the scone. Even though Mon pointed towards me, he placed it in front of her like a sacrifice. She politely thanked him before fingering the plate to my side of the table. "He is determined to serve me."

Mon waited for me to take a bite. "So, are you telling me you think Jessie is the one?" She used air quotes. "You know the one takes time to develop into the one."

I became defensive. "No, I don't know what she is. All I know is that she seems pretty special, and I like her. I think about her a lot. She makes me feel...I can't explain."

"I get it, Babe. No need to identify what you are feeling. That's great. Follow what you are feeling, wherever it goes."

I felt my face flush and tried to hide my smile by drinking the Diet Coke.

"I'm happy for you. Your face tells it all. That's how it should be."

She checked her watch as the afternoon began cooling off. "Mon, I know you have to go, but can I ask you a question?"

"Babe, I wasn't checking my watch in order to tell you I have to go. The funny thing about the world these days is that you can't look at a watch for the time without someone thinking you are in a hurry. I guess everyone is rushing somewhere, but I'm not. This is where I want to be. Tell me what's your question, my apprentice?"

"How do you make things work with David?" The rich, buttery taste of the scone comforted me.

"If you are looking for a magic formula, there is none. And I really think anyone who tells you there is, is lying." Mon delicately placed her sunglasses in a leather case. "We have our own careers, and we both are busy, but we try to make the most of when we are together. The key thing is you don't try and control the other person. At least, that's what I've always believed.

"You know, we can't really control anything in life, so I never understood why people get into relationships and try to control who they love. It makes no sense

Alex came to the table to see if we wanted anything else. After I demurred, Mon asked for the check. "My philosophy has always been if you treat a man like a wind-up monkey, he is going to wind up with someone else. That's why I've always given a lot of space. Thankfully, your brother feels the same way. We know we work together, so we figure out a way to stay happy. Being happy is relative, Babe. If you and Jessie continue on, you'll have to figure out what's the path to your happiness. Sometimes, it's a warped, crazy road."

I ate the scone in a few bites and waited for Mon to finish her tea.

"My student, now you have your homework to do," Mon said, pointing to the books while checking herself in a makeup mirror. Carefully, she reapplied her lipstick. "Am I ready for the world?"

I laughed. "You realize I ask that question every day."

"Babe, sweetie, remember this. The question you should always be asking is, `Is the world ready for me?'"

Twelve

The summer of anticipation and exhilaration dissolved quickly. Jessie and I fell into a routine of running and fucking, fucking and running. I naively thought nothing would ever change and somehow believed that we'd reached some sort of exalted state of grace. It's the disarming deception love-struck fools are seduced by when every day feels like a Teddy Pendergrass song. And like most new couples discovering the joys of each other's bodies, we had constant, intense, glorious, and imaginative sex.

We fucked on my apartment roof in mid-afternoon, in the dunes amid a tornado of mosquitoes on the eastern part of Jones Beach, in the back of an empty Westbury Theater on Sunday nights, and in different fitting rooms of our local Macy's. I even managed to slip it in Jess through the side of my shorts as we huddled together beneath a blanket on the great lawn of Central Park. A homeless man munching on McNuggets and blades of grass cheered us on. We were like children playing doctor in the basement. Unfortunately, as we moved forward, we discovered that such wondrous, innocent joy is virtually impossible to sustain.

Jessie worked throughout the summer in Manhattan as an assistant in an art gallery. We hardly talked about my leaving for Boston in September. Every time the subject came up, she redirected the conversation or we fell into each other's arms. Things were going so well, there were days when I regretted my decision to move, but I knew staying on Long Island was a death sentence. When we were forced to confront the future, Jess kept assuring me that grad school was the right move, and we could work things out as a long-distance couple.

While she worked each day, I killed hours by watching baseball or trying to finish *Ulysses*, which was like doing a jigsaw puzzle with most of the pieces missing.

David frequently called just to ask about what chapter I was reading. He was livid when I told him that I was thinking of putting it aside because it was too confusing. "Don't you dare quit on *Ulysses*," he barked into the phone while I watched Letterman. "Few people have actually gotten through it. There are too many college kids wasting time syncing up *The Wizard of Oz* with *Dark Side of the Moon* looking for cosmic significance instead of reading Joyce.

"Don't be part of the bullshit generation. That book is like life—you plow through it and take the best from it you can. You won't understand it all, but that doesn't matter. Ultimately, part of it will make sense. You'll be better for it. Fuck Mike, you've got the time now. All you're doing is spending time with Jessie and working at Alesso's, right? You still that ace salesman?"

Ah, yes, indeed, I was still working nights at Alesso's, an off-price department store in one of the Island's biggest malls. It was a boring part-time, peon job that I had held on to for two years because I loved talking to people and listening to their stories. Everyone had a fucking story.

Each night I got involved in long conversations with customers, who were desperate to reveal something deeply personal or strange about their histories or families. I heard about the cop suing his own police department for millions because the stress of the tough Long Island streets and his high job-related sugar intake prevented him from getting a boner. A weed dealer told me about a saintly school superintendent pimping out teenage escorts and selling dildo bongs like Avon products to her friends. In life, if you listen carefully, people will tell you anything.

I was like a nonjudgmental priest hearing illicit confessions while pretending to peddle toys, chaise lounges, and outdoor gas grills. The grills were my favorite thing to sell. I knew nothing about grills, gas, or the outdoors, but I greeted customers and feigned knowledge by confidently showing them how to open a few valves. They'd ask me for grilling techniques as if I was Bobby Flay.

My diet at the time, though, consisted of nothing more than yogurt, salad, and bananas. To compensate for my ignorance, I would conjure elaborate grilling stories to move thousands of the damn things and keep my manager happy. Storytelling was my game. That was something I felt good about, and I took pride in cashing my $5.15 an hour check each week.

Patrolling the sales floor, dressed up in a button-down shirt and tie, I was now confident enough to flirt with all the girls wearing men's shirts tied up in a knot over bikini tops—thong straps peeking out of the back of cutoff shorts.

They seemed more interested in playfully peacocking around the store and having hard-ons like me stare at their asses than buying anything. Some were cute with short, asymmetrical haircuts. They were clearly itching to make the leap into Manhattan for a whole different lifestyle. Most, though, were Long Island lifers—young Mariah Carey lookalikes with hair teased to the light fixtures and cheap butterfly eyelashes.

I thoroughly enjoyed engaging with the parade of lovelies. It was thrilling to play the game I had never been privy to previously. I derived the most fun from flirting with many of the older women who shopped behind huge sunglasses. They preened around the floor with Stars of David or crucifixes hanging between their fried-to-the-crisp, liver spot stained breasts.

These divas were the mainstays of the Long Island I knew too well. The women's balding, potbellied husbands, wearing white shoes and loud bowling shirts, turtled sheepishly behind them. I usually ignored the Catskill crew of men and just fantasized about fucking all those toasted cougars with washed-out bottle blonde hair and boobs dropping faster than the Hindenburg.

I would never have imagined things like that before I met Jessie. She changed the rules for me. When it came to women, suddenly everything seemed possible. I saw the world in a new light, and all I thought about was sex.

One night, though, after I spent forty minutes trying to sell two grills to a beautiful, slim, fiftyish redhead, who was surrounded by a group of gawking older men, Jessie surprised me by showing up in shorts and a tank top. She rarely visited me after her tiring, daily commute home from Manhattan.

Her hair was tucked beneath a weathered Mets cap. "So, grill master, you finally figure out how to keep your Diet Coke from sliding through the grill?" she said, eyeing the woman heading to the cashier. The men—decked out in pastel pants and straw hats—backed away. Each one stared when Jess moved in next to me.

"Oh, say hi to these men, Jess. I'm sure they'd be happy to meet you." The group, all smiles and googly eyes, stared at her.

"I caught an early train from the city. I wanted to see you slaving for the Man. Have you ever grilled a steak on one of these, Mr. Salesman?" Jessie delicately touched the grill with her fingertips. I pulled her aside while the men talked amongst themselves.

"Jess, you okay? Is something the matter?" I was unfamiliar with the steeliness in her voice.

"I'm fine and dandy," she said through a taut smile. "Do you intend to cook a steak again someday? I would love a steak. Oh, who knows maybe even tonight?"

She pivoted away to address the men. "Hello, sirs. Yes, you good looking gentlemen. Snappy dressers for all the women, I bet." All of the geezers started giggling like all crazy, fucking men do when their dicks get hard.

"Do you men enjoy a good steak? According to the salesman here, and I can vouch for him because he's a smart guy, this grill makes a great steak. That would be a big selling point, right? Who doesn't like a perfectly cooked steak?"

"Jess, stop." She had this unsettling tendency of circumventing direct discussions by finding a different way to deliver her message. I hated it.

"Relax, Michael, I just want you to see if these men like steak." She didn't even look at me.

One of the men with a knit shirt engraved with a U.S. Open logo grinned, "Will you be cooking the steaks, my dear?"

"No, no, c'mon, I'll leave that for your wives. I'm just in the mood for a steak. That's okay, don't you think?"

A chorus of "You bet" emerged from the four gladiators. The selling floor was empty except for our small party. Jessie's unsubtle attempt to say that she'd had enough of my eating like barnyard animal rattled me. I remained silent with a smile cemented on my face.

"We'll buy you a steak," one of them said as he playfully reached for his wallet.

"A porterhouse?" Jessie grinned.

"If you were wearing a Yankees hat, I would say yes. A Mets fan only gets a New York strip." He emphasized strip before they all offered slightly deranged, wanton laughs. One man had two gold teeth on the side of his mouth like an octogenarian Eazy-E of Mensches With Arthritis.

"I'm not a Mets fan, but I do like the color of the hat," Jessie said. "And I confess, I'm not a Yankees fan either. I don't like black hats. I side with the cowboys, not the villains." The men leaned backward in unison. I was losing my potential sale. Jessie's voice deepened as if narrating a movie. "I don't understand the majesty of baseball. He does." She pointed to me.

"You a Yankees fan?" a man with thick glasses asked. "Convince your girl to trade in that Mets hat for one from a championship team in the Bronx."

"I like both." It was a convenient lie because I liked neither.

"You can't live in New York and like both the Mets and Yankees, son. It's either one or the other. If you can't pick one, then you definitely have to buy the young pretty lady a steak." The golfer winked at Jessie. Beads of perspiration on his forehead forced him to take off his hat so he could wipe his eyebrows with a fresh handkerchief.

I gave up. Jessie had played the men just right to get exactly what she wanted. "Yeah, that looks to be what's going to happen. It's amazing how things work that way," I sighed.

"Would any of you men like to buy a grill tonight?" I figured since Jessie was making the men all giddy, horny, and chatty, maybe they would reach for their credit cards.

"No, no, we were always just killing time and enjoying engaging the pretty lady while the wives spend our money in the Ladies Department.

We better go meet them now," Eazy-E smiled sheepishly. Just before they all stepped on the escalator, he turned back to us. "Friends? Boyfriend and girlfriend? So, you two are what?"

"Becoming vegetarians," I said.

He wheezed out a cough before saying with mock disdain, "Vegetarians. Bite your tongue. It might taste better." With a deep swallow, no doubt to solidify the teeth in his mouth, he continued. "Do me a favor and buy the young woman with the million dollar dimples a steak before you go to the dark side."

They laughed conspiratorially and shuffled away.

"What was that Jess? You couldn't just ask me to take you out to dinner? Wouldn't that be quicker?"

"Michael, spare me, there's no one in the store tonight. They are just old guys who want to talk and flirt a little. I was having fun." She removed the Mets hat to let her hair fall free. "It's not like I prevented them from buying anything. It's almost time to close, anyway. You aren't going to sell anything, so lighten up. If I embarrassed you, I'm sorry, but it really was no big deal."

"That's how you tell me you want to eat meat? That's not kosher."

"No, but they were." She grinned with narrow eyes. "I was just talking about steak. You are very temperamental tonight." Jess reached out to fix my tie. After a few moments, she brushed some lint off my shoulder. "You look cute and handsome in a tie and all dressed up. I'm sure you've been told that tonight. You're even cuter when you're angry. Listen, no harm done, is there? Maybe it wasn't the smoothest thing I've ever done, but, well, I am incredibly hungry.

"I had a shitty ride home next to a fat, miserable dude who was sweating all over me. I want to go to Legends after you get off. You up for it? I won't even order a steak. I promise."

She proceeded to give me the irresistible eye flutter that always immediately closed the deal. We were headed to the sports bar to eat steak.

"Michael, let's go out and have some fun tonight. Don't argue over something silly."

"I'm off at ten. Meet me at the employee exit."

"Sounds good, I'll leave Willy Loman alone." Jess adjusted my tie once more and blew a mock Marilyn Monroe hand kiss while stepping backwards.

Twenty minutes after she walked away, a tall, stocky girl with soft, slate blue eyes walked into the department. She wore purple lipstick with multiple rings in her eyebrow. Her midnight black hair—a cheap dye job—was discordant for such a pretty face.

I completely ignored her while sitting on the edge of the lawn chair display. She perused the grills before disappearing into the music department nearby. My manager, Al Gordo appeared from the camera department, shaking his head.

"Did you sell that Amazon Goth girl a grill?" he said with arched eyebrows. Al was an old-school Italian, the kind of guy my mother called a ginzo. He always wore a chain with a red devil horn around his neck. I had no idea what it signified, but my mom told me that people who owned horns would be protected from bad things in life. It magically warded off all evil spirits for Italians, like some kind of marinara voodoo.

"Is she coming back to buy something?" He said while spying the girl.

"What? Er, no. I wasn't paying attention."

"You're a salesman, Mikey. You're supposed to sell some of this goddamn shit. You realize you're not here to field blown kisses." I was caught off guard by his reference to Jessie.

"Yeah, you know I see everything." He pointed his index finger to his eyes, and then towards me. "Nothing gets past me, brother. Is that little Missy in the Mets hat your girl? Now, she's a hottie." He winked while shifting his hips like he was fucking someone.

"I would think the Nine Inch Nails Rosie O'Donnell chick would be more your speed. I like you Mikey—you're a good worker and a nice guy. But what would a hot girl like that be doing with a guy like you? And I say that with love."

While singing the chorus of Tom Petty's "You Got Lucky," Gordo spun on his heels to walk away. "You know I'm just kidding. You're my best salesman. I need you down here. I do want to see you selling grills next time instead of flirting with your girl, though."

He left to cash out some of the registers, but the damage was done. His words confirmed all my suspicions about what other people must have been thinking.

I retreated to the stockroom, now furious and humiliated. Stalking between the tightly spaced shelves on the crowded, dank floor, I wildly punched the boxes of rakes and lawn chairs with Ray Leonard combinations until they all tumbled over. I was so hyped up, it felt like I had been tasered. One last vicious right hand shattered a plastic lawn gnome to pieces.

As every one of Al's words about Jessie repeated in my head, I suddenly felt ashamed about how I'd shunned the girl on the floor. What the fuck was happening? I was rapidly turning into the kind of asshole who would have ignored fat Michael years before. So, this was my great becoming?

The girl was standing by one of the most expensive grills when I returned to the floor with my tie off. "I know you are closing, but I do want to buy a grill for my dad," she said. "Do you get commission?"

I placed my hand behind my back in an attempt to hide the cuts on the knuckles. My stomach was convulsing.

"Commission? We don't know the meaning of the word. It's just suburban slave labor here." I tried to conceal my rage.

"I just thought if you got commission, I might buy one from you to help you out." She looked into space over my shoulder.

"I need more help than you know, so I'm here almost every night over the summer..."

"Well, I don't come to malls a lot, so boring. I'm not sure how you work here." Gordo walked in behind her to extend his tongue between the index and middle fingers of his right hand.

"The job keeps me sane. I'm Michael, in case you come back. I think they go on sale next week." I watched Gordo furiously waving his arms. Telling customers about upcoming sales was taboo. "They're definitely on sale next week. You should check back. Hey, I'm sorry, I was zoned out before when you walked in."

"Oh, no worries," she smiled before reaching out her hand. "I didn't notice you not noticing. No one pays attention to anyone anymore. I kinda think life's easier that way. And It's Jane, by the way."

Blood was running off the fingertips of my right hand, so I awkwardly offered her my left. "See you again Jane by the way."

"Okay, I see what you did there. Cute. Lame, but cute. Maybe I'll see ya, and maybe I won't. We come, we go—it's all the same," she said on her way to the elevator.

Gordo abruptly loosened his tie knot and unbuttoned the top of his shirt. "That's a wrap to this shitshow." He snatched my bicep. "If she comes back this week, go for a threesome. I bet she can eat plenty of your girlfriend's steaks. Yeah, I heard that too. Now get the fuck out of here."

He walked away without ever noticing the pool of blood on the floor.

Thirteen

Jessie ran a towel through her wet hair while sitting on a couple of boxes in my room on a muggy August morning a few weeks later. We'd decided to go to a Sunday matinee Mets game at Shea Stadium after getting back from a quick four-day trip to a deserted beach in Truro out on Cape Cod. A few weeks before, I met Mr. Stacatella on my old high school track, and he graciously offered up his summer house to me.

I jumped at the opportunity to get away with Jess for a respite from all the packing. I thought some time alone with Jess would help assuage my fear that our relationship would implode once I moved. Throughout my life, the end of summer was always a fraught time for me, filled with an uneasy sense of inevitable loss.

Seemingly, nothing had changed.

The brief Cape trip was an opportunity to leave my sleepless nights and increasingly rigid daily regimen behind. I accommodated Jess's request to temporarily take a break from running and made sure I ate full meals without hesitation or qualification. They were small gestures, but clearly very important to her. She was becoming increasingly impatient with both my intense discipline and diminishing appetite.

I never remember Jess more relaxed than during those days by the water. She slept topless in the sun while reading *Prozac Nation* during the blazing days and convinced me to go midnight skinny dipping with her after our late dinners. On the last evening, I watched her, so lovely, diving into the water under the dim moonlight. She quickly emerged, shouting my name with a smile.

Naked and trembling from the cool evening breeze, I was left alone to wonder what my life would be like without her. From the water's edge, I watched Jess bobbing serenely with arms spread. She floated in the undulating water with the moon reflecting off her glistening shoulders.

"Michael, I love this—it feels so great," she yelled into the night. I walked back towards our towels by the small fire we'd built. Instead of following me, Jessie swam further out to the cresting waves. By the time I picked up my towel, she was far from the shore.

"Michael c'mon, c'mon. Don't leave me out here. The water is so warm," she shouted. I slowly made my way to the edge of the tide, but Jess was now well in the distance, drifting away. "I see shrinkage there, Michael. You are shrinking. Ha, ha. I'm going to go out a bit more."

Her voice was barely audible in the mist. I reentered the water to decipher what she was saying. With a backward flip, Jess aggressively swam deeper into the ocean. She attacked the increasingly violent waves before finally stopping in the distance with both hands above her head. As I ran unsteadily into the surf, I completely lost sight of her—it seemed as if she had disappeared. After minutes of searching, I finally heard small yelps of joy to my far right.

There she was, surfing back like a dolphin towards the deserted shore before a tumultuous wave hurled her onto the sand. Undeterred, she sprinted towards me and threw her hands around my neck. With her legs latched to my waist, we kissed, her lingering tongue licking the salt off my lips.

"There's something about this, so freeing," Jess exhaled as I held the arch of her back. "I don't want to leave. Why can't life be just like this? Michael, you sure we have to go back?" I could feel her warm breath on my face as she talked. "If I could live life without clothes, I would. Can't we just stay right here like two kids on vacation?"

. . . .

"Michael, you have a t-shirt I can wear? You must have a Mets shirt or some baseball related shirt, right? I love going to baseball games." Out of the corner of my eye, I watched Jessie carefully cup her breasts with her bra. "Up Michael, up. We've got to meet the Mets, greet the Mets." She sang the Mets fight song slightly out of tune. Jess reached under the sheet to grab my numb, unwilling cock. My legs had cramped up from the night sweats, and I could barely raise my head off the pillow. That didn't stop her. "Step right up and meet the Mets. Up, up. Time to wakey. Stand to attention."

"Give me a few minutes. Please, I need some water. I'm so dehydrated from last night. I think you're trying to kill me—I feel like a prune." The room was damp from the humidity of the ninety-degree morning.

"You're the guy sleeping under a sheet. I'll play waitress for a sec and get water but, c'mon, get your ass out of bed. I wanna go watch some baseball. You get like three more minutes before I yank you up by Mr. Met here." Jess reached towards my crotch before slapping my ass. "You're lucky I spared you. Now tell me, where are the good t-shirts?"

After changing into a pair of running shorts, she returned from the bathroom with two cups of water, "Look in that box there. Right beneath the one you were sitting on," I said from the chair next to the bed as Jess, now wearing her Mets cap, rummaged through the overstuffed box. After sorting randomly, she pulled out a royal blue Mets t-shirt.

"You have a Mets shirt? Since when? You hate the Mets."

"I hate nothing. You know I'm a lover." I mumbled.

Jess carefully fitted the tee over her shoulders, straightening out the creases.

"A little self-love wouldn't hurt, Sylvia Plath." She checked her ass in the mirror. The sight of Jessie in the shirt made me lightheaded.

"That's my dad's shirt. I can't believe amid all that crap, you actually found the shirt my dad used to wear all the time. There are a lot of others in that box." I was struck by a vision of my father leading me by hand through the loge tunnel toward the field at Shea.

"Wow, I feel honored," Jessie smiled. "This is great. Michael, you've never talked about your father."

"Yeah I know. I will, don't worry. It's a long story. I'll tell you more..." I was falling back to sleep in the chair with no intention of saying another word.

"Should I not be asking? I'm sorry. I didn't know it's a sore subject. You really never talk about your parents."

I knew I should have been more forthcoming about my past like

Jessie, who had frequently talked about the brief memories of her parents. There were some things, though, I was not prepared to revisit with her. "I know I should let you in more. My dad sure didn't look like you do in that shirt." Her breasts, accentuating the cartoon script of the Mets logo, were making me hard and fucking up my head even more.

I realized that if I tried to convince her to wear something else, it would lead to too many questions, so I tried to distract her instead. Of course, that just ended up peeling off different scars.

"If you keep looking in that box, it actually has a few things from my parents."

"Michael, where are your shirts? Show me the box with your stuff. I don't want to wear your dad's shirt if..."

I patiently tried to act as if nothing was awry. "Jess, wear that shirt. My dad would have been happy to know you are wearing his shirt to the Mets game. No one loved baseball more. There are other things from my mom and dad in the box. Keep digging," I implored.

"What am I looking for?" Jessie dug out a few more t-shirts, placing them on the bed.

"A picture frame, look for a frame."

"Michael, how many of these boxes are filled with your parents' things?"

"Just a couple. I don't have much. Every box with the 'Mom' printed on it has random things from them." She looked towards the hallway at the other cartons before continuing to search through the box in front of her.

"Is this what I'm looking for?" she said, staring at the bubble wrapped frame secured in a towel.

"Yeah, yeah, that's a picture of my mom and me. There are some photo albums in one of the other boxes of us all. That's my favorite picture, though. That's how I try to remember my mom. I was like eight or a bit younger. I don't know for sure."

Jess reached for the lamp to get a better view as she held the picture closely in front of her eyes.

"You look so cute—love the haircut all short and combed—and your mother is so beautiful. How come you don't have pictures of her or your family anywhere in this apartment? I can't believe this is the first one I've seen of you with her. Where was this taken?"

I looked into my mom's eyes once again and remembered the day we sat together on the perimeter of the pond at Eisenhower Park in East Meadow. She'd insisted on feeding the pigeons by the water after we'd finished a picnic on the lawn. In the picture, I was holding a slice of bread with one hand while throwing small pieces with the other. My mom, her brown hair pulled tight and pinned in a bun on the back of her head, was laughing with eyes alight.

We went to the park infrequently, even though it was close to our home and one of the few open spaces in the suburban spread suffocated by strip malls, supermarkets, Mickey D's, and gas stations. The outing almost didn't happen because my father spent the morning arguing with David, who opted to stay home by himself. It was one of the few days I could recall when my parents were completely relaxed and seemingly at peace with the world. We sat under the sun throughout afternoon without any sense of time.

"What are you doing with the bread here?" Jess said, laughing.

"I think I was probably going to eat it, but I guess I was throwing it to the birds."

"There are no birds anywhere near you."

"I was throwing it into the air with the hope they would catch it. In my mind, that's how birds ate. I think that's why my mom is laughing."

"Why is this in the box, Michael?"

"I'm packing. It's all going with me." I had stuffed everything in the boxes—stored away and taped up forever.

"I know that, but you weren't packing when we met. I mean, this is such a lovely picture of your mother. If I'm out of bounds here, let me know and I'll stop. I don't want to pry, but the way it's so carefully wrapped, it obviously means a lot to you. It doesn't belong in a box. Pictures are meant to be seen."

"I guess some are meant to be seen and some maybe aren't. Or at least not very often." Jess neatly folded the bubble wrap around the picture again as she sat next to me.

"I'm sorry I don't know what you mean. Why not? Pictures are how we remember," she said quietly.

I looked out the window towards the train tracks nearby as tears welled in my eyes. "And maybe there are some things you want to forget. I love that picture. It was one of the few days I know my mom was truly happy. But that blouse. The royal blue blouse. It's the same color of the one she had on the night she died. When I see that picture, that's what I remember also. It's so, I don't know what you want to call it. It's still kinda like a nightmare to me. So goddamn vivid. You know, Jess, I think I gotta tell you…"

I was getting nauseous and felt the sudden need to purge that part of my past. I began talking to prevent from getting sick.

"The night my mom died…"

"Michael, you don't have to…" Jessie interrupted—her hand touched my shoulder.

"You wanted to be let into my world? You want to know more about me, right? That's what you said. Then let me tell you at least this now. Okay, please? I was watching television with her."

I placed the water glass on the night table next to the box of condoms and bottle of Diet Coke from the previous evening. "It was a few days right after my eighteenth birthday, and she asked me to stay home with her and my dad. She was fine—I didn't see anything wrong. In fact, I hardly remember my mom ever getting ill throughout my life. She was the strong one.

"We spent part of the night playing Monopoly. It was one of those games that looked like it would last for days, so she asked to put it on hold. The two of us decided to watch television in our living room while my dad stayed in the kitchen to read the newspaper. He enjoyed spending the late nights by himself." Jessie listened, the picture to her chest and her face contorted. "We ended up watching old reruns of *I Love Lucy*. My mom liked the crazy, old comedies. That was her favorite show. She could recite lines from almost every episode. Any time I would tell her some sitcom made me laugh, she would invariably talk about Lucy stomping on the grapes in Italy as the funniest thing she had ever seen. You ever see that episode?"

With a quick shake of her head, Jessie chugged the Diet Coke straight from the bottle.

"That Lucy and grapes show was the litmus test of funny for her. She was having so much fun, so we probably watched four episodes together. I was about to call it a night when the show with Lucy and Ethel working in the chocolate factory came on. My mom begged me to sit through it with her. Of course, we had seen it a thousand times together. I can still see my mom laughing at Lucy throwing chocolates down her shirt and eating one after the other—her eyes popping out of her head with a mouth stuffed with chocolate. You know what I'm talking about?"

"I'm not Lucy literate. I liked *Three's Company*. Those Lucy shows are old, aren't they?"

"Ancient, but she loved them. And you gotta see that one show. Even I love the chocolate orgy episode. You know, there are times when I'm watching television inside at night, I can imagine my mom sipping tea and rocking back and forth with joy at the sight of Lucy jamming chocolate into her mouth."

I breathed uneasily while thinking about my mom laughing. "During a commercial break, she asked me to get her a slice of Entenmann's coffee cake. She used to eat that with her tea practically every day. It was a ritual. Like communion or something. After bringing the slice of cake to her, I left her alone and sat with my father for a bit.

"When I was in the kitchen, the phone rang. I don't know, it was probably around 11:30 or so. I remember checking with my dad to see if he was going to answer it or ignore it like he usually did at that hour. As I expected, it was David calling for me from San Francisco. So I spoke to him before he talked to my dad for a few minutes while I took the garbage out. It was stinking up the kitchen. There was this smell. Just terrible. I can practically smell it right now.

"After I got back, my dad handed me the phone. Before I could get into a long conversation with my brother, I shouted to my mom because I knew she would want to talk to David. And when I called her, there was no reply. I could hear the television still going and the sound of studio audience laughing.

"I figured she couldn't hear or she was eating, so I called again. And again. David's voice was in my ear. He was saying, 'Mike you there? What's going on? Say something.' Kinda panicky. I yelled to my mom again, and when my dad glanced over from the newspaper towards me, it felt as if the world suddenly shifted. I could hear David shouting. 'Michael, will you say something.' I tossed the phone on the table and ran into the living room.

"The back of my mother's head was against the armrest, her eyes staring at the ceiling. There was white powdered sugar around her open mouth. It was so like a horror movie, unreal to me. The cake was sitting sideways on her chest. That blue blouse covered in brown topping crumbs. I grabbed her shoulders and shook her, yelling like crazy for my father. But she was totally limp, like a ragdoll or something.

"I remember tossing the cake to the floor before feeling her chest. I wasn't even sure where her heart was. And then I grabbed her wrist, but her hand just tipped over. My dad—I don't think I ever remember him so, so I don't know, so alive. He pushed me out of the way so he could cradle her. He was yelling 'hon, 'hon, 'hon.' But there was nothing, just nothing. Her body collapsed in his arms.

"I just couldn't look at her eyes. Those eyes just staring blankly into emptiness. Then seeing the tears falling off my father's chin. Fuck. That was the beginning—that was it. I know it. Nothing was ever the same. He was never the same."

I paused after swallowing those final words, desperately hoping Jessie would not pick up on them. She was silent with her head hunched over her knees.

"You know Jess, I really don't think it's possible to feel that way again—just totally lost. It all happened so fast, so abruptly. She was laughing, and then silence. Part of me has this sense that the feeling of that night is never going to disappear. I still feel it sometimes. You know, I can see her jaw covered with powdered sugar when I go to sleep at night."

Jessie ran her fingers through my hair, but I recoiled. She pulled me to her anyway. "Michael, I'm so sorry. I had no idea."

"Of course, you didn't. How could you?" My laugh was shrill, ridiculous. "I barely mentioned my mom until now. I had never heard of a brain hemorrhage until the doctors explained it to us in the hospital. Who thinks that it's going to happen to your mother?

"My mom died when I was taking out the garbage. I was taking out the fucking garbage."

I scanned through the bureau for underwear as if I had never said a word. "Let me take a shower. We have to go. I'm sorry for all that. I shouldn't have told you."

"I don't know if we should go to the game," Jess reached out her hand, but I ignored her.

"Jess, we most definitely are going. We're not sitting here all afternoon. That is the last thing we are going to do. I didn't bring all this shit up to ruin our day. I want to go to the game. Let me shower and clean up. If there's one thing I absolutely have to do right now, it's wash up."

"Michael…"

"Jess, no, please, trust me." She lovingly wrapped the frame one more time before placing it in the box. Jessie carefully covered it with a few of the shirts that she had emptied onto the bed.

All the forgotten anger churned inside me once again. I remembered precisely why I kept the picture buried in the box, and felt guilty for dumping so much on Jessie. I knelt down to hug her waist.

"Forgive me, please. I'm so sorry for telling you that. I never should have said a word. Please, let's go to the game. I need to let it go. This is going to sound wrong, but the only way I'm going to feel better today is by forgetting about all of this. We're going to the game. And I need you there with me. Somehow, I feel that would make my mom happy. I know I'll forget it all after I shower. Just let me wash up. I need to get clean."

Fourteen

Jessie and I listened to Madonna's *Bedtime Stories* without talking throughout the interminable stop-and-start drive on the Grand Central Parkway towards Shea Stadium. When we finally arrived and strolled around the perimeter, she gazed up at the weathered white cement promenade with childlike awe. "Wow, this is the first game I've been to here. They need to redo this place. I love stadiums, but it looks like a junkyard."

"Wait, I thought you loved going to baseball games?"

"I lied," she said. "I've been to two games at Yankee Stadium with my cousins. That was kind of fun, but I can live without the Bronx. I'm hoping the people at Mets games are nicer."

"Oh, Yankee Stadium is totally different than Shea. It's a different kind of New York mean. You didn't wear a Mets hat at Yankee Stadium, did you?" I lazily trailed Jess as she pulled me along with her finger in my belt loop.

"I did, actually. I know I was a bad, bad girl, but sometimes that can be a heck of a lot of fun." Jessie winked while waving to random people as they walked past us. It was clear she had moved on from my potential day-killing story. Her childlike enthusiasm allowed me to finally relax in one of the few environments that always felt like home—the ballpark. We were there to have fun, and put reality aside for a few hours. And honestly, I think that's precisely why they created baseball.

When we finally exited the rotunda to see the groundskeepers watering down the manicured infield, Jess jumped into my arms and yelled "Yeah, baby!" Two teenagers behind us mimicked her.

Jess defiantly screamed "Yeahhh, baby" back to them. We settled in the field box after squeezing past a man and a woman eating ice cream sundaes out of an inverted mini Mets helmet. Next to them were their two portly young boys with puffy, white marshmallow cheeks. Their blue and orange Mets t-shirts were two sizes too small. I quickly pivoted my eyes away to focus on the outfielders playing catch and stretching down the right-field line.

The grand, green beauty of the perfectly trimmed diamond immediately put me at peace under the cloudless sky as Jessie playfully asked questions about each player on the field. "Is number 45 good?" "He's got a cute ass, where does he play?" "Why is that player so out of shape?" "Don't they have to run or something on their off days?"

They were very different questions than the ones I had asked my dad years before. I was persistent and probably annoying as I peppered him throughout each game. Lost in the boyish delusion of playing in the big leagues one day, I wanted to absorb as much information as possible and understand everything.

"Watch and learn," my dad would say. And learn I did. We only went to a few games each year, but my dad and I watched all the Mets games on television, and I listened to everything he said.

When Jessie walked away in my dad's t-shirt, I heard his voice again. "Michael, watch the pitcher's legs as he throws. Developing strong legs is the key to pitching. It gives you the strength to push off the rubber. If you don't use your legs, you'll hurt your arm. That's why I think you should start running more. Your legs are kind of like Jell-O, and your Little League coach said you'd be much better off if you lost some weight to balance the lower half of your body."

"We want a pitcher, not a glass of water," Jessie screamed at the field upon settling in next to me. An older man sitting two rows behind us shouted, "We'll take a pitcher of beer here."

Jess adjusted her cap, ponytail popping out of the back. "Michael, you paying attention here or are you lost?" She clapped her hands in front of my face. Was he messing with me?" I was now busy counting how many bags of popcorn the couple next to us was eating.

"What, oh, what? Forget it. He's probably just having fun. It's a baseball game. If he does it again, I'll go beat him up."

Jess whispered, "I thought you were going to say beat him off."

"I can do that too."

She looked directly at the vendors patrolling the stands. "That reminds me, I'm starving." It was a strange non-sequitur, but somehow very Jessie at the time. She was always hungry.

"There's an ice cream guy there," I replied, uninterested.

"Hot dogs, Michael, hot dogs. People eat hot dogs at the game. I can eat ice cream at Carvel, for God's sake," she said with cartoon anger.

"Okay, okay, when I see the guy."

"He's right over there, Michael. What are you blind? Get four hot dogs."

"Two, I'll get two." I quickly amended.

"C'mon batter, c'mon," Jessie shouted before lowering her voice and leaning close to me. "I'm not going to get into this now. I'm having too much fun. Buy four hot dogs."

I called to the sweating vendor for two franks. Jessie marched down the aisle, bent over—her ass to my face—and sweetly whispered to the kid struggling with his steamer. "He meant four, give us four, will you please?"

All the men in the row in front of us were checking her out. She skipped back to plop four hot dogs in plastic bags in my lap before snatching one away with her right hand.

"Thanks, dear, next time you pay," she said, grinning ostentatiously at the men.

Jess rolled her eyes after a quick bite of the shrunken wiener in a bun. "Wow, so this is a ballpark frank. Tastes like chicken. I'll stick with Nathan's." She voraciously finished it off without a breath. "Michael, I'm going to get a beer. Hold onto my frankie for me. I'm coming back for that."

When she disappeared up the aisle, the man sitting in front of me and sipping the head off his beer smiled. "She's coming back for your frankie," he said.

We both laughed as he raised a hand up for a high five.

With Jess out of sight, I offered my hot dogs to the two young boys. The parents nodded agreeably to the little Poppin' Freshes when I handed over the franks in a magnanimous, guilt-relieving gesture.

Jessie bounded back, hat slightly askew, with a beer and a Diet Coke.

"Here you go, rot your insides out. I'd rather get a very mild buzz on a hot day." She plucked her one hot dog off my lap. "Wait, you ate yours already? Really? I don't believe you."

I didn't flinch. "I swear. I was surprisingly hungry from all that last night." My friend angled his head around once more and laughed.

"I'm going to try and believe you. I'm impressed. Progress, finally," Jessie said. "Now, what did I miss? Anyone hit a home run? Who's this guy Ordonez on first base? Is he any good?"

"You didn't miss much, still no score. Ordonez is a very good fielder. Not much of a hitter," I replied as Jessie took a long pull of her beer.

"Not much of a hitter? Don't be so critical of the guy." She spread the mustard on her hot dog before chomping.

"Speaking of critical," Jessie said as the crowd around us booed after Edgardo Alfonso bounced into a double play. "After all this time, I finally researched some of your brother's stuff. I didn't read the books, but I read his long article on Prince and some other things and, well, I don't know." Her head swayed side to side. "Don't take this wrong or anything, but is he as big as a jerk as he sounds? He just comes off so arrogant. I hope when I meet him, he's not like I am imagining."

I was taken aback. "Well, I'm not sure what you are imagining, but that's his voice. That's how he always writes."

She shivered after finishing her frank. "Reads like `hey I'm cooler than you' to me. Half the time, I don't know what he's talking about. I mean all the hip-hop stuff. Who cares? It's noise to me, and he's writing about it as serious music. I'm sure he's a straight-up guy, but I was not impressed. What I read turned me off."

"A lot of people read what he writes. He's one of the most widely published music critics." I realized I sounded like a defense attorney or a publicist. Or a brother.

Jess sat back confidently after draining half the beer. "Oops, struck a nerve. I knew I should've kept my mouth shut."

"You didn't strike a nerve. I'm just telling you the truth. I mean, haven't you read Robert Christgau, Lester Bangs or Greil Marcus?

Opinionated and maybe arrogant. That's what they are supposed to do. Who wants a boring critic?"

"Oh, Michael stop with this nonsense. I never heard of those guys no, and I don't need to. I get it. He's your older brother. Maybe, I shouldn't have said what I did, but we need to be honest with each other. He just sounds like a know-it-all."

"He's supposed to fucking know things. That's his job." This time, all three men ahead of us turned their heads.

"We're done here." Jess ignored me while watching animated players chasing Mr. Met on the scoreboard. "Relax, Michael, and don't you ever curse at me. I don't fucking like it. Capisce? What you don't seem to understand is, I'm not going to read those big, boring critics or whoever you mentioned. And I surely won't read your brother again. I really don't care. I hate critics. Why do I need some person telling me it's okay to like Janet Jackson? I like what I like. Music and film critics make no sense to me. Why is their opinion better than mine?" She shrugged and ran over to the muscular, surfer blonde vendor selling pretzels.

The innings breezed by with the Mets getting shut out in the muggy August afternoon heat. Jessie drank one beer after another while cheering every out for both teams. Her t-shirt was soaked dark blue—I could see her bra strap every time she stood up.

After the seventh inning stretch, she grabbed my hand. The section around us had emptied out, but Jessie still whispered. "Listen, Michael, I was thinking. Maybe this is crazy, I don't know. I talked to my boss, and she says she knows some people in Boston.

"There are galleries on Newbury Street. I looked it up. It's a great area like the Village. And there are a few in some place called Copley or, I don't know, Copley something, and she said maybe I could get a job in one. It's a possibility."

I immediately translated where she was headed.

"So, I was thinking…" She hesitated before looking into my eyes. "What if I move up to Boston also? I looked at rents. I'll get my own place. It's kind of expensive, but I have some money saved. You don't know where you are moving to yet, right? We can get studios or something near each other. I know it's not smart to move in together at this point—it's way too early. But we can be together. I really think it would be good." Whatever remained of the crowd cheered a John Olerud home run to break the shutout.

"Michael, hey, are you listening? Did I say something wrong? If you think it's a bad idea, I understand." Jess gazed at me with heavy-lidded eyes.

"I think it's a great idea. I'm not sure why I didn't think of it." I said, feigning enthusiasm. Jessie and I would be together all the time.

I had been obsessing over us breaking up or drifting apart, but the thought of us in Boston together just never crossed my mind. I figured we'd have a long-distance relationship while I studied and worked my way down to my ideal weight. That was what really mattered.

"That's great. Great," I replied. Her drooping, overheated body rested in my arms. "I'm not sure how that's going to work, but it will be so great to be together." If I said great one more time, I could have endorsed Frosted Flakes.

"We will figure it out, Michael. There's no point in living four-hundred miles apart when all we have to do is be careful with our money. We can have some fun while you study. Hopefully, I'll get a good job. I've been thinking about this for a while."

The Mets scored another run, and despite the nine-run deficit, Jessie jumped out of my arms and shouted, "Yes, yes, yes." She obviously wasn't reacting to the score.

I laughed nervously with my hand on her spine to prevent a backward flop.

"What's so funny? They just scored." Jess finished her beer just as she fell into the chair.

"I don't know, you saying `yes.' You love to say that, and it's making me really horny now."

"I love what?" Her crimson face twisted.

"Yes, yes, yes. Your favorite phrase." It was a quick and hopefully effective misdirection. I tried to put Boston on the back burner, where I hoped it would stay.

"I never say yes. What the hell are you talking about? What's yes?"

Clearly drunk now, Jessie waved for the beer guy who was counting his money.

I figured she'd never remember what I was saying. "You can't be serious? You scream `yes' when you come. I mean all the time. I swear. Half the time I think I'm fucking Molly Bloom and the other times, Marv Albert."

"Fuck you, I do not," she shouted. "And I'm not a screamer. And I don't even know who those people are, or care. What are you talking about?"

"I just finished this book and this character…" I lost my train of thought while still fighting the lingering notion of settling down together in Boston.

"Michael, I don't care about a damn book your reading. All you think about is books. What is wrong with you?" she demanded, suddenly snapping back to lucidity. "Okay, now I'm going to be self-conscious for sure."

"No, no, you are definitely not. One of us is enough," I hoped Jess would smile. Instead, she defiantly ordered one last beer to nurse without a word throughout the final innings.

After what seemed like the slowest game of the year, we crawled out of the parking lot onto the Grand Central Parkway. The sweat was dripping off my arm onto the seat. Jessie adjusted the air conditioner nob, but a whoosh of hot air rushed into in our faces.

The traffic, stacked for miles as we crawled past the World's Fair hemisphere in Flushing, compelled Jessie to walk towards the front of the car in the next lane. She stood angrily with hands on hips like Mussolini, searching for the problem.

"Get back in the fucking car, skinny bitch," someone screamed out from the traffic jam.

Jessie leaned into the adjacent car's window and talked to the driver. Within moments, a half dozen people were straddling the lanes of the parkway and peering into the distance.

A voice rang out from behind us. "Look what you started, sweetheart. Get in the muthafucking car 'fer Chissakes." Jessie stormed back toward her seat with both hands raised in triumph.

She hopped in to nestle next to me.

"Michael, go beat the shit out of that guy yelling at me. What a moron. If you don't, I'll kick his ass." Jess touched my face with her sweaty hand. "Can I be serious with you? So you think it's okay? Me moving to Boston with you? I do think it's the right thing. I really love you, Michael. I do. I want to be with you."

My body quickly went slack at the sound of "I love you." Those were foreign words, a different language. Something I'd never heard. I suddenly felt so vulnerable. For months, I was toughening up and getting stronger—shedding all traces of childhood vulnerability. I believed I loved Jessie, but I was afraid if I told her, it would be a clear sign of weakness. I'd be regressing. If I allowed myself to be sentimental, I would become soft again.

And I knew I just couldn't accommodate that. Too much work and energy had been put into getting beyond any hints of indulgence. I could not—would not—return to the days of Mr. Softee.

I remained stunned in silence for minutes. As the traffic slowly inched ahead, I finally yielded while dazed by the maze of red lights before me. "Jess, I love you—I mean I do." The words just poured out.

The cars finally spread wide enough for me to accelerate, and Jess's limp body fell into mine until a long honk of a car horn forced her to move away. "You better drive. Just drive." Her eyes were closing as she breathed quietly with her head against the seat. I was sure she was going to pass out. "Michael, I don't know why I never said I love you before, but I need to say it. I honestly don't know what it means," she whispered to herself.

We merged with the stream of cars heading back to the Island. The warm breeze blew my hair back, literally giving me a second wind. Jessie awoke from her stupor just as we finally sped out of Flushing.

"I think Boston could be our own little adventure. It could be a lot of fun. Our own apartments in the city. Pretty good, don't you think? I mean, it's better we're together than apart. That makes sense, doesn't it? And it's got to be better than Long Island," she said.

"Yes, yes, of course, yes," I replied, smiling and completely without thought.

Part Three

Shelter From the Storm

Fifteen

Zach Wheat
Pepper Martin
Cookie Rojas
Chili Davis

I jotted names for my All Food Baseball All-Star team in the margins of *The Boston Globe* sports section while sitting with David and Mon in the therapist's waiting room at Massachusetts Central. My right leg bobbed uncontrollably until Monique placed her hand on my knee. "Relax Babe, it's going to be fine," she said, readjusting herself in in her seat. I continued to flip the pen between my fingers.

"Give me that back. Just sit still for a moment." Mon snatched the pen and dropped it in her handbag.

"What do I tell him? I have nothing to say." I knew I sounded desperate.

"You tell him the truth. Tell him the crazy shit you've been telling Monique." David was sitting directly across from me with his leather jacket in his lap. He impatiently examined the freshly painted walls and ceiling. The hospital was undergoing extensive remodeling—the world seemed to be in transition. "You've been through this before. It's a waste of time if you are going to bullshit the guy. You've got to talk about what food represents to you. Dr. Graynor discussed this after you went chop-socky on your arm, and it's time for you to deal with some real things.

"Mike, you can't pretend you can fix things by yourself. I know you went through therapy, but you really just must have just watched the clock. This time, you have to work."

David's voice was missing any hint of levity or the usual what-the-fuck bemusement. "I really never actually heard of male anorexics.

I mean I just haven't," he said, looking directly at Monique. "I have seen girls all the time in my classroom over years. I knew they were going through something—it was as clear as their hollow armpits. The way they look just screams 'illness here.' So many times, I've spoken to them in my office and wanted to say, 'Get some kind of help, please,' but I knew nothing for sure. Who knows what's really going on in their lives?

"You, though, well, this is the first step, and it won't be easy. You have to start showing some fight." He suddenly slumped in his chair while massaging his scalp. "Damn."

"Am I giving you a headache?" I said timidly.

"You aren't giving me anything. Headaches come when you don't sleep much, and you can't figure things out. You aren't doing anything, so stop blaming yourself."

My fingers rhythmically tapped the arm of the chair as David cracked his knuckles.

"Okay, guys enough with the ambient noises here. I feel like I'm hanging with Kraftwerk," Mon demanded.

"You know, sometimes I wonder why. Why is this happening?" My eyelids were so heavy from two sleepless nights—it was hard to believe it was barely midday.

David shook his head quickly like a cartoon character coming to his senses. "Don't even ask that question. Those kinds of questions, 'Why this?' 'Why that?' They're useless. It's a waste of time at this point, so just deal with it. There are better questions to be asked and answered. That's why we are here.

"You will get through this. It's crazy, I don't believe in the whole 'Whatever does not kill you only makes you stronger' thing our fucked-up culture has appropriated for a Hallmark card slogan to help people rationalize pain, but I do know that if you confront it now instead of ignoring it like you, and we..."

He turned to Mon before continuing. "Have done for the last few years, well then, you can come through on the other end."

"Let's face it, Babe, we all confront these trials, and you need to trust me here." Mon hovered near me with arms stretched over her head. "How you deal now is important. Adversity really doesn't build character. That's nonsense. It reveals character. The next few months are really going to be make or break. The real you is going to emerge. I don't believe you want to live like this. I mean, I just don't. You can't."

She sat next to me again, covering her eyes with her hands. I turned to see if she was crying. How I lived my life had always been my own business. The way my choices affected Mon or David just wasn't part of the equation. I was putting so much energy into holding on to the one thing that made sense to me, I didn't see or care how it possibly could tear them apart. David's headaches and Mon's exhaustion and tears were clearly all my fault. If the doctor couldn't help, I feared I would lose the only two people I had left in my life.

After long moments of uneasy silence, Mon abruptly snapped to attention. I was scanning a two-year-old *Sports Illustrated* with Brett Favre on the cover. She leaned in towards me. "I must tell you, I was sitting here thinking about the problems you had in the past with therapists. I still remember those phone calls. We've never talked about this, but I never thought you took those situations seriously. You understand, you can't jump around to other therapists again. It's not a game anymore."

"I'll be fine," I tried to reassure her. "It won't be like the past. I'm good, Mon. I know what's at stake. I gotta be honest, though, I really don't want to talk about it now."

"Fine Babe, I'll let you be," she said quietly.

"I think we've said that too much. Letting it be. That's the fucking problem. We enabled him, but when that door opens, it's going to change. As weird as it may sound from me, I feel good about this guy. My guess is, you still don't think there's anything wrong. That's been the root if you ask me, am I right?" David's eyes were burning a hole through my head.

"That's how you interpret it, not how I do. There were complications," I replied.

"There are always complications. Life is one long complication. That's why we go to see psychiatrists. You need to take this seriously."

Unfortunately, David was right. My past efforts in treatment, collecting and discarding doctors like used baseball cards, were, at best, half-baked. They were mostly camouflage for my desire to continue living on my terms. When I did make attempts, I merely said the things I believed the doctors thought I should say. I never wanted to change anything. The whole process was nothing more than a charade, something to be endured.

Jess and I chose the shrinks randomly. The ones we settled on had no clue how to deal with a male anorexic. I thought every doctor would have some kind of plan to treat my inability to eat, but I quickly found that wasn't true at all. I was just another patient with problems.

As I watched David gaze at the floor with his head halfway between his knees, I drifted back to my first visit to a therapist, maybe eighteen months before Jessie left. His office was just outside of Kenmore Square where the C trolley line disappeared underground on Beacon Street.

The waiting room was very quiet and lovely. Framed reproductions of Klimt paintings dotted each of the four walls. I sat across from a teenage girl wrapping strands from her long, stringy hair around her fingers before placing the frayed ends in her mouth. The points of her shoulders stuck out of her blouse like the corners of a hanger. When the nurse called out a name, she stood while trying to hold up the waist of the weathered jeans slipping off her elfin hips. I thought to myself, "Now, that girl has a real problem."

I ended up waiting over an hour for Dr. Eckstrom. I've always remembered the names of all the doctors I dealt with—they were seared into my brain. There were so many of them. Throughout my years in Boston, talking to physicians, dealing with emergency doctors, and choosing therapists seemed like part-time jobs for me.

With his thick mustache and unruly hair, Dr. Eckstrom seemed to fall straight out of a *New Yorker* cartoon. He played a tape of ocean waves and wind chimes—I thought I was at a Yanni concert—before asking question after perfunctory question.

"How long has this denial been going on?"

"What is your relationship with your mother?"

"Do you have any recollections of abuse?"

He kept staring out the window as if I wasn't in the room. There were a few knowing nods and deep sighs. Even though I calmly answered each question, I refrained from revealing too much detail about anything. After about a half hour of watching him scribble notes on a pad between sips of coffee, I grew restless while listening to the waves crashing against the shore.

The clock ticked off seconds before one query gave up the game. "Okay, tell me if you don't mind me asking, are you menstruating?" he said, tapping the pad with his pen. That was enough to send me reeling into a rage—the fucking guy obviously wasn't paying attention. I remained silent while eyeing him gazing into the sunset with a shit-eating grin. He was probably thinking about sniffing his secretary's panties throughout the session. I could have gotten more insight from Dr. J. As the time ran down, he asked me if I wanted to take one of his tapes home. They were on sale for $15 each, five for fifty.

The forty-five-minute hour felt like a quarter of the shitty little life I was walking back into once the door closed behind me. I furiously punched the dashboard of my car while sitting behind the wheel in front of the lovely ivy-covered brick building next to a basement bookstore. What a nightmare. Those fucking waves. I knew I would've prefrred to shove a tampon up my ass than go back.

A few months later, Jessie was reading *Rumi: The Book of Love* when I returned from work one night. She recoiled after I took off my shirt. Looking warily into my eyes, she said, "You're still losing weight, those bones in your back. Jesus Christ. This is getting out of control. I want you to see this doctor I got. You need to talk to somebody besides me—someone who can listen and not lose it. You said the last doctor wasn't really listening, so maybe this one will."

The thought of going to another psychiatrist seemed like a waste of time, but honestly, so did every day of my life.

Dr. Soolame was in Brookline near Cleveland Circle, not far from where we lived. His office, located in an old, decaying building, had a cramped waiting room that smelled like wet paper. Every seat was filled, so I stood silently next to a tall, dying plant.

Sitting beside the funky fern was a tall, barrel-chested man who seemed to have wandered in from a New Mexico reservation. His dark skin, ruddy face, and broad shoulders were imposing. The hands in his lap looked to be as thick as slabs of beef.

I thought about the big chief running away after McMurphy was lobotomized at the end of *One Flew Over the Cuckoo's Nest*. My first instinct was to flee all the all the crazies also, but I remained in the corner to analyze the other patients' possible afflictions.

Did the woman across the way with pink toenails angling out of her sandals have a slight neurosis that kept her from having a vaginal orgasm or did she place her three-year-old in the dryer that morning? Was the trembling guy, wearing a moldy Red Sox jacket, a slightly neurotic family man known in his neighborhood for being affectionate to little kids or was he on parole for that reputation?

Was big chief upset about his wife leaving with a bigger chief? Or was he traumatized by the realization that he was the only fucking Native American in all of Boston? There were at least a dozen patients, and I couldn't stop that endless either/or game in my head.

Waiting rooms make everyone more paranoid than Cypress Hill at a police checkpoint. I was sure all of the others were all staring at my bony hands, sunken eye sockets, and chicken neck with suspicion. I must have looked like the Unabomber after one too many juice cleanses.

Upon finally getting to see Dr. Soolame, I sat sheepishly on a reclining chair. He was Indian or Pakistani with cocoa skin and a big mole on his cheek. The first thing I noticed was his narrow, bony wrist as he played with his watch. The wrist was so thin that every time he raised his arm in contemplation, the souped-up Swatch slid down against his rolled shirt sleeve by his elbow.

The man's arm was like a breadstick on steroids. There I was, trying to figure out my food obsessions with Gandhi. He could not have weighed much more than me at the time. It reinforced my dogged belief that I had no real problem at all. There are skinny people in every corner of this world. And then there are really skinny people. No big deal.

I ended up talking non-stop for an hour without interruption until a large fly buzzed by my eyes. I swatted it away with my right hand.

After I missed, Dr. Soolame said his first words. "What was the significance of that gesture?"

"There was a fly in my eye."

He placed his hand on his chin. The watch descended again. We sat together in stone silence before Dr. Soolame finally sighed at the clock on the wall. Time was up. "Michael, I think there's more to that hand gesture than you know. It is something you can talk about next time. I want you to think about what you were trying to say with that."

"I'm trying to say there was a damn fly in my eye. Nothing more. Nothing. You didn't see the fly?"

He stared me down, his eyes ping-ponging in his head. Quietly, he said, "Perhaps, perhaps. Have a good day." That was it. Not even, "What do you think of when I say bratwurst and pitted avocado?" Nothing.

Afterwards, I told Jessie I'd made another appointment and would eventually go back. Of course, I had no intention of returning to break down the significance of a fly in my eye. On the night before the next appointment, *One Flew Over the Cuckoo's Nest* happened to be on Turner Classic Movies. Sometimes life works like that.

Jessie had never seen it. I sat through the film again, even though the ending always infuriated me. Jess remained rapt while holding a pillow to her chest until the credits rolled.

"That's such a great movie. How did I miss it before?" she said. "It's so sad, but so hopeful."

I thought back to the desperation I felt while sitting in Dr. Soolame's waiting room.

"Where's he running to? I mean where the fuck is chief running to? He has nothing. He knows no one. He's just running away."

"He's free. He's running to freedom," she replied firmly.

"Freedom? C'mon, what is freedom in that situation? He put himself in the ward in the first place. He created the precise situation he was running from." I angrily changed the channel.

Jessie pecked at a bag of potato chips while huddled under her old, faded blue blanket. "I don't agree. He's free to choose how he wants to live now. He can make up his own rules. It's kind of beautiful. He knows what he left behind. Now he's going to find what's in front of him. He can live with the freedom to choose. That's the freedom I'm talking about."

"He's just running." I was adamant. "It's way too romantic an ending if you ask me—just makes no sense. There's nowhere to go."

"I don't know, Michael. I think there's everywhere for him. He starts over. That's something." She eyed me carefully. "Michael, you are going back to the doctor tomorrow, right? I didn't forget. You're going."

And yes, I did indeed drag my ass to Dr. Soolame's office each week to talk. And talk. And talk. He always remained completely silent while watching my every movement. I figured I had to be gaining some kind of insight through osmosis.

Talking actually felt quite good, though. I talked about everything I wanted to eat, everything I refused to eat, and everything people should not eat. I even detailed how my food-oriented lists were getting more creative.

Words here, words there, words everywhere. But I was getting nowhere because my obsession was getting worse.

The more I talked about food in the office, the more I thought about food while I wandered around in Boston. I saw obscure images of food or references to obesity in everything—billboards, television, clouds, flushing toilets, and graffiti. My weight plummeted and fatigue set in as food seemed to circle the wagons—I never felt more trapped.

I lasted a good three months before I left Dr. Soolame's silent treatment. It was so goddamn exhausting talking about food. My head was so far up my own ass that I could have watched a dental hygienist clean plaque off my teeth.

Jess was angry, but I promised to hook up with another doctor as soon as possible. Completely quitting was not an option. The bottom was dropping out of our relationship. Jessie was becoming more and more remote as we drifted further and further away from each other.

Our sex life shriveled up like a raisin in a microwave. Our dreams were not deferred—I just decided to nuke them. Pathetically, I did not miss the sex or worry about our distance. There were too many other things preoccupying my mind.

I would never have believed there would come a day when I would lose interest in sex, but, sadly, it had arrived. I barely had the energy to jerk off, let alone fuck Jessie. There were times when I felt twinges of desire after she walked naked through the apartment. Sometimes I was turned on when I realized that she was masturbating during all of her endless evening baths. On most nights, I simply couldn't be bothered. I just shrugged it off, completely content to let her come alone.

Now, I do know what you're thinking: "I love to fuck. That can't happen to me!" Yeah, that's what I thought, but let me tell you, it can. It sure as hell can if you get sucked into that black vortex just like I did. Blink once too often, and the world changes before your eyes.

My final therapist was recommended by Monique's yoga instructor, who once had a studio in South Boston. This time, the shrink was into imaging or something called sense-synthesis. When we discussed the treatment over the phone, I didn't understand what she was talking about.

She carefully explained imagining the inner workings of my mind and trying to visualize the turbulence or distress. The woman said that by giving an image to my oppressive thoughts, I'd be able to vanquish them through finding associations and making adjustments to my reality. It all sounded like complete horseshit, but I figured maybe a radical approach was needed.

I sat hesitantly in the rustic, fussily decorated office in a large house in Newton. Doubt crept in immediately when Dr. "Call me Marie" walked in. By the sight of her, I needed to call a waitress. Marie's entrance was preceded by the sound of corduroy chafing between her thighs.

I thought I wandered into the final battle of *Ghostbusters*. Everyone always said I was exaggerating, but I knew what I saw. When Marie sat down in the large, burnished-brown plush chair, her body seemed to congeal into the upholstery like a mound of vanilla pudding.

I processed her image with awe.

Thunderthighsmassiveassbazookaboobswhatawaist.

Her side drooped over the armrests as she juggled a glass of orange juice in her little, chubby hands. She must have eaten everything I refused over the years. Images of food flashed before me.

I visualized a head of lettuce when she said, "Let us start."

"Alrighty, Michael, just slowly allow the first things to come to the surface. Some images will arise as we wait. When they do, I want you to describe them so we can discuss."

I inhaled and pretended to meditate for ten minutes before she whispered, "Breathe deeply, free your mind."

Nothing appeared in the far recesses of my brain. The only thing I could think about was an old VH-1 documentary on the Mommas and the Poppas. It included the rumors of an obese Mama Cass Elliot choking on a ham sandwich. Now if there ever was an example of the cosmos offering life lessons, that was it.

Marie exhaled and said, "What do you see?"

I thought death by cold cuts. "I see a demon."

"That's good. What kind of demon?"

My eyes were still closed. "A dark demon. Very bad. He's laughing."

"You said he. It's a man? We can trace that. What else do you see?" she replied with hope.

"Besides Devil Dogs and Deviled Eggs? Underwood's Deviled Ham."

"Michael, we can't continue if you do not take this seriously. What do you really see?"

I saw money being pissed away. My starvation wasn't going to be cured by conjuring floating, Jungian dream images—save that silly shit for people with restless leg syndrome. I needed a real fucking doctor. After a yell-until-the-neighbors-complain fight with Jessie, I told Monique it was impossible to work with someone like Marie.

It was the first time I'd ever heard Mon yell. "Michael, stop this now. Your view of the world distorts all things out of context. You see what you want to see. I don't believe she was fat. I just I think this is just another excuse to avoid therapy."

A few days later, she encouraged Jessie to help me make an appointment with a physician. Jess cornered me one morning before I headed out to work. "Monique gave me this name of a doctor who will refer you to a therapist. She's the doctor of her assistant's sister here in

Boston. She's supposed to be good. Do you believe this? Because I don't." Jess handed me a post-it note.

"The sister of the assistant of your sister-in-law. Michael, do you realize how many people are trying to help you? Make the damn call. You left that Marie lady, you left the Indian doctor, you left everybody so far, but you are not leaving this. You owe me that much."

The next week, I was in Dr. Rigatta's office for the first time.

Sixteen

Monique had just finished stretching with arms towards the ceiling before she picked up a month-old copy of *Newsweek* featuring a smirking George Bush on the cover. "Where is he? Now you realize why we are called patients. I was thinking the other day, and it's just a suggestion, but maybe you can get a life coach also. I had two friends who had life coaches, and they liked them."

"No life coaches for him. He doesn't need someone who got her degree by spending six weeks in a correspondence course singing 'Don't Worry, Be Happy,'" David said with a wave of his hand. "You can buy a life coach degree from the crackhead selling blowjobs in the back of Wal Mart for Chrissakes.

"Only in America do they invent jobs for people to pat you on the back, and rub your belly. What are life coaches qualified for besides cashing checks from vulnerable people? What schooling did they have besides getting an online certificate of self-affirmation from Mary J. Blige?"

"A yi, yi, David you can be so negative sometimes," Mon seemed fatigued from boredom. "It was only a suggestion. Then I've got nothing else. I'm going to get something to drink and take a walk. I can only inhale fresh paint for so long. Babe, you want anything if I get back before you have to see the doctor?"

"Diet Coke." I hadn't had my fix yet and was twitching from the lack of caffeine.

"Get him water," David said brusquely. "If you go to the bathroom, see if they have one of those cheap dispenser machines with Tylenol, tampons, and condoms. I need some Tylenol or Advil to get rid of this headache."

"We're in a hospital, not a club, David. There happens to be a pharmacy here. I think that's a little more efficient." Mon was already halfway out the door.

David laughed with two fingers forming the okay sign. "Yeah, right. Whatever. Maybe what I need is a tampon. This is brutal."

I sat listening to a Muzak version of "The Long and Winding Road" as David paced the room.

"David, you alright? You know you guys don't have to stay. I'm fine here by myself. I can hop on the T home."

"Mike, stop worrying about me. The doctor has to be out here soon enough, and you'll have plenty to deal with. This is your moment. It needs to stick. Hopefully, he can begin to unravel years of dysfunction. You've written the book, *How Not to Live a Life*. Now it's time to rewrite things."

"I'm worried. I mean I don't know how to talk about this," I mumbled. "You said before you don't understand this whole thing. I don't understand it myself, and I'm living it."

He sidled up to the doctor's door while laughing. "Well, the last person to understand it is the person going through it, so you shouldn't expect to understand the irrational. The reason you are here is because you don't understand it. So just tell him everything he asks about. He's going to ask about me, about Jessie, about dad, about a lot of things. The past, your sex life, and your eating habits. Wherever you lead him. Just talk honestly."

I recoiled at the word 'everything.' "He's going to ask about our sex life? I don't want to talk about that."

"And I sure don't want to hear it, but you know he will. This is going to be hard, so be prepared, Mike. You are not going to come out of his office shitting rainbows each week. It's going to hurt. If you think Jessie leaving you was hard—and I know it was—now you are going to have to relive it. It's the only way to get beyond the past.

"Everything's that happened will come up. I bet the fat kid stuff is just a footnote to all the other things. He's going to force you to deal with Jessie and with your relationship with me.

"You have to tell him about it all—all the fucked-up things including Jessie's anger at me." He sat once again, holding held his head in his hands. "Nothing ever seemed to go right there, starting from the first day. You remember that disaster?"

I did. I'd stored everything without ever wanting to revisit it all. I knew dredging everything up again was inevitable, though. I remembered all of their fights along with all the constant quiet tension. In fact, not only did I continue to relive their first godforsaken meeting, but I also still heard them yelling at each other on the night of the trivia party.

"Jessie always thought I had an agenda. She was always angry at me for something. You know what I mean?" David said nonchalantly.

The blood was coursing through the veins in my neck—it was simply impossible to contain myself anymore.

"David, no, in fact, I don't know what you mean because we have to deal with some shit. I can't bury it anymore. I have to ask you a question. I just can't get past it, and I haven't been able to get past it. Especially since Jessie walked out. I really wish I could." I hovered over David, seemingly hoping to intimidate him.

He looked up, his face pale and weary. "Go ahead. What? What is it? You look upset."

"Upset? Upset isn't really the word. You have to tell me the truth here. You remember that shitty trivia night Jessie and I had with Les and her friends a few years ago?"

David squinted at me. "Barely. All I remember is Jessie telling me to go fuck myself."

"You don't remember the fight you had with Jessie. You telling her to leave me? You remember that now? Did you tell her that? And I mean, why the fuck would you do that? Why would you tell my girlfriend to leave with Les?" My face was burning. "Why? Tell me why? I need to understand. That's one why question that has an answer. I need an answer."

He shifted to his feet and reached into his pocket for a piece of gum. "Did Jessie tell you about that? Is that what she told you?"

"I need you to tell me that you told her that." This was new territory for me. I couldn't remember the last time I raised my voice to David, but I felt that he had to come clean with his betrayal. "I need you to tell me the truth."

After a deep breath, he tossed the gum in his mouth. "You want to know? Yes, yes, I did. I'm sorry she told you that, but I was hoping she wouldn't. That night was complicated. I told her that yes, and I think I was justified in doing so. I never told her to leave with Les. I just said leave. Yes."

I bent over to brace myself with hands on my buckling knees. "Why? It was you who gave her the idea. And now she's gone. Are you happy now? Your grand design was fulfilled."

"What exactly did she tell you? Is that what you think? Her walking out on you was my plan? You can't be serious, Michael."

"She didn't fucking tell me. She didn't. In fact, she never mentioned it and acted like it never happened. I heard it. Heard it all. I was outside of the apartment listening to you both yelling at each other like an old married couple. The two of you shouting about me so the whole building could hear. I still remember the words."

He grabbed me by the shoulders as if he was squeezing an accordion. "You were outside the apartment listening to us? Are you kidding me?" His hands, jerking me upright, were surprisingly powerful. I heard his slow breathing.

"How long have you kept this in? This has been churning in your gut for this long, and you never mentioned a word to me. Every time we've been together you couldn't muster the courage to ask me about this? I can't believe you." He released me before tucking his fingers behind his head. A lock of thick black hair fell to the side of his face. "Why did you swallow this till now?"

"I don't know. I just couldn't ask. There never was a good time." All my resolve dissolved, leaving me shaking.

"And you think this is a good time? In the doctor's waiting room? I mean, I'm glad you are getting this out, but why didn't you ask me about this right after Jessie disappeared? I would have explained it then. If you want to know the truth, I'm relieved she left. I hate to tell you that, but you have declined so badly ever since you met her. You ever think she was part of the problem? You ever think she might have been the wrong person for you to be with? You were a healthy person before Jessie and half a person after her. So yeah, I think I did you a service."

"Relieved? How was Jessie any of your business? That was my life."

"And you, yes you, are my fucking business. I was relieved for you. I was relieved that maybe, just maybe, whatever the dynamic sending you into the goddamn abyss was over. I don't give a fuck about Jessie. That might be terrible to say, but I love you, and I need you to reclaim yourself. I'm sorry, Michael. I'm sorry I told Jessie to leave you, but am I sorry she's gone? Fuck no. I'm just not."

I turned away in disbelief, ultimately dropping back into a chair.

"You must hate me, Michael. I don't know. I…Listen, I'm sorry. I mean I really am. And I'm sorry you had to hear that in the hallway. I wasn't trying to break you two up, but I was trying, and I am trying, to put you back together. If you hate me…"

"Stop it. Enough with that." I looked up at David. I desperately needed to cry to expel all the noise in my head. Instead, I simply ended up sitting limp and defeated. "I can't hate you—you know that. I don't know what I feel. I'm exhausted. I'm just so exhausted."

"Mike, I don't know what to say. I'm trying to figure out just how much anger you've been carrying around. Where is that anger been going? Where?

"I can't imagine what it must have felt like to listen to that argument. I just can't, but you can't seriously believe Jessie left because I told her to. Do you? Jessie was never going to listen to a word I said. I think more than anything, she was going to defy me at all costs. But please, please, think of what you have done to yourself, and then ask yourself why Jessie gave up. You need to think this through. Maybe this is the first thing you should tell the doctor. Now I don't even know how much of that night has contributed to what I'm looking at here.

"I don't know, Michael. Again, I'm sorry if I hurt you. None of that fight, none of it was…I just never expected it to get back to you. What the hell were you doing listening outside the apartment?"

My left leg was going numb as I recalled huddling outside the door. All that fucking shouting. When I slept each night, I still heard Jessie's piercing voice. It was so vivid, I was often forced to cover my head with a pillow.

"It really doesn't matter what I was doing there. I was just there. There was a moment when I was walking that night—you remember how cold it was? Well, I felt like I didn't want to come back. I just wanted to escape and disappear. I ended up on the floor in the hall until you left. You walked right past me without even seeing me. How could you not see me?"

"Jesus Christ, Michael, that was an awful night, but what I was trying to do, well, I don't know what I was trying to do. I was just so frustrated. I have to say I was frustrated with you most of all that night. I think I told you that. Seeing you like that with your friends there. You sweating so terribly, so goddamn gaunt and not eating.

"I honestly don't think you'd be here in this office if you were still with Jessie believing everything was normal. That's what I saw that night. I saw a guy who was completely fucked up acting as if everything was normal with his girlfriend in tow making nice with everyone. And, at the same time, she was also flirting with your friend, Les.

"It was an absolute fucking horror show for me to witness. And maybe that's what I was trying to tell Jessie. It needed to stop. We needed to get you to where you are now right here.

"It's strange, but I think this—this step—might save your life. It has to. And that's all I give a shit about. I didn't want Jessie to leave you like she did, but I knew things had to change.

"I've got to be honest, you scare me, Michael. You used to worry me, but now you just scare me. You think you are invincible. That night you kept telling me you were alright. You are always alright. And everything about you has been telling me you are not. I see you now. I barely recognize who I'm looking at. Monique and I, we bite our tongue, but I guess what you heard that night what I'm thinking and have been thinking. If that's wrong, well then, I don't know…"

He trailed off. There was nothing for me to say. Hearing the words "You scare me, Michael" was unbearable. I wasn't angry at David because I was genuinely frightened also. Everything he said was true.

Every day, I flinched when I saw my reflection in a parked car's window. A ghost always looked back. David's words articulated everything I could not tell myself.

My initial question to David and Mon was finally answered. I needed to tell the doctor I was scared for my life. I was as scared for myself as I was of myself. I needed help.

After I finally settled down, we remained silent for over five minutes until Monique returned. She was smiling while holding a cardboard tray. "You guys are still waiting? He's very late. That's ridiculous and rude. What have you two been chatting about? Dude talk? I have to tell you, they have a nice new cafeteria here. I just love the remodel they did. It looks great. I've only been here one time, right after we moved. They were still under construction."

She sat next to me and crossed her legs regally. "Babe, here's a water." I let the bottle fall into my lap. "David, the coffee is probably kind of cold, but there's nothing I can do about it. Here's the Advil." My brother grasped the paper cup with the pills and raised his left hand to Mon.

"Are you guys alright?"

"We're fine," David said as he reached for a pack of Oreos on Mon's thigh. "We're fine. We're going to be alright."

"David, it's okay, you can tell her. I don't care. I understand. I really do. I know what you were trying to do. I just wish I'd asked earlier."

Mon looked to David while clasping my arm. "Wait, what? You understand what? What happened here?"

"I'll tell you later," David said in a voice barely above a whisper.

"Babe, look at me. Are you alright?"

I took a tentative sip of the water. "I'm fine. Really."

The office door finally opened. A tall man in his early forties with thinning blondish hair and a pockmarked complexion emerged. "Hello, I'm Dr. Hampton. I'm so sorry for the long wait. There were things in the hospital I had to attend to. They were beyond my control. Sometimes that happens. No excuses, though, and it will never occur again. You are my only appointment for today. A rare day. Again, I'm sorry. Okay, so Michael is…"

Monique pointed to me just as the doctor reached out for a shake. "Well, nice to meet you, Michael."

Both David and Mon stood when Doctor Hampton approached them with a welcoming hand. "I'm his sister-in-law Monique, and that's Michael's brother, David." Mon winked at me before touching my shoulder tenderly.

The doctor echoed her smile. "It's terrific to me you all are here. I see you have a support system. Always important. So, are you ready to begin Michael?"

I didn't hesitate. Finally, the answer was yes.

Seventeen

Doctor Hampton's overly bright office looked like it was still in need of some final furnishing—the walls were almost barren with nothing more than his mounted diplomas near a framed print of Edward Hopper's *Gas*. The room had oversized, naked windows looking out to the Charles River. As he checked some paperwork behind an impressive mahogany desk, I scanned the two densely packed bookcases covering the freshly painted wall behind me.

"You can sit in either chair, Michael, whichever one you feel most comfortable in. I'll be with you in a second," he said. I wondered if he would be judging my decision. I had the choice between a plush brown chair that seemed to belong in a living room or a wooden rocker next to a small table. I focused on Mon's voice in my head, "Relax, stop over-thinking, and just talk. There is no road map in therapy."

After I plopped in the rocker, Dr. Hampton stepped from behind the desk and pulled up a chair to sit across from me. He readied his pad on his lap.

"Okay, Michael, I'm glad you are here. Before we start, I want you to know I spoke with Dr. Graynor from Boston Mercy after getting her very extensive notes from the night of your accident. I also spoke to Dr. Rigatta, who is very concerned about you. I know you disappeared from her, but she obviously has all your records. I've looked over them all after talking with her, and she has agreed to be part of the team. So, you will be working with her again. You have to commit to this, and we are going to monitor your weight to keep an eye on things.

"Our first goals are to get your weight up and you eating again. Now, I know that is very scary. You are probably already feeling immediate resistance and anxiety, but that's expected. Nothing happens here overnight, especially with anorexia.

"There is no magic pill. There is no abracadabra that is going to change your life. It's going to take work, a lot of hard work. That's what I'm here for, and, of course, that's what Dr. Rigatta is here for. We just need you to be all in. You made the appointment—that was the first step. Step two was coming in. Now it's a collaboration. But you are going to be doing a lot of the heavy lifting with our help. It's going to seem like a struggle at first, but it will get easier, trust me. And yes, I know that's going to take some time. Trust is earned. Right now, you probably want to put a stake in my heart, and go back to life as usual."

I offered a slightly dazed smile and thought steak, but I resisted the urge to wander into fantastic food associations. I could not repeat my misadventure with Dr. Marie. With an absent-minded nod, I considered whether I was ready to put food in my mouth again. Sweat trickled down from my side, so I absorbed the stream under my t-shirt with firm pressure from my arm.

"So how is the arm healing Michael?" I quickly realized Dr. Hampton was going to be reading my body language. "I see a few bandages must have been removed." He re-crossed his legs while clipping his pen to the edge of his pad.

"I wasn't trying to commit suicide," I blurted out defensively. "I just want to make sure you know that."

"You know, I don't think you were either, Michael. I believe it was an accident. An accident in which you got very lucky because you came very close to slicing a major vein. Thankfully you missed. That was the good news from the situation. Now, you didn't answer my question. How does your arm feel? I genuinely want to know." He sat back with a compassionate smile and pointed to my arm with the pen. "That had to hurt."

"And it still hurts," I said, relaxing into the wooden chair. "I guess it aches more now than anything. It throbs when I squeeze my hand. I don't think I'm going to pick up scissors ever again."

"At least not to cut a bagel. That's not the preferred method we used when I was growing up in Manhattan. You know, the problem of living in Boston is you really can't get a great bagel here. Well, maybe in Brookline. They get it right. From what I understand, you grew up on Long Island, so you must sympathize."

I silently nodded when Dr. Hampton walked over to crack open one window before slowly peering over his shoulder. "And Michael, the thing about bagels is they should be eaten fresh. Not when they are rock solid and inedible, right?"

"Okay, so Dr. Graynor did take careful notes." I laughed for the first time.

"Yes, she did. She's very comprehensive. When I talked to her, she was very concerned about you also. Now, I know your first response to my question about how your arm felt was to affirm to me that you weren't committing suicide, which I never brought up. I'm sure you know that, yes, that's what Dr. Graynor and the nurses initially thought when you were at emergency. I know you assured her also that you weren't trying to harm yourself, and you said it was all an accident. But let me try to put Dr. Graynor's concern in context for you. You insisted to her, and you were adamant right now, that you weren't trying to commit suicide. We get that."

"I wasn't. At all."

"Michael, please. Listen. I said I believe you, and I do. I sincerely do. That said, I need you to understand the urgency of your situation. You need to realize that over the past few years, your actions, your refusal to eat, and your willing emaciation are in themselves forms of slow suicide.

"There's no sugarcoating this. You need to recognize what's been going on, and why there is so much concern. We are going to prevent further damage by trying to change your behavior. It's going to be incremental, but the behavior has to change. The isolation, the refusal to eat, and the inability to eat with other people. All that must be modified.

"We are going to deal with all the issues surrounding your need to control your food intake, but our first priority here is getting you to slowly commit to eating again. And you need to understand that this is not something that can be delayed. We don't have the luxury to do anything but try to get your weight up.

"I know you don't want to be hospitalized. No one is going to force feed you, but we also can't have you losing weight or remaining where you are. This is a serious problem, and your health is tenuous. I'm not trying to scare you straight. That doesn't work in these situations. We will be working to make you feel comfortable eating and comfortable with yourself again."

He strolled over to his desk to pour himself a glass of water. "Would you like some?"

"No, no," I hastily replied before realizing I was already denying his first request to intake something. "Okay, a little maybe."

"Well, there's no point in pouring just a little water, so here's a full glass—you drink as much as you want."

As I eased into the rocker, my backbone was immediately irritated by the wooden spirals. "I guess we are going to start with the glass full." It initially seemed like a witty comeback, but I realized the line sounded like it needed an accompanying rimshot.

"Optimistic. Yes, indeed. That's a good place to start." Dr. Hampton placed the water on the table next to me before sitting down once again.

"Let's just straighten a few things out now. I met your brother and your sister-in-law just before. They're your only remaining family, am I correct? Your mom and dad have passed. Your brother is David," he mumbled as he glanced at his notes. "And your sister-in-law's name is…"

"She's Monique Jacob." He jotted on his pad, and then looked up quizzically.

"Okay, Jacob. Not your brother's surname."

"No, she's Monique Jacob, the model. Retired now." I felt slightly wounded because it didn't compute. "You don't recognize her name?"

"I'm sorry but no, I don't really pay attention to many models' names. The last model I recognized was Kim Basinger, but she might be slightly before your time. Before she became Kim Basinger, the actress. I think she won an Academy Award, didn't she?"

"Yeah, she did, *L.A Confidential*. Of course, I know her." I immediately knew I had found the right doctor. "She's so beautiful. In fact, I just saw *9 ½ Weeks* on television again. I've seen that movie a bunch of times. It's not very good, but I really like it. The first time I saw it, I couldn't get it out of my head for some reason." I was leaning out of the chair with my hands between my knees, now ready to talk movies.

"For some reason," Dr. Hampton said with a smile before sipping his water.

"No, it wasn't because of the strip and the sex scenes, which are pretty great, I have to say. But it wasn't that. I don't know, there's just something about it."

"Well, at least you know who Kim Basinger is. I thought she might be a bit old for you."

"Cheekbones like that do not have expiration dates." I amused myself by talking as if I was boning Basingers when, in fact, I'd forgotten what a vagina smelled like.

"I'm glad we established that. Cheekbones do not have expirations dates. I'll have to remember that one," he laughed. "We can come back to your brother, Monique, and your fascination with 9 ½ Weeks, which is interesting to me, but for now tell me about your girlfriend." He paused to check his notes, "Jessica."

"Jessie," I corrected.

"Okay, great." Dr. Hampton replied, writing with a flourish. "From what I understand, you two were living together, and she left you right before the incident with your arm, which yes, I know, was an accident. I'm not correlating the two." He placed his hand in front of his chest as if to say, "Yield the impulse to reiterate there was no slitting wrists over Jessie."

"How do you feel right now that you are alone?" Dr. Hampton had one eye on me and one on his notes.

"She left with my best friend. How should I feel?"

"I'm asking you. Yes, I'm sure that unfortunate situation definitely complicated things. So how are you coping? Are you eating at all? Are you going out of your apartment? Do you miss her? In essence, I'm asking are you moving on with your life?"

"I don't know. I'm angry." I shrugged, unsure whether to express just how angry and betrayed I felt.

"Angry she left you, angry she decided to move on, or angry she left with your best friend?"

"Yes, yes, and yes."

"Alright good. Drink some water, Michael. It's there for you. Take a breath. Now tell me, you didn't have any idea Jessie was unhappy with the relationship and the way it was affected by your disorder?" He took a quick look out the window towards the graying afternoon. "According to what you told Dr. Graynor, you haven't had an actual meal, breakfast, lunch or dinner in what? She writes here over two years. How long were you with Jessie?"

I calculated the time in my head, fully knowing the no-meal zone had been much longer than two years. "Well, I got my master's degree before she moved in, and we dated for about half a year before we both moved to Boston so..."

"That's fine. I don't need a strict timeline. I'm getting an idea. We'll soon flesh it out. Would you say you did not share a meal with Jessie for at least two years while you lived together?"

"You are saying it's my fault she left me?" I felt as if I was being attacked.

"I'm not saying anything, Michael. I'm asking you a question."

"No, I didn't share a meal with her. Ever in that time. Ever."

"Alright, so what did you do when she ate? I'm not clear on this. Did you leave the room? What happened when you two went out to eat?"

"She ate by herself. I watched and talked to her. Sometimes, she just ate when I worked nights at the music store I worked in. I just left that job—I'm temporarily done working for now. But no, I never ate breakfast or lunch. She knew that, so she just ate whenever she wanted, and I just went on with my life." I slumped in the rocker again while considering my words.

"I'm digging my fucking grave, right?" I looked at the doctor nervously. "Can I say 'fuck?'"

"You sure can. You can and should say anything you want. And no, you are not digging your grave. I'm just trying to understand the dynamics of your relationship."

"Well, it was more complicated than just my eating problem."

"I'm sure it was. Any relationship has its own complications, but this kind of denial or absence had to complicate things even more. Let me ask you, did you ever feel compelled to eat with Jessie just in order to eat with her? To share things with her. Eating, as I'm sure you know, is a big part of a relationship. It often helps connects us." He was writing on his pad while flipping the pages more quickly than I expected. I didn't think I was all that interesting and tried to figure out what he could be noting down. I ended up sitting silently for a few minutes.

"Michael, you with me?"

"Yeah, yeah, I guess I realized I needed to eat with Jessie when she first moved in. But after she moved in, the fear of eating intensified to the point where I thought if I started eating with her, I'd eat so much I'd gouge myself. And I knew I couldn't live with myself or I'd have to run extra miles the next day while also starving more."

He leaned forward, inhaled deeply, and began writing even more quickly. "So, you understood you were starving yourself?"

"I did, but I couldn't stop. When she moved in it all—the voice in my head saying no—just took over. It became uncontrollable. It wasn't an actual voice. I'm not hearing things or talking to myself. It's just like a force. And, at the time, I noticed my pants were beginning to fall off of me. I didn't put a name to what was happening—Dr. Rigatta did that." I hesitated. "Can I tell you a quick story? Save your place where you were, but let me just tell you this."

His eyes went on alert as he turned to a fresh page.

"It's not all that revelatory, but I remember like about five months or so after Jessie moved in. We were still having sex at the time. I guess I'm also telling you that we really weren't at the end. I'll throw that out there too.

"But, one morning after we had sex. Jessie got out of the shower. I was still in bed. She sat down next to me and spread her thighs. She showed me these red marks right up high on her thighs to the side of her vagina. I remember her looking at me and saying, 'Look what you are doing to me.' Just like that. She wasn't malicious, just angry. My pelvis bones were becoming so narrow and, I guess, sharp, they were bruising her. Almost cutting her.

"I remember touching the red marks, like slashes, and then leaning back in bed and looking at my body. My pelvis bones were sticking out really high. I knew I was losing weight like really quickly. She never had those marks before she moved in. I'll never forget the look on her face when she felt the curve of my bones."

I couldn't actually express to him the shame and hurt I felt when I saw those bruises on Jessie's thighs. I barely got out of bed for two days afterwards.

"Well, I'm certainly glad you told me that," Dr. Hampton said with concern. "I'm sure that was a difficult time. Can I ask if that made you at all want to eat more that night or the next day?"

"No, I didn't want to keep on going that way." I slowly rocked in the chair and shook my head. "I hated myself for hurting her, but the fear was too great to even think about eating. I felt bad about those marks, but it felt worse to consider eating. A lot worse. I figured we could change positions. Changing the sex was easier." I was forced to glance toward the empty space over the doctor's head. I couldn't believe my own words. "That's pretty sad, isn't it? Pathetic."

"Beating yourself up right now is not going to help. Let's not judge things or get too hard on yourself right away. I think you know that you were dealing with something that felt bigger than you. It was destroying everything in your path. But let's slow down just a bit. Now, you are telling me that when you were living by yourself while going to grad school, you were eating?"

"Not a lot. Things I could manage and definitely didn't make it feel like I was eating a formal meal. But yeah, I was able to eat. I just sat in my apartment reading and eating whatever I could. I liked it by myself."

Dr. Hampton reached over to his desk to retrieve a tissue and delicately wipe his nose. "So, the word meal sounds like a four-letter word to you?"

It seemed ridiculous, but he was right on. "Yes, I guess so. I never thought of that. Obscene is a pretty accurate word for how I saw a full meal. It was forbidden."

"Good Michael, this is hard I know, but I appreciate your honesty. Now take me back a bit then. When you moved to Boston, you two did not live together, right? You lived in separate apartments."

"Yes, that was the plan from the beginning. I moved into an apartment on Commonwealth Ave. Monique actually found it for me while I was packing on Long Island, and David was meeting Jessie for the first time after he flew in from San Francisco. That first meeting was bad. I have to tell you that story sometime."

"Yes, of course, I want and probably need to hear it. So, your brother and Monique were living in San Francisco, and Monique actually had time from her schedule—you are telling me she was still modeling at the time—to rent you an apartment? You didn't rent it on your own?"

"Monique was slowly transitioning into all her businesses at the time. She had, and still has, a bunch of things she's involved in. But I didn't want or intend for her to get me an apartment. I was going to head up to Boston, stay in a motel, and get an apartment before classes started. When David drove me up in the van, though, he drove directly to the apartment as a surprise.

"Mon was shuttling to Boston from Manhattan, where she always worked a lot—she also has a place in midtown Manhattan. At the time, she was in Boston to oversee the opening of House of Fitness. She was one of the initial investors in the chain. She did the commercials also. You might have seen them on television." Dr. Hampton nodded repeatedly, but it was clear he had never seen Monique running in a sports bra on a treadmill.

"Yeah, she rented me the place right by Boston College. I wasn't going to BC, but it was a great location. I was there until I finished school. It was an accelerated year-and-a-half program."

With his hand over his mouth, Dr. Hampton scratched at his slight stubble. "Okay, so you lived in that apartment while Jessie lived…"

"She lived in a small place in Somerville. That was complicated, too. She first said she was fine with getting her own apartment, but when she helped move me up, she saw my place. It got weird. She asked if maybe we could live there together. After that, there was this big argument between her and David. I told David I was thinking of having Jessie move in with me. And he was really not happy at all. He said it was a bad, bad idea. He told me to say no to Jessie. I ended up helping her find an apartment."

I had a headache just thinking about it. "Can I get some more water please?" I surprised myself with the request. I'd already had more water in a few minutes than I had in three years. Dr. Hampton sprang to his feet to carefully pour from the pitcher.

"We sure have a lot to get to in the coming weeks. I need to hear all these stories. Now tell me, your brother didn't want you to move in with Jessie initially, correct?"

"No, he said I was moving to get my degree. I'd get nothing done if we were living together."

"And you agreed with him?"

"Well yeah, he wanted me to concentrate, and I wanted to do well. I wasn't sure if I was interested in doing the things you do when you live together. I didn't want to be my parents."

Dr. Hampton nodded rhythmically as if listening with headphones. "And did you tell all of this to Jessie or did you just repeat what your brother said?"

"I said David thought it was a bad idea."

"Okay, I understand that, but it sounds like there's a bit more to the story. A lot. I do want to go back to a few things before I let you go." Dr. Hampton sat on the window ledge while I quietly rocked—I was calm enough to go to sleep. "I want you to meet with the nurse and get a blood and urine sample after this. They're for Dr. Rigatta." He placed his pad down on the table by the window and leaned forward with one foot resting on the table top.

"Tell me one thing, Michael. Why didn't you get continue to get your Ph.D. or go to law school or pursue an advanced degree? You really can't do much with a master's in literature."

I paused because I didn't know the answer. It was the question I'd spent nights brooding over. "I honestly have no clue. I don't. I was going to get my Ph.D., and just didn't. When Jessie asked to move in together, there was no way we could afford things if I was going to school on a stipend. It was either live with her or do my own thing at school."

I watched Dr. Hampton stare at his notes with a tight smile. "Really quickly Michael, I'm assuming it was Jessie's idea for you to live together after you finished your schooling. Is that correct? She asked again after you lived separately."

"Well, we both decided, but she suggested, yes. Things changed.

Jessie gave up running—I never understood that—and she kind of flitted from one job she hated to another. Jess asked to move to Allston near her friends, so I let my apartment go. Doing that, I hated. There's a lot of hate here, right? But my place was big with huge windows and a lot of light. I came and went when I wanted. It was great."

"Michael, did you actually want to live together?" He grinned, tapping his chin with his index finger.

"Well, I guess so I mean, I loved her, so I thought her idea was good."

Dr. Hampton's eyes lit up as he walked back to his chair.

"What I say? Did I say something wrong?" I retraced my words.

"Not at all, Michael. That was just the first time you said you loved Jessie."

That wounded me deeply. It felt as if I had betrayed her.

"I did love her."

"I have no reason to doubt you did. That's for us to pursue. We'll leave Jessie for next time. Michael, indulge me here for a second. Tell me just a bit why you like 9 ½ Weeks so much, besides Kim Basinger's cheekbones. What do you think that movie is about?"

"Are you serious?" I wasn't sure how we got back to the movies.

He laughed and said discordantly, "Dead serious."

"I don't know, I think it's about a guy obsessed with control as he manipulates a woman. She finds something about herself through their fucked-up relationship. She feels letting go sexually is kind of liberating until she realizes that he is controlling her freedom. She ultimately finds herself by actually letting go of his control. Control and breaking free. And yeah, lots of hot, sunlit sex with Kim Basinger's incredible body. That's it. Three stars."

"That's good. You have watched the movie carefully," he said, scratching at the pad.

"Am I right about it?"

Dr. Hampton broke out into another audible laugh. "Michael, you have master's degree in literature, and something tells me you have seen a lot of movies. You know there is no right or wrong answer there. It's how you interpret it based on the content. I just want you to think about what you just told me about the movie for next time, okay?"

I looked around the room for a clock. "That's it?"

"Yeah, that's a lot, Michael. Do you feel comfortable with this?"

"Comfortable no, drained yes."

"That means you definitely want to come back then despite feeling drained?" He moved behind his desk before carefully placing his notes in a folder and dropping it in the top drawer.

"Yeah, I'm coming back. I've got no choice."

"Oh, you most definitely do have a choice," he replied.

"I didn't mean it that way. I meant I'm at a point where I feel I have no choice but to go forward."

"That's good. What we want to hear. The nurse's office is right down the hall to your left. You can go out through this door for the urinalysis."

I stood motionless near his desk. Urinalysis? I laughed, thinking yes, I'm in analysis. Again. How the fuck did that happen?

"Before you leave, I just have one question more for you," Dr. Hampton said with a smile. "Yes, I know, always one more question."

"Uh-oh, this worries me." I looked at him uneasily.

"Relax. I know you know this, but let me ask you, what is the word for when eating too much and feeling like you are about to burst? You used it before."

No hesitation. "Gorge. Gorge yourself. It's what I am constantly thinking about."

"Okay, yes. Now, I'm not a Freudian by any means, Michael, and this kind of stuff is the last thing we are going to dwell on. In fact, we won't. Our goal is to get you eating but bear with me here. I couldn't help but notice you said 'gouge myself.' You said you were afraid to gouge yourself. You know the difference, right?"

I'd been caught with my hand in the cookie jar, and froze in the doorway. Of course, I remembered using the word. "Goddamn. I can't believe that. That's sad. I don't think I'd make a very good witness for my own defense. I'd be shot at dawn."

Dr. Hampton grinned while spinning in his chair towards me. "You are not on trial. Please don't think of this as a trial, Michael. I just pointed it out because I couldn't let it go. You can think about it.

You did great today. If you keep working like today, you are going to be okay. I believe that. Now also go out with your sister-in-law and brother and make sure you eat something. Whatever you can, please. There's a whole world out there for you to taste."

Eighteen

On the Monday after the Superbowl in late January—always a reminder of winter's slow death march—I arrived at my apartment after a laborious mile walk from my car. The long trek gave me time to rewind another exhausting session with Dr. Hampton. By the time I reached the lobby, I was ready for a nap. I sat on the stairway to gather myself and saw a package beneath my mailbox. It seemed unusual because the only pieces of mail I was getting were credit card statements and straggling envelopes for Jessie that had eluded the post office's rerouting process.

The package had no return address, but it was postmarked in North Carolina. After I trudged up the stairs, I placed the box on the table before rummaging through the kitchen cabinets for a can of soup. I'd promised Dr. Hampton that I would eat something—anything—and now I was genuinely determined to keep my word.

Weeks before, David taped a sign with "You can get with this or you can get with that—the choice is yours" in black magic marker on the refrigerator. It seemed like a kitschy thing to do but after that whenever I walked throughout the kitchen, I heard Black Sheep in my head. My choices took on heightened importance. Eat or not eat. I was going to feel guilty either way, so I had to choose which option I could live with most easily.

When I told this to Dr. Hampton, he was stern. "It's not what kind of guilt you can live with most easily. It's whether you can live to make future choices. Guilt won't kill you. Starving will." His blunt approach was the one thing I liked most about him. And I was genuinely getting to like the guy.

His words floated in my head throughout each day. Fuck "What would Jesus do?" That didn't apply. Even he had a last supper. I thought,

"What would Dr. Hampton do?"

I heard his voice every time I scanned the shelves filled with dozens of cans soup and vegetables. "You can pacify me here in the office, and then you can go home and eat nothing, Michael. I get that, but what we're doing here is just empty talk if you are not taking concrete steps to break the patterns and put food in your body.

"You've got to eat some kind of food during the day. You can lie to me, and you can lie to yourself. That's what you, and most people with eating disorders, fall back on. But we need to get beyond the familiar. We need to get into the uncomfortable to deal with that. You say you are going to eat something, and I can trust you here. The question comes down to this: Are you willing to trust yourself?"

I dumped a can of chicken and stars into a pot. I knew I could drink the broth while eating just a few of the tiny, twinkling pieces of pasta. While the soup simmered, I went back towards the heavily taped package with a knife in hand. My arm throbbed on cue—it immediately triggered a momentary flashback to the dark night with the bagel.

I quickly changed course in self-preservation. After I retrieved a big bowl of boiling hot soup, I warily eyed my North Carolina surprise with trepidation. Steam from the bowl clouded my eyes, but I impulsively went samurai on the box. Thankfully, the blade went directly into the tape. Inside was an envelope and a small package carefully nestled in bubble wrap. It was a familiar kind of neat. I'd seen this type of meticulous wrapping many times before.

My mother's statues of Jesus and Saint Anthony from her car dashboard were taped under the bubble wrap. I remembered that Jessie had found them in the box of my parents' belongings after we returned from the Mets' game just before we moved. She mysteriously asked if she could hold onto the statues for me, and I'd long forgotten them.

I placed the weathered statues upright on the table before ripping open the envelope to read the note:

> *Michael, I think you should have these. I know you*
> *don't believe, and you know I didn't either, but these*
> *always seemed important to you. I saw how you packed*

them away years ago. I know you kept them as memo-
ries of your mother. I just think you should have them
now. When I cleaned out my bureau drawers from the
apartment, I accidentally took them with me. I've held
onto them for you over the years because even though
I know you denied what they meant to you, I thought
someday you might need them. I really hope you are
taking care of yourself. I think of you often. Les and I
are fine and happy. I want you to be happy too. You
know I hope you find a little peace with yourself. Maybe
these can show you the way.

    Nothing else worked. And I know I couldn't make
you happy either.

    Something will someday. I know it.

    Take care,

      J

The phone rang as I read the note again. "I think of you often." "I want you to be happy." I picked up the receiver, hoping it was Monique. She would understand what the fuck Jessie was trying to say.

"Mon?"

"Michael, no, it's me. I'm coming over. I'm just making sure you are home," David sounded out of breath.

"What?" I had to steady the receiver against my shoulder because my hand was shaking uncontrollably. I sat in the middle of the room on top of a large plastic garbage bag filled with a collection of Jessie's CDs.

"What do you mean what? I'm coming over, for Chrissakes. What's not to understand?"

"David, I, I'm not sure this is a good time. I'm…"

"You can jerk off later. I'm leaving the Brookline Booksmith, so I'm on my way. Don't tell me this is not a good time. We need to talk. I'm bringing a friend. You need anything?"

I threw the envelope and letter on the table, knocking over Jesus.

"Michael, you want some Diet Coke or something?" David seemed distracted by a voice in the background.

"Is Monique with you?"

"I said I'm bringing a friend. Mon is in New York. Are you okay, Mike? You sound…"

"David, I'm really not feeling well."

"You are not listening to me. I'm coming over. We need to talk. If you are not feeling well, drink some chicken soup. You have ten thousand fucking cans Mon bought for you. Do yourself a favor, and open one. You will feel better. Trust me."

I laughed uncomfortably while staring at the congealed fat on the top of the cooled soup bowl sitting on the table. "How long 'til you get here? Give me some time." I couldn't think of a valid excuse to stall him.

"The longer we keep playing twenty questions, the longer it's going to take us."

"Who's us?"

"Oh shit, Mike, c'mon, you'll take guests for $200, right? It's a surprise."

I thought he might have met Jessie. "Who? Who you got? I think I've had enough surprises today. I don't need another."

"I have no idea what you are talking about, but just be there. We'll be over in fifteen minutes. I'm bringing someone you need to meet. That's all you need to know. Now hang up. You can tell me about your surprise when I get there. Seeya"

I stood Jesus upright again. The poor guy now had a faded red robe and slightly chipped beard. My heart accelerated as I picked up the letter to re-read Jessie's words.

I laughed out loud at Jessie's ludicrous notion that I kept the statues as memories of my mother. Of course, she didn't know the truth. How could I possibly have told Jessie that Jesus was all about Christina, though?

I'd saved the statues as monuments to lovely Christina, my first failed attempt at a girlfriend. I'd never forgotten her or what I'd experienced with her. Well, I didn't really experience anything *with* her, but she always remained a vivid reminder of what I so desperately desired. And precisely what I feared most.

I only went out with Christina for a month or so, right after I got my driver's license. She was a thin, shy Latina, who loved to smoke pot. In fact, Christina was stoned most of our time together. Her large, searching eyes always seemed at half-mast. I thought the pot smell on her clothes was some kind of exotic perfume until one of my friends told me she lit up for lunch each day.

I first noticed Christina when she magically showed up at every baseball game I pitched. She cheered with her friends out in the grass by the left field foul lines, far from the bleachers. I figured she had a friend on the team. After the season ended, though, Christina would linger by the gym each day while I threw to Mr. Stacatella. It was a little over a month away from graduation, so coach encouraged me to ask her out. When she miraculously agreed, I knew for sure she must have been doing some really high-grade Dr. Dre weed.

We only dated four times, and I always felt so intimidated by standing next to her. She was the kind of girl horny all high school boys fantasize about. I used to think she was some kind of dream—someone I magically conjured up. It was hard to believe she was real. Christina had such remarkably beautiful breasts, almost cartoonish for such a little, lithe girl. Her confident stride—shoulders back and chin out—betrayed her timid demeanor. She looked like she was always on the verge of laughing at a joke only she was privy to.

Of course, we had nothing in common, but I was thrilled to be seen with her—a lovely, mocha skinned Jessica Rabbit, high as a fucking satellite.

After we sat through a laughably miserable Bruce Willis thriller on our final date, she asked me to park the car I'd borrowed from my mom behind an abandoned Dunkin Donuts near her home. As we sat in silence, she said, "I'm so glad you are religious. I come from a very Catholic family. Jesus shows us the way. We just follow. It's beautiful, I was named after Jesus. You know, Saint Anthony is the patron saint of lost things. He's my favorite. I pray to him all the time."

She genuflected beatifically, kissed her hand and touched the statues of Jesus and Saint Anthony on my mom's carefully decorated dashboard.

I just bowed my head toward Jesus while staring at Christina's skin-tight, powder-blue Led Zeppelin *Zoso* t-shirt covering the keys to the universe. There were blonde highlights in her hair and thoughts of my first blowjob in my head. I was ready to split the seams in my pants while sweating like Albert Brooks in *Broadcast News*. There simply was no logic for us being together, but there we sat with the Lord under the parking lot lamp's glow.

"I'm not religious, actually. This is my mom's car. She's also super religious like you," I said, lovingly touching the rosary beads hanging from the rear-view mirror. "We have statues like those all over our house. My mom goes to church each week and prays all the time. You two would get along." Indeed, my mother had placed a statue of Jesus and crucifixes in almost every room around the house.

When I was eight, she mounted one of those scary, magic-eye pictures of Jesus in my bedroom above the light switch. His twinkling, blinking eyes followed me everywhere, even to the darkest corners of the room. He was watching when I stared into my neighbor's window as she got undressed each night. I knew he was looking while I frantically masturbated to *Playboy* centerfolds. And he was judging.

The picture remained on the wall until I was fifteen when I finally got the backbone to toss the creepy, roving-eye dude in the bureau drawer. I've never felt more paranoid than the moment I yanked that fucking guy down.

When I cheerfully told Christina about my mother's devotion, her red-rimmed eyes widened. "And you don't believe?" she said, her features going limp.

I panicked momentarily. The blowjob had probably already flown out the window with the Holy Spirit, so I quickly lowered my expectations. A lie was necessary to get in enough good graces for a possible Hail Mary handjob.

"I'm trying to get back to believing. I'm just not sure. When I drive this car, though, it reminds me of God's power." The truth was I always drove my father's Chevy wagon and rarely resorted to using my mom's car. I'd just forgotten to put the statues, rosary beads, and other auxiliary nonsense in the glove compartment after I left our house.

Christina immediately perked up at the possibility of my redemption. We talked for another half hour while she slowly closed the gap between us. Soon enough, I found her in my arms.

I had never even kissed a girl, so the whole marvelous fuck fantasia running through my head was ridiculously optimistic. Christina was more than responsive, though. When she leaned into my chest and pressed her wet lips to mine, it was obvious she knew exactly what she was doing. I made a silly pop with my tight-lipped pucker. She laughed while tenderly touching my chin. We kissed again, her tongue sneaking through my lip lock.

"Breathe, breathe," she whispered. When her whole tongue slipped into my mouth, I was transported into all the porn movies I'd watched in my best friend's garage.

All those years of imagining kissing sweaty, big-boobed women with mouths cracked open suddenly disappeared. I was lost in my own real-life passion play. The sensation of Christina's thin, slippery tongue—something like an eel swimming around my mouth—felt a bit disgusting at first, but after a few minutes, I was madly in love.

Unfortunately, I had no idea what to do with my hands. Gently touch the breasts or grab them like a macho man? Reach around and squeeze her ass? Undo the button on her jeans?

I simply held her tiny waist with limp noodle arms and continued to kiss as if someone had cut my spinal cord. Every so often, Christina placed my hand on her right breast. I just rubbed in a gentle, circular motion—she must have thought I was polishing a doorknob.

While I explored her mouth, she lovingly ran her fingers through the curls in my hair and twirled, making small braids in the back of my head. We kissed for two, and then three hours until my tongue went numb.

At one in the morning, she gently pushed me away before placing her index finger to my lips. "That was sweet, really sweet." She straightened her hair, reapplied her lipstick and asked to go home.

Confused and in a daze, I drove very slowly to her house. Christina kissed me on the cheek and said, "You're really nice, let's do this again." She took one step out of the door before stopping to reach back and lovingly touch Jesus and Saint Anthony.

I panicked immediately after watching her small hips disappear down the path. She wanted to do precisely what again? I didn't do anything. I knew Christina had to think I was the lamest virgin on Long Island. Mother Theresa had more game. I drove recklessly towards Jones Beach to figure out what the hell had just happened—I must have done something wrong.

A half hour later, during the approach to the toll booth on the Meadowbrook Parkway, I experienced a sudden sharp jab in my crotch. It felt like I was getting stabbed by knitting needles. The pain forced me to drive with my ass raised out of the seat and shoulders hunched over the steering wheel. I leaned towards the windshield like a crash-test dummy in flight.

The car wavered across lanes as my speed neared one hundred. Finally, I swerved into the main lot at Jones, beneath the water tower, and surveyed my surroundings. When no one was looking, I took off my pants and underwear to air out my balls. I thought maybe freedom would alleviate the pressure. Something had to stop the charges of electricity.

Freeballing definitely didn't help, though, so I redressed and scurried through the dark tunnel. Desperately hoping that exercise might cure whatever the fuck was going on, I jogged towards the boardwalk, past moony lovers holding hands. I made my way amid the straggling night owls gazing towards the cresting sea. There I saw an ice cream vendor next to an old man selling heart-shaped balloons in the mist.

As the pain intensified, I was convinced that if I applied a couple of ice cream bars to my balls, I could numb them into submission. It would be my version of a make-shift ice pack. As I crumbled to one knee while waiting in line, I was surprised by a tap on the shoulder from a grey-haired woman with glasses.

"Are you alright?"

"I'm in pain," I winced. "My lower stomach."

"Oh dear, you want a doctor? I hope it's not a kidney stone." I had never heard of a kidney stone, but her diagnosis gave me hope I was just experiencing a serious kidney problem instead of a cause for castration. I offered her five dollars for two ice cream bars.

"You're hungry?" she said, squinting. "I thought you were in pain? Why don't I call the police to help you?"

"No, no, no, please, I don't need no police. Buy me the ice cream." I was kneeling like a quarterback running out the final seconds of a game and refraining from cupping my balls.

"What flavor do you want?" she said tersely.

"Your favorites are my favorites." My words echoed directly into the wooden slats of the boardwalk.

She returned with two chocolate covered vanilla ice cream bars and a dollar in change.

Running back to the car, hunched over like Quasimodo, I was resigned to my fate: I was headed to the emergency room with cancer of the testicles—a just punishment for wanting to fuck Christina.

I sat behind the steering wheel, stared at the dirty car rooftop with my pants around my knees and placed the frozen ice cream bar on what remained of my balls. The other bar went on my cock, which looked like a diseased, purple mushroom head on a droopy stem. People walked by— obliviously staring at the stars—as I frantically massaged myself with ice cream.

The pain moved up into my asshole and stomach, leaving me gasping for air. I drove the car—the ice cream resting between my legs—to die in solitude in the back corner of the lot. Unfortunately, the chocolate coating was slowly melting. I had no choice but to put my pants back on and go to the trunk to retrieve a few of my beach towels to protect my mom's immaculate seat.

After reapplying the softening ice cream bars, I realized I was going to have to explain why I had melted ice cream on my cock to the emergency doctors. I conceived grand tales of being raped by the Good Humor man and having wild fuck sessions with Dolly Madison.

The ice cream felt so, so good—all rationale evaporated. Within moments, I was giving glory to Jesus and Saint Anthony with a choc-olate-flecked, vanilla cream hard-on.

Christina would have been so proud of my piety.

I proceeded to rub the cool, smooth ice cream all over my lower body. It was the most sensual thing I'd had ever felt in my sensation-free life. The head of my penis—freakishly blue with hints of white and brown— was quivering, prepared for liftoff. I felt remarkably powerful holding my messy, hard cock as pain coursed through my balls. While stroking with my frozen right hand, I dripped small pools of sweet cream into my mouth with my left.

It was immersion in a sea of pure pleasure. Such a wonder! I rested against the window, drenched in ice cream, and thought about Christina's breasts and warm mouth. It took one manic yank to release a laser shot of come and ice cream all over the windshield. Another quick jerk ended up shooting a confetti spray directly at Jesus and Saint Anthony.

The sweat dripped off my arms onto the ice cream-soaked towels. When I came back to earth, I couldn't see out of the jizz plastered windshield. The rosary dripped freshly minted beads of come. And, of course, the pain in my balls quickly drained out, leaving me limp. Come seeped down the milky white windshield onto the dashboard. It completely engulfed Jesus and Saint Anthony.

They looked like the pods in *Aliens*—traces of figures encased in white ooze. I laughed uncontrollably while thinking about Christina words: "Let's do this again." Yes, yes, and again and again.

Once the initial rush dissipated, though, I was overwhelmed and terrified by my indulgence. Just what had I done? Coming had never felt that good.

After starting the car, I turned the defroster to full blast. Come slid down into the crevice of the dash next to the windshield. The car had to be back to my mother in the morning, so I wiped down Jesus and St. Anthony. The statues needed a good soaking—maybe even a baptizing in the beach surf—but there was no chance to get out of the car while still covered in ice cream.

I simply wrapped the soaked, sticky towels around my balls like a diaper and drove back home. In minutes, I was hard again. The drive on the Wantagh Parkway was exhilarating. I was glancing through a come encrusted windshield while giddily licking ice cream off my fingers. I'd never felt more alive. Or strangely conflicted.

It took a few hours, but I finally got the car cleaned up in the early morning as my parents slept. Jesus and Saint Anthony were sadly beyond redemption, though. I just couldn't wipe away the small spots of come in Jesus's beard. Saint Anthony's base had a dried layer of white film no amount of Lysol could clean.

I packed the statues away in my bureau in memory of my gorgeous, sweet temptation, Christina. Sadly, I knew I could never see her again. The fear that Christina would make me feel like a manic, fucking Caligula and so out of control again was much too terrifying. I ignored her throughout the rest of the summer. It was quite clear I needed to bury my desire.

Before my mother had to go to work, I drove to our neighborhood Catholic artifacts store to buy expensive replacements for Jesus and Saint Anthony. I also added new rosary beads and statues of Saint Patrick and Michael, the archangel. I neatly placed them neatly in a revamped hall of fame on the fresh-smelling dashboard.

My mom was so thrilled by the display of newly-minted statues that she treated me to a big dinner at my favorite Italian restaurant. Of course, she thanked me over and over again for my thoughtfulness and generosity.

I simply told her it was all my pleasure.

Nineteen

"Mike, this is Richie Incaviglia. You guys are going to have a lot in common. He played in the Yankees' minor league system, so you can talk about baseball as much as you want." David was carrying two cartons of Ensure and nodding over his shoulder to a tall man with a buzzcut and a trimmed beard. He looked like a tight end in his black Oakland Raiders jacket.

I suspiciously stared at him as he lugged two large grocery bags while stepping into the apartment and reaching out his hand. "Hello, brother, nice to meet you."

David put the cartons near the kitchen entrance. "Richie come on, in, put that on the table. As you can see, this is a life is in transition here. He's got a garbage bag in the middle of the room. It is décor to die for. Wait, Mike, what the hell are those? They look like mom's old statues." He delicately picked up Jesus. "Shit, he's seen better days. I don't remember him looking this ratty."

"I would put that down if I was you," I said.

"What are you doing with these statues? You didn't keep these, did you?"

Richie tossed his coat over the chair. He towered over me—clearly an ex-athlete with broad shoulders and imposing biceps bursting at the seams of the short sleeves of his Nike t-shirt. I pushed the seat towards him and peeked into the bag on the table. "What's that?"

"A jar of protein powder. It's for you, and it should last a few months. I'll show you what we're going to do with it."

"We?" I said, wondering when we became a team.

"I want to know what is going on with these statues here, Michael. You are scaring me again. But first, listen to me. Richie is going to work with you. He's going to help you with nutrition. When you gain some weight, he's going to be your personal trainer. Get you back to running. Get you back to being Michael."

"Running?" It seemed silly at that point. "That's a bit overly optimistic right now, don't you think?"

"Nothing wrong with optimism is there?" Richie chimed in, smiling. His teeth were much too white for Boston living.

"You're not from around here, are you?"

"Is that a prerequisite?" he quickly replied with a laugh.

"Another San Francisco guy, Mike. I'm bringing the old gang back together. He trained Monique for years. He knows what he's doing—we've been friends for since I can remember."

"Too long," Richie said, evoking a knowing smile from David.

"I moved to Boston last August. Kind of an untapped market. We opened shop in Cambridge and down outside of Kenmore Square by BU." Richie surveyed the apartment, leaning into the main room where my stereo system was spread out on the floor next to the couch I was trying to sell. He scratched his head, turned to me and shrugged before proceeding into the kitchen.

"You need help moving some stuff out of here? It's kind of, I don't know, cluttered?"

"I will need help, yeah, getting a lot of this shit out of here. It's a mess because I'm just waiting to throw most of it out. I have a lot of CDs here if you want some." I dragged the garbage bag towards the kitchen entrance.

"I'll look later, Mike. No need to show me now," he said with a bemused smirk while inspecting the refrigerator and cabinets. Luckily, the army of cockroaches was hiding somewhere deep in the woodworks.

"Let me get this straight, you do professional personal training and nutrition consulting, and you are going to work with me? What am I missing here? I'm barely eating."

"Who better to work with?" he said before picking up the cartons of Ensure and placing them in the cabinets. David laughed as he shuffled through the garbage bag of CDs. "Michael, you need someone to help you figure out what to eat, and slowly build your body back up. That's what we've been preaching, but he's the man to help you put it into action. It's that simple."

"It actually is pretty simple," Richie said with a bottle of water in his hand. "We've got a lot of time to get to know each other. Monique has told me a whole bunch about you, and what you've been going through. We'll talk about things, but from what I understand, you put tons of effort, and probably too much energy, into losing weight. So, you obviously have the discipline. You just need to redirect that energy into a positive force. I heard you were a dedicated runner once. True?"

"Yeah, I ran for a bunch of years," I said as David picked up Jessie's letter again.

"We'll get you back to doing it," Richie demanded. "If you were a runner once, you always have the capacity. You just have to tap into that part of yourself again. My feeling is once a runner, always a runner. Not everyone has that kind of discipline. It's hard to teach. But we need to get your body healthy first. That's what we'll be working on."

"When you say working, that means?" I was seeing Dr. Hampton and Dr. Rigatta, and was now hesitant to have to deal with another person doling out advice. Doing it my way was the only blueprint I knew. Suddenly, it seemed like life by committee.

"It means Richie is going to work with you a couple of days a week. He's gonna be your guru, your Yoda, Master Poe, Mister Miyagi, Morpheus, he's going to be your fucking Yogi Berra, and you are going to listen to him," David shouted as he scanned the letter.

"It's going to be a collaboration," Richie said quietly.

"And what's the Ensure for? You want me to drink it? Old people drink that."

"For a good reason. And we're all going to be old one day. Part of the process. The bottom line is it helps people, and it's better than all that Diet Coke in the frig you have here. It will help in the beginning. From what I understand, you're having a tough time eating solid foods, so we need to get some good calories in you as a supplement. You are going to get back to eating solid foods, though. There's no getting around that. We need you to gain weight in a healthy manner first—whatever way we can."

He saw me flinch.

"That's scary I know, but you are dealing with your therapist. He can help you with that." Richie nodded knowingly before draining the water bottle without a breath. "I want your permission to meet with him and Dr. Rigatta soon to coordinate things and see how I can help them. I can tell them what my plans are. I want to get an idea what your vitals are, and what you need."

"Whoa, whoa, whoa. You want to what the what? Can we slow down here?" I raised my hands over my head.

"Michael, we are not stepping on your toes here, but Monique and I have told him everything. We need you to be with the program. The more help you get, the better. You can have a three-headed monster help you battle this. So just give him permission to meet with the doctors. Didn't Rigatta want you to make an appointment with a nutritionist? You haven't even done that yet. So...." David massaged his forehead as he folded the letter and placed it into his back pocket. Slowly, he walked into the bathroom.

"Did you read that letter?" I said. "You believe that?"

"One thing at a time," David replied with a cough. "I don't know why she's sending you this. I really don't, but let's deal with the plan first. Are you okay with Richie talking to the doctors? Monique wants you guys working together like yesterday." He closed the bathroom door, leaving Richie and me alone.

"You played minor league ball?" I said as he gazed over the bookshelf.

"I did. Got to AAA, played third base, but I blew out my knee and realized I was never going to make it. Sometimes life makes decisions for you. You follow them. So, tell me about you. They said you love baseball."

"Too much, they say also," I shook my head.

"That's impossible. You just can't love it too much. It's the greatest game. Too slow for Americans these days. That's why football is going through the roof, but baseball's still the only sport that matters."

This was a guy I could work with. "Man of my heart. Jesus Christ, why couldn't you have said you liked rugby or throwing fucking darts or something, so I could tell you thanks but no thanks. It would have been a lot easier."

"I don't want you to agree because I love baseball. I want you to agree because you want to get better. If baseball makes it easier, then I'm fine with it. You ready to get working?" Richie extended his hand again for another shake.

I was wary to let him see the veins popping out of the back of my pale hands and the small bandage I kept on my forearm.

"You really think you can eventually get me running again?"

"That's going to be up to you, brother, but I know I can help you get there if you have the same will and determination to get healthy as you did to get in the position you are in now."

"I'll try," I said with a glimmer of hope while contemplating ways I could slither out of the agreement.

"That's all I can ask. It's alright for me to talk to your doctors?"

"Yeah, of course."

David returned, holding a towel in one hand and a bottle of Advil in the other. "Michael, why do you have like five bottles of this in the bathroom?"

"Why else? Because everything hurts. It makes the pain go away," I shrugged.

David took two pills without water. "We good then, guys?" he said with eyes wide.

"I wouldn't go that far, but yeah," I replied.

Richie picked the bowl of chicken soup off the table. "Okay, first thought. I'm not a food Nazi, but you know how much sodium is in this bowl of canned soup? I just looked at the number of cans of soup you have in those cabinets. Way too many, man. They load this stuff with salt. I doubt you have high blood pressure, but it's still not good for you."

"We bought that for him. We just want him to eat something. Our fuckup," David interrupted with a laugh.

"Monique bought all of those?" Richie said. "I'm going to have to talk to her. That's funny. She should know better. Well, I'll show you much better options than Campbell's soup. No worries now. Hand me the jar over there. I'm going to make something good for you—I see there's a great new blender here and a lot of fruit. Fantastic.

"That I bet was from Monique," he added while glancing at David, who nodded. "I'll make a smoothie, and show you how to make it, okay?"

"You think I'm going to drink a smoothie now? Really? C'mon."

"I'm going to hope you drink a smoothie," Richie replied without hesitation. "I'm never going to make you eat anything."

"He won't, but I'm going to mainline it in you if I have to," David replied angrily. "There is no fucking smoothie yet. It's a conceptual smoothie he's proposing, and you are already resisting. Michael, when are you going to see Dr. Hampton again?"

"I saw him this morning."

"You better see him again soon because we have to talk about this letter," David ripped the paper out of his pocket. "Are you okay after this? When did it come?"

"Of course, I'm not okay with it. I got it today right before you called. That's why I told you I didn't want you over now. It came in the box with the statues."

Richie disappeared into the kitchen as David hovered over me. "I'm sorry, I obviously had no idea. So now tell me, Jessie had mom's old statues how?"

"She got them from me."

"And you kept them from mom's car because…"

"You don't want to know."

"I'm sure I don't," he shook his head. "Some things I don't need to know, and most of life should stay a goddamn mystery, but why is Jessie sending them back to you?"

"I don't know."

"So, we should go and ask Alanis Morissette who oughta know? Fine, fuck it, we'll just remain oblivious to Jessie's motives for sending you a letter telling you she's thinking of you with Jesus statues. I'm lost here. Jesus statues for you—of all people? This has nothing to do with fasting, right? It's not a crazy Easter or Lent thing. Please don't say that. Tell me this isn't some weird fucking code between you two."

The whirring of the blender from the kitchen sounded like a cat crying.

"There's no weird code. Jessie really has no idea why I kept mom's statues. She just thought they made me think of mom. I don't know why she wrote to me. It would have been better if she wrote `go fuck yourself' instead of `I'm thinking of you.' I just don't know what it means, David."

"Fine. That's what I want to hear. Now fuck Jessie. This is too much. She's out of bounds. Here's what you gotta do." He took a lighter out of his pocket. With a shaky hand, he torched the corner of the letter and envelope before grabbing the statues and walking into the kitchen. I followed like an obedient dog. David placed Jesus and Saint Anthony in the sink, and then tossed the burning paper on top of them.

Richie stood back from the blender filled with a greenish liquid. "Dave, Dave, no, no, don't do that. C'mon. Stop. You can't do that. We're going to burn with them if you do that."

"Fuck it. You gotta burn the past before it devours you, Michael." The bright fire swayed, nearly singeing David's hair. Streams of smoke made the alarm go off.

Richie was tall enough to pull it off the wall with an extended hand. He started blessing himself and solemnly bowing his head. "Dave, man, that is so, so wrong." We all hovered around the sink to watch the fire licking the statues. Richie yanked David back by the shoulder. "It's all going to come back at us you know that, right? It always does. My mom is saying like a hundred novenas for us right now."

"Everything comes back to you," David whispered. "They're just action figures for Christ sakes. Let them fucking burn, and let's all move on. Just let it burn."

After a few minutes, he finally extinguished the flame with a burst from the faucet. I stared at the disfigured statues covered in wet, black ashes. Somewhere Christina was crying. We all stared silently into the sink.

"We are so fucked," Richie said. "I mean royally fucked."

David turned to me before glaring at Richie. "And that is news somehow?"

Twenty

"Richie, open the window behind you. Really wide." David gathered the remains of the statues and smoldering paper with a dustpan and tossed them in a white plastic kitchen bag. He held the tightly wrapped bag like a football to his chest.

Richie winced. "Dave, c'mon man, it's ten degrees outside. The smoke is already gone. What are you doing?"

"Oh stop, just open the window and look down."

Richie carefully did as he was told. "You have a dumpster outside your apartment?" he said, squinting at me.

"It hasn't always been there. They did some work on an apartment downstairs a few months ago, and left it there," I looked down to the half-full, blue dumpster. David nudged me out of the way. "Steve Young back to pass, sees Jerry Rice, corner of the dumpster and throws."

"You are not going to toss that in the garbage from here," Richie said, reaching out before David proceeded to sling a wobbly spiral right on top of a cracked full-length mirror.

"Just did." David replied while slowly walking towards the hallway. "We're in Allston Rock City. You know someone will have a half-melted Jesus on his dashboard by the morning."

"I don't believe you," Richie's head dropped. "I don't think all those years of Catholic school are going to save me."

"Jesus forgives, remember. That's what they taught you." David was gathering the garbage bag of CDs by his feet while sitting at the table in the main room.

"I doubt he's going to forgive immolation. A thousand Hail Marys on Sunday won't get us absolution," Richie laughed.

I glanced at the counter with the smoothie glass, hoping he was too distracted to remember it.

"Did you really go to Catholic school growing up? And you go to church now? Really?" I actually didn't give a shit about how often he did the stations of the cross—I just needed to stall the inevitable.

"I sure did, sure do, and really. Each week. It gives me peace," Richie said quietly.

"He even does yoga and goes to Buddhist temples too. He's so fucking peaceful, he's barely breathing. The guy is the only Zen Catholic I know. Not a bit of guilt in him. Until now." David carefully pulled a handful of CDs out of the bag and placed them on the table one at a time.

"And that's how we've gotten along all these years. Total opposites make for interesting conversations and good arguments in loud clubs."

"Usually, each one of them is more of a one-way conversation. Your brother talks while I listen and disagree," Richie replied.

"Beautiful music has been created by dissonance throughout our lifetime, but I'd stop short of saying we make beautiful music together," David added.

Richie genuflected ostentatiously after taking one last glimpse at the dumpster. He ran a few fingers through his closely cropped hair just before grabbing the refrigerator handle with his lumberjack hand. "You know I don't know if I could live like you guys do, believing in nothing.

"I don't get it—there's no comfort in that. I've told your brother a hundred times before that art will never save you."

Finally, he pulled a yogurt out of inside the refrigerator door.

"Okay, here we go again," David said, gritting his teeth. "See, we go through this every few months. He says art can't save you and I say…"

I darted my eyes at each one of them.

"What do you need saving from?" Richie finished David's thought in a deep baritone voice.

"Michael, let's just say, I think life is easier if you believe in something. It's not complicated, and I'm not some devout Catholic or anything. I just feel more at ease believing that there is something bigger than me, and I'm not alone in the world. It helps me sleep. And it definitely helps when I work out. It just helps. There doesn't need to be an explanation does there?" He looked to me with a shrug. "You either believe or you don't."

"I get it," I said. "I mean I don't, but I get why you do. Jessie, my ex-girlfriend who used to live here…"

"You mean the girl we just torched Jesus and Saint Anthony to forget about? Yeah, I heard all about her," Richie said as he stabbed a spoon into the vanilla Yoplait.

"Yup, her. She didn't believe but used to say if I believed in something I never would be going through what I'm going through. I think she was hoping that believing in some higher power would magically make me eat."

"And you don't think that's a possibility? That maybe the whole thing is tied to, say, maybe an emptiness inside you?" Richie asked.

I turned to David, who extended his palms out as if to say, "Go ahead and answer."

"Wait, are you saying the anorexia is some kind of metaphor? A literary construct? It's not. It's how I've lived my life." I had to rein in my voice because I was yelling at someone I had just met.

Richie snatched a bottle of water out of the refrigerator while laughing uproariously. "I have no idea what you just asked. Wrong guy here. Literary constructs?" He said the term gingerly. "You sound too much like your brother, and that's precisely when I tune him out. I went to Cal State Long Beach. We didn't do constructs or metaphors. We did shots. All I'm saying is that people, including me, believe in God because it brings me some comfort I think those who don't believe don't have. You know what I'm saying?"

My knees ached from standing so long. "I get what you're saying, yeah, but what you have to understand is, well, let's put it this way. You, yourself, said you either believe or you don't. And I just don't. I can't just start believing in a God in the hope he will ease my problems."

Richie barely let me finish. "You're right Michael, but maybe if you believed in the first place you wouldn't be so conflicted with yourself."

I was getting dizzy as a rush of cold air made me feel feverish. "But if I believed in the first place, I'd be a completely different person, living a completely different life. That's not who I am."

"And well, who are you? Do you know?" Richie opened the window wider to throw the empty yogurt container down towards the dumpster. "Convenient," he added.

"Do you know where you're going to? Do you like the things that life is showing you? Where are you going to?" David sang off key with his head in his hands.

Richie tossed a Delicious apple at my brother. "Okay, I get it, enough bullshit. I'll leave that to you."

"Glad that's over. He obviously doesn't have a fucking clue who he is or what he wants. That's why he's seeing Dr. Hampton," David said with a hint of good cheer. "I say it's smoothie time. Then we're going to go through these CDs. You are not going to throw them out in a garbage bag. You can sell all of these and make some money."

"Didn't Jason Giambi go to Cal State Long Beach? That's a great baseball program," I said.

Richie's eyes brightened. "He did. And Steve Trachsel. All proud Dirtbags. You're right. It is a really good baseball program. I loved it there."

"See Richie, you fell into his trap. My brother is the master of avoidance and misdirection. He's going to ask you to name every damn guy who ever played baseball at Long Beach. Will you just take the smoothie and drink it, Michael? After you drink, you can ask him who rubbed the balls for the umpires before games. I don't care. Let's get to drinking."

David took a sip from the glass the glass, grinned crookedly and handed it to me. "Fantastic. I don't have a clue what's in it and don't want to know. I already feel stronger. Now drink some, Michael."

I wiped off David's faint lip prints with my shirt—one eye on the thick, green liquid.

"What am I about to drink?" I said.

"It's a honey banana shake with vanilla whey protein and a little spirulina in it," Richie replied as if he was Emeril serving Christmas dinner.

Richie and David remained silent and motionless. I had no choice but to down it. The icy liquid slid down my throat, chilling my intestines. It actually tasted sweet, but I couldn't admit it or else they'd end up making me drink it all.

"Who made this, Socrates?" I said with a grimace. "I kinda think this kind of tastes like ass." I was hoping to generate a smile from one of them.

"Jesus Christ, I'm glad you know what ass tastes like, but you are full of shit. You know that is sweet. Drink more. Here, let me have another sip. It sure tasted fine to me." David yanked the glass from my hand to take a quick pull. Mike, c'mon that's good. That smoothie is… smooth."

"It is good. I drink different flavors at least once every day. If you drink more you will come to like it." Richie was a bit too happy for the gray afternoon.

David poured what remained in the blender into a red plastic cup. "We'll drink together. Cheers." He reached the cup toward me. I hesitated before finally clicking glass to plastic. As the smoothie oozed like lava throughout my system, I quietly licked the film off my lips.

David quickly drank the rest with one long swallow. "Hey, you know what? We need to make progress on cleaning this place up so it looks like an actual apartment. It can't look like a cave a sad person lives in.

"Let's start by throwing out that maroon couch with the stains on it. I don't want to know where they came from either," he said. "I have bad memories of that couch. Lots of depressing nights trying to get you to eat or dealing with Jessie's stink eye. Rich, let's take it out, and just leave it in the dumpster."

"No way, I was going to sell it." I was ready to dismantle what remained of my life with Jessie, but I wanted it to be on my own schedule. The CDs were the easiest to part with—minor fragments of our lives. The furniture, though, felt like a punctuation mark on the narrative.

"And what do you think you are going to get for that, Mike?" David said. "A bag of hair? It's garbage. The cushions have ass marks deep enough to bury a body in. We're throwing it out now." I took a mournful look at my withered couch fit for a crack den.

"It's for the best. We'll be back in five minutes," Richie said. He picked the far end of the couch up to his shoulders. After David followed accordingly, they were in the hallway before I could think of an excuse for why it should remain.

"Okay, open the door, Michael. When we get back that glass you are holding is going to be empty. You don't think you are just going to look at it all afternoon, do you?" David's eyes were twitching.

"You need help negotiating the stairs?" I shouted when they approached the stairwell.

"Drink that up, Michael. What are you going to do, carry the lint? We'll be right back," David hollered as they descended.

I never finished anything, and that certainly was not a moment to begin a new approach to life. The glass was visibly shaking in my hand. After a quick trip to the window to watch David and Richie artistically angle the couch in the dumpster, I rushed to the bathroom and flushed the remainder of the smoothie down the toilet.

Dr. Hampton's voice simply was not as strong as the familiar, friendly one I had relied on for so long. Throwing the smoothie out was so easy. So natural. And so wrong.

I sat at the table feeling depleted and exhausted. Whatever rush of relief I felt while watching the smoothie circle the bottom of the toilet quickly turned into hopelessness. I had failed again and was left to wonder how the punishment would be meted out.

"Great, now what else can we get rid of?" David huffed as he sprinted into the room. "Let's look at this big mess of CDs and get the bag out of the center of the floor."

"That wasn't that bad, was it?" Richie picked the glass off the table. "One down. We're going to try another flavor this week. We are going to integrate meals, though. You with that?" He seemed so satisfied with his small victory.

"Monique and I bought a bunch of different things we can try that won't be too heavy or make you feel uncomfortable. They'll be good for you. I'll stop by tomorrow. Don't worry, it'll be in the afternoon." Richie sounded like he was talking to a kindergartener. "We got some chicken, some fish, some avocados, peanut butter. I know peanut butter is probably scary, but it's great for you."

"You always this cheery and enthusiastic or is it some kind of afflic-tion?" I was kidding, but his ebullience unnerved me.

"I can be an asshole if you would prefer that, but your sourpuss outlook on life is part of the problem if you ask me. Let's start off thinking positive. You know you've got a sister-in-law who will do anything to help, and your brother is gung-ho to get you back on the beam. I'm here for one reason—to help you. Not everybody has people in your corner like you do. You gotta know that."

David snuck in behind me. "Monique is still really concerned, and all in. You know we all are, right?"

I sat silently, feeling like a selfish prick while replaying the smoothie swirling down the toilet.

"Alright, tonight we can go to Nuggets in Kenmore or Looney Tunes on Boylston and sell these. The beauty of used record stores. You can make a lot of money." David squinted at the spine of each CD he'd already stacked on the table

"Hey, I'm not a hoarder—you sent most of these from San Francisco. You brought me like fifty a week for the last year-and-a-half." I rear-ranged the piles. When Jessie and I first moved in together, I would get a FedEx box of brand new CDs from David each week. After he arrived in Boston, he would randomly drop by our place with a large carton of discs before taking me out to a local rock club.

David wrote mostly about hip-hop and soul at the time, but he seemed to gravitate to trip-hop or noisy catharsis in the clubs. I couldn't resist the quick thrills, even though I felt like I was just tag-ging along. I'd never heard of most of the bands before. Jesus and the Mary Chain, Portishead, Tricky, Slowdive, Morcheeba, Ride, and The Sneaker Pimps. They were all a fucking blur.

He always invited Jessie to go with us. Every time, she turned him down. She thought I was taking handouts from my brother and spend-ing more time with him than with her.

One night, months before she left, Jessie confronted me as I got out of the shower after returning from an Erykah Badu show at Avalon. "Michael, do you see what's going on. You are always out with David. You just follow him everywhere. It's ridiculous. You don't even give a damn about Erykah Badu. You went because he said she was good. Do you even care about what is going on here when you are out? You are clearly just sick of your life as it is and sick of our lives. Just sick. Do you see that?"

Of course, I did and went to bed. The next day, I went out to buy *Baduizm* at Tower Records while Jessie got her hair cut on Newbury Street.

David dropped a couple of CDs in my lap after creating a jewel case tower near the bookcase. "These classic rock records I know are Jessie's. Richie, c'mere. You're a classic rock guy. Maybe you want some of these."

Richie walked back to us from the kitchen with a dishrag in his hand. "I'm not sure I need any music, but what are you dealing with?"

"Besides bad memories? Lots of Bon Jovi. Lots." David nodded knowingly to me. "Jessie just loved him. Look in the bedroom, she has a cardboard poster of the guy. And this guy," he said, pointing at me. "Allowed a poster of Jon Bon Jovi in the apartment."

"Hey, I like Bon Jovi," Richie grinned. "I don't want the CDs, but I kind of like his music."

"I'm glad you kept that secret from me all these years." David selected a few more discs. "Okay, we got Van Hagar *OU812*. If ever a band should have quit it was Van Halen."

"I'll actually take that," Richie said. David tossed it to him with a flick of the wrist.

"Red Hot Chili Peppers' *Blood Sugar Sex Magic*." David raised it over his head. "Going once, twice and…" Richie waved him off.

"Those fuckers don't know how to write songs. Good decision." He held another CD before his eyes. "Let's see, REO Speedwagon. A classic, classic rock record, *You Can Tune a Piano, but You Can't Tuna Fish*. Actually, pretty good pop songwriting."

Richie disappeared into the kitchen before yelling over his shoulder. "Pass."

David arched an eyebrow at me. "If I dig into this bag one more time and pull out *Eat a Peach*, I'm going to think Jessie was trying to gaslight you."

I could hear Richie washing the blender and thought, if nothing else, he was going to make a good maid.

"David, we are not going through them all, are we?" I said, ready to kick them both out so I could go back to sleep.

"One more," David said, holding Richard and Linda Thompson's *Shoot Out the Lights*. "Jesus, where did Jessie get this? This is genuine genius, and probably the last record you should ever listen to at this point in your life."

"That, Les gave it to us for a Christmas stocking stuffer."

David marched toward the kitchen window. "Damn, the guy did have good taste in music. I'll give him that. This, I'm throwing in the dumpster. The one thing you don't need is the greatest record about loss and breaking up. Great, great music, but bad, bad karma."

"What are you talking about? Something I should hear?" Richie was now standing next to me.

David leaned out the window. "You, of all people, shouldn't hear this. Wait until your divorce is final. Ten years from now, I'll buy you a copy." He looked both ways before throwing the CD like a Frisbee. I heard the distant noise of plastic cracking.

"You're not the only one whose life's in the shitter," Richie exhaled. "My wife was a Buddhist, in case you are trying to put the Zen Catholic equation together."

I wasn't. I was thinking about a flushed honey banana shake with vanilla whey protein and a little spirulina in it.

"To really answer your question, no, I'm not always this cheery. I just know you have to make the best of a bad situation."

"I had no idea you were getting divorced." I genuinely felt sorry for the guy. He offered a dismissive wave and headed towards the door.

"No worries. How could you know? See, we have plenty to discuss. Hey, I've got to get out of here. I think you guys have things to talk about. I'll see you tomorrow, Michael. You're going to be alright. I can tell. It was great to meet you. Dave, I'll take the T home this afternoon. I think I might stop off at Kenmore to see how things are going."

I reached out to him. "I'll drive you. It's not a problem. Think of it as a first thank you."

"You guys have a lot to talk about. Thanks, that's cool, but no need. I'll let you guys be." Richie eyed David as he quietly snuck out.

When the door closed, I turned to David. "Hey, I don't understand. What's he mean by we need to talk?" My brother rubbed his forehead with his index finger and thumb before massaging his neck.

"Michael, listen. I know it's a bad time, and you need all the support you can get, but I'm going to London for a while. I'm not sure how long, maybe a few months or more. I'm going to work with Eric Clapton on his autobiography. I was asked to collaborate, and I'm going to do it. Obviously." He paused while looking down at his shoes for a few minutes as I tried to process another absence.

"You are leaving now? When?"

"Next Monday. A week. I know this isn't optimal for you."

"And what about Mon?"

"Monique will be here most of the time. She's got business. You know that. And when she's not in New York or L.A. she's going to be helping you. I won't be here, but she will. She's going to do what's necessary to get you focused. You need to lean on her. She wants that. You're going to go over to our place to eat whatever you can eat a few times a week. We don't want you rotting here by yourself. The loneliness and isolation are gonna to kill you. Literally."

"I don't need a babysitter." I couldn't hide my anger.

"Michael, please. I know you were bitter as a kid when I went to school and left you behind with mom and dad, but you know that's what we do. We grow up. I know this is going to bring up a whole mess of issues about dad, but you realize this has nothing to do with me leaving or with that. You can separate them, right?"

"I will be fine. This isn't about me."

"It is. It is," he said with a weak smile. "My going to London isn't, but this is about you. We've talked about it a hundred times already, and this will be the last time for a while. I'm not going to mention it at all over the next week. But Dr. Hampton, Rigatta, Richie—it's all about you. We're doing this for you. Whatever it takes. It's that simple."

David went to the refrigerator and returned with two ice cubes held against the back of his neck. He tossed a bottle of water to me. "I will check in with you by phone. I want to hear progress. Start clearing all this stuff out of here. You can stay at our place when Monique is out of town—even when she's home.

"We have two extra rooms, you know that. Right now, you have to start working toward a life beyond here. A new apartment, a new city. But first, you have to get better. Have to."

I blurted out, "What about your classes?"

"Are you listening to me?" David pivoted into the bathroom. "I need you to focus." He stepped back with the bottle of Advil again.

"David, you just took that before."

"And I'm taking more now." He nonchalantly held two pills before his mouth.

"Am I causing this again?"

"Stop. Stop. Stop," he said, swallowing the Advil with a quick tilt of the head. "Everything is not your fault. My classes are covered. I'm easy to replace."

"I don't know about that."

"I do. Now, you good with all of this? I mean, I know it's a lot to absorb at this moment, but it's only for a few months. Not a big deal."

"I don't know if I'm okay, but I'll make myself okay with it." It was all slowly sinking in. I'd have to make do again, just as I had to adapt without Jessie. "You are going to help write God's autobiography? After today there's something so wrong about that."

David just looked out of the window into the early evening darkness. "I know, right?"

"You are going to pick me up tonight to sell the CDs?" I said with anticipation. Sweat ran down my neck. Suddenly, it felt oppressively hot.

"Yes, indeed. I'll call before I leave. We can talk more about everything tonight. If you want to sleep over our place, that's fine. Might be a good idea."

"I'm fine here in Allston." I waved my hand like a *Price Is Right* beauty offering up a view of the showcase prize.

David reached into his pocket for his keys. "Drink some water when you finish cleaning up the CDs. Just put them in stacks. We'll crate them, okay?"

I could feel his fingertips press against my collarbone as he squeezed my shoulder. "Mike, one thing. I, uh, I don't know how to say this. I'm not saying you did, and if you did, I don't want to know. I genuinely don't. It's for you to live with and decide what you are going to do when I'm gone. But if I was a betting man, I'd go to Vegas and bet everything Monique and I own on you pouring that smoothie down the toilet. Like I said, I don't want to know, but if you did, I hope you realize you can't—just can't do that anymore. We are past that. I'm going to go. I'll see you tonight."

I remained silent as David walked out the door. As the sound of the keys jingling and his muffled footsteps dissipated, I went to the bathroom to stare at my sallow, sweat-soaked cheeks in the mirror. In an angry burst of frustration, I poured the entire bottle of water over my head before scrubbing my face.

Twenty-One

Dr. Hampton's waiting room was empty as I read an article in *The Sporting News* on Ichiro Suzuki preparing to play his first season in the major leagues after a spectacular career in Japan. I ripped the page with the picture of his wiry frame out of the magazine and put it in my back pocket.

With late February snow covering Boston, the mere idea of baseball gave me something to look forward to. I knew Richie would want to see Ichiro and the Mariners when they came to town, so I decided to stop off at Fenway Park in Kenmore Square on the way home to pick up a Sox schedule. I was also going to check out a foreign film at the nearby Nickelodeon Theaters. I wanted to do anything to avoid going home.

The cold, dark apartment had been emptied of the most visible traces of my life with Jessie. The front room was barren except for my stereo system, books, and crates of CDs I'd yet to sell. I spent most of my nights listening to music while sitting on the floor or watching CNN and The Food Network in the bedroom.

When I wasn't at a doctor, I explored the classified sections of *The Boston Globe* and *The Boston Phoenix* for apartments with the hope of settling into a new life in a vibrant, well-furnished place once I got healthy enough to move. It was a small dream, but those slivers of hope kept me going.

After Dr. Hampton's assistant popped her head in the room to tell me he'd be late, I mindlessly paced the floor next to the office door—a silly, nervous impulse as futile as pushing the UP button while waiting for a delayed elevator. I began doing deep knee bends when a tall auburn-haired undergrad with a wide-brimmed fedora and a long, black overcoat entered the room. I stood rigidly, as inconspicuously as possible, next to the moldings. Her eyes never looked away from the beige carpet. She sat on the far side of the room—shoulders hunched and legs crossed—meticulously folding her coat on her lap.

Her wan, makeup-free, hollowed out face reminded me that Dr. Hampton was probably listening to slightly different variations of the same story with the same common denominator all day long. I sat back down next to an exotic potted plant and thumbed through a withered *People* magazine with George Clooney on the cover. Someone had drawn Elton John glasses around his eyes. "Tomorrow has been canceled due to lack of interest" was written in block letters across his teeth. The ink was fairly fresh.

I stole quick glances toward the girl while pretending to read an advertisement for tampons. She wore a form-fitting black button-down blouse and knee-high black boots over black jeans. The blouse collar was open to the top of her small breasts, revealing sharp collarbones and a severe chasm at the base of her throat. Long feather earrings dangled nearly to her shoulders. Her right foot spun in circles as she inspected the back of her veiny hands and gauged the edges of her nails.

Dr. Hampton finally appeared to apologize for being late and walked to the girl.

"Hello Brittany, it's a nice surprise, but you realize your appointment isn't until five." He waved me into his office, but I hesitated until I heard her answer.

"I'm going to wait. I've got nothing better to do, so I figured I'd get here early since I was late last time," she said quietly.

Dr. Hampton calmly nodded. "Michael, go on in, I'll be with you in a moment."

I could hear them talking through the closed door as I slowly stepped towards my favorite rocking chair.

"Is she okay?" I said after Dr. Hampton entered.

"She's fine," he replied, deflecting the question before settling behind his desk. "I'm sorry I'm a bit late, so we will go over the hour today if that's good with you. If you have someplace to be I understand, but this is the second time I've been late with you. Yes, of course, I remember our first meeting," he added, tilting his right index finger to the side of his head.

"I've got nowhere to go either," I said out of the corner of my mouth.

"Great, then, well, I don't mean great in that context. We always want you to have a place to go. It's great you have some spare time so you can stay. Tell me how are things going with Richard and the food intake? I spoke with Dr. Rigatta, and she told me you have been diligent with the weigh-ins. She said you're doing better. Have you been okay with that?"

I looked out the window towards the ashy afternoon sky. "You think the sun is ever going to come out or you think this winter is going to be forever? It's sure been a cold, cold winter." I tried to sing the line like Mick Jagger, but it came out like a dying cow.

Dr. Hampton smiled while sitting back in his chair. "Am I supposed to recognize the song?"

"I don't think I would if I heard me sing, so no. I'm not sure why I did that. I guess, I'm just cold, but I'm always cold these days. Maybe it's just a condition of life. As far as the weigh-ins go, well, if I said I had no choice but be okay with getting weighed, you'd say I do. So, I guess I'll just say I'm doing it. You know scales spook me."

"Just to hear you say you are going to do it is positive." Dr. Hampton gazed toward the window while rolling up his sleeves, determined to work. "I know this seems like an endless winter for you—it has been bleak, no doubt. But you are undergoing major changes, which makes it even more difficult. I guarantee you the sun will come out."

"Please, don't say tomorrow," I laughed.

"You know I avoided saying this is the winter of your discontent, and I swear I will not say the sun will come out tomorrow either." He smirked with a hand raised as if taking an oath. While he talked, I kept thinking of the sharp toes of girl's boots and her thin thighs in those black jeans.

"Michael, I want to hear how things are going with you day-to-day, but I hope you recall what we talked about last week." Dr. Hampton raised an Igloo cooler to his desk. "I asked if you would be willing to sit down with me and share some food sometime soon. Remember, we talked about how important it was for you to break the cycle of isolation and that private religious ceremony surrounding your eating process? We want you to move on and try to eat with people. It should be part of the everyday life process again, not something secret."

Of course, I remembered the conversation, which seemed like a nice, theoretical possibility for another day far in the future. When he moved the cooler to the desk's edge, I began getting queasy. I'd begrudgingly eaten some vegetables and two scrambled eggs with Richie only two hours before and just couldn't contemplate more food. My walking and weak-ass imitations of exercises in the waiting room were attempts to burn off some of the calories. An all-too-familiar stomach bloat had me stretching the waist of my jeans throughout the afternoon.

"Now, I'm not going to ambush you, Michael, and you have every right to say no here, but you've told me more than a few times you like yogurt." I was nodding my head as the sight of the girl's black boot circling counter clockwise flashed before me once again. Dr. Hampton continued speaking, but only every other word registered.

I jumped up to stare at the ice-covered waters of the Charles River. The sound of the wind just outside the glass seemed comforting.

"Michael, are you with me or are you tuning me out?"

"I'm not tuning you out. Trust me, I'm here. I just need to know that life is going on outside of this office. Just to see life happening. I want to see the T going over the Charles. I ate something today, and it's tough to describe, but I'm not sure I know how to live with it. I'm not sure I know how to live anymore. I know this is not normal. I'm not sure what happened along the way or how I got to this point, but I'm really uncomfortable right now."

"Who'd you eat with?" Dr. Hampton moved towards me.

"Richie. It was like two hours ago. I actually ate with Monique the other night also. Nothing big. She just asked me to eat, and I couldn't turn her down. She makes it impossible to say no." My voice wavered as I struggled to swallow.

"You know, the only other time I'd actually eaten with anyone in like years was the night I stabbed myself. That was out of desperation because I actually felt like I was dying that night. I don't mean like something inside of me was dying. I mean literally dying.

"It really is a crazy fucking thing. One minute I'm scared of dying, and then when I finally eat something, I can't live with it. It happens every time I don't eat alone. When I ate today with Richie, I felt so…" I leaned with one hand against the window.

"Why don't you sit, please?" Dr. Hampton looked at me warily. Another image of the girl's thin, angular thighs appeared in the window. I remained standing silently, wiping sweat from my brow before finally taking a seat once more.

"I ate with Richie before and felt ashamed as if he was watching. And that's how I feel all the time. I didn't sense that with Monique, for some reason. I didn't want to eat with her, but there's this, I guess you'd call it safety. It doesn't feel like she is judging.

"I know you probably have yogurt in that cooler, but I just don't think I can eat it. It's not just because of eating together, but believe it or not, I feel really fat right now." I pointed to his desk. "It's crazy I know, but I do. I'm also afraid of you judging me. I hate it, but I'm going to fail your test today."

I gathered my thoughts, the word 'fail' echoing in my head. "Let's meet again this week. If you want, I will try and eat with you. But the way I feel right now, I just can't eat more. I know you are thinking I'm failing, but I can make it up another time."

"This isn't a test, and you are not failing, Michael. That's the last thing I want you to feel. I'm happy to hear you ate something today. Of course, I want to make sure you eat something later in the day also. Something more substantial, but it's not a test of will.

"As I said, it's about breaking the isolation. But if you have been doing that, I'm proud of you. Yes, we can do this next time, if you want to schedule something later in the week. You will feel safer because it won't be a surprise." Dr. Hampton spoke in measured words, his weathered voice echoing through the room.

"Let me try to explain." I tapped my fingers rhythmically against the seat between my legs. "When I was eating with Richie, and when I think about eating in public, I'm afraid people will say I'm weak. Over the past four years or so, when I didn't eat, I felt strong. I mean really powerful, almost invincible. You know, I felt I was stronger than everyone else because I knew I could do something that they couldn't. I could do what nobody else around me could do. Do you realize how that makes you feel? It feels…"

Dr. Hampton didn't flinch. "Special?"

"Yes, yes, of course, yes. I was different. There's an incredible rush to that kind of feeling. If I eat I become…I don't know. I become like everyone else. Weak. And people eating with me will recognize it. They will say you can't do what you once did before. I would be failing. I had already set the bar so high, and now what am I left with? I'm just going to end up eating like everyone else?" My thumbs were rattling against the rocking chair handles. I could hear Dr. Hampton's breathing as he sat on the side of his desk.

"Yes, Michael, like everyone else, but it doesn't make you weak. I want you to understand the distortion—how you invert the equation. Eating is going to make you stronger. Down deep you know that. I'm sure of it."

"But I feel so…I don't know how to put it. Not only do I feel like I've been outcast from the special circle I was in, but I feel like I'm nowhere. I was the ringmaster of that circle. Now I have nothing. And I have to deal with this stomach. Jesus fucking Christ. I feel like Buddha. I just hate it. I hate the feeling, and I hate that I allowed myself to feel this way."

"You mean you allowed yourself to eat?"

"Yeah, it's about eating, always eating. I have this Buddha belly. You know I have never worn a belt as an adult. I've always hated belts. They make me feel confined, like I'm in prison. I don't wear any jewelry either. I hate that feeling. I sold my high school class ring right after graduating because I could feel the weight on my finger.

I waved my clenched fist at Dr. Hampton. "See my wrist? I couldn't bear to have a watch on my wrist. The idea of watches makes me uncomfortable. I even hate to wear socks. They make me aware I have a body."

I was breathing heavily—my t-shirt sticking to the sweat on my chest. "Dr. Hampton, you see that belt you are wearing. It makes me nervous because it reminds me of how I used to feel so suffocated while wearing one when I was a chubby kid sitting in the middle school cafeteria. All that fucking pressure against my stomach, reminding me I was fat.

"I have no belt on now, but it feels like I do. And you know what? I feel like a balloon. A fucking grotesque balloon. This is what happens. This is the panic when I eat. We can talk about it, and I can intellectualize about what eating means to me, but you see me now? Look at my hand."

I held it, fingers quivering, out in front of my face. "I'm like out of control. This is what I deal with. People say just eat, but they don't know."

"Michael, you are barely over a hundred pounds." Dr. Hampton eased himself off the desk calmly. "I know you know you are not fat. Sit for a second, and compose yourself. Recognize what you are feeling is not reality."

"But it's my reality. You get that, right?" I wanted to cry and get it out but there were no tears. There was nothing.

Dr. Hampton stood with shoulders back and hands in pockets as he walked towards me. "And your reality is a false one. You get that, right?" Of course, it made sense. I understood exactly what he was saying, but the feeling in my stomach betrayed all rational thought.

"I'm embarrassed. I mean, I'm seriously ashamed. I sound like the most fucked-up person. You must think I'm crazy. How does someone get this fucked up? Someone must know."

"Michael, you can't think about those questions. You are beating yourself up. It's just another form of self-torment. Life doesn't have to be this difficult. You are not alone with what you feel, trust me. I know that doesn't help, but there are other people who are struggling with what you are going through and doing the same thing you are doing.

"The only question you have to ask yourself is, 'How do I get well?'"

I held my face in my hands between my knees while rocking back and forth. After a few shaky breaths, I begged him to take a ten-minute break because I wasn't sure I could go on.

Dr. Hampton clapped his hands and put the cooler beneath his desk. With a peek at his watch, he said, "That's a good idea. We still have plenty of time. I'm going to get some water."

"I don't need water." It was an instinctual response without hesitation.

"I want you to stand up, Michael, walk around, take a look out the window, and I'll be right back." He paused while watching me carefully. "With some water."

"I swear Dr. Hampton, I'm really going to eat that yogurt next time, I promise. I'm positive you are disappointed in me and probably think I'm a sad excuse for a person. I'm disappointed in me. It's ridiculous. I'm thinking about what I just told you. If someone outside these walls heard me, they'd say buck the fuck up, you crazy muthafucker. Who the fuck needs to be safe while eating? I know that's what they'd say. And they'd be right—I know that.

"I honestly never even told my brother or Monique this. Jessie never saw me actually break. I tried to avoid scaring her, so I never told her what I was going on in my head. All of this has been bottled up. Every minute, every day for years. It's all I think about. You can't imagine how tiring it is. Sometimes, I think my life is just one long exhausting experience I'm not going to recover from. I'm sorry to come apart like this, but you have to know. You have to understand this is how I feel every time I put something in my mouth. It's easier just to not even try."

Before he could respond, I corrected myself. "I know how that sounds. That circles us back to the beginning where I don't want to be. That's just what I'm thinking, but I am trying. I'm really trying."

"I'm not disappointed in you, so stop thinking that way." Dr. Hampton stood by the door with the empty water pitcher in his hand. "I think you have the answers to some of your own questions. You began the very important process today.

"Up to now we have been doing a lot of good work, but I think you are getting beyond your intellectual barriers and digging beneath the surface to deal with feelings that are going to arise in here. And it it's alright to be scared of them. What we need to do is to continue to figure out what triggers them and how you can cope with the feelings when you are not in this room."

He paused momentarily to let his words linger for a minute, and stared me down. "Are you a little better now? You okay? You look okay."

I was surprisingly tranquil while listening to him speak. "I'm okay, yeah, yeah, go get some water. I'm fine. I guess, I just never had a meltdown like that in front of somebody. Inside, I feel like the Wicked Witch of the West, and I haven't even had any water yet." I forced a forbidden smile.

"Here's something to remember Michael, the Wicked Witch of the West had to be vanquished before Dorothy could go home again. That's definitely the most important thing to take from that film. Sit tight, and I'll be right back. You take a few breaths, relax, and take a look out the window again. I'll be right in the nurse's office across the hall. I'll be checking on you. Now breathe."

Twenty-Two

The blur of passing headlights on Memorial Drive across the river hypnotized me into a wonderful, dreamlike trance until the sight of my reflection in the window forced me to step back in fear. My hair was getting mangy and out of control—the curls tumbled down wildly, completely engulfing my narrow face. Now angry and completely disgusted with myself, I suddenly thought about the girl in the waiting room again and wondered if she was still sitting, sadly alone. She had been on my mind ever since I first took a glimpse of her—I just couldn't get her out of my head.

Dr. Hampton had been teaching me about triggers—the little, random things in daily life that tip me into obsession. There were so many in my life, but over the weeks I'd slowly begun to identify some of them by myself. And while staring into the descending night, I realized that the sweet looking, impeccably dressed girl was a fucking bony-ass trigger on the .44 Magnum aimed straight at my temple. She had opened the floodgates from the past I so desperately wanted to blot out. Those black clothes—Jessie. Yes, I understood that Jessie had been hovering beside me while I talked throughout the session.

Jessie and David.

My initial glimpse of the girl immediately evoked the first time they met: the lunch that fired the match leading to the fireworks display after our trivia party and, ultimately, all the bickering that followed. I could still hear them my head. While I slowly bounced my forehead against the chilled, tinted window, that whole goddamn afternoon on Long Island replayed like a haunting, bare-bones Roger Corman horror movie. David couldn't have written a more terrifying script.

He and I were sitting at the restaurant's bar, waiting for Jessie to meet us at the Garden City Hotel, where he was staying with Monique.

They had just flown in from San Francisco to help me finish packing before my move to Boston. David was dressed in head-to-toe black—a rock critic cliché he owned and always managed to laugh about. I was wearing my usual Levis and a powder blue, button-down shirt while nursing a whiskey David had ordered for me.

It was barely two in the afternoon, but he insisted we drink something. Of course, I hadn't eaten after squeezing in a nine-mile run in the morning, so I was slightly buzzed before Jessie even arrived. Mon was in New York, leaving the unholy trinity together to bond over food.

Jessie walked in twenty minutes late. She wore tight black jeans tucked into black boots and a white top under a black vest. Her fingernails were painted red and her hair fell to her shoulders with one braid on each side of her head. I barely recognized her and prepared for my lunch with Johnny Cash and Chrissie Hynde.

Jess gave me a wispy graze of a kiss. "You okay? You look like you saw a ghost. Are you going to introduce us?" she said. I took another quick sip of my drink to fuel what I'd hoped would be a lift-off into oblivion. A restaurant was the last place I wanted for all of us to connect.

"Yeah, sure, Jess, this is my brother." She cautiously reached out and leaned slightly towards David as he took her palm with both hands. I was expecting some kind of hug instead of the Bill Clinton meets Lady Diana greeting.

"Well, finally," he said. Jessie's eyes were heavily rimmed with eyeliner. She had jangling bracelets on her right wrist and large hoop earrings bigger than my forearms. David bowed playfully, a gracious host. "What can I get you to drink?"

"I've read so much of your work that I feel I know you already," Jessie said before taking a glass of white wine.

"If you've read my work, don't confuse that voice with me. They are not the same. Ask any writer. It's dangerous when people think they know the writer from his voice," David said as I nodded vigorously.

Jessie smiled. "Yeah, I know, I've heard that before from some people. Michael chats you up you all the time—you have a lot to live up to."

"Oh, okay. I guess the pressure is on. Now, I'm worried." David was smiling broadly and fully attentive.

"No, no, don't worry," Jess replied with an easy laugh as we headed to the table behind the hostess. The click of Jessie's boots echoed throughout the mostly empty restaurant.

When I finally settled in across from Jess, the table seemed much too high, so I felt like a child sitting with his parents.

The waiter, a tall, pretty boy with crystal blue eyes and slickly combed hair, handed us the menus. David placed his on the plate while Jessie took a quick glance at the first page. I simply turned my menu front side down, near the far left of the table. It would wait. I watched businessmen and women in pants suits sitting for a power lunch nearby as Jessie and David yammered on about their personal histories. They hardly acknowledged me—it seemed like I was an extra in a David Lean epic.

I faded in and out as the whiskey took hold, but I had enough clarity to follow David after he placed his napkin on his lap. I had never felt more out of place because the last time I had been in such an expensive restaurant was for David's college graduation many years earlier.

Jessie took another long drink of wine before looking around the cavernous room with a slight daze in her eyes.

"Why don't we order?" I said, hoping to get the food formalities out of the way.

"Michael, hey, chill out. We're here making conversation, getting to know each other," David snapped with one eye on me.

"I want to eat, for Chrissakes." I blurted out impulsively—they were instinctual words I barely recognized.

"Jeez, that's one of the few times I've ever heard you say that since I've been with you," Jessie said with a squint.

"So, now you are hungry? I've been on the Island for two days, and he's barely eaten a thing," David replied. "Jessie, I knew he was dieting, but he does eat, right?"

I looked at my brother suspiciously, wondering if he was he was slipping in a David innuendo.

Jessie smiled cautiously. "I think he's probably going to eat more while you are here. This is probably the first lunch he's had in months."

"I doubt that. If he's not going to eat for you, then he won't eat for anyone."

"What does that mean?" I glared at David.

"It means if you are not going to eat with your pretty girlfriend, why are you going to eat with me? What did you think it meant?"

"I don't know, I thought you were saying something else."

"Like what? Huh? There's no subtext here, Michael. Brother, please don't tell me that you looped already. That's kind of embarrassing. I expect more from you."

As she peeked at the menu, Jessie asked David why Monique was absent from our small party.

"I know, and that's really a shame, but she was called to New York for a last-minute photo shoot she just couldn't turn down. She's definitely sorry she missed you, but you'll meet her soon enough."

"It's fine. I was just curious. Michael also talks about her a lot. What kind of ad is she doing?" Jessie said nonchalantly, feigning an interest I knew she didn't have.

"It's some sort of group shoot with others," David said in the same blasé tone. "A passing of the generational torch thing. A few younger girls with her. For whom or what I don't know. It's probably a cosmetics thing at this point in her career."

"What do you mean at this point?" Jessie added. As the waiter buzzed by our table, I asked for another whiskey.

"And bring a bottle of the wine she's drinking," David quickly replied.

"I don't need," Jessie raised a hand.

"Doth protest too much. That was actually written by Shakespeare for that asshat, Al Sharpton. Now that's a little-known fact." David hoisted his glass to us, forcing me to extend my trembling hand. David and Jessie clearly noticed the shakes.

"To Jessie. I look forward to many more of these together," David said.

"So do I," Jessie punctuated the toast with a crooked smile and reached across the table to grab my fingers. "Michael, you are freezing. It's like ninety degrees today. How can you be cold?"

"I don't know what it is," I said before putting my cool, clammy palm to the side of my face. It felt like a fish. "Where'd the waiter go?

I really would like to eat something."

"You ran this morning, didn't you?" Jessie said.

"Yeah, I did."

"Did you eat?"

"Don't worry about it, no, I'm fine."

David quietly watched us ping-pong back and forth. "I didn't eat, no. I just figured I'd wait to eat a big lunch here," I explained.

Jessie shook her head and turned to David with her neck extended. "Did you eat breakfast?"

"Me? You joking? Of course, I'm in New York again this week. You think I'd pass up an opportunity to have onion and garlic bagels? I've got to indulge in all New York things while I can."

"See, Michael? Forget it. Let's not talk about that." Jessie stopped just short of exasperation. "There's only so much to say. You know, David, if I'm honest, I'm pretty disappointed Monique isn't here. It would have given our little toast and meeting some symmetry."

"That's true, but we know life isn't about symmetry. It…" David said.

Jessie didn't let him complete his thought. "I don't know about that. I pretty much believe life balances itself out, and everything comes full circle. Uh, David, when you were talking before about Monique's photo shoot, what did you mean at this point in Monique's career?" I scrambled for something to say, hopefully, to fill the dead air as my brother savored his wine.

"From what I said before? I don't know. I meant what I meant. Now she is pretty much about cosmetics exclusively." It was one of the rare times I saw David become defensive. "A few years ago, it might have been lingerie. I'm not sure why you picked up on those words. 'At this point' means at this point. She's older now, and the lingerie models today are usually younger, probably younger than you. And, well, probably thinner than ever."

Jessie grimaced and leaned into my brother's words.

"Thinner? From what I've seen, she's pretty thin. Women can't get much thinner," her voice went sharp.

David took a deep breath while looking quizzically at Jess. "Uh, well, she is, of course, but to be honest, there's always a younger, leaner, fresher, skinnier version of what they are selling and, ultimately, Monique is in the selling business. We all know she sells fantasy. To women, to guys, to whoever is buying or fantasizing. That's her reality.

"It's no secret it's a stealth cloak and dagger game of seduction and deception. I'm sure you know this year's model is always going to come along, and that's who people will glom onto. That's the world we live in. Remember Elvis Costello, album two. He nailed it with his music and then lived it. He was the guy, then he wasn't. Now, he's just a singer-songwriter again.

"I really don't know much about Elvis, but the pictures of Monique I've seen are...are..." Jessie was sitting at full alert while glancing into the space above my head.

"You're looking for airbrushed," David said, laughing.

"No, not really, I'm not." There was genuine defiance in Jess's voice. "She must be beautiful. Obviously, I don't know because we haven't met, but she is beautiful, right? I doubt she needs airbrushing." I coughed ostentatiously as if choking and called the waiter over to refill the water. I was hoping the Rob Lowe wannabe could take some of the acidity out of the air.

"You don't need to convince me. Of course, she is." David eyes inevitably narrowed slightly. "You're getting me wrong here," he said with his hand in front of his face. "I think my wife is the most beautiful woman in the world, no offense to you." Jessie waved him away, allowing him to continue. "And I'm the luckiest guy on the planet to be with her. Guys like me don't usually get to be with women like her.

"On the surface, you are right. But we all know that her marketable beauty is only going to last so long and with age, things change. She knows that. We don't have to like it, but we have to recognize the reality. It's our culture. She'd be the first to tell you, it's a short shelf life. And that's what I meant before by saying 'at this point.' She's made a great living, she still earns fantastic money, and I'm a beneficiary. I really don't have to worry while I work. I can write novels and reams of words about music. If it wasn't for her, I'd be like every other asshole with a Ph.D. who opines about rock music for a living. You can't beat it."

Jessie smiled with glassy eyes, tilting her head back to finish her wine.

David just continued as if on autopilot. "Mon knows it's all temporary, and she has to sell something else to people. If she makes the right decisions—and she will because she's really smart—people will buy into all those things because we have an insatiable need to stay young and beautiful."

"David, can you take a breath?" I said, frantically looking to both him and Jessie for answers. "Why do we have to wait so long to get served here? Is that usual in these restaurants?" Jessie completely ignored me and swallowed another glass of wine like she was sitting on the beach swigging Gatorade. David was oblivious—staring out the window into the lush green gardens or checking out the hostess who was seating couples at various tables across from us.

"I think I still see her in magazines, maybe they are Michael's old ones, I don't know," Jess said to no one. I spotted a few beads of sweat circling my cheeks with my napkin while the room slowly began to spin before my eyes.

"I don't buy the age limit you are talking about. Those are artificial limits. I don't believe it, and I don't want to believe it." Jessie was insistent, tapping her index finger on the edge of her dinner plate.

David grinned wanly with a shrug. "Two or three years in her business make a huge difference. If you don't think so, you are wrong. It's not a matter of belief, it just is."

"Okay, I'm wrong. I don't know if I'm wrong, but let's say you are right. That doesn't make it right, does it?" Jessie gratuitously cleared her throat as she peered toward the table of elderly men next to us.

"And what is right in this world?" David said, dead-eyed. "In the world Monique is in, it's right. It's all about business. Millions of women and men buy into it. They have to be doing something right. Right is relative in what they do. If you were making marketing decisions, it sure would be AOK. I think we agree on the ethics, but you arguing against the basics of advertising. You know ethics have virtually nothing to do with that."

"It's kind of ridiculous, don't you think?" Jessie said, topping off her wine.

I finally chimed in. "Well guys, I think we should order. You two look famished."

After a brief moment's pause, David asked, "And Jessie, you think that an entire industry built around the most beautiful and the thinnest of the thin is worried about being ridiculous? It is all fucking ridiculous. Tell me now, what isn't? It's about selling. Selling products, selling an image, selling a brand, selling an entire mindset to the world. You have to know this."

"But you agree it's the wrong message," Jess almost leaped out of her chair. "And kind of sad. It creates a ridiculous standard that women can't live up to. I look through magazines, and I know that I can't live up to what I see." Angrily, she brushed her hair off her shoulders with a long sigh. "It's frustrating to think about."

After a brief respite to nervously wipe the corners of her mouth, she went into overdrive. "What I'm saying is, I think what Monique does—and it's not about Monique, just whatever the big picture she kind of represents—well, those ads screw up a lot of women. I hate them. Not only do women think that we are supposed to be size zeroes or else there is something wrong, but their boyfriends seeing the ads think the women they are with don't live up to…"

"To what? The jerk-off fantasies? You are saying it's like porn," David said, accenting his words with a phony chuckle.

I quickly looked around to see if anyone was listening. The senior citizens at the table to our right were engaging in private conversations and smiling like they had one too many Lorazepams for breakfast.

David's words "like porn" reverberated through the room as I remembered the first time I saw one of Monique's ads after David told me he had married her. She was wearing a black bra and panties in a *Vanity Fair* I was reading while killing time during a baseball game rain delay.

I mindlessly fixated on how the tight, curving lines on the sides of her smooth stomach led down to each arcing pelvis. Without any impulse control, I unzipped my pants to rub one out before realizing what I was doing. It was crazy, borderline insane, wrong. Wrong squared with a dollop of unforgivable. My brain just shorted out, as it tended to do whenever I reached into my pants. I wasn't sure how I would ever face Monique upon meeting her. I knew I'd committed a chop-your-dick off sin.

David and Jessie continued talking, but nothing they said registered. My head had drooped so far down toward the table, it was practically sitting on the plate, like St. John the Baptist's.

"Michael, Michael, you okay?" David grabbed me by my right shoulder. I quickly popped up, pretending to be fully alert.

"Yeah, all good, fine and dandy, ready to go. Just need some water."

David stuck his fingers into his glass to playfully squirt droplets at me. "I bless you son, now wake up and join the conversation here."

"Jesus, now I'm getting hot," Jessie said while waving her hand in front of her face. "I think I've had enough wine. I'm not really saying it's like porn, but some of those ads, well, they make women feel bad and..."

"Guys feel good," I said deliriously with a honking laugh.

"Calm down, sober up. We'll order in a second. Jesus, you know you sound like a hyena," David demanded with Jessie looking on, seemingly embarrassed.

"I'm fine, I'm fine, I'm just following along and thinking of things. And I will add here that ads are why we read magazines." I was trying not to fall out of my seat.

"What? What the...Michael? That's most definitely not why anyone reads magazines. I don't know sometimes. Can you tell me what are you talking about?" Jessie seethed between her teeth.

When I looked at her, I thought I was squinting through a kaleidoscope. "I'm just listening in my own world here, and trying to put all the pieces together."

"The pieces together? What pieces?" Jessie's voice went sharp. "I mean do you ever look at those ads as a turn-on?"

"I'm not saying anything anymore. I'm going to listen to you two debate things. You should have your own radio show. Ads are ads. I don't think about them at all. Ever. I was just kidding."

"Now tell me, you see all those bra and underwear ads as turn-ons, Michael?"

"Yes, of course, he does. All guys do in some way. That's how they function," David answered while laughing.

"David, that's kind of gross, don't you think? How do you deal with it if you know guys are thinking about your wife that way? I'm not going to bring up the idea of your own brother...I mean that's way too sick. My God."

"Whoa, no, whoa, whoa, no, please, c'mon now. Who said anyone thinks about Monique that way? Jessie, you are crazy. Never in my life," I shouted just before the waiter finally arrived.

"Can I get you any appetizers?" The muscular, dimpled pinup towered over me.

"Where you been, my friend?" I whispered. "Definitely no appetizers. I think I'm going to have, well, I..." After checking the menu again, I didn't recognize any of the dishes. My choice was completely random. "Char-grilled branzino. Sounds like the guy who was choked to death in *The Godfather*. I'll have that."

"Beautiful fish. You'll enjoy it very much, sir," He replied as if he'd just made a left turn off the soundstage of *Upstairs Downstairs*.

"Aha, see that you guys, I'm having a beautiful fish. Can't wait to eat. David, what are you having?" I asked as the corners of the restaurant circled before me.

David gestured grandly over his menu, "I'll have...Jessie, you like lobster?"

"Well..."

"Don't worry. I want to know if you like lobster because then we will get two. I really don't want to get messy all by myself here."

Jessie looked to the waiter.

"He's not asking you, I am," David added firmly.

"Of course, I do," Jessie answered, now irritated.

"Two lobsters please," David demanded.

I was genuinely disgusted by their indulgence. "David, you're not seriously having lobster in the middle of the day?"

"Yup, Mike. And what did you order?

"Branzino. It's a beautiful fish."

"I'm going to the men's room before the food comes," David excused himself. "You two carry on. I'll be right back. I'm really not sure how we got talking about Monique and the ethics of what she does for a living, but that's fine. I'll see you guys in five minutes." He gently tapped me on the shoulder before glancing back at Jessie and walking away.

"Your brother is really condescending, and just as I expected him to be," Jess said after a Falstaffian gulp of wine. "Remember, I asked you about this? Well, I certainly hope he isn't always like this all the time. Is he? And Michael, why are you like you are today? You look like you are about to pass out. For God's sake, you had one drink."

"Is he always like what?"

"Does he always talk like he's lecturing someone? You don't find him obnoxious?"

"He's my brother. Of course, I don't find him obnoxious. That's who he is."

"You haven't seen your brother in years. He's been mostly absent from your life. You talk to him by phone, and you know who he is?"

She was going in and out of focus, but I managed to answer. "You've only met him for a half hour. That's hardly time to make a judgment. And you are asking me what's up with me? What's going on with you? You forget your holster? Why are you dressed like Wyatt Earp?"

"And you? You are in powder blue shirt and jeans? Who goes to lunch dressed like a Smurf? Michael, I..." She hesitated and added, "I like to dress like this. You never saw me dress when I went to clubs with my friends. With you, it's different. We just don't get dressed to do anything. Your brother is dressed in black, too. Somehow, I should have known that."

Jess aggressively fanned herself again before standing up. "Did you hear what he said? 'On the surface,' and 'you have to know this.' Let me translate those terms. Even a dummy like you should understand."

"Oh Jesus, stop Jessie. What time is it? It's gotta be almost nighttime already."

"Michael, it's barely three. You need to sober up fast. I need you to be present with me."

"I need to sober up yes, sure do, yup, but maybe you are over thinking things here. Just ignore him. That may be the best way."

"Michael, no, no, don't do that. I'm not being the bitch here. I'm just saying, I don't like being talked down to."

"Now stop with the bitch stuff. There is no one here accusing you of being a bitch. This isn't N.W.A," I giggled.

"What?"

"N.W.A. One of David's favorite bands."

"Of course. Why did I know you were going to say that? Who cares what his favorite band is?" She craned her neck to see if he was returning. "That does remind me. I have to ask him…"

"I don't want to know what you have to ask," I replied while wiping streams of sweat from my neck.

The waiter snuck in to apologize for the delay.

"Michael, are you going to make it through lunch?" Jessie demanded.

I wasn't actually sure. "I'm great, but what are they doing, reeling my beautiful fish out of the ocean?"

David finally sat while Jessie had her back turned. "Hey guys, the runner is right behind me. How are you two doing? Everything good? Where were we?"

And right on cue, the runner in a black uniform eased in next to me to put the tray on a folding stand. He carefully placed the large steaming lobsters in front of David and Jessie before presenting a plate with a fleshy fish in front of me.

"We were talking about music." I warily poked the steaming branzino with a fork.

"My kind of talk. That's a good change of pace. Jessie, do you like music? What do you listen to?" David surveyed his lobster while adjusting his napkin.

"I really don't think you would like what I like. I read your reviews. Michael told me some of the bands you think are great, and most of them I've never heard or don't like." Jessie was now in a new dimension of indignation as she sat back, seemingly uninterested in the lobster.

David cracked a lobster leg, "Well try me. What do you listen to?"

"I like the kind of bands you seem to hate. I don't know, but from what I can tell from all I've read of your work, my music is not your music. It seems like you dislike every popular band. You think most of the rock I listen to is superficial. You know David, you just said the word surface before. Well, I guess I just like surface rock. I read something by you about the band Husker Dü. I never heard of them. Michael gave me one of their records. You said they were one of the great bands of their generation. It sounded like noise to me. That's not why I listen to music. To be assaulted. That's not great." Jess's face flushed with her eyes on fire. "Those are the bands you always like."

David nodded agreeably, but his nostrils were twitching. "Don't say always. I don't write about anything in the always. That would imply I'm predictable. And I definitely do not think I'm predictable."

"From what I read, you clearly hate pop music," Jessie said as our water was being refilled by the waiter who was hovering like the spaceship in *Close Encounters of the Third Kind*.

"Who says I hate pop music? I love pop music. Chic is one of the greatest bands ever. Abba. Who doesn't love them?" David's replied.

"You wrote Mariah Carey over-sings, right?" Jessie insisted after finally biting into the lobster meat.

"That's true. She does. Great voice. Over-sings a lot." David barely looked up.

"You wrote long really negative reviews of Phil Collins and Journey."

"Self-explanatory."

"They are all good," Jessie said, laughing to herself and shaking her head. "I like them, and so do millions of people. I'll give you another example. I like Bon Jovi. I mean I really like him a lot. I think he's great. Michael told me you hate him. I don't get that. He writes music people can relate to—he writes about real people."

"Jessie, it's great you love Bon Jovi, and you are right, millions of people love him. But you can't be serious to say he writes about real people." David vigorously wiped his fingers like he was wringing someone's neck.

"What Bon Jovi plays is not what I'd call rock 'n' roll. To be honest, I think he's in the same business as the advertisers selling airbrushed fantasies. His music panders just as much as the ads you hate. His whole catalog is filled with fake songs about fake people. To me, there's the same kind of cynicism involved in selling that music as there is in selling bras and panties. And Bon Jovi is a prime purveyor of that."

After a long sigh, Jessie tossed her napkin on the table. "That's bullshit, and you know it. And guess what? I can't believe you just said purveyor with a straight face."

I couldn't stop digging into the branzino, which was the best thing I'd tasted in my life. The afternoon felt like a wild, hazy dream. Any anxiety about eating had completely vanished. I just kept shoveling down forkfuls of fish and broccoli while they talked. I figured at any minute, Jessie would turn into Ignatz Mouse and throw a brick at Krazy Kat David so we could all go home.

When Jessie moved her seat away from the table with a huff, she talked while completely oblivious to the waiter staring at her ass. "So wait, let me get this straight. You hate Bon Jovi, which is cool. We don't have to agree on that, and never will. But from what I've read and what you are saying…"

David interrupted her. "You don't need to continue to say from what you've read. If you want to know where I stand on something, just ask me. I'm right here."

"Fine, but what you've written represents what you think right?" With a flourish, Jessie pulled her hair back with her hands.

"Of course."

"Well then, you are always, not always, but you have frequently criticized our culture and pop music—like you did just now—of being superficial. And you do agree that the business Monique works in is the ultimate epitome of superficial American culture at its worst, yet you are not against reaping the benefits from that culture. You don't think that's a bit of a problem?"

"Uh guys, I'll be right back." My stomach heaved as I abruptly stood up. My feet tingled, and the floor felt uneven. "Hey, play nice. I need to go to the men's room. You can order dessert or something while I'm gone. Maybe you can talk about kittens in the summer rain for a change."

"Mike, you alright? You look like you are about to fall over." David reached out a hand while Jessie looked on with wrinkled brow.

"Michael, you are sweating so badly. You sure you are alright?" Jessie said. I looked down to see my sweat-stained blue shirt.

"Never, ever been better. Feel like James Bond with Domino Petachi." I walked very slowly with one hand extended towards the bar while waiting for a trap door to drop. The bearded, heavy-set bartender in a much too tight white dress shirt and bow-tie politely pointed me to the men's room.

It was immaculate with a waxed floor, bright fluorescent lights, sparkling stainless steel sinks, and expansive stalls. I carefully bent down toward the sink with the water running from the faucet. Breathing uncontrollably, I finally splashed my face and arms before making my way inside the stall at the far end of the room. Water dripped off my chin onto my pants while I sat fully clothed on the toilet.

Exhaling quietly and silently repeating, "Easy, easy, easy," I managed to wipe my face with bundles of toilet paper just as someone sat down a few stalls away. I remained frozen, listening to a man letting out an uninterrupted, laser-like piss at the urinal for nearly five minutes.

When I realized that there no choice but to go back and join the pleasant afternoon repartee, I began my slow, patient exit from the stall. After a few tentative steps, a *Point Break* wave of nausea surged through me. Everything I'd eaten rushed up from my toes. I pivoted toward the toilet to spew out an intergalactic stream of vomit until it felt as if branzino and broccoli were oozing out of my eyes. It was such a beautiful relief—all the poisonous alcohol had been purged.

After meticulously cleaning the toilet, I moved three stalls away from the scene of the crime and sat down with head in hands. I was exhausted—thoroughly depleted. And freed.

I finally felt calm enough to get on with the afternoon and ended up re-entering the restaurant with a smile after rinsing out my mouth under the faucet.

Of course, David was standing with his hands behind his head, just outside the door. "Where the fuck have you been? We've been sitting waiting for you."

"No worries in the world, brother. I just finished. I actually stepped outside before to get some air for a while. Such a beautiful day."

He immediately grabbed my arms and squared me by the shoulders. "Jessie asked me to check on you. What the fuck is wrong with you? She's rightly concerned. We've been waiting for nearly a half-hour. Let's go back. You want dessert?"

"Dessert sounds yummy, but no, I'm stuffed. That fish was delicious, though. Best I've had." On the way to the table, we passed a woman bartender with big almond eyes and ruby red lipstick. I could see Jess re-applying her makeup in the distance. "Are you two still arguing?" I asked David.

"We weren't arguing. It was a discussion. Interesting discussion." He tapped me on the back before I sat down at the newly cleaned table. Of course, I knew David was completely full of shit, but sometimes ignorance needs to be bliss, so I opted for a moment of happiness.

"He went outside for a breather," David said to Jessie who looked at me with a pained grin.

"Fresh air does wonders. I'm ready to run miles now," I smiled.

"I can drive you both back if you want or give you money to take a cab. Jessie, you had a lot of wine. We both have. If you want to take a cab, I'll drive Mike's car to his place. You two can drive to the hotel for your car tonight." David made a play for his wallet but Jessie nervously brushed him aside.

"We're fine. Thanks for the offer, but no we definitely don't need your money."

"Hey, I doubt we all will be going to many concerts together." I offered a fake laugh to Jessie, now sitting stone-faced.

"A small disagreement," David said. "Not everybody can agree on music. Some people like Pink and some people like Floyd."

My throat burned with the sour taste of vomit still in my mouth as we spent the few remaining minutes discussing the details of our upcoming trip to Boston while David paid the check. Just before we left, Jessie asked David if he'd ever move east again.

"Only if I had a genuinely compelling reason. You never know what life has in store for you," he said dramatically. "Only a fool makes plans. Just ask John Keats."

Jessie and I made our way home without a word. When Jess pulled into my apartment complex driveway, she grabbed my thigh. "Michael, I wish you hadn't disappeared on me."

"I didn't disappear. I just needed to get away."

"That was one long getaway. Not right at all." She aggressively yanked me back after I opened the car door.

"I don't know what to make of your brother. Not yet, at least. One minute he's pretends to be Prince Charming, and the next he's comes off like a cancer."

"Well, that's great, Jess. I don't think I'll tell him that." I was standing outside the car on an unsteady leg.

"Maybe that's really extreme. I don't know. But he seems…" She paused before putting the car in reverse. "He seems extreme. I don't know how to explain it."

"Maybe, it's more than words," I answered, smiling weakly.

"You know, I'm sure he hates Extreme, too," she said as I closed the door.

. . . .

"Michael, here is some water," Dr. Hampton was standing next to me. "What are you thinking about? You seem to be lost in something important. Are you alright? Has that Buddha feeling passed? Are you thinking about that? Or is it something else? Why don't we talk?

I audibly exhaled. Fatigued from the memory, I said, "I don't know if you want to hear it. It has nothing to do with what I ate. And it really doesn't have all that much with what I'm feeling right now or with any food today."

"It usually never does, Michael. That's the core of this. Let's sit down. Why don't you tell me what's really on your mind?

Part Four

What Was It You Wanted

Twenty-Three

"**A**re you alright, Michael? I'm going to turn the speed up a notch. You tell me if we are going too fast. You are going to begin to walk pretty quickly now. If it's too much just tell me. Use the bars on the side if you need them."

I stared ahead at the bright yellow wall with the cheap painting of a river headed to oblivion. The grooved treadmill belt was moving much more slowly than I expected. Doctor Vondu, the cardiologist overseeing the stress test, dutifully checked a large blood pressure monitor connected to the treadmill.

"You are doing fine. Don't think, just keep going. We only have a few more minutes to go. Everything is spectacular so far. Your blood pressure is great. Here we go Michael, you ready? These are the last two parts. Breathe and relax." His gentle voice never registered beyond a steady monotone.

When the treadmill kicked into another gear, I was forced to grab the bar with my right hand. Once I finally regained balance, my feet squarely pounded the rotating belt, and I knew I was home free.

The blood pressure cuff folded around my right bicep looked like a flotation device for a preschooler learning to swim. I must have looked ridiculous to Dr. Vondu, a kind, balding man with glasses and a classic white overcoat. It was tough to tell because he smiled like the Jack-in-the-Box clown throughout the test while making notes on a paper attached to his clipboard.

Out of the corner of my eyes, I could see Angie, the stately black nurse who had administered the echocardiogram of my heart.

"Here we go, Michael. How's your breathing? You feeling alright? You look great." Dr. Vondu's encouragement sounded straight out of a workout infomercial, but it was exactly what I needed to push through the anxiety. I was shocked by how strong I felt—completely free of the lightheadedness I'd suffered when I walked only months before.

"This is the last section. And you said you weren't going to finish, Michael. Once you put your mind to it, your body responded beautifully. Now you are going to be walking quickly, so be prepared. Don't try to run. I know your runner's impulse is going to kick in but don't. That's not what this is for. I'm going to push you and then it's done."

When the treadmill shifted gears, there was a quick, euphoric jolt of recognition throughout my body. It felt like I was taking the final steps before heading out onto the winding paths of Long Island all over again. My gait was so steady that I knew I could withstand whatever speed the treadmill could generate.

"I'm ready. Let's go."

My first few steps at the new speed were awkward, but I quickly adjusted to the timing of the belt and kept pace. My eyes remained focused on one small crack in the painting where the river met the horizon.

Even though I was merely walking like an octogenarian for a few lousy minutes, it seemed as if I was on Boylston Street after finishing the Boston Marathon. The muscles in my thighs were thrumming, and heat coursed through my knees. Once my breathing evened out and I adapted to the rhythm of my steps, I was ready to complete the test.

Finally finishing something felt exhilarating.

"You made it, Michael, excellent. You did that like a champ. We're going to slow it down now, taper off. Be careful. Adjust now. It's going to slow to a halt. You did great. You see? Remember all that fear you had when you walked in. Now, look where you are. Through the whole twelve minutes." Dr. Vondu leaned casually against the wall and quietly nodded his head to me.

"Angie, take the pictures of the heart—let's see where we are at. I'm very encouraged."

The treadmill eased, this time forcing me to grab both sidebars to maintain my balance. When the belt stopped, my momentum hurtled me backward. Dr. Vondu rushed to steady my shoulder. "Stand up straight and collect yourself. We'll get you unhooked so you can relax."

I huffed and puffed like a junkie running from the cops. After Angie released the electrodes, everything in the room—the pictures of the heart's anatomy on the wall and the numbers on the treadmill monitor—all came into focus. I stepped back to sit on the examining table. Angie was next to me with a smile and a cup of water.

"Relax, here have a drink. You are all finished. We'll just take one more look at the heart to see how it is after the test. Lie down now so I can take those tabs off. It's going to hurt a bit. You are lucky you don't have much hair. I feel genuinely bad for the Grizzly Adams guys. Take deep breaths and rest. The doctor will explain everything when we are done with this."

"How was my heart before the test?" I said through slow gasps. I had barely slept the night before while thinking there might be some kind of damage: a leaky valve, an irregular beat, or a knife wound in the center.

Angie never answered my question—she just gently smeared gel on my chest once again.

"Is silence good or bad?" I said with a faint smile.

"Doctor Vondu will go over every one of the tests, but in case you are worried Michael, you shouldn't be." She slowly caressed the wand over my heart. When the back of her slender wrist accidentally brushed up against my nipple, I felt a quiver in my running shorts. A small sign of life from the touch of a woman. Progress.

I smiled for the first time all afternoon.

"I knew I would see that big smile and bright eyes before I left." Angie wiped the gel off my skin with the finesse of an artist. "More smiling suits you. Now go out and face the world that way. We're all done here. The doctor will be in a minute or so."

I tied my badly weathered running shoes before pulling some of the frayed rubber off of the sides of the soles. After inspecting the cabinets for tissues and splashing my face with water from the sink, I strolled back onto the treadmill. An unsettling dream from the night before rushed back to me: I was running on a large, scaffold treadmill in front of thousands of people cheering for my death in The Los Angeles Memorial Coliseum. The belt furiously rotated while my father clocked the time. I woke up precisely when the floor dropped out and the machine swallowed me up like a snapdragon.

"Michael, I have good news," Dr. Vondu bounded into the room after closing the door. "I see you are ready for another run. It's best if you don't stand on the treadmill, though. Please come here and sit down."

He looked over the charts and x-rays. "I'm very pleased and you should be, too. I can see from the echo, it's clear that structurally, your heart is very sound. As you know, living like you have could have done serious damage, but you definitely have a runner's heart. You eating more again also certainly makes a difference. Your heart is very strong while your blood pressure is quite good. Perhaps on the low side, if anything. Make sure you keep yourself hydrated. We will get you more water. You need to drink. Have you been drinking enough?"

"Well, I just started again," I said while stealing glances at the x-rays from my seat on the examination table. They looked like blurry pictures of vaginas.

"Again? Meaning you stopped?"

"Uh, stopped for years. I actually didn't have a drink of water since I moved to Boston. Didn't start again until a few months ago." He cringed, put his palm under his chin and tapped the charts with his thumb.

"Okay, so you already know that was a very wrong path that will lead to problems you don't want to face. Damage to your kidneys and heart. Listen, I think you are on the right track, but you cannot veer off of it. I'm sure that Dr. Rigatta told you there is no safety net here. You have to use today's test as an affirmation that your heart is healthy, and you can do the things you doubted when you walked in."

"Do you think I can get back to running sometime?" I was ready to jog home.

"Eventually. You need to gain weight and drink plenty of water first. I recommend you start walking every day. Take long walks. Build up to running eventually. From what you told me about your running history, I'm sure you want to get back to that, but don't put the cart before the horse." He scratched his head. "Do they still say that? It doesn't make much sense anymore, does it?" His clipped, rhythmic way of talking in short declarative sentences relaxed me.

"You know what your priority is. One thing will follow the next. I can understand the desire to get back to running. Few things offer what running gives us. If you want to run, you do what you have to do to get yourself in the position to run. Your head is telling you to run again. This heart tells me you have the strength," he said with the x-rays nestled to his chest.

I hopped off the table to stand next to him with new confidence.

"Now, I want to see you back a year from now for another stress test. I expect it will be easier. Hopefully, if you follow the program Dr. Rigatta has set out for you, you will improve with leaps. I understand you have someone helping you with your nutrition."

"Yeah, he's out in the lobby waiting for me. He's a friend. We came over on the T, and we're going to get baseball tickets after this," I said, giddy with the dream of running free again.

"You are a lucky young man then. A lot of people are looking out for you. You realize if you keep to the program, you might even be running before I see you again next year.

"You should be happy. You have a good heart. Now it's up to you to be good to it." He gently tapped the clipboard on my arm.

"I'm sure others have told you this already, but your weight will go up when you take the weight off your shoulders. You've got a lot of living ahead of you. Embrace it. If you have any problems, don't hesitate to call my office. On your way out, I want Angie to record your weight."

I grimaced at the thought of getting on a scale.

"Don't look terrified. Embrace now, Michael, embrace." Dr. Vondu carefully raised his index finger. "One more thing before we go get weighed. Now that you are going to walk more and hopefully start running again, please get yourself some new running shoes." He spied my feet with a dismissive shake of his head. "You owe yourself that much. Those have seen their best days and many miles. Treat yourself right. We must be good to ourselves. That may be the first key to good health. I will see you outside on the scale."

. . . .

"Will you wait, for Chrissakes? Don't go Emmitt Smith on me now. Where you rushing to?" I yelled to Richie bounding up the steps of the Kenmore T stop. He reached the street level and waved me on.

"The doctor said you have to do more walking and climbing stairs is even better for you." I looked up at him standing square-shoul-dered with legs spread like a general, hands tucked into his San Jose Sharks hoodie. My legs were throbbing when I finally emerged onto the wet pavement dotted with patches of black snow from a late March storm.

Richie wrapped his heavy right hand around my shoulder and playfully yanked me ahead as I sidestepped a filthy, crushed green top hat left over from St. Patrick's Day.

We walked to the corner of Commonwealth Avenue and Brookline Avenue past construction on the site of the demolished legendary rock and roll club, The Rathskeller.

A cluster of construction workers in neon vests milled around the cordoned off area. "You know what they are building there?" I watched a patchwork, light-blue station wagon attempting to parallel park into a curb space fit for a VW bug.

Richie was walking backwards down the sidewalk. "I think a hotel. I really don't know much about this area, but a lot of my clients tell me it used to have charm. Looks like just another street to me. How much character can a place with Pizzeria Uno have? I do love the Citgo sign, though."

He gazed up at the towering neon monolith, which always evoked the Red Sox for me. "When I was growing up watching games from Fenway on television, I'd always see that and think if I played here someday, I could hit a ball off of it." Richie laughed knowingly. "Stupid, stupid."

We stood silently on the sidewalk, looking up at the faded, chipped sign towering above the square. "You know, you realize you didn't have to come all the way down to the hospital with me. You have to have better things to do," I said. When Richie offered to accompany me for the test, I felt as if he was doing it out of some kind of obligation.

"Nobody has to do anything. I came along because we all need some moral support when taking those tests. I came to de-stress the stress test. How's that?

"I also had a conversation with one of the nutritionists of eating disorder program while you were taking the test. Dr. Rigatta is encouraged by your progress. I know she's told you that. She talked to the program head about it. He contacted me and said the nutritionist there wanted to know more about the things we are doing. Basic stuff, but they are always looking for ways to help the patients. That's the way it should be."

When the light changed, I wandered into the street. "Wait, Dr. Rigatta said she was encouraged after only three months. You're shitting me."

"I'm not, my friend. Mike, you've been starving for over three years. You've gained weight in three months by eating real food. They know that's great."

Gained weight. Two words—two nuclear bombs. I stopped right in the middle of Comm. Ave. as a bus passed. Richie barely noticed and kept walking before abruptly halting near the curb. "Will you come on? The light is going to turn green." He marched back to grab me by the arm. This time he pulled like he was yanking a recalcitrant dog. His hand could have snapped my forearm in half with a quick twist.

"Where the heck are we going? Fenway is back there," I said, pointing with my thumb over my shoulder. I was momentarily paralyzed. Had I been putting on pounds too quickly?

"I'm hungry," Richie said over his shoulder. "Let's stop in at Bruegger's, and get some bagels. I haven't had lunch. You haven't had anything since before we left for the hospital. Then we'll get tickets."

"No, I'm not eating anything," I yelled as I walked ahead after he released me. I let out my frustration just before stepping onto the sidewalk. "Now wait, let me get this straight. You went down to the hospital with me to see the nutritionist with the eating disorder program as what? A trainer? So maybe you can get some new clients? Should I interpret it as a business opportunity? Don't tell me anorexia is going to become a cottage industry for you now."

Right after the words slipped from my mouth, I knew I'd made a terrible, impulsive mistake. Life has no delete key, though.

We ended up facing each other on the corner of Commonwealth Ave. and Kenmore Street. Richie braced me with his hands on my shoulders as an elderly man and a woman—still bundled up in scarves and parkas—walked past us. It had begun to drizzle.

His dancing eyes prepared me for whatever admonishment was coming. "Normally, I'd either tell someone to fuck himself or most likely, I'd deck him for saying something like that, but that's just not going to happen. That's what you want. You are not going to do this to another person. Not this time.

"You heard you are gaining weight, and you are acting like an asshole to drive the people around you away. That's what you do. That's all you know. I'm sure that's what you did with your girlfriend and with God knows how many other people in your life."

He jabbed his finger in my face. The veins in his neck, thick as lawn hoses, were popping through his skin. "I bet you think I'm getting paid to help you? Am I right?"

"I don't know. Yeah, well of course." I had always thought David and Mon had hired their friend to fix me.

"You are a piece of work. Don't you get tired of living this way? I've known your brother for over two decades. I've been friends with Mon for well over ten years now. I trained her, and she helped me get my business off the ground. But we are all friends, and we will always be. They were desperate to help you, so they reached out to me. I've been glad to do it, and I'm going to help you beat this. You being a prick is not going to change that.

"I recognize why you are like this right now, so you better get over it. You are not going to derail this day just to go home and sit in the dark. That's what comes easy to you. You've been coddled your whole life, and now it's time to get real. I consider you my friend, so now we are going to get some bagels and tickets to see Ichiro play baseball because baseball makes us happy. And it's damn good to be happy. Why is that so hard for you to understand?"

He let go of my shoulders and marched off towards the entrance stairs of Bruegger's to leave me standing limply in shame.

I knew I couldn't let another person walk away from me. "Richie, wait up. Hey, I'm sorry. I really am, I swear. I don't know what happens. It's like the Hulk. I get so fucking crazy. I normally don't say anything, I just…"

Richie paused momentarily as a pretty blonde closed her umbrella while smiling at him. "You just withdraw. I know. That's not going to happen now. What you are used to doing is turning the Hulk on yourself, so yell away. I guess it's progress you are redirecting your anger at me. That's okay for today.

"For. Today. But I'm telling you from now on, if you ever say anything like that again to me, I will break your jaw. You will be drinking nothing but smoothies through a straw for months. You understand? Maybe your girlfriend should have broken your nose or something. Someone needs to call you on your bullshit." Stepping back and quietly exhaling, he reached out to me. "We straight?"

I tentatively shook his hand. "I'm sorry, I really am."

"I heard you the first time. Apology accepted. Now don't use it as an excuse to beat yourself up. We're already moving on."

We waited in a long, snaking line in Bruegger's—the sweet aroma of onions and garlic gave me a contact high. Richie leaned back towards me while staring at the menu. "I'm going to get a dozen. I have an idea. After we get tickets, we're going to change things up a bit. Why don't you just head back with me? You can stay the night in the extra bedroom. Monique told me you have been staying over with her sometimes. Since she's in New York, I know you can use someone to talk to."

"C'mon, no, I really don't think I can. You don't want me at your place. Not after today, not after all that," I said, pointing to the street.

When Richie laughed dismissively—there were small crow's feet around his eyes. I'd never noticed them before and realized he was older than David. "We're done with that," he said. "Over. Someday you're going to want to break my jaw, too. Give me one reason why you can't."

"I don't have any clothes. What am I going to sleep in?'

"We're not having a week-long sausage party. I have t-shirts. It's one night. There is plenty of room, so that's one lame-ass excuse. You have your own television if you want to hide in the bedroom. If not, we can watch ESPN or there is probably a Celtics game on."

"I'm not really good without my routine. It's kind of..."

"Different, I know. I know you better than you think, Michael."

The sales clerk, no older than nineteen with freckles and frizzy auburn hair pinned back, asked Richie to order. "What kind do you like?" he said, facing me.

"Anything. I haven't had a bagel since the night stabbed my arm. I never got to eat that one. I know Monique told you about that."

"Oh yeah, Edward Scissorhands, I heard that story a while ago." He covered his face with his hand, feigning embarrassment. "Pick a flavor will you."

The smell of the onions worked subliminally.

"Good choice. Hi, Miss, we'll have four onion, four sesame, two garlic, and two poppy. I want one of the sesame now with cream cheese." Richie watched the girl calculating bagels in her head. "What do you want on the one to eat now?" he asked over his shoulder.

I hesitated, still replaying my ugliness in the street. "Nothing on it."

"Give me one onion too with a slight graze of cream cheese. Like a sad schmear," he said to the beaming teenager. We waited while watching the thin girl fumble with a knife after bagging the dozen. Finally, Richie broke the silence. "So, you are coming over, right?"

"You're not going to play Bon Jovi records, are you?" I said.

"Ah yes indeed, boy, your brother gave me the lowdown on that crazy Jon Bon Jovi dynamic between you all."

I grinned in deeper shame. "You probably only got the Cliff Notes to that narrative. Jess and David together could get crazy ugly, fucking bad, especially the last few years."

The freckled girl handed Richie the bag before placing the plated bagels with cream cheese out on the counter.

"You still have Jessie's poster of Bon Jovi in your apartment by any chance?" he said while handing me the paper plate.

"I sure do. I don't know, I just couldn't toss it."

Richie took a healthy bite of the bagel before speaking with his mouth half full, "Why did I know that? You have to ask yourself why that's one of the last things standing."

After draining half of the bottle of juice, he added, "Think of it this way, if you stay at my place, it's just one less night you have to stare at Bon Jovi. Pathetic, Mike, pathetic. Throw the damn thing out. Someday, it's gonna feel real, real good when you do. Like your letting go of something from deep inside of you. Trust me. Now, let's go get tickets. One day I'm gonna buy you a Fenway Frank. Something to look forward to."

Twenty-Four

I examined the tickets and carefully folded them into my wallet as Richie peeked into the tunnel of the Auditorium T stop. A pretty, petite Chinese girl with oversized horn-rimmed glasses was playing the saxophone solo from "Jungleland" on violin with her instrument case open before her. A sizable crowd had gathered. Richie approached me with starry-eyed wonder at the girl's dexterity and lyricism.

"Damn, she's so good. Has to be a student. The thing I've learned from my short time here is that the only Asian people in this city are students. Kind of weird, isn't it?" He was swaying like a teenager lost in the music. "I never realized Boston was so..."

"White?" I punctuated with a muffled laugh. "It's no accident Kevin White was mayor for so long here. It doesn't get more vanilla. I feel like I'm living in a low-rent Woody Allen film." I squatted to stretch my calves while watching a woman next to me in aqua Nikes marking up a worn copy of *Infinite Jest* with a red pen. As the final mournful chords of "Jungleland" lingered in the underground station, there was scattered, but enthusiastic, applause.

Richie strolled over and dropped a five-dollar bill in the violinist's case. "If I had a ten, I'd give her one."

I was long past tired and felt like taking a nap on the bench beneath an advertisement for Keith Lockhart and the Boston Pops. We'd walked from Fenway Park to the Massachusetts Ave. stop so Richie could buy Pearl Jam's *Binaural* at the Tower Records located above the station. "I am really stiff and cramping up. My legs are killing me," I said.

"It's because your muscles have probably atrophied, and you've already done more exercise today than you have in three years. If you keep walking like the doctor said, it will all go away." Richie offered me some of the bottled water he bought at Store 24. I casually waved him off as the girl broke into a languid version of Nirvana's "All Apologies."

"Jesus, I think I could fall in love with her. And I love this song too. You see how cute she is behind those glasses?" Richie said.

He eerily read my mind. She was wearing Doc Martens and a plaid skirt over black tights. Such thin hips and lovely eyes. "That girl's about 20 years old," I whispered.

"Okay, you're saying I'm getting too old for college girls?"

"I would think so, yeah for fuck's sake. She's closer to my age. Thing is, I know the little girls understand, and they'll go after an older you instead of a younger me all day, every day. All you gotta do is give them that arm flex you like to do. What do you do spin your t-shirts in the dryer like fifty times so they shrink to Bart Simpson size?" The woman put *Infinite Jest* away in her leather briefcase and grinned cautiously before letting out a giggle.

Richie glanced at her stepping away from us. "Alright, I'll give you the license to break balls today. Laugh away. But you know what you need to do is to get back in the saddle sometime soon. You should be going over there and dropping money in her case to say hello."

The sharp metallic scraping of steel on steel screamed out of the tunnel. I incrementally stepped forward towards the tracks, and finally saw a headlight. "No worries, we're out of here. I hear the train a coming." Richie was focused on the violinist, his right hand undulating to the music.

I thought about the tickets in my wallet again, still disappointed David would not be going to the game. He had told me there was no chance he'd be back before September. All I wanted was for all of us to enjoy a game together while sitting under the sun, but I'd come to realize that I needed to temper my expectations—they were never going to coincide with reality.

The train slowly crept into the station as the girl segued into "Over the Hills and Far Away." We waited as the crowd huddled before the car.

Richie tapped my arm as I walked towards the T. "Wait Mike, how much money you got on you?"

"What? I don't know. I don't carry much cash. I charged the tickets."

"Check how much you have." The doors to the car slowly pried apart, and people jostled in. I quickly looked through my wallet to see a five and three singles.

"Give me the five." Richie said with eyes alight.

"For what?"

"Michael, give me the five," he ordered. I hesitantly handed it over.

He immediately gave the bill back to me. "Good, now go over and put it in the girl's case."

I stood motionless. Richie implored, "Go now, and let's get on the damn train."

I dropped the money in the case. It evoked a smile from the girl, who was now completely enveloped in the music at her fingertips. Richie and I leaped onto the train just before the doors closed. As we sat down in the middle of the car, he grabbed a *Boston Phoenix* off the seat in front of us.

"Didn't that feel good?" he said. "See her smile at you? Gotta love that. Those are the smiles that keep us going. Five bucks is a small price to pay for that."

The T stuttered towards Kenmore, forcing everyone standing to rock backward. Richie opened the *Phoenix* and gazed out the window towards the dark tunnel. "You ever read this?" he asked over his shoulder.

"The *Phoenix*? Only for the concert ads."

When we hit Kenmore, our car emptied out. A beautiful, athletic Filipino girl, no older than me, grabbed a handrail across from our seat. She stood shoulders back with long black hair falling to the side of her breasts. A woman with a bad wig whispered something in her ear. The girl thought momentarily before breaking into a lovely, relaxed smile.

Her dark charcoal sweater and leggings muted the radiance of her lustrous skin. With such fully, defined lips and easy confidence, she reminded me of an extremely exotic shade of Christina, my teenage kryptonite. Fearing an oncoming involuntary grade-school hard-on, I quickly adjusted my place in the seat. "Rich, give me that water—I really need a drink."

He handed over the bottle with his head still buried in the newspaper. "You know I read an article about the Catholic Church in here. About these creepy pedophile priests. It actually made me embarrassed to be a Catholic—it gave me such nightmares," he said while briskly leafing through the pages.

The girl was laughing conspiratorially with her friend. She stood with her right hand on her hips, as if the train belonged to her. And, of course, it did. All the men's eyes had gravitated her way. A goateed teenager, wearing a Dead Kennedys t-shirt, was slumped in a seat, head between his knees. He gleefully spied the graceful curves of her long legs.

She seemed far out of place in Boston with a real-deal tan—not a trace of the typical sun lamp crisp of club girl poseurs. "Michael, are you listening?" Richie followed my eyes and shook his head. "Of course, you aren't. Did you hear one word I said?"

"I heard you. I did. Fuck those priests. They should all be in jail. I read that article, too. But what do you expect from this Irish Catholic city?"

"You know that old sayings, `life's a bitch but karma's a whore—she will fuck you good every time?' Someday, every one of those priests' karma will arrive in jail in the shape of a big, ugly, fat cock."

Richie quickly looked around the car with paranoia. "Okay nice, now tell me really how you feel? That's not some old sayings, that definitely sounds like a David sayings."

I acknowledged him with a smile. "Probably right, think it is, but forget those sick, pedo priests for a second or two. Look at that girl over on my left. You can't have skin like that and live in Boston.

"No way you survive this kind of winter with that glow." I took another sip of water. I simply couldn't remember the last time I had such an urge—a desperate need—to fuck again. It seemed so startlingly primal and unfamiliar. I was embarrassed by my desire but thrilled to be turned on. I had forgotten what it felt like.

Richie folded the *Phoenix* as he squared himself in the seat. "Why don't you stand up? Either right here or walk across to that side of the car way in the back. Make her notice you. Don't go anywhere near her and be an ass, just get in the field of vision."

"No, that's too weird. It's too obvious. How am I going to make her notice me? She must be deep throating some tall boyfriend with big muscles every night," I said, recoiling and redirecting my line of sight.

The car emerged out of the Kenmore tunnel into daylight onto Commonwealth Ave.

Richie tugged at my shirt. "You know, I'm actually surprised you've ever seen a vagina in your lifetime. Just stand like you are stretching your legs, for God's sake."

"When I was running, and Jessie and I first started going together I might have, but not now," I whispered as he rolled his eyes. "Look at her. C'mon, be serious." Just as the car headed past Boston University toward the Paradise rock club, a small boy in a Red Sox hat jumped out of the seat in front of us and ran to his parents next to the girl.

"See, lookie, the kid there has more balls than you. Did you really just get out of an extended relationship?" Richie collapsed the paper in his lap. "When did your confidence go into the toilet? You know let's get real, I think what you really need most is to get laid again. That will give you a boost. I think you need to come to the gym, and hang out. There are women who are even hotter than your girlfriend over there. Now I know the kind of girl you like. I will find one for you."

The car sputtered and stopped again just past Star supermarket. "No, you won't—thanks very much. And no gym for me. I won't fit in. I just don't fit," I said as the seats emptied out.

"It's not about fitting in—it's about showing up. Who said eighty percent of life is showing up? It's true. Just be a part of something. Worse comes to worst, maybe someone will give you a charity hump." Richie let out a silly laugh.

"Just come by. I will introduce you to some women." He paused, pawed through the paper one more time and added. "And by the way, your next, almost, nah, never girlfriend with the tight ass just walked out of your life. Next time you have to make her know you exist."

I looked out the window to catch my vision of Christina walking past two leering cops into an Indian restaurant. A hunched back man in a Bruins cap sat in front of us.

"Rich, hey, do you pick up most of the women at the gym? Do you date your clients?" Looking at the back of the man's head, I mouthed silently, "Do you fuck your clients?"

Richie covered his face with his free hand as he placed the bag of bagels between us. "No, no, no, it's bad for business. The last thing you want is to be known as a predatory trainer."

"But it must be tempting," I said with raised eyebrows.

"Life is tempting. It's all around us. Sometimes you yield, and sometimes you hold the line. But you need to at least allow yourself ..." Richie stopped when the man tilted his head in to listen. He dragged me by the shirt to the back of the car.

"You can't live like this. You need to allow some temptation into your life. You've built up a wall that nothing penetrates. No food, no women, no pleasure. It's just impossible to go on like that. We are not wired that way.

"Brother, let me tell you a story," he said, taking a bite from a bagel. "I'm not sure why I'm telling you this, but I feel like you need to hear it. I was in Los Angeles about seven years ago before I was married. I was still struggling with my baseball career was over. I was really lost just like you. Feeling everything you are feeling. Just numb. You know my whole life since I was a kid was geared to playing ball, and it disappeared.

"When I lost that hope, there was nothing. It was like the world ended. Your brother and Monique really helped me when I did some weird shit. They've always been there for me. I was running out of money, taking painkillers, drinking."

His words surprised me, and I wondered if he was bullshitting just to make me believe there was a community of broken people. Over our three months together, I'd never heard him mention drugs or alcohol. I thought Richie spent his life mainlining wheat germ and yeast. He finished the bagel and stood up. "It's Harvard Ave. We can walk to my place from here. You need to walk. That's why we didn't take the C line."

While we ambled down Harvard Avenue towards Coolidge Corner, Richie told me about how he channeled his anger into exercise, which replaced baseball as his new obsession. By the time we got to his apartment building, Richie had described years of maniacal training, uncomfortably reminiscent of my routine before I stopped eating.

As the elevator took us up to the fourth floor, I couldn't help but think about what would have happened to my life if I had taken the off-ramp towards health instead of the detour to the boneyard. When the elevator doors opened, a woman with a pixie cut and a tight, lavender t-shirt stepped back, startled. "Oh, c'mon Richie, you scared me."

She extended her palm as an invitation to step forward. We both entered the hallway as she tugged at her sweats and yanked the bottom of the shirt. Her breasts were big enough to tip over her small body.

"Amanda, this is my friend, Michael." Richie casually waved to me. "Amanda teaches English at Northeastern. She lives next door. You two sure have a lot in common." The elevator closed, but Amanda remained standing in the hallway. "Mike has a master's degree in literature. He's having dinner here. Have you eaten? I'm just about to cook."

Amanda smiled hesitantly before pressing the elevator button again. She raised her thin, finely chiseled arms to the back of her head while thinking momentarily. "I was going to get my mail, but I haven't eaten...."

I definitely did not want her to join us and forced a quick smile, hoping she was going to say she had plans for anal with the boyfriend.

Richie pointed towards his door after touching her shoulder affectionately. "Why don't you stop by, and eat with us? I have plenty of food. You like scallops and angel hair pasta?"

The elevator arrived—this time she stepped inside. Amanda squinted while tapping the doors to keep them open. "Who doesn't like scallops? It will take me a little bit, though. I need to take a quick shower and change."

Richie, suddenly transformed into Rachael Ray, applauded cheerfully. "I'll cook something extra special just for you. Take your time. We have all night. Just come on in when you're ready. We'll see you in a while."

When Amanda disappeared, Richie shrugged.

"Aha, now that's how it's done," I said. "A twinkle of the eye, some scallops, and you end up playing hide the cannoli. I bet you're sorry I'm here tonight."

He struggled to open the door to his roomy apartment. "I did it because you are here, Mike. Amanda and I are just friends. She's a sweetheart. Really hot too, am I right? It'll be good for you. You two can discuss *Crime and Punishment* or something. When was the last time you ate dinner with a pretty woman who wasn't your sister-in-law?"

"Wait, let me figure this plan out," I laughed. "You want me to eat dinner with someone I don't know, and sleep over, all in one night? You're kidding. You know that's a bit much for me to handle. I honestly think I might have been better off letting you break my jaw before."

Twenty-Five

Monique looked fatigued as she waited for me outside the café Better Latte Than Never in the heart of Harvard Square. She was huddling in the doorway with hands stuffed into the pockets of a motorcycle jacket covering a white New Order "Bizarre Love Triangle" t-shirt. Wild gusts of wind had cooked up amidst ominous rain clouds overhead. As I approached, a teenager with a wispy beard, chiseled features, and a wiry, angular body, decked out in a neon lime colored windbreaker and skinny jeans, moved in next to her. It seemed like I was walking into a Jean-Jacques Beiniex directed perfume ad.

"Hey Mon, so how was New York?" I said. The kid never moved when Monique gave me a quick hug. He tapped me on the shoulder and asked if I had a cigarette. When I demurred, he checked out Mon as if appraising a statue. "You?" he mumbled.

"Someone must have told you smoking is bad for you?" Mon pushed the door open while the kid continued to eye her body.

He stepped onto the sidewalk and caressed the carefully curated scruff on his chin. His jacket had the Stiff Records logo neatly monogrammed on the right side of the chest. "Someone must have told you life is bad for you. You probably wouldn't know about that, would you?" he sneered.

"Move on little stiffie," Mon said through gritted teeth.

He walked away with hunched shoulders, flipped her the bird and shouted, "If it ain't stiff, it ain't worth a fuck, bitch."

"What a silly mutherfucker. Now that's a Harvard trust fund punk who wouldn't know Lene Lovich if she sat on his face. What a douchebag. I'm losing my patience with people these days, Michael." Mon yanked off her beret before surveying the small café. She carefully aligned the part in her hair.

"Sounds like you had a really fun time in Manhattan. You're so cheery," I said, a bit unfamiliar with Monique cursing like Richard Pryor and so easily irritated. We found a table near the window just before a waitress handed us the menus. The girl with ink-black, asymmetrical hair—probably a part-time keyboard player in a damaged art noise band—refused to make eye contact with either of us.

"Something to drink?" she asked after I took my sweatshirt off.

"Herb tea please," Monique said without hesitating. I flashed back to my brunch with Mon on a summer day in the coffee shop in Manhattan, just after Jessie and I met. It seemed like a distant memory from sunnier times. A lifetime had been lived in the interim.

With Jessie, Les, and David all gone, my existence revolved around meetings with Mon and Richie. I had no friends and didn't want any. How could I even begin to explain what I was going through to outsiders? My neighbors always kept their distance. I was the forgotten crack addict in the building—a phantom neither seen nor heard.

My appointments with Dr. Hampton and Dr. Rigatta felt like moments out of time in an incubator, sealed off from real life. All of the restaurants and café talks with Monique took on a heightened importance and became the only real contact I had with the outside world. She was retraining me in Eating 101 while also reinforcing the basic fundamentals of living.

"I'll have a Diet Coke," I whispered to the waitress standing next to my chair.

Monique smiled with a slight roll of her eyes. "Uh yeah to start, but the next choice better be something you can chew. I'll have the roasted eggplant sandwich and sliced pears, please. That sounds yummy," she said while cleaning her knife with the napkin.

I considered ordering toast, but some kind of lunch was ultimately mandatory because I could not disappoint Mon, and I knew how important it was to prepare for David's return. There was no way I would let down him down.

I was determinedly persevering despite my worst instincts. The only thing justifying my consistent eating was the hard, undeniable truth: I felt so much better—more energetic and alive.

I wasn't sleeping until afternoon or early evening anymore. There were doctor appointments to keep, and Monique and Richie called me every morning to make sure I was out of bed by noon. At first, it was difficult to realize those were good things, but I knew dreaming the day away would eventually lead to dreaming my life away.

Honestly, I only had one genuine motivation to eat, though—running again. The next time I got on that fucking treadmill with Doctor Vondu, I would be running, even if he told me to walk.

Monique toyed with her phone while bobbing her head to Donna Summer's "She Works Hard for the Money" playing on the sound system.

"You okay?" I said.

"Yeah, I'm fine," she answered with a sigh before waving for the waitress. "I just have a lot going on that's all. Nothing for you to worry about. How are you? You look better. Some color in your cheeks. Tell me, how's things going with Richie? I was thrilled to hear things went so well with the cardiologist. Hearing you happy about something was so great. I'm sorry I wasn't there with you. The last three weeks have been crazy. I'm also sorry we didn't talk more." She checked her phone one last time before placing it in her purse.

"Mon, stop apologizing. You sound like me," I smiled weakly.

When the waitress returned to the table, she took a double take at Monique before squinting at me. She was probably thinking, "Is this skinny bitch the best you can do, lady?"

"I'll have a turkey sandwich," I said with the panic instinct fully kicking in. I figured I could eat half, and send the rest of the demon turkey to its next life in the garbage.

"What kind of bread?" the waitress asked with quick a glance at a woman hobbling past our table.

"Whole wheat." White bread definitely held no wonder for me.

"Mayo?" she replied, bored.

"No, no," I bleated out. The waitress gave me a half-lidded, what-the-fuck sigh.

"You have to put something on it, Michael, no one eats a dry sandwich," Monique interrupted. "The goal is to make food appetizing again. Give him mustard."

It seemed silly—I wondered what the hell was wrong with a bareback sandwich as rain began pelting the windows with force.

Without looking directly at Monique, I said, "So when is David coming back? I spoke to him last week—he sounds kinda weird. He just didn't sound like he was having very much fun at all over there."

She grabbed her neck and stretched her shoulders back as the waitress slipped our drinks before us. "It's not fun. He's working. It's going slowly, so I genuinely don't know when he's going be back."

"I guess work is work, but he sounded kind of disconnected when I talked to him. I'm used to the hearing the jump in his voice over the phone. Like he's going to pop through the line. You know what I mean? Like David. I really miss seeing and talking to him."

Mon quietly circled a spoon through the tea. "I wish he was here, too. I do, but there's nothing you can do. I'm sure he's fine." There was an unfamiliar uncertainty in her raspy voice, and her weary eyes betrayed the meticulous makeup. She collected drooping, wayward strands of hair with her index finger before tucking them behind her ear.

"Michael, why are you so stooped shouldered? You look like a hunchback. What's going on?" I was surprised Monique noticed. My back had been hurting for months—getting out of bed each morning had become increasingly difficult.

"I don't know. It feels like I'm carrying a piano. I think I need a massage or an execution. I can't tell if it's an extension of all the other aches and pains or if it's something new."

"It's that old damn lumpy mattress you are sleeping on. That should have been the first thing you threw out." Mon turned animated. "You should have burned that damn thing. How can you sleep in it after all this? After all you know. Oh, my God. Buy yourself another one, even if you intend to move. You can't wreck your back. I'll buy you a new bed set."

"No, you are not buying a mattress. I will get one. I promise."

"Okay, I'll leave it at that. Get one soon. I'm going to make sure. I may do a bed check every so often. Now c'mon, tell me what's going on with Richie. I spoke to him last week, and he told me you slept over his place the night you saw the doctor." The small café was emptying out as our food arrived. The plate lingered before me for a few minutes.

"You feeling better working with Richie?" Mon took a quick bite of her sad, wilted sandwich and leaned in while she waited for an answer.

"I do. Working with him is good and hanging out is fun too, but I think he's trying to set me up with girls half the time we are out. You know he invited his neighbor over his place to eat with us that night? Some teacher from Northeastern. And I've got to tell you the truth, I don't think he was really setting me up. You know bottom line, I think he was setting himself up. Each time we're out, he keeps introducing me to different women. I kinda believe he's really interested in them."

Monique held the cup of tea before her mouth while smiling momentarily. "That sounds like Richie."

I bit into the corner of my sandwich, hoping no one in the café was watching. "It sounds like Richie because…now, Mon, don't leave me hanging here. He gets a lot of women, yes? He's always got the flex going and that sly eye flutter he makes when he talks. He's an easy guy to be around, so he must be knee deep in women."

"Uh, well I didn't need that image, thanks, but how much you want to know about Richie?" Mon said. There was a manic glint in her eyes.

I suddenly realized that maybe a little ignorance goes a long way with all new friends. "This doesn't sound too good. Does he fuck goats or something?"

Mon raised her eyebrow and whispered, "Not goats. Richie ruined his marriage because he, well…let's just say he has a…call it a weakness." She delicately wiped the corners of her mouth with a napkin and looked around at the empty tables. "His wife Jane was great. She would have done anything for him. She did do everything.

"She's an accomplished lawyer—a high stakes prosecutor in San Francisco. And a gorgeous Thai beauty. I mean gorgeous. But he slept with some twenty-three-year-old Vietnamese girl who was his massage therapist. Jane caught them in his car by the gym of all places. What a fucking idiot. Excuse me, you know I don't speak like this, but sometimes…"

I squirmed in the booth at the thought of Richie's wife watching him fuck in a car. Mon spoke with seen-it-all nonchalance. "Oh, that girl was only one of many, though. The sad truth is some people don't know how to get out of their own way, and Richie is one of those guys. He has the best intentions. I mean he's so sweet, but he has a self-destructive detonator he can't help but press sometimes.

"And he knows better. Ever since his career washed out—he was supposed to be a guaranteed major league player—he's been compensating, I guess. He still regrets not making it. He used to talk about this all the time when he trained me. He's such a fantastic trainer. He made me go places I never thought I could. He's so patient." She smiled to herself. "Fantastic trainer who can't train himself.

"I think since the injury, he's been trying to fill the void. Maybe all the conquests give him back the sense of power he lost. I don't know and can't explain it. I'm not going to analyze him, but all I know is he…" She finished her tea and flagged the waitress.

"He was in a relationship before he met Jane with this wonderfully friendly and pretty Chinese pro tennis player. He screwed that up by sleeping around also. David says he goes after more pussy than Purina. I'm being terrible here, I know."

The waitress returned to refill Mon's cup. I gave her the thumbs up, even though I had barely eaten a quarter of the sandwich. "Richie sleeps around. Who'd a thunk it?" I said, laughing.

"Not with anyone." Mon was now slumped in the booth. "The dirty truth is he's got yellow fever. I don't know if you'd call that a fetish or not. He just loves—I'm not sure that's the word—he's got a thing for Asian women. Typical juvenile attraction to the exotic. Of course, Jane is Thai, but she's a woman, if you know what I mean. I think she intimidated him. Ever since I've known Richie, he's been chasing younger Asian girls. That's his weakness."

I started laughing uncontrollably. "You are seriously shitting me. I don't believe it."

Mon waited until I calmed down. "I don't want to know why that is somehow funny to you. Are you guys watching Asian porn together? That's probably where it all starts."

"No, no, but I now know why he doesn't really like Boston too much. Now this, I really need to know more about."

"I'm being bad here, but I feel like gossiping today," Mon said, hesitating slightly. "Something different in my life for a bit. Just to put this in perspective, like six years or more maybe now, right before he got serious about personal training when his knee fully recovered, he went on a crazy bender."

I jumped in immediately because I was disappointed I had already heard the story. "Is this the pills and alcohol thing he told me about?"

"Pills and alcohol? Richie?" Mon looked at me incredulously and laughed. "No, of course not. He told you that? No. As long as I've known him, and I knew him when he bottomed out, he's always been a pure body, pure mind kind of guy."

I ate half of one of the quarters I'd cut as Mon watched. "I'm not going to be your mom, but you need to finish that," she said.

"I know. Slowly," I replied before reclaiming my thought. "Richie told me that you and David helped him out when he was down. He said it was about alcohol."

"What? There was no alcohol with Richie." Monique folded a NutraSweet packet into small squares while frowning. "He's crazy. It was…I shouldn't be telling you this."

"Mon, c'mon you've already passed the confidentiality threshold. Spill."

"Escorts. Upscale Asian escorts. He owed like $35,000 to an escort agency. It may have been more, I don't remember. I just told my accountant to write a check for whatever he needed. He came to us because he needed to pay off the debt. For some reason, he was charging up his credit card for these high-priced Asian escorts. He said it was like an addiction.

"He called it a fever dream when we talked. Love that term. How appropriate." She offered a sinister smile while looking around the room and rubbing her forehead. "Two girls a night a few times. He said he loved tattoos. I don't know. Don't ask me."

"Why? He can walk into any bar and pick up anyone. Everywhere we are together women are checking him out. Why would he pay?"

Mon looked blankly out the window at the rain flooding J.F.K. Street. "Danger? Who knows what the high-dollar girls do. Anything, I'm guessing. Anyway, explaining these kinds of things is impossible. It happens. It's human nature." After a long sigh, she raised her hands in the air. "You can't explain people when it comes to sex. It changes them.

"So, of course, we loaned him the money. It wasn't about the money. I don't care about the money, and I knew he'd pay us back. I trusted him. He did too, once he started getting clients.

"He trained me, so I connected him with friends, and then Sarah James, the actress, worked with him for a movie. She recommended him on the *Today* show. He became the guy for a bunch of Hollywood people. With that, his career skyrocketed like you wouldn't believe. And honestly, I was happy for him because it seemed to keep him focused."

I tried to absorb it all—the lingering escort story somehow seemed incredibly hot. I was getting hard while sitting across from Mon and struggling to digest the tasteless turkey. I'd never felt more uncomfortable with so many conflicting emotions and I tried to change the subject. "I don't get it. If he was so successful with movie stars, what the hell is he doing in Boston?"

"What happened with Jane was really nasty. He said he needed to leave the west coast, and get as far away from her as possible. I think that's the shame mechanism kicking in," Mon said with a quick check on her face in a pocket mirror.

"He's still healing too. He needs to be around friends. He screwed up with Jane. You know there's a price to pay when you do that."

"And that price is working with me?" I smiled, but Monique's stared severely at me.

"No, Michael, no. I think working with you is helping him, actually. He wants to help you. I know he wants to see you get stronger. Maybe you and I can run the Charles someday. That can be a goal. I'm counting on you."

We sat together, quietly watching the Harvard students stream out the door in groups. When the silence became unsettling for us both, Mon abruptly went to the bathroom. While she was gone, all I could think about was Richie and the endless escorts—all that restless fucking and sweaty mess of beautiful bodies colliding. I just couldn't imagine what it would be like.

"Michael, I'm sorry I just needed to make a call." Mon sat down again, her hair now combed carefully and lipstick neatly reapplied. Hearing her say "Michael"—as she did throughout our entire conversation—jarred me. When I was driving to meet her, I realized she had been calling me by my name for weeks.

"Mon, why you don't you call me Babe these days? You haven't called me that in, damn, I don't remember."

"I wasn't sure you would notice that," she replied. "Let me ask you. Why would you want me to?"

"You've called me that since we met. I'm used to it. That's why. Why else?"

She reached across the table to squeeze my hand momentarily before letting go and nervously picking up her teacup once again.

"Yeah, yeah, I know I called you that for a very long time and, to be honest with you, I really regret it. I genuinely do. You know it's just something I called you. It was playful and harmless, I thought. You had such a baby face. You still do, but I really didn't know what I was reinforcing. I mean, I didn't do anything intentionally."

"Reinforcing what? Am I missing something here? I don't get it. Babe is a nickname. What's the big deal?" I was trying to focus on Mon's words while daydreaming about naked masseuses with coconut oil dripping off their breasts, tatted-out escorts, and skinny tennis players in short white skirts, bending over to hit backhand, baseline volleys.

"Listen, I'm going to talk straight with you here. I've spoken with doctors over past couple of months. Some of them treated a lot of girls I've known who've suffered from what you are going through. And I've done a lot of research. I think a lot of what is been going on is, well." Mon looked away toward the kitchen. "Michael, take this the right way, please.

"I'm just afraid you don't want to grow up. All these past years, you've done everything in your power to stay thin and small. Like a boy, almost. You don't want to take the next step to become a man."

She rested her head in her right hand before pulling her hair back tight. "Please understand, I'm not saying you're not a man.

"You're a smart and wonderful person, and I love you. You know that. You are my brother-in-law, so I'm saying this because you need to hear it. I think you need to come to terms with growing up.

"Maybe I'm not saying this right, but you have spent the last few years preserving the body of a boy."

Mon's hand shook as she put the cup to her mouth. "I know this is hard for you to hear, and it's so hard for me to say. This is probably the worst place for me to say it in, but you asked and things need to come to a head. I've wanted to say this for a long time. It just never felt right.

"You are not a babe or a child. Something inside me thinks that's how you perceive yourself."

"Is everything alright here?" The waitress stuck her head in with a forced smile.

"Yes, yes, thank you everything is great," I said unconvincingly as Mon's words brought me back to reality in a hurry. What she was saying, though, was a mere variation of what I'd already discussed extensively in therapy.

"Monique, I know," I said softly, but she just kept talking in an unsteady voice.

"I think you need to take the leap of faith in yourself, Michael. I can't call you Babe anymore. I probably should have never done it. Sometimes, I wonder if I was part of the problem."

"Mon, please stop. It's okay. Trust me, you were never, ever part of the problem. You could never be part of the problem. You are always there to talk to me, and you are here now. It was a just a stupid nickname. All this adult stuff is what I've been talking with Dr. Hampton about. It's all things I've been going over and over. I never want you to blame yourself. I'm not sure where I'd be without you."

I thought Monique would smile, but a tear fell from her eyes.

Finally, she let out a small, uncomfortable laugh. "I'm usually not this emotional Michael, you realize that. I'm sorry. I must look terrible too." She reached into her purse and took out the mirror again. "Jesus. It's embarrassing."

Of course, she still looked as lovely as the first day I met her. "We should all look so terrible, Mon."

After taking a final bite of her sandwich, she touched my plate. "I'm so happy to see you eat. It's the only thing saving this afternoon from a total trainwreck. I feel bad about telling you things about Richie— that was stupid of me—and I've been thinking about the Babe thing for so long now. There's so much going on," she said, clutching the table with both hands.

"Michael, listen, I realize I just got back, but I'm going to New York again next week. I know again, and I'm sorry. It has to be done. I'll be gone for a while this time, but I'll be back for your birthday, I swear. I know it's a bit away. I've got it on my calendar. We're having dinner over my place. We'll plan something special then. You can stay at our condo again while I'm gone."

I wasn't surprised—actually, I was getting used to her absence. Mon had been shuttling back and forth to New York and L.A. for meetings since I started therapy. She was my rock when we were together, but she also had a business to run.

When the waitress finally arrived with the check, Mon reached for it after straightening her jacket. I quickly intercepted. "I've got it."

"Michael, no."

"Mon, let me pay," I said firmly. I had been living off the money from the sale of my parents' house, and even though it was beginning to run out, I had enough to survive for months. I gave my credit card to the waitress.

"Now check this out, Michael. It stopped raining out just for us. It's perfect. I guess the red sea parted," Monique said before redoing her lipstick and brushing her hair back with her hands.

The waitress thanked me while staring at Monique one last time.

As we made our way out the door, Mon said, "Will you look out there? I don't remember it looking like that in this city after a rainstorm. Crazy, crazy colors. So beautiful. Those clouds. What a strange day." She tapped me on the back. "That's a generous tip you gave."

I saluted confidently. "Indeed, boss. You realize that's the first time I paid for my own meal in a restaurant since I left New York. It feels good. And it'll help her pay for about ten pages of a textbook."

Mon nudged me with her elbow as we walked past the doorway of the Garage marketplace, and into the mist descending from the Chagall sky. "Silly me, here I thought it was because she had a great ass."

Twenty-Six

After the typically cold, stormy Boston early spring, we seemed to skip a season in April. The baseball games I anticipated all winter were ushered in by a shock of intense heat and sustained sunshine that continued throughout most of the month. The deceptive but welcome premature blast of summer and the sudden appearance of girls in shorts walking down Commonwealth Ave. were most befitting for my year of complete disorientation.

Of course, I was still prepared for a possible surprise foot of Easter snow, but the sight of students mingling again on the streets, runners dashing along the Charles, and crowds of people strolling through Harvard Square in t-shirts and dresses was wonderfully comforting. A switch flips in Boston when the sun finally emerges—people seem to reclaim their better selves as they shed the seasonal armor of frustration, and yield to the light.

And that was especially true for me. I felt surprisingly determined and reinvigorated while reveling in the warmth defrosting the city as I drove to a late afternoon appointment with Dr. Hampton.

Despite a bottleneck of cars on Storrow Drive near Fenway Park, I arrived much earlier than expected. With plenty of time to spare, I walked up the three flights of garage steps, scurried back down and repeated the process twice because I finally could. It seemed like a small but hard-fought victory.

Exercise had become part of my new daily routine: I'd shower, drink a smoothie, stretch, do laps around the Chestnut Hill Reservoir, read, and then head off to see either Dr. Hampton or Dr. Rigatta. If it was an appointment-free day, I pushed myself to take an additional walk through the neighborhood sometime before dark. I knew I could be running a mile or two—maybe even moving on to distances again—by the time September rolled around. The regimen was all carefully planned out, and my goals were all ahead to grasp.

I'd also started a daily journal, which helped me detail and identify my infinite anxieties and hesitations. By putting the ping-ponging thoughts on paper, I managed to dilute the power of the voice that questioned every bite and decision I'd made over the years. Developing the writing muscle again was almost as arduous as getting my legs back in some semblance of fighting shape. I struggled to get through pages but refused to go to sleep without making each day a complete chapter documenting the journey back to running. Someday I could reflect and make sense of all the chaos in my head.

I had my journal with me when I arrived at session while Dr. Hampton was out getting coffee. I sat by the window, taking the sun in on my cheeks. He returned wearing a checked, baby blue short-sleeve shirt without a sportscoat.

"I brought you some water, Michael. It's a bit hot these days for me, but I'm sure you are loving it." After placing a glass on the table next to me, he pulled his chair around the desk and sat with a stack of files. "If you don't mind, I'd like to start by having you sort something out for me."

I usually allowed Dr. Hampton to direct the discussions, but this time I needed to hijack the moment.

"Before we go on, can I just mention something. It'll be quick."

He offered an open palm, "Of course."

"I have a friend, maybe not a friend, more of a friend of a friend. I got a call from her last night. She teaches English at Northeastern. Apparently, they're looking for part-time teachers. She asked me for a resume and said with a master's I can teach writing. Maybe even some intro literature courses if I did okay. Who knows? She talked to the head of the program and was confident because they are always looking for part-time teachers. Cheap labor, I guess."

I was surprised to hear Amanda's voice on the phone while watching the Red Sox game the previous night. And quite frankly, I was shocked she even remembered my name. It was genuinely exciting to receive a call from someone other than Richie or Monique. My life had become monastic—on most days, the only person I talked to face-to-face was my friend, the Indian clerk behind the counter of 7-Eleven.

Dr. Hampton placed the folders on the desk before leisurely sitting back in the chair.

"Now that is indeed excellent news. Something like that is just what you need. It gives you something to do and look forward to. I'm sure you are very qualified. That's the opportunity you have been waiting for. Do you feel good about it?"

I was desperate to work and do something. Anything. Eating had become my job. "I guess so. I've never taught before."

"The only way to learn to teach is by doing it," Dr. Hampton said cheerfully. "You'll do fine. You have a thoughtful friend there. See, and you told me you had no friends."

"Well, I actually only met her once."

"That one time was enough to make her think of you, so I would consider that a friend."

"I really don't know if it's going to work out, we'll see. It's kind of minor anyway. So, what did you need to talk to me about? We can get down to real stuff."

Dr. Hampton smiled weakly as he picked up his folders again with a pen. "Michael, that's certainly not minor, so don't diminish it. You must see you are doing that. Accept it for what it is—an opportunity. It's important." He let his words echo.

"Now, I just have a discrepancy I'm hoping you can clear up for me. I was talking to Dr. Rigatta in her office the other day about you. She's very encouraged by your obvious improvement and how serious you have been about seeing her. I saw your latest lab results. They were very good, much improved."

I felt an unusual sense of pride as Dr. Hampton gingerly stepped behind his desk. "Anyway, as I was saying, when I was with Dr. Rigatta, I went through her complete file on you dating back to when you first saw her, and something popped out at me.

"I happened to look at her initial notes from your first visit. She has your father deceased by a car accident. Wrong-way accident on a parkway, she has written. I made a copy of her notes and even asked if that's what you told her." He tapped the sheet of paper with his index finger.

I immediately knew what he'd discovered and tried to figure out how I could rationalize all the lies. The truth was unavoidable, though. What happened with my dad was going to surface eventually—the bill had now come due. My initial fear was that Dr. Hampton would now doubt everything else I had told him.

He peered at me over his glasses. "According to my records, and I remember you telling me because I thought it was significant, you said your father died of stomach cancer. Now trust me, I'm not trying to cross-examine you, and I'm not accusing you of lying, but those are two very different stories."

I just didn't know how to tell him I lied, so I bought some time by explaining why I conjured the first story. "I told Dr. Rigatta what I did because I needed to say something. I know all this is totally unforgivable, but you have to trust me when I say I have never lied about what I've been through. I'm sorry about that first lie to Dr. Rigatta. I mean really sorry." I stood and reached for the water, the cup shaking in my hand.

"Michael, it's okay. Sit down. You can stand if you want, but it might be better to sit. Just tell me what's going on or what happened. You lied to Dr. Rigatta? Why?" He dropped the files on the desk.

I walked to the center of the office and stared at a new Hopper print on the wall. It was beautiful—a sun-dappled house in a green field next to its charcoal-stained companion. "I don't know why. I guess I just didn't want to...I don't know. When I first met Dr. Rigatta, I just wanted to get out of her office. I mean, I didn't think I had a problem, so I just was talking as if none of it mattered. She asked about my mom. I told her, and when she asked about my dad, I just said he died in a car accident. It's the first thing that came to my mind." I spilled exploding droplets of water on my leg and dabbed the small mess on the hardwood floor with a tissue.

"I didn't want to tell her what happened, so I thought of Jessie's parents. That story came into my head. Jessie's parents, they were killed when a car jumped the divider. That's what I thought about. I ended up telling it to Dr. Rigatta. It came easy. It didn't feel like a lie."

"Alright, so you lied to Dr. Rigatta. You didn't tell her about your father's stomach cancer, why?" Dr. Hampton said, alternately writing on his pad and eyeing me.

"You don't understand. I lied to you too. My dad didn't die of stomach cancer either. This is really terrible. I'm totally ashamed. I'm sorry. I know how bad this sounds."

"Wait, are you saying you told stories about your father's death to both of us? Why would you…?"

My first instinct was to step toward the door, but I was trapped with my own lies and past. There is no escape from that. "I don't know. I really wasn't ready to talk about it when you asked me after Jessie left. You remember how I was when I walked in here? I thought I would break down. My whole world was such a fucking mess at the time. It was all so overwhelming.

"If I didn't have to talk about it, I thought it would be better. It's just easier that way. It's wrong, I know, and goes against everything we're doing here, but I figured if we could just focus on the food. That's what you said. Attack the food and get me eating again. We could deal with the other stuff later. I was scared if I told you, we never would have gotten to the food stuff."

He crossed his arms as if he was about to scold me for wrecking the family car. "Deal with what Michael? How did your father die?"

"I honestly don't know—that's the truth. I actually don't think my father is dead. He just left. He left our house one night and never came back. I mean he just disappeared. You really don't know what it's like. You can't. So, I don't know if he's either dead or if he's out there. There are days I think I'm going to walk into him or he's going to show up. I walk around doing double takes, thinking I'm going to see my dad."

"You mean your father is alive?" Dr. Hampton squirmed to the edge of his chair and held the corners of his desk with his large hands. My mouth turned sour as I walked back to the rocking chair for water. The cup was empty.

"Michael, sit down, please. Take it easy. I'm going to call the nurse's assistant next door to get you more water. Relax. I'm not really sure I understand what you are telling me here."

"I'm saying I don't know where my father is. He's dead, I guess. I don't know, but I've been searching for him ever since he walked out because no one ever proved he's dead to me. The fucking Long Island cops are useless. Fucking Dunkin Donut patrol, they gave up looking. I don't even know if they were looking from the start. Nobody cared except for me and David."

The young assistant knocked before entering with a bottle of water. Dr. Hampton thanked her, slowly walked over, twisted the cap off and placed it next to me. "Drink, please. Okay, listen, I think we are approaching this backwards, and that's why I'm confused. This is very important. Tell me what happened."

I sat slumped in the chair, trying to explain the ineffable reality. "What happened is my mom dying. That just crushed my dad—he just changed. Changed to the point he hardly talked anymore. He was there but he was gone. I never saw him so quiet all the time. He was already bad, probably seriously depressed for years after losing his main job. But my mom's death, I think that killed him. You gotta understand, I was the only one in the house with him at the time, and I didn't want to be there either. I missed my mom. I still saw her around the house wherever I went like it was haunted. So, I hardly stayed home.

"My dad, he had nothing. His whole world was my mom. David was gone for a bunch of years while I was busy doing other things to just forget it all. I was playing baseball all the time. When I couldn't play ball, I went out with my friends. I wasn't there for him and, honestly, I think my dad just checked out. He never left the house other than to go to work or to eat. That house was so empty and dark without my mom.

"And my dad had no friends. Our neighbors were just people, you know? My mom and dad never did anything with anyone. You know how all couples on television go out with each other? My parents never did. They never had parties or went to parties. They went to the mall and to eat. Together. That was fine for them, I guess.

"Like I said, David got the fuck out as quick as possible. We had no relatives. My mom had no family, and my dad's brothers treated him like shit. They lived maybe twenty blocks over but they never visited, never called, never did anything. When we went to visit them when I was young, they acted as if they couldn't wait for us to leave. I'll never forget it.

"My mom told my dad she wouldn't see them anymore, so we didn't. One of his brothers owned a big Italian restaurant in New York, but he never invited us there. Ever. Could that be so difficult? When I was a kid I didn't think anything of it, but when I grew up I realized what was going on. It was like they didn't want to know my dad. Fuck them. You'd think when my mom died, they'd reach out, but no one did. It was just the two of us—my dad and me—and I didn't want to be there. Fuck them, and I guess, fuck me."

There was nowhere to hide. I had to tell him everything. All those goddamn memories just cascading out. I tightly squeezed the handles of the rocking chair with the hope of launching into space and disintegrating. Dr. Hampton sat with a firm jaw resting in his hands, glasses propped on his head.

"Michael, I know how difficult this must be, so let's go slow please, but let me be fully clear. I need to know everything. He just walked out the door without telling you?"

I yanked the rocking chair out of place and moved it out of the sun's path. It felt like I had been baked to a crisp.

"The night he left—it was August 15th, you don't forget that—he just told me he was going out for dinner. He was doing that. Going to like Denny's or Red Lobster by himself. At first, he used to ask if I wanted to go with him, but I used to say no, mostly.

"I mean, I went a few times, but then stopped. It was just so, so shitty just the two of us. It was a reminder that my mom was missing. She always seemed to be with us at the table in an empty chair. You know what I mean? Instead of going to eat with him, I either went out with friends or just stayed home and watched the Mets while listening to music. I thought he would be okay going out by himself all the time. I should have gone with him, I know, but I didn't. I figured I'd go another day. There would always be another chance until there wasn't.

"The last night, he was getting ready to go out to eat and standing in the doorway, just outside the room. I was watching the game. The Mets were playing the Padres. I remember that. He walked halfway into the room to look at the television. He never asked if I wanted to go with him. He said to me, 'Michael, you going to be okay?' But he said that every time he went out. And then, when the Mets made the last out of the inning, he walked away.

"I remember him looking over his shoulder and saying…" I paused and laughed foolishly while shaking my head. "He said, 'Gotta love the Mets' and gave a wave. Like a little salute."

I offered a weak imitation of his slow, amiable adios.

"And he never came back. When he didn't come back that night, I knew. I didn't know what, but I knew something was wrong. My dad was punctual. If he didn't show up, it was time to worry. He and my mom ate dinner at seven every night without fail.

"You have to understand, this was less than a year after what happened with my mom, so I panicked. I called David, and he told me to call the cops, but they wouldn't take a missing person's report until a day or two. And even then, they kept saying they were doing shit but…I don't know. They didn't find him. David flew in to talk to detectives, but that went nowhere. The two of us actually went out searching. We drove all over Long Island like fools chasing a ghost.

"Where do you look for your father? It was just so fucking insane. Like something you read about, only you are actually living it and nothing of what you are doing makes any rational sense. Weeks, and then months and months went by. It was a local story at first, but then people forgot about it. I was stuck in the house, totally abandoned. David was married and busy with work. He had a life. I couldn't help but still go searching in malls and parks like I was going to just run into him. It was all so pathetic."

Dr. Hampton put his glasses away and placed the folders in his drawer. "Let's take a break for a moment."

I stood again and leaned against the window. Kids were throwing a football by the water while two crew teams streamed through the Charles River into the sun. "No, I don't want to break, please. Let me finish and get it over with. I never should have lied, but you see?

"How could I have told all this to Dr. Rigatta? And if I told you early on, we would just be talking about this. I was going to tell you eventually, but it's so hard for me to understand, let alone try and explain. It's just easier to say he's dead. That's what I have to believe. If you keep saying it to people, it becomes the truth."

I spied a gangly teenager, wearing a red cap and holding a ball just out of reach from a ginger-haired young girl. She repeatedly jumped to grab it, only to come up a foot short each time. The tension drained out of my body as if someone had unplugged my nervous system.

"'Just gotta love the Mets.' That's the last thing he said to me. Every day I watch a baseball game, who do you think I think of? What a sick, fucking joke. After I realized he wasn't coming back, I had to take over the house. I searched through all his papers for a clue like a detective. His office was all neat and clean. All the bills were paid—he owed nothing—the house had been paid off for years and transferred to a trust with David's and my name.

"My father asked us to sign the papers a few months after my mom's funeral. I had no idea what it meant when we did it. I was in school, so I just signed. I remember there was a lawyer sitting in our kitchen with all of us. David later told me that my dad had been intending to transfer the house into a trust for years, and never got around to it.

"He said he never saw it as a sign because my dad wanted to protect us in case he got seriously sick. We wouldn't have to leverage the house. I don't know how it works, but who thinks of those things?"

"Well, fathers do, they do," Dr. Hampton said while leaning against his desk a few feet away from me.

It took me a few minutes to regroup as I wondered how we could continue now that Dr. Hampton knew I had lied. "I think David and I were the only ones who missed my dad. He worked as a taxi dispatcher, so he wasn't missed there. They just plugged somebody in. No one really gives a fuck. People are interchangeable."

I warily watched Dr. Hampton walk over to the couch near the window and sit down. It was like a stage performer entering the audience. "Michael, has your father been declared legally deceased?"

"He was, but they never found anything. No body. It's called in absentia. I think after six or seven years or so, they just say fuck it, get real, and get on with life, folks."

"You have never talked about this to anyone, have you?" Dr. Hampton's eyes were heavy as he nodded his head solemnly. "You have been carrying this around."

"Other than with David when it happened, no, and now it's just an acknowledged thing between us. It's not only too complicated to tell people but why would I tell anyone? The only time I felt this way was when I told Jessie about my mom dying. That made me realize I could never tell her about my dad. I told her he died of colon cancer. It was so much easier. I know this is all unforgivable and fucks things up. I'm really sorry for lying to you. I am.

"If people only knew what it's like thinking your dad could be out there somewhere or on the streets. I sometimes think he could be on the T when I go to see Monique. At times, I still have that hope, but I know it's a lot better to just to let hope die."

"No, I wouldn't put it like that, Michael." Dr. Hampton quickly raised his hand to me. "It's obviously important for you to move beyond it, knowing it had nothing to do with you. You know that, right? Your father was probably suffering from severe depression. Whatever happened, you just don't know. I realize certainty is always more comforting than uncertainty. And in this case, it may be true. You can't go through life looking over your shoulder."

Clouds shrouded the sun as a child's shrill laughter echoed from below. The drying sweat on my body left me cold, so I plucked some tissues from the box to wipe down my arms. "I just need you to know that I need you to trust me from here on out." I was pleading.

"I'm not a liar, and I'm ashamed. You have to understand. What I told you about me and Jessie was the God's honest truth. I know you don't know Jessie, but the Jessie I've talked about is the Jessie I know. That's my truth. The eating, the fear, everything else is my story.

"When we started, I missed Jessie. It was all happening all over again. The absence. And then I was thinking about telling you when David went away. That brought up more shit for me, which I know was unfair to him. I can't have him carry my baggage. I miss him too, but I know he's coming back so I can deal with that. All the rest is true—it's something I can't get out my head."

I sat down again, prompting Dr. Hampton to tap me on the knee and walk back to behind his desk. "We obviously have a lot to deal with going forward. This is a lot to process—we have to deal with it fully. But me trusting you is not the problem right now. I do trust you, and I do not doubt a word you've told me. I need to know you trust me. I know you weren't totally comfortable when we first met. That's why you held this back. Do you fully trust me?"

After draining the bottle of water, I didn't hesitate. "I've trusted you since after the first couple of meetings. You asked me about my dad like the second time we met, and I wasn't sure I'd make it past another week or so. I lied because I didn't think it would matter."

"Michael, you know everything you say at all times matters. Our words always matter. I know you well enough to know you recognize the power of your words. Of course, it would have been better if you opened up instead of trying to hide your past and what you were feeling, but that's done. The last thing we are about to do is assign blame.

"What we need to do is to figure out a way forward so you can deal with all of this. Getting you healthy is our goal, and nothing will get us off course. I'm just worried about you right now. This is a lot to come to terms with today."

"That's putting it mildly, I guess." I crushed the bottle in my hands and tossed it in the basket before sighing. "But you know what? I'm going to be okay. I starved for these last years because I thought I was stronger than everyone else. That was obviously fucked up, but getting here tells me I'm strong enough to deal with this now."

"You are strong, Michael. Of course, you know your starving was not the way to prove your strength. It was a way to block out your feelings. Dealing with all of this will show you your path to strength. It's alright to be vulnerable, though. I believe everything you've told me. I need to know—there's nothing you haven't told me, right?"

"No, I swear." I rocked slowly in the chair while realizing this wasn't going to be a *Good Will Hunting* moment. I wasn't going to have a good cry, hug Dr. Hampton and become completely healed before heading out to California with the pretty girl.

This was going to be more fucking work.

"Dr. Hampton, I don't want to go backwards. I can't be forever chasing something I can't find. I'm not going to return to where I was in the winter. I don't want to be who I've been. I'll come to see you as often as possible. Whatever it takes."

He walked towards me after placing his pad and folders in the drawers. "We will figure out our schedule if you want more time, of course. What I'm worried about is how this is going to affect your eating. You obviously have been eating. Did you eat lunch today?"

"I usually eat a sandwich after we meet. I'm trying. I really am, and it's a struggle."

"Fine, there's a courtyard cafeteria downstairs. Why don't we get something to eat together? I am free for ninety minutes. Are you okay with that? It doesn't have to take long."

"You mean the two of us? Is that allowed in your job?"

"Michael, I think that is precisely my job here. Of course, I'm worried about you eating when you get home and tomorrow, but one step at a time."

"Can we talk about something else besides my dad? I have nothing else to say right now." I was hesitant but confident that I could eat with Dr. Hampton watching me.

He took a few steps toward the door before looking back. "We can talk about anything you want. I know you like music. I don't know anything about rock, but I've always been a Miles Davis fan."

"Now, that's great. Seriously. Miles is pretty much all my brother talks about when I'm at his place. He's always played his records for me."

"Then it sounds like a plan. Ready?"

I hesitantly walked past him to the hallway. "I've got nowhere to go. Let's go."

Twenty-Seven

D
r. Hampton was right. The next two weeks became a queasy nightmare that nearly subverted whatever stability I'd achieved. Every bite turned into a landmine again, and each day I found myself staring at the smoothie in the blender convinced I was about to drink toxic waste. As much as I tried to focus on the life ahead of me, all of those easy triggers, old habits, and familiar, grotesque feelings kept flooding back.

One afternoon while watching Mario Batali sauce his gnocchi on television, I yanked the full-length mirror off the back of the bedroom door, carried it down the stairway and tossed it out onto the street. I could not let it mock me anymore. It leaned next to a light pole down the block for a few minutes. A stoned white girl with a nose ring and knotty blonde dreads rushed up to me and asked if she could have it. She quickly balanced it on her head with both hands and bounded away. It was such a relief to transfer all the torment in that funhouse mirror to the blithely unsuspecting waif.

I was fully cognizant of the black hole sucking me back in, so I called Dr. Hampton to set up three two-hour sessions for each week. I was finding refuge in the one place I had so assiduously avoided for years. There just didn't seem to be enough time to quell the incessant static between my ears. So much revisiting, rehashing, and remembering.

We were drilling deep, but I frequently found myself sitting in the rocking chair, wondering if, perhaps, some things should just stay the fuck buried. I had opened the temple of doom only to realize there would be no Indiana Jones or movie magic to set the world back on its axis.

I had to be my own hero, but the therapy was so, so emotionally taxing. There had to be some kind of shortcut to a semblance of well-being. I'd always read about celebrities or movie stars going into analysis and coming out the other side. The bookstores had thousands of self-help books by smiling, happy people who used to be miserable.

What if I was just not fit to join the club? Maybe some patients never get fully rehabilitated or find their true selves—they either slowly shed their old skins in the process of evolving into completely different people or quietly self-destruct without anyone noticing.

Each session felt like a twelve-round battle. Dr. Hampton spent half of the time as a neutral referee and the other half as a trainer insisting on different combinations. By the end of the meetings, I was badly bruised and ready to quit. I knew that that was the easy, familiar response, though. Relenting to the tumult was not an option anymore. I had come too far and worked too hard. I knew if I couldn't beat my demons, the least I could do was get off of my fucking knees to stand up and fight harder.

And so I ate what I could to maintain my strength and daily exercise schedule. Exercise brought a measure of pleasure to my life again. My walks became more frenetic and unsettled—it felt like someone was following me. I barely noticed the late-blooming flowers around the reservoir and kept my head down as the onslaught of cheery joggers passed by with quick hellos. The pain in my back and neck stiffness became more severe with each morning. I was downing four Advils with a gulp of milk each day before soldiering on.

The brief heatwave had yielded to the kind of ferocious spring storms everyone was expecting. I walked through raindrops with muddy sneakers, hoping to find renewal through my wet journeys. The dream of running once again became the one reason I put food in my mouth. It may have been the wrong reason, but it was a motivation. And that was all I needed.

Richie had gone back to San Francisco for a few weeks to deal with his divorce, leaving me without reinforcement. Mon called almost every day, though, and one night she even had a pizza delivered from Oregano Kind of Guy, her favorite pizzeria in Brookline. She hung on the phone until I ate a slice and made me promise that I would finish the pie over the next few days.

"Michael, you sound strange tonight. You alright there by yourself? I told you to stay at our place. You know, I won't be back for a while, and you have everything there."

"I'm fine here, no worries. Here, there. It doesn't make much difference. You know what they say, 'Wherever you are, that's where you are.' Jessie used to say it all the time."

"Stop, I know you are joking with me. You realize that's not how it goes. It's 'Wherever you go, there you are.'"

I didn't care if it was "I am what I am, and that's all that I am" because it all was cartoon philosophy to me. "I like mine better. It really doesn't matter, does it, Mon? You have to go someplace for that to apply. I don't think 7-Eleven counts."

Monique's voice was chilly and clipped. "Listen, let's simplify it for you and make it 'wherever you go, there you eat.' Call it Monique's rules of order. That's the only thing you have to worry about. Now, I want you to finish that pizza. I will check in with you tomorrow. Before I let you go, promise me you are eating."

It was a silly game we were playing. "Mon, you make me promise that every day. You should just make a tape recording." The hope in her voice was consistent and very, very predictable. It broke my heart. "I promise. I'm trying."

"Try harder. I'll talk to you tomorrow, Michael."

Of course, I took one slice from the box and cut it three ways for the next day's breakfast, lunch, and dinner before tossing the rest in the dumpster. As I watched the pizza box wilt in the drizzle, my mother's voice echoed in my head. "Shame on you, Michael. Somewhere in Africa, a child is starving." When I walked away, a rat emerged from the pile of garbage and gnawed at the cover of the pizza box. I felt much better knowing the pie would not go to waste.

The only way I managed to survive each day was to escape the silence of the empty apartment and deadly glare of the computer screen. I ended up strolling aimlessly through malls in Watertown and Chestnut Hill. Almost every night, I headed to the movies. On the days without a doctor's appointment, I went to the Coolidge Corner Theater or hopped between theaters at the Fenway multiplex.

After sessions, I took the T to the Harvard Film Archive and The Brattle Theater in Harvard Square to see double features. It didn't matter what movies were playing—I sat through Godard, Fellini, Chaplin, Sturges, Mike Leigh, Chris Marker, Herzog, and Jarmusch.

I drew the line at Bergman. Did I really need to see sad, pale people living through a glass darkly? Bergman understood the world's pain, but he also fucked Liv Ullman throughout all those years. We should all be so tormented.

If I wasn't hiding out at the movies, my nights ended alone in the corner of the Middle East Upstairs in Central Square. I'd get drowned in sound by a random noisy, brooding Boston garage band.

At the end of the second week of my mindless wanderings, I happened to stumble into the Brattle's Monty Python retrospective. It took the silly, Spam-loving Brits to pull me out of my rabid rabbit hole. I laughed like a high teenager throughout *The Life of Brian* and almost joined the crowd singing along to "Look on the Bright Side of Life" during the crucifixion scene.

A Wile E. Coyote sized keg of TNT detonated in my head during *The Meaning of Life*. And I never saw it coming. Through the spaces of my fingers covering my eyes, I watched the blimp-shaped Mr. Creosote projectile vomiting and eating to the breaking point before exploding. The scene's grandiose absurdity and outsized slapstick evoked grimaces of disgust and uproarious laughter from everyone in the theater.

As often happens when sitting anonymously in the dark with strangers, I found myself caught up in the communal hysterics. It brought on a strange, wonderful sense of freedom. On the screen was my worst nightmare—an obscenely fat man bursting open from morbid obesity. For years, I'd imagined my waist rupturing after one too many imaginary donuts.

And goddamn it, there I was, watching someone do just that. And yes, of course, it seemed beyond the boundaries of ridiculousness.

I sat amid everyone in the theater—sallow-skinned skinny women, squinty-eyed, chubby men and popcorn eating, finger-licking teenagers—squirming in fits of laughter. The girl next to me had tears of joy running down her cheeks. They were laughing at my most terrifying fear. I stared at the disgusting, vomit-stained restaurant on the screen and thought perhaps my whole life was just one big, fucking joke. The entire crowd was laughing at me. For the first time I wondered if maybe, just maybe, it was time to just laugh along with them.

I wasn't going to explode like Mr. Creosote.

No one explodes like Mr. Creosote.

It was comical and ludicrous. And it was my life's obsession. Perhaps the only way I was going to survive was by acknowledging that my very existence had become a sick, self-indulgent farce. Somewhere in a village in Africa, a mother was telling her son, "An adult in Boston is starving because he's unhappy. He's unhappy! Those Americans and their unhappiness."

I left the Brattle dazed and wandered around Harvard Square with the audience's delirious laughter still ringing in my head. It was like a beautiful morphine dream. In the Massachusetts Avenue music pit, a saxophonist played a slow, sensual take on "Just Like a Woman" while a bearded man with a long, braided ponytail and an acoustic guitar sang "The Ghost of Tom Joad" in front of Au Bon Pain.

While frantically navigating through the crowd of students, I was sure I saw my dad—the thick tufts of black hair and wounded eyes— tossing money in the guitar case. And, for a quick moment—barely a flash—there was Jessie. Her blonde hair gently flowed in the breeze as she walked past a double-parked Hertz truck on J.F.K. Street.

They were there. I saw them.

When I opened my eyes, a woman with thick glasses kneeled before me while holding my wrist. A small group of stern, concerned men and women stared down at me.

"Do you need the police?" the woman shouted. "He passed out. Call the police."

I was on my back next to the Out of Town News rack in the heart of the Square. "I didn't pass out, did I?"

"Yes, dear, I watched you go down. You just collapsed. Are you okay?"

The newspaper vendor rubbing his long beard tied in a knot with a rubberband reached down with a bottle of water. I jumped to my feet. "Easy, easy," he said. "You took a tumble."

Dozens of eyes were on me as if viewing an animal in a cage. I waved them away after grasping the bottle. "I'm fine. No worries." Upon finally regaining my balance, I remembered my knees buckling and the black night spinning.

The woman took my arm again to check my pulse. "Your heartbeat is very slow. You sure you are okay?"

A tall, bald policeman placed his hand on my back. "We need an ambulance here? What's the situation?"

I brushed the dirt off my sweatshirt and shuffled backwards to the T station. "I'm fine. I don't know what happened. I'm just probably dehydrated. Going to drink the water and head home. Thank you. I appreciate your concern, but I'm fine."

The cop gave me the obligatory double-check before moving on as the crowd dispersed. I thanked the woman while heading woozily down the escalator into the bowels of the T station. After downing the bottle of water in two long gulps, I waited for the trolley next a homeless man with the sports section of *The Boston Globe* sticking out of the waist of his gray, checkerboard pants. The last things I recalled before falling were the sound of laughter and Jessie's face.

On the long slow, numbing ride home, I knew my movie binge had to come to an end—you can only spend so much time in the dark. I had to get a grip on my life again and eat a sandwich. Maybe two.

When I finally arrived at my place at one a.m., there were two messages on my answering machine. I played back the tape while manically scavenging through the refrigerator. Monique's voice sounded so intimate and fragile like she was sitting near me.

"Michael, where are you? I know you said you've been going to the movies, but this is three days now, and I haven't heard from you. Call me back when you get in whatever time it is. I don't care. Call me for Christ's sake. One day, I understand. Three days, no. Call me. I've been having a bad feeling about things. I need to know you are alright."

I picked up the phone receiver to dial her after biting into the dry chicken sandwich I had slapped together. The next voice I didn't recognize.

"Hi, Michael, this is Kathy Myers from the Northeastern University English Department. I received your resume from Amanda Crosetti. I'd like to see if you could come in for an interview for a writing instructor position in the department. You can reach me at…"

I stopped the tape to get a pen and paper. After scribbling the number on the back of a yellow pad, I shoved most of the sandwich into my mouth, closed my eyes and sat at the table waiting to explode like Mr. Creosote. After three deep breaths, I dialed Monique. She needed to know what was happening.

When I finished the sandwich, I was still in one piece.

Twenty-Eight

"**Y**ou done, brother? Hang out by the bikes for a few minutes. I'm glad you finally came to your senses and got down here. I'll be back but I just have to finish with a client, so wait," Richie sprinted past me after I stepped off the treadmill in the far corner of the gym. After getting back from San Francisco, he had called earlier in the day to demand I work out with him.

Initially, I didn't want to be anywhere near all those buff, pretty boys grunting, sweating, and flexing. I used to call all the peacocking men pumping weights while sculpting their torsos to perfection the body artists. Of course, I realized I should have embraced them as kindred spirits instead of trying to avoid them. Their rigidly controlled diets and obsessively dedicated workouts were routines I understood much too well.

Down deep, we were really just different sides of the same coin. That's probably why I hated them. Our goals and means to an end may have been vastly different, but we all were ultimately transforming our bodies well beyond the norm.

Maybe what they represented—the juiced up, vein popping, hyper-ventilating, sweat saturated, testosterone-fueled mentality of the gym—was what really nauseated me. Preening dudes trying to out dude each other. It was like a secret, unwelcoming society with no room for outsiders, and I did not have the password to enter.

Richie, though, always had a quietly persuasive way of helping me focus and work toward my one true goal—running again. So yes, despite my deep reservations, I showed up at the gym to work out.

I sat on a recumbent bike next to a gray-haired man calmly reading the comics in *The Boston Herald*. A girl near him was dressed in a black Wu-Tang Clan t-shirt. She peddled furiously like Lance Armstrong after an injection. I was watching her muscular, spandexed legs spin into a Roadrunner blur when Richie tapped me on the shoulder.

"Here, take my cell. It's Mon, for you. She's been calling your place."

"And she called you?" I said, laughing.

"Take the phone and talk to her."

"Hi, mom, what's up? You putting a tracer on me?"

"Michael, pay attention. You need to be back at your place between four and six. It's three now. Be home in an hour and wait."

Richie chatted with a tall peroxide blonde in black sweats holding a toning weight in each hand.

"Mon, you didn't order me another pizza, did you?" I said into the phone as "Train in Vain" played overhead.

"Hell no, my sense is that the other one is still in the refrigerator, so no more pizzas until I get home. Just make sure you are at your place. You got me? I can't talk long, but I've been calling you all day, and I left a message for you last night. You didn't get it, right?"

"I haven't checked my messages in a couple of days so..."

"I guess that's a no. Please, Michael, just go into Verizon and get a cell phone. We've got to get you into the twenty-first century. Put Richie back on, willya. I gotta go. I'll talk to you later."

I held the phone in the air above the bike's control panel. "She wants to talk to you again."

Richie looked confused before chatting with Mon with one finger in his ear. I started peddling aimlessly while he repeated "Yes" over and over. As the conversation continued, he rolled his fingers to signal me to keep my legs pumping.

"Okay, Mike you did a nearly an hour on the treadmill. I'm going to get you to forty minutes on the bike. It feels good to exercise again, doesn't it?" The Wu-Tang girl walked away, hips swinging as if in a Lansdowne Street club.

"I know you are not listening to me if you keep staring at her. You're heading home, and I'm coming with you, you understand? Pop your eyes back in your head because we need to get our asses in gear." Richie tossed a towel my way.

"I'm lost. Why are you going with me? Mon said I need to be back by four. You don't need to go."

"Don't ask me. I'm the messenger, and she wants me to go with you. I'm actually done till seven when I need to be back here, so it's no problem. I have to get something to eat too. You have your keys? You can drive and shower at home."

"We are going now?" I said as the girl returned and smiled at Richie with the bottle of water to her ruby red lips. The mustard yellow Wu wings on her shirt were perched to fly away.

"Sorry to disappoint you, but yeah." Richie waved his hand before my eyes. "You sure seem pretty intrigued by the scenery for a guy who wanted to block out all the gym distractions. I'll get you a few more towels before we split. Sit here," he said.

I didn't have time to change, so when we arrived at my Corolla in the garage, I looked like a demented pool boy wrapped in white towels. Richie wiped a streak of dust off the window while peering into the car.

"What is all this crap on the seat? You clearly have not had a girl in this for a long time. It's such a mess." After adjusting the seat all the way back, he tossed the CVS receipts and the empty Diet Coke bottles on the floor before gathering my journal and writing pad in his hand. He fingered through the journal as I negotiated my way out onto Commonwealth Avenue through a downpour of rain punctuated by lightning. We were going through a strange Filipino-like monsoon season—rain fell every other day, drowning the city. It was just past three o'clock, but a cluster of dark clouds had turned the afternoon into charcoal ash.

"You writing a book?" Richie said, still flipping pages.

"A journal, it's different. Put it in the glove compartment." I was afraid he was going to read my confessions.

"So, you are taking after your brother after all. This is definitely something I don't want to look at. I already know too much about what's going on in your head." He switched the radio off and pulled me by the shoulder. "Mike, don't take this wrong, but were you eating while I was gone? You look a bit thinner to me like you lost some of the weight you gained. Your cheeks need filling out again."

"I had a tough few weeks. Really tough. Let's put it that way." I struggled to concentrate on the road.

"When are you going to Rigatta to get weighed again?" he said while scanning my pad with the incomplete All Food Baseball All-Star team.

"I'm going tomorrow. I don't know if I lost weight. I really hope not because she'll be really pissed. She is take no prisoners these days."

"It's not about her, it's about you. Hey, we're going to eat later after we get to your place and get this done." He slowly recited the names of the players on the pad. "What is this nonsense? Food names? Johnny Oates? Are you kidding me?"

"It's nothing. Just keeping my mind occupied." The heavy traffic was bumper to bumper as we headed to Brighton Avenue onto North Beacon Street.

"This is precisely what you should not be thinking of. What the hell, Mike?" Richie ripped the pages off the pad before carefully folding them.

I awkwardly reached towards him, letting go of the wheel. "No, leave them. C'mon, Richie, I've been working on that for…"

"Too long. Now drive carefully, I want to live. I'm going to hold this for now. Don't worry, I'll keep it safe. I just don't want to see you thinking about this. There are better things to occupy yourself with."

He placed the folded pages in the back pocket of his pants. "Back on the beam, Mike. Tell me what's going on."

"Nothing, nothing. I'm fine."

"You say `I'm fine' to everyone. I don't believe you. Just get us to your place, and we'll talk about what's been happening." He wiped the foggy windshield with a 7-Eleven napkin from the glove compartment. "How's your back?"

"My fucking back is killing me. That I'll tell you. It's like I'm carrying around Popeye's anchor. How did you remember that?"

He smiled knowingly. "You'll see in a few minutes when we get to your place."

A small, black Mercedes Benz cut me off. "What the heck does that mean? Is there some hot Vietnamese masseuse waiting for me?" I couldn't resist pushing his buttons.

"Maybe, maybe not. You know, that might have been a better idea."

Richie rolled down the window to gather rain in his cupped hand. "Mike, you don't have to answer. I get it, but what's bothering you? You can talk. I'm not playing shrink. Just between us."

We got stuck at a light near Dave's Donuts, the decaying 24-hour coffee house with the large, neon donut on the roof. As the rain suddenly turned to mist, I was hypnotized by the sign's methodical cycle. The blurry glow began at the base as sections slowly illuminated clockwise until the full circle was complete—the D in Dave's flickering and faltering intermittently. The kitschy sign lit up the gloomy late afternoon sky before going completely dark and starting the process all over again. Ongoing and never-ending.

I finally broke the silence. "I'm not sure we should get into this now, but I'll ask you anyway. You know anything about my dad? David ever tell you about what happened?"

He turned the defroster on hot while wiping his hand thoroughly with the mess of crumpled napkins. "Er, what? Alright Mike, yeah. Honestly, I never brought this up with you. I didn't know how."

"I'm asking you. You're not bringing it up. So, then you know about it all?" The light went green, allowing for a pickup truck and a minivan to jockey in front of us.

"Of course, I know. Your brother was all ripped up about it when it happened. That's all we talked about at the time. Dave couldn't get past it. It's been a non-subject for years between us, though. At the time, your brother, man, he was in bad shape. He was worried about you, and how you'd handle it by yourself. He was in hardcore therapy, just like you are now."

"Wait. David was broken up by my dad leaving? Are you sure?"

"What do you mean am I sure? Of course. I referred him to the therapist because I was seeing one at the time for my crap. I never saw David like that. If it wasn't for Monique, I'm not sure where he would have been. He wasn't leaving the house or showering. He looked like Einstein there for a while, kinda just plain lost. Monique was flying back and forth from L.A. and New York. Do you remember when she took some time away from the business? That was to help him get back on his feet. He was really gone. He's always struggled with depression."

This stunned me. There was so much I didn't know. I thought David left it all behind once he went back to San Francisco after dealing with the Long Island police. That's what he encouraged me to do. We never talked about it over the years. And I never wanted to involve Monique until calling her after I passed out in Harvard Square.

"Mike, drive the car, don't fall asleep here," Richie tapped the steering wheel, jolting me upright.

"I thought I was the only one. David never brought it up. I figured it was all dead to him."

"Jesus, Mike, no. He probably didn't talk about it to preserve himself. Are you just dealing with this now in therapy? I would figure that would be the first…"

"No, I fucked up. I never mentioned it to Dr. Hampton 'til now."

"I'm so sorry this is all coming up again for you. We definitely need to go out to eat tonight and talk. Tomorrow and the next night too. No wonder you look thin," Richie sighed.

I searched for a space after turning down my street. There was a large furniture truck parked outside the building. "What the…is that truck what we're waiting for? Are you shitting me? This is not you, right?"

"Monique. All Monique. Your back, she was worried," Richie said. "She knows you've been sleeping in that old bed that your girlfriend and that guy were doing the do in together." He pointed to a car pulling out at the end of the block.

I rolled down the window and stuck my head out to take a closer look. "Shit, I definitely don't want a new bed."

"Mike, it's too late, way too late. Just go with it." He waved to the movers, gave them a thumbs-up and eyed me. "Before we go deal with these guys, tell me one thing. Have you talked to David since all this stuff about your dad came up again?"

I parallel parked in the classic Boston bumper car tradition without leaving too big a scar. "He called me yesterday. Jesus, it was the worst conversation I can remember. I don't know what's going on with him but he, I don't know what. He asked me how I was. I guess Mon told him I was struggling. We talked, but he sounded…I can't describe it. Out of it.

"You know, I know he's busy and all, but sometimes my brother gets so far into his own shit with work and all caught up in his stuff. He sounds so, I don't know, distant. Like his exhaustion or his fatigue from work takes over everything.

"That's why what you said before surprised me. I honestly don't think any of the stuff about my dad or anything else matters to him." I quickly stepped out of the car, but Richie yanked me back in.

"Brother, you're wrong here. I don't know what to say. There's, well, you have to trust me. He cares. He cares a lot."

I walked into the light rain with Richie following. A burly man with a pen stuck behind his ear below a blue Red Sox hat approached me.

"You Michael? We have a bed set here for you to sign for. Let us in, and we'll set it up." Another worker straggled in behind him while the third opened the truck door latch to reveal a thick, king sized mattress and box spring next to a large, mahogany headboard and frame.

"No, no, I don't want this. You can return it. It's a mistake. I'll call the person who bought it, and tell her." I was angry Monique would even think about wasting money to put a brand-new bed in the tomb I called an apartment. The crew chief with the clipboard looked at me cross-eyed.

"Sign the papers and let them start. He's signing. No worries." Richie grabbed the keys from my hands and ran to open the front door. "Sign the papers," he shouted over his shoulder before instructing the gatekeeper of the truck to start unloading.

The man pointed his long, craggy index finger to the lines inked with x's on the invoice. "This is a hell of a bed, man. Wait until you see what it's going to look like. The headboard is beautiful. Top of the line. You don't want to send this back. These are beds of most guys' dreams."

Richie tossed me the keys from the sidewalk. "Now, you know why Monique had me come with you. She knows you better than you know yourself. She said you were going to ask them to take it back. We have to stop by my place later to pick up the sheets, pillows, and comforter. Two sets of silk sheets, Mike. Silk. She had it all sent to my place yesterday when I got back."

He held me by the shoulders. "Brother, I told them to take the old bed away and burn it. And when they are done setting this new one up, you are going to going to call Monique and thank her twenty-times over. Then we're getting something to eat. You understand?"

"So, you were in on this all along? You knew about this, right?" I couldn't help but laugh at the whole charade while Richie bounced enthusiastically on the balls of his feet in the soft mist.

"Tell me, is it nice?"

Richie's eyes turned to cue balls. "Beyond nice. Mon swore me to silence. And I knew you'd warm to it. I'm going to ask her to buy me one. You know what that bed is for?"

"Sleep and a long, long dream I don't ever want to wake up from. That's the only thing in the realm of possibility now," I said as the crew chief walked toward us again.

"You can sleep when you're dead," Richie choked out a laugh. "Warren Zevon. Your brother first played me that song. I live by the words. You realize I'm gonna quit if you keep on saying crazy stuff like that. Sleep, c'mon. Wake up, please. Breaking in—the bed's for breaking in. You have to make that thing rock till your neighbors complain." He momentarily chatted with the movers before tipping the chief.

"I was going to tip them." A VW bug swerved through the street, nearly hitting me.

"No worries. You're buying dinner. We're going to Legal's for fish. I can taste it already. And you are going to enjoy it. Mike, make sure you hear me, seriously. You're wrong about your brother. However that conversation went down, forget about it. He's not around, but he cares. Now let's go watch them finish. We gotta see what an empty apartment looks like with Michael Jordan's bed in it."

We stopped at the truck where one of the men tossed my old mattress and metal frame into the cabin before locking it away. Richie took the invoices from my hand.

"Sorry there was no cute Vietnamese masseuse hiding in there. Maybe next time they'll be three for you. Before we go up, I hafta ask, Mike. I see that cardboard Bon Jovi poster is still in your bedroom behind the door. What's it doing there? Shame on you, man. What the heck are you thinking?

"Let Jessie go. I was going to tell them to toss it away with the mattress and box spring, but I'm counting on you to do the right thing. You know what the sad truth is, though. I know for sure, even Jonny BJ approves of the bed. He'd know what to do. He's up there right now, observing through the eyes of a hair metal God, and preaching, 'Make it rock, Mike, make it rock.'

"And starting tonight, my friend, your mission is to find yourself a slippery when wet little Gina on the docks who will milk you dry. You can eat all morning and never worry about calories. That's the real breakfast of champions."

Twenty-Nine

When I got to Mon's just before eight after a slow, scenic walk from the Government Center T stop, there was an elderly woman, resting against a brick column at the bottom of the staircase. She held a Chihuahua in one arm. A warm breeze in the humid June night blew through an unruly patch of white hair she attempted to control with her free hand.

"Are you looking for something?" the woman asked.

"Not really. I'm just visiting," I said, heading up the stairs while watching her rub noses with the tiny dog with the sad face.

"You look a little lost. I do like your flowers. I hope she appreciates them," she replied with a sly smile. I had bought Monique flowers from the small, makeshift florist next to a copy shop on Cambridge Street. It was an undeniably corny impulse gesture. I had been embarrassed while carrying them throughout my walk past smiling couples and considered giving the entire bouquet to the old woman.

I glanced back towards her. "You know, they're not for my girlfriend."

She cautiously placed the dog on the ground while nodding, "They usually never are, they never are. That, I know, sweetie. Have a good night with your friend."

Mon pulled the door open just as I waved to the woman slowly strolling away with a grin.

"You making new friends?" She glanced over my shoulder out toward the sidewalk.

"New, very old friends. I'm pretty sure she thought I was a junkie stalker or some kind of pathetic, piss-poor gigolo," I laughed. "You know you didn't have to come down to get me. Why didn't you just buzz me in?" Mon looked unusually thin in a red San Francisco 49ers t-shirt and deeply faded blue jeans. I never remembered seeing such a prominent chest bone and frail shoulders.

"I needed the exercise. I've been sitting around all day. Wait, those flowers are for me? What's the occasion?" She stepped carefully, in bare feet, to pull me into the building.

"It's ridiculous I know. Flowers. Who buys flowers anymore, but I wanted to thank you for everything while you were gone. It seems like a long time, and you did so much." I handed the bouquet over, the blood rushing to my face.

"You didn't need to buy me anything. C'mon. They are so lovely—let me look at these." She tipped her nose into the petals.

Mon tenderly touched the top of each flower as she adjusted the stems in the elevator. When we stepped off onto the fifth floor, The Fugees' "Ready or Not" echoed in the hallway from inside the condo. I walked in to see a multi-colored Happy Birthday banner hanging near the kitchen.

"It's real low tech, I know. Walgreen's party department decorations. I spared no expenses on this one. Happy birthday, Michael," she said with a squinty smile.

David and Monique's place was spacious and warm with high ceilings. I loved visiting it during my years with Jessie. She often said I spent too much time there, but it was where I felt most comfortable. I knew their lifestyle was the one I eventually wanted to have. The condo had a large bay window with an expansive view of the Charles River.

I would always go over just to talk or watch a baseball game with David. Sometimes, all I did was listen to music and watch the runners jockey down the pathways next to the water while he worked in his office. Most Mondays nights in the fall and winter, we'd watch football together on their widescreen television.

Mon always made an effort to disappear between nine and midnight during each game. She usually went to Lansdowne Street rock clubs or enjoyed late dinners with her circle of neatly dressed, fine-boned friends—the beautiful people society.

With both Mon and David gone, the condo became a familiar pit stop for me again. I'd pop in for a few hours every so often just to get away from the Allston gloom. There was a framed print of Miles

Davis taking a break on a stool during the *Kind of Blue* sessions on the main wall. In the corner was a large, abstract pen and ink sketch capturing John Carlos and Tommie Smith with their fists raised at the 1968 Olympics medals ceremony. Above the couch loomed a large Alex Katz original portrait of a severe woman glaring over sunglasses. The place was always refreshingly bright, tidy, and welcoming.

I sat down on the couch next to the plush chair with three blue balloons. Each had "Happy birthday Michael" clumsily written in magic marker on the side.

"Monique, I told you nothing special."

She poured a glass of wine and playfully tossed a balloon at me. "Oh stop, I know you are joking. I found three balloons in the drawer and bought a buck ninety-nine banner. When we do something special, you will know. You want some wine?"

I waved her off as she drained the glass. "You bought me the bed for my birthday, so three balloons are just about right then. Just so you know, that bed is unbelievable. I do love it."

"No, no, the bed wasn't for your birthday. That was for your back. Your present from us is coming." When the last notes of *The Score* ended, I filtered through the cabinet of alphabetically ordered CDs.

"Play Maxwell. Love me some Maxwell," Mon shouted from the kitchen. I popped *Embrya* in the CD player and "Everwanting: To Want You to Want" filled the room.

"Monique, no more presents. Enough," I said as we met at the dinner table. She pointed me to sit in the chair.

"Too bad, David and I have a present for you, so shush. Let me see your cell phone."

I dug into my pocket and pulled out the small flip phone I'd gotten earlier in the week. "I think it's a cheap one."

Monique quickly programmed numbers into it. "It's not bad. You can upgrade. It's a beginner. At least you are finally connected to the world. This is a huge step forward. Go get something to drink. The Diet Coke's in the lower inside door. You know where it usually is."

"Want another step forward?" I was waiting for just the right moment to tell her I had gotten a job. Somehow, things finally seemed to be turning my way.

"You are going out with a cute girl from the gym?" Mon craned her neck to me while holding the wine glass inches from her lips.

"Ah no, that would be nice indeed. There are a lot of crazy hot girls at the gym. Guess that's the next step. But no, I'm going to be teaching English at Northeastern. I interviewed with the head of the writing department a few weeks ago. I'm going to get a class, maybe two. I think in the fall. They're on the quarter system, so I have to find out when they send out contracts.

Monique jumped up to embrace me. "That's fantastic. Oh, my God. I'm so happy for you. I bet you got dressed up for the interview. Finally."

"I did, kind of. She said it wasn't a formal interview, more casual, but all the clothes I had looked ridiculous. My pants made me look like a puppet. I went to Filene's and got a bunch of new shirts, dress pants, and a couple of ties. Calvin Klein, Geoffrey Beene. And shoes—you believe that? Imagine me in shoes?"

"You are blowing my mind here. I bet you looked fine." Mon finished another glass of wine before pulling a fresh bottle out of the cabinet. "You do look so much better than before I left. I've been so worried. When we spoke about your dad and everything you were going through in the spring, I didn't know what to think. I thought you'd regress. That's what I told Richie. That's probably why he's been pushing you. I was afraid I was going to come back to see you looking…"

"Like a scarecrow. I realize that. I was heading that way too, but I don't know. Richie has been so great. He's been getting me out all the time. As I've been telling you on the phone, we go out to eat a lot, and I've been religious at the gym. I mean, I walked from downtown here without a problem. He's kind of forcing me, but I'm getting in the flow a bit. So much has gone so wrong. I realize I know nothing anymore, so what the fuck? I have to at least try."

Monique slowly brought out a large platter from the refrigerator, carefully placing it amid the porcelain plates before me. "All this good news is the cue for the birthday dinner. You can eat whatever you can manage. I feel lost. I don't know where you are at, but I think you can handle this. At least you have to taste.

"You ready for some fresh sushi and sashimi I just bought before you got here? Go turn Maxwell up as I get everything ready." As she walked back to the kitchen, I braced myself for the wild unknown. There was no way I could tell her I was not ready for sushi yet. I had made strides, but raw fish—Neneh Cherry territory—was still way beyond me.

I nervously watched Mon carefully rearrange the various pieces of sushi and sashimi on a large platter with a pair of chopsticks.

"It doesn't need to look like a painting," I said, sniffing the fish and hoping it didn't talk back.

"Says you. Find the beauty in everything," Mon replied tartly before handing over chopsticks. I hesitated momentarily.

"You need a fork?"

"No, believe it or not, I'm okay." Monique ignored me and placed a fork next to my plate.

"Really, I don't need it," I said, smiling. The chopsticks reminded me of Les. He had taught me how to use them when Jessie and I visited his place for Chinese nights. We'd go over for Chinese food once every two weeks. Les, Jessie, and Patty would eat their mu shu pork, lo mein, and shrimp fried rice while I watched with my Diet Coke.

One night I told Les I had never used chopsticks in my life. He was shocked and seemed possessed to teach me the proper technique. He placed ten cigarettes on the table, illustrated the correct way to hold the chopsticks and meticulously guided my hands until I could pick up one cigarette. I fumbled with the silly sticks until the early morning while he played acoustic guitar.

At the end of the evening, he gave me a pair to take home so I could practice. While Jessie slept each night, I stabbed at buttons, pens, dry spaghetti, and marbles. I was obsessed with becoming a master chopsticks technician. By the time we went to their apartment for Chinese again, I picked up all ten cigarettes with ease. It was a dubious achievement—kind of like a vegan learning how to caramelize a steak, but I was fiercely proud of my little victory.

And I never thought I'd actually use chopsticks until Monique handed me a pair.

"What we have are sushi rolls and some sashimi. There's scallop, tuna, Masago and Unagi there. I got a variety for ya. Salmon, Tuna Tataki, California Roll is easy for you.

"Just take a look at them and see what you might like. If you want, I'll tell you the difference." I curiously examined the platter as she pushed a bowl of noodles towards me.

"Those noodles are delicious, Michael. They are so fresh. You have to try them." There was enough food to feed the Celtics and Tommy Heinsohn.

Mon patiently placed a few slices of sashimi on my plate. "I started you off with scallop, so yummy, and tuna," she said.

I poked at a couple of pieces of fish. "Now, what is this?"

"It's what the Japanese like to call food, Michael. Surprise yourself. This is your year of living dangerously. You will like it. Just pick it up, put it in your mouth and swallow. Say to yourself you are eating pizza if you have to."

She plopped a sushi roll in her mouth before walking to the sound system on the far side of the floor.

"I think I heard this CD too often. What do you want to hear? I have this urge for *Appetite for Destruction*, something loud and nasty. You know I love my Axl, but not while we're eating. After we finish I'm going to blast it so I can clear out my head. This is good for now," Mon said after replacing the CD in the player.

The first gorgeous notes of Glenn Gould's *Goldberg Variations* floated through the apartment.

"Eat something, Michael, just something. I swear that the sashimi is going to change your life."

"Then you should have given it to me three years ago."

I tossed back a sushi roll because I absolutely refused to hear Mon say "Eat" one more time. It slid down my throat after a few quick chews. It could have been a crayon.

Mon sat again to hunt eagerly through the tray. "Try the scallop sashimi." She picked up a piece with the chopsticks and placed it before my mouth. "It doesn't bite back. Try it." I snagged it with my eyes closed eyes and head tilted back.

"It looks like you're forcing down a dose of castor oil," Mon said. It just tumbled down my throat. "Now, it looks like you just ate a slug," She was holding her hand before her mouth as she laughed.

"I wasn't? That did not taste like food. Who eats this?" I could feel the fish descend into my stomach and get lost like Jonah in the whale.

"Just everyone except you. Take a sushi roll now. Dip it in a sauce or some of the wasabi. That will really open up your sinuses." Monique was now eating voraciously while taking generous drinks from her wine glass. Her eyes were slowly dimming.

"Okay, what's wasabi?" I felt truly ignorant.

"It's got a stiff kick, and will remind you that you are alive." Mon pointed to a small bowl next to the platter. "Your taste buds have been dormant for years. That'll give them a jolt."

I cautiously dipped a sushi roll in the wasabi bowl, inadvertently coating the whole piece. A quick flip of the chopsticks sent it to the middle of my tongue. Monique reached out with alarm before placing her hand over her eyes.

It felt like someone set off a stick of dynamite inside my mouth. I leaped out of the chair. "Oh shit, oh my God, oh shit. You've got to be kidding me. What did you feed me?" My eyes watered uncontrollably as my nose flared.

Mon pointed to the refrigerator. "Go drink some milk." She was now laughing with mouth wide.

"Is fire coming out of my nose?" I yelled while holding a towel to my eyes.

"You are just supposed to dip it," Monique giggled. "Are you okay?"

"I'll let you know when I can talk." I was coughing wildly.

"Drink milk, milk," Mon shouted.

"Oh yeah, yeah, easy for you to say. As if I'm just going to drink a gallon of milk." I took a small sip of milk while wiping the tears from my eyes.

"It's all trial and error. Trial and error, just like life," Monique said between chews. She pointed her chopsticks towards me. "The more things you try, the richer your life will be. And I see that smile on your face, so I know you are smiling inside. It's all in good fun."

I couldn't help but grin back. She made indignation impossible. "That was a trial and an error. Goddam."

I sat down again—this time placing a two liter of Diet Coke on the table. "Never again," I said as Monique tried to stifle her laughter.

"I'm sorry to laugh, but that was really pretty funny. You are supposed to taste the wasabi, not inhale it. I'm actually very proud of you for trying. You get a gold star. You know what? I think it's time for your present. It's right here." She grabbed a wrapped box from behind the couch. "Don't stare at it. Open it."

I ripped the careful wrapping apart. There were two yellow clasp envelopes inside folded tissue paper. "What's this?"

"Something for you to look forward to. Something to set your sights on." I reached into one envelope to find an airplane ticket.

"Monique? What? Where are we going?"

She laughed once more. "That's just for you. You can go anywhere you want. That's for when you gain some more weight, get better and want to travel. It's a round-trip open-ended ticket. Pick where you want to go in the states. Just don't go to Newark. You need to change scenery, go on vacation, get some sun, sit on a beach or go to the mountains, somewhere. But you have to get fully healthy."

"I've never been anywhere. The furthest I've gone is the International House of Pancakes." I said while skeptically holding the ticket. "You know I'm not going on vacation. Why?"

"It's not for now, Michael. I know you aren't going anywhere. This is for the future, so you can get away from Boston for a few weeks or maybe a month. Who knows?"

"Are you trying to bribe me? Eat, then I can travel?"

"No, but if that's what it takes you damn well better believe I would."

"Monique this is really nice but…"

"You are a tough crowd, Michael, you know that? No buts here. Say, `Great Monique, I'm looking forward to going on vacation.' And that…" she said pointing to the other envelope. "Will allow you to enjoy it more. They are travelers checks, and David opened up a bank account under your name. Look, you said you are starting a job, which we didn't even know about—now we want you to have a head start.

We don't want you to have to worry. Michael, we want you to put the past behind you."

I dropped the box as I stepped from the table. "I can't accept that. I will keep the ticket and maybe go on vacation sometime, but I don't want money. You have given me so much already. No, Mon I can't accept all of this. I thank you so much, you know that. I know you mean well, but please, I'm not a charity case. That envelope is thick. I won't even count how much in travelers checks is in there. And I certainly can't accept any bank account." I walked away with hands over my head.

Monique followed. "First, the money was David's idea, but Michael you have to understand something. I have spent a lot of money because I have always had a lot of money."

"You earned it. You work hard. What are you talking about? You…" I said, sitting on a stool next to the kitchen counter.

"Michael stop—listen to me. You and I have really never talked about too much before Jessie left. We didn't talk like we do now. You really know very little about my life, and I haven't been that forthcoming. We haven't been open. What do you know about me? I mean really know?"

Mon was right. While I had a lot of conversations with her, they were unfortunately always about me. She continually advised and encouraged, but I had never asked her anything about her childhood or family. "Well, I know…" I didn't get much further.

"Yup. Pretty much nothing, but you need to know I'm a trust fund baby. David and I never told you. Why would he? And I'm not proud of it. I made a lot of money throughout my career, but I didn't need it. I did the work for me because I needed to do something. And it was important. So much in my early life came so easy. I had everything growing up. Everything.

"The only thing I didn't have was friends. I grew up around adults—rich adults—in a large estate, and was homeschooled." She opened another bottle of wine. "I created my own public story. Of course, no one really looked into it. There was no Internet when I started."

"Wait, what? How did I not know this? Where was I?" My lack of curiosity throughout our time together embarrassed me.

"You had other things on your mind. And honestly, I just never told you. It never came up, did it? We talked about..."

"Oh shit, me, always me."

"No, don't take it that way. Let's put it this way, now don't make *this* about you. That would be wrong. You just didn't know. But let me tell you now. You know Jacobson steel? It was just sold to a Japanese company. Right? You heard of that company?"

I just listened and absorbed while Mon stalked around the kitchen. She pointed to her chest with her thumb. "Mona Jacobson. I changed it to Monique Jacob when I was seventeen and left home to begin my career. There was no risk for me, so I could go out and become whoever I wanted to be.

"There really is no Monique Jacob, I guess. I'm just Mona Jacobsen who needed to become somebody else." She glided her hand over her face. "And this allowed me to do it. So yeah, I grew up in a life of insane money, and then made even more money. That's the way life works sometimes. It doesn't happen to everyone, but it happened to me and, sometimes I don't know why.

"Michael, I gave to you because you needed it. You are not charity. Your brother and I saw how you were twisting your life up. If I could make it easier for you, I did. Sue me. You know how many people suffer from what you do, and don't have the means to get help? They suffer in silence without doctors. But I can help you. Who cares what it costs? That money over there on the table is nothing."

"I understood when you and Jessie refused to take the money we offered over the years. And I understood when you refused to move after Jessie left, even though I told you I could find you an apartment. David and I let you figure it out on your own. Paying for therapy isn't charity. It's saving your life. I'm going to pay for it as long as you need it. And to beat this, you are going to need it wherever you are."

She walked back to the dinner table and picked up the box. "This is a reminder for you to realize you have a life waiting for you. It's just money. You can burn the travelers checks if you want. Ignore the account. They're meaningless. We can get you more anytime. But what David and I can't give is whatever is missing inside you. You have to find that."

Mon was holding me by the shoulders when the phone rang. She frantically sprinted to her cell. Her hand trembled so much that she nearly dropped the phone. After listening intently, Mon raised a finger in the air towards me.

"Are you sure? Really? Wait a second. Give me a second." She breathed quickly—her small chest heaving—and pushed a couple of stray plates away from the edge of the table. "I'll call you right back," she whispered before ending the call.

"Michael, Jesus, I, listen, I've got to call somebody back. It's going to take a while. I don't know how long, so I may have to leave." Mon snatched a dishcloth to wipe her nose.

"What is going on?" I said, stupidly. "Can I help?"

"I wish you could, but not right now. It's just something I need to deal with. I'm so sorry, but I do need to return this call."

"Mon, stop bullshitting me. This doesn't sound like everything is okay. You need to tell me…"

She grabbed my hand when I reached to her. "I'm sorry, Michael. This is so shitty of me. I'm screwing up your night. Listen, I'll be by your place tomorrow morning, first thing. Ten o'clock. There's more I wanted…"

She rummaged through her handbag sitting on the kitchen counter.

"Michael, don't take the T home. You know I'd drive you home any other night. I've got to stick around here. Take some money, please. I will see you in the morning."

I took a few steps back, waving like a football referee signaling incomplete. "Are you kidding me? I don't want your money tonight."

Monique rushed me, pulled open the front pocket of my baggy jeans and stuffed it with crumbled twenties. "You have it now." She ran toward the table to pick up the box with the envelopes before scrambling to the closet in the hallway. After squeezing the box into a leather bag, she handed it to me. I tentatively gripped the handles.

"Michael, please take a cab back. I don't want you on the T tonight. I know it seems like I'm kicking you out—I obviously am. But you have to trust me on this. It's important."

I meekly stepped towards the door. "You can't tell me what's going on?"

"It's just something I have to do. For one night, don't ask questions." Mon lunged to hug me. "Your birthday continues tomorrow. Don't hate me here, please. I know this sounds fucked up and abrupt, but I'm going to say it again. Trust me, please?"

What was there to say?

I eyed her walking towards her bedroom before I slipped out the door. When I finally hit the street, the skies opened with slanted rain. As if on cue, there was an idling cab at the far end of the block. Either Monique conjured it, or I was dreaming. I ran towards the taillights with the bag under my arm and rain against my face.

The black driver was talking to dispatch, the stub of a cigar in his mouth. When I opened the door, he tossed the butt out the window. "Where we headed rock star? Get out of the rain."

I jumped in. "Just go anywhere, please. Just go."

Thirty

The taxi rolled about a block and a half, jerking and coughing until we sat at the light.

"You believe all this rain, boss? I think it's mother nature telling us something." I was still catching my breath and inhaling stale smoke as the cabbie spoke.

"You have to tell me where you want to go, my man. We can just sit in idle."

I listened to the dispatcher bark out an address over the two-way radio. "Drive for a block or two—I'll let you know."

What had just happened with Mon hadn't quite sunk in yet. I sat in a daze, wondering if I'd be shitting out a can of tuna in a few hours.

"You're going to pay for going nowhere here. Where to?" The cabbie was clearly agitated as he fiddled with his weathered blue Red Sox cap and scratched his gray stubble.

"Fuck it, I don't know. Let me out. I'm going to walk."

"Brother, it's raining out there."

"I'm fine. It's letting up. I don't have far to go." The waist of my pants felt unbearably tight when I glanced over my shoulder back to Mon's building. "I need the exercise."

The hack turned to face me. "Look at the rain coming down. Are you crazy?"

"Might be, just might be." I reached into my pocket, pulled out a twenty and handed it over.

He flinched before accepting it. "This is way too much."

"It's always too much. Sorry about the confusion, but I got it from here," I said, stepping out into the storm.

The tail lights faded into the gloomy darkness as water kicked up from the tires rolling on the slick pavement. I looked towards the solitary light in Mon's window before walking to the Arlington T station. The sidewalks were deserted and the whoosh of cars rushing through the flooding streets echoed in the stagnant air.

After ten minutes, I finally rested near the edge of Boston Common. Nausea seemed to rise from my toes as I bent over with hands on my knees and the leather bag tucked tightly under my arm. I breathed deeply to prevent a massive upchuck of an aquarium of fish. Finally, I regained enough composure to step on into the night's silence.

During my years in the city, I had never been afraid while walking around Boston—crime was just something I read about in the Metro section of the *Globe*—but that night I was strolling around the perimeter of the Common with hundreds of dollars of travelers checks and my mystery bank account information. I didn't want to end up a corpse in one of Robert Parker's Spencer novels, so I kept moving briskly with my head down. Intermittently, I stopped to look through the park towards the deserted intersection of Boylston and Tremont Streets. The newly renovated, brightly illuminated building tops hovered over the Theater District.

When I made it to the stairs leading down to the T station at Arlington, my Adidas squished and squashed with each tentative step towards the toll booth.

The platform was empty as I gazed into the tunnel. In the silences between the static of the sound system and the distant scraping of metal on metal, I heard heels clicking on the cement behind me.

I turned to find two slightly staggering girls in stilettos. One had an unusually large, pointed nose and scattershot, highlighted hair all teased up as if she'd just stepped out of a Long Island bar. The other strutted in a navy-blue, form-fitting dress extending down just past her crotch. She was thin with a jackknife shape and small, half exposed breasts.

When the near-empty T finally pulled in, I breathed more easily after slipping into a seat by the front window. The girls had followed right behind me but they ended up in the middle of the car. Each one gripped the poles next to the seats along the aisle.

Both struggled to stand upright on their heels as the trolley tossed sideways. I nodded to the wafer-thin girl as her friend adjusted the top of her dress, which clung to her like Saran Wrap on a sweaty bowl.

On the way towards Copley, the car stopped abruptly in the middle of the tunnel forcing them to grab one another's arm. Seemingly without reason, they suddenly broke into spasms of laughter when the lights sputtered out. I could see the faint silhouettes of their asses while they chatted in the shadows. As I sat in the darkness, wringing water from the bottom of my jeans, someone swooped into the seat behind me just before the electricity sprang to life again.

"3B, that's you. I knew it was." I felt a tap on my shoulder.

"3B, hey. That bony chick caught you checking her ass out. She's so drunk. They both are. I knew for sure you didn't see me. I was in the corner of the train back there. You were way too preoccupied."

I frantically tried to connect the face to a name while staring at the girl with the jet-black, Louise Brooks bobbed wig.

"It's me upstairs, 4B. At least I used to be 4B, remember? C'mon, look carefully. Only think blonde hair." She snuck in next to me. I followed up from her pink sneakers to the black fishnet stockings covering angular legs to the edge of her black miniskirt.

"Look up here, 3B." Her index finger, punctuated with pink nail polish, pointed to her large, oval blue eyes.

I laughed upon finally recognizing our upstairs neighbor, who always offered big, gracious hellos to Jessie and me whenever we saw her in the hallways. She raised a bag containing black, strapped high heels into her lap, and collapsed back into the seat.

"A-ha, now you recognize me. Long time, no? Months. I moved out late last year. That building was a roach motel. I got a really nice place now. Movin' on up in the world." She blinked nervously while pulling a cigarette from her purse.

"You think they'll see me if I smoke?"

I shook my head dismissively. There was a NO SMOKING sign next to the beer ad on the divider in front of us. She pressed against my shoulder, laughing. "I'm just messing with you. I'll hold onto it, though. If I can't smoke, having it in my hand makes me feel at ease. So, you still in 3B, 3B?"

"Depressingly, I am, but it won't be for long," I said, as embarrassed as I was hopeful.

"Excellent, excellent," 4B replied with a vigorous nod. "You and your girlfriend moving out? Where to? Maybe we'll still be neighbors."

The train lurched sideways. She clasped her purse in one hand, dropped the cigarette in her lap, and steadied herself with a palm against the wall. Her bag tumbled toward me. "My bag is not nearly as nice as yours. Fancy stuff, Mr. Big Shot. Who knew?" she said with a smile. A man in his early fifties with gray, wind-swept hair sat across from us.

I handed her the bag back as she crossed her legs. The upper inside of 4B's right thigh was slightly concave, and her fishnets had two small ripped threads behind the calf. She squiggled in her seat before pulling the hem of her dress down.

"You coming from a party?" I said, eyeing the high heels in the bag.

"You can say that I guess," she shrugged. "What about you? Looks like you went swimming. What's got you walking through the rain on a night like tonight?"

I nonchalantly gazed straight ahead at the advertisement for Budweiser with a buxom blonde girl exploding out of a bikini. She stood tall in the snow banks while holding a big, frozen bottle to her voluptuous lips. *Bud Ready When You Are.*

"I had a really strange, strange night," I sighed.

4B brushed against me again with her shoulder. "They all are strange. It just depends to what degree. Hey, don't mind me being the first to tell you, but your hair is a mess. Like a wet mop. You do realize you are soaking wet, right? I have a tissue in here." She opened her black purse to pull out a napkin.

"Yeah, here you go." She pushed my hair back with her fingers before handing me the napkin.

"Try and dry off a bit. Lucky thing the air conditioning hasn't worked on the T since Reagan was president." We pulled into Copley Station, and when the train decompressed after the doors opened, 4B squinted at me. "You know this guy next to us?"

"No, am I supposed to?"

"You tell me. You keep looking at him. I figured if you keep staring you might recognize him like you did me." I continued to wipe my hair, completely unaware I had been fixated on the man in a disheveled, olive-green pea coat, who was now sleeping against the window.

As I leaned over to get a better look at his mud-caked, fluorescent orange sneakers, 4B re-crossed her legs before squaring herself in the seat to face me. She placed her bag between us. "So, you never told me where you and your girlfriend were moving to? You going to get out of Allston? I swear that's where hope goes to die. I'm in Brighton, near Boston College. It's a really nice building."

I valiantly tried not to laugh—I thought for sure she might have relocated and gone upscale to downtown or the South End, but she only went movin' on up about two miles. "You didn't really go too far. I walk around the reservoir right by BC. I'm surprised I don't see you."

"Hey now, you know there's a really big difference between the Boston College area and downtown Allston, home of sad wannabe rock stars," she said with comically faux fury. "You and your girlfriend need to get out."

"I'm the only one moving. Just me. My girlfriend is gone. She moved out just before Christmas. It's a really long story."

Her lovely ocean blue eyes slid to half-mast. "Oh, that sucks. Sorry to hear that—she was nice, like you. Hope it wasn't ugly. I hate ugly."

The lights in the car went out once more to groans from the two club girls, who had crept their way next to us. "I guess ugly is determined by who is telling the story," I said to the darkness. While the power slowly regenerated, I brushed my hair completely back with both hands.

The train stuttered towards Auditorium station as 4B handed me a mirror from her purse. "Take a look at yourself. If you are not trying out for the next singer of Poison next week, it's time to cut that Peter Frampton hair. With it all combed back like that I can see your face now. You look so different. You know you have great eyes. Bigger eyes than mine. Jesus."

I quickly glanced at my face in the mirror—my cheeks had filled in, and the deep rings around my eyes were disappearing. I definitely looked healthier, but I wasn't quite sure I liked what I saw.

"You know 3B, I was looking for you with your girlfriend when I saw her recently at Bread and Circus. I figured I'd see you both. I was so used to seeing you together." 4B tucked the mirror into her purse and craned her neck to take a look at the driver.

"What? That's impossible. No, no. She's not around anymore." My stomach did somersaults while I contemplated her words. "Bread and Circus? No, she moved away with my best friend. They live in the south now. Wait, you saw her?"

4B looked alarmed, leaned forward and pressured my knee with her fingers. "No. Then it wasn't her. It was night. I was probably high. Don't listen to me. It looked sorta like her. It wasn't. Forget about it. I'm sure I was high."

When the car came to an abrupt stop at Auditorium, the two girls stumbled next to our seats. 4B placed her hands on the base of the back of the girl with the teased hair. "Steady, Secretariat, steady. I don't want you falling in my lap. A little less Tommy Girl next time, honey."

"You sure it was not her?" I said, still holding the leather bag tightly to my chest.

"Was not who?" 4B replied, somewhat oblivious while standing to adjust her dress.

Thin, greenish veins in her inner forearms were visible through her pale skin.

"My girlfriend."

"Oh, I'm positive. Forget I said that. It just kind of looked like her, but she had way different hair, and if it was her, she would have said hello. You two always said hi when I saw you. I didn't see you two too much before I moved. It became less and less. I used to see you leave at night. We would both going out at the same time. Remember?"

I did. On the nights I went out to clubs or to meet David, I'd often hear her clip-clopping down the stairs in heels and ass hugging dresses with deep, plunging necklines. Jessie used to call her Sharon Stoned. When I'd see her, we'd exchange anonymous pleasantries while descending the staircase together to go our separate ways.

4B stared bemusedly at the two girls huddled by the door as the car trudged into Kenmore.

"So, what you think? You think they're hot?" She wiggled her eyebrows while angling her thumb towards them.

I placed the leather bag between my feet, ignoring the question.

"Oh, stop with the too-cool-for-school stuff. Talk to me like a guy. Hot or not?" She kept alternating glances to the girls and back at me. "You sure were staring at them like they were hot before I so rudely interrupted you." With a loud laugh, she tapped my arm. "You were zombie staring like you did with that homeless Michael Douglas over there before. C'mon, give it up. I love to hear what guys think. Hot or not? Both, one, or neither."

"No, I wasn't staring that obviously, was I?"

"Maybe they didn't recognize it because they're drunk. But you were doing that Superman x-ray vision male gaze thing. The feminist police would be all over you if they saw. Especially those Harvard ones. So bad, they'd arrest you, and throw away the key. You don't want to get on their bad side," she said with hands on her cheeks like Macaulay Culkin in *Home Alone*.

"Was I creepy?" I was genuinely embarrassed by my transparency.

"Nah, heck no, I know what creepy looks like, and it wasn't that. You just looked horny. To me, there's definitely a difference."

I inched away from her. "Oh shit, that's just as bad. Pretty pathetic. Hopeless."

"Oh, no, 3B, no, c'mon. You don't need to move away from me. Relax. You lost your girlfriend. I get it. You get a pass, and I know every guy is horny. It's just to what degree. Just like strange nights, remember? You were a sad, puppy dog kind of horny." She squeezed my bicep with a smile.

"I'm kidding, you know that. You were fine. Sometimes, the whole world feels like you do. No worries. You don't know what sick, creepy guys looking at women on the T look like. If you were like that, you think I'd be sitting here? Okay, stop feeling sorry for yourself. Now tell me, hot or..." she said mischievously.

I shook my head, unwilling to play along, but she kept silently mouthing, "Hot or not?"

"The skinny one. There's something about her. The other one looks like she's going to sing Taylor Dayne karaoke."

The doors opened at Auditorium to free the girls who descended with hands clasped onto the platform. 4B yanked me out of the seat after grabbing hold of my fingers. "Let's go. We're going to get a cab, my treat."

"What? No. I don't want," I protested. "We're not following those girls if that's…"

"In your dreams, 3B, that's definitely not what I'm thinking. I'm not following, I'm leading. They're going to end up face down, ass up in front of a toilet." She stood in the aisle shouting, "Hold the doors" to the driver. The doors did indeed remain open as the people nearby glared at both of us. Sprinting out of the car with her hand extended, 4B commanded, "Now. Let's go."

I gathered my bag to follow her onto the platform and up the stairs. We stood next to each other, laughing in the cool night on Commonwealth Ave. The rain had completely stopped. She leaned over with hands on her thighs. "I'm so out of shape," she said with a cough. "Damn. This is your ass on drugs, girl. You okay?"

"I'm fine," I replied while taking long, deep breaths. Walking miles on the treadmill was finally paying dividends. After we hopped into a taxi idling on the corner of Brookline Avenue, the cabbie with a salt and pepper ZZ-Top beard and thick glasses asked for a destination.

"Cleveland Circle," 4B said.

I waved her off, but she immediately snagged my hand. "I know where you live, and we ain't going there. First, we're going to Cleveland Circle to get some beers. And then we're headed to my place. You got me?" The cabbie hesitated before looking at me. He angrily took off when 4B pounded her fist on the divider. "I said Cleveland Circle. Do you need an invite? Just go, man."

When the car circled around to Beacon Street, she turned to me to finger a few wet curls of my hair behind my ears. "Don't think sex tonight, so take that off the table, and completely out of your mind. I don't want sex to get in the way of us having a good time. Not tonight. I need a friend, okay? Can you be that? I trust you. Can we have some beers, laugh and just talk? Guys can still do that, right?"

"I can do that. These days I'm probably not good for much more."

"Don't say something so silly," she grimaced. "It's just that's not what this is about tonight. You smoke?" She pulled a thick blunt out of her purse. Beacon Street was empty as we sped past Richie's place in Coolidge Corner.

"Hate to disappoint you, but no."

"You straight edge?"

"More like control freak."

"Okay, and that's exactly the reason why I smoke and drink, and do a whole bunch of other things you don't want to know about," she said. "I'm probably more of a control freak than you, but I had to let go. Sometimes, I think I go too far, but you know what? I realized life is way too short. If I die tomorrow in a car crash, I'm okay with it. I'm living my life my way."

The cab pulled next to a crowd of similar taxis idling at the corner of the Store 24 in Cleveland Circle. 4B opened her purse, but this time I seized her hand. I took out the four remaining twenties Monique gave me and reached towards the driver. 4B pulled out one bill. "For beer," she said.

I handed the surprised cabbie $60. "Keep the change," I said, pretending to be Bill Gates.

4B reached back while stepping out onto the slick pavement. I followed obediently. "I thought for sure you were going to call him Harry," she pushed my shoulder playfully. "I always wanted to say 'Harry, keep the change.' That's one of my mother's favorite songs. She used to sing it to me when I wouldn't go to sleep. Any mom who sings 'Taxi' to her daughter is definitely hoping her girl turns into a prom queen just like me."

We walked past a beefy Boston College student in maroon shorts vomiting into a paper party hat. Store 24 was filled with shouting college kids, looking over a rack of stale ham sandwiches and pouring oversized Mountain Dews. 4B began talking to a bearded, homeless man in a bulky, faded maroon overcoat. While chatting with him, she pointed me toward the refrigerator case. "I'll be right there. Pick something good."

I watched her give the twenty-dollar bill to the man before shaking his hand. Gazing into the display of beers, I suddenly felt her palm on my back. "Here, hold these," she said, handing me three packs of Slim Jims, two packages of yellow Hostess cupcakes, and a Snickers bar.

"Let's get a six of Heineken, and get out of here. I'm not choosy. Is that enough food for you?" she whispered.

I shrugged while still thinking about guppies and goldfish swimming throughout my stomach. 4B tried paying with a hundred-dollar bill but resorted to her Amex when the short, bloodshot Hispanic man behind the counter pointed to the sign: "No bills bigger than $20 accepted."

"The hunnie's not real anyway, handsome," she said to him with a wink.

We walked silently up Chestnut Hill Avenue into a tall building on Commonwealth Ave.

"We're home," she announced after ripping open a package of cupcakes and obliterating one with two bites in the hallway.

The security guard behind the desk perked up from a book. "Hi Phoebe, home early tonight?"

"I won't make it a habit Russ, don't worry."

I suspiciously looked at her. "Wait, your name is not Phoebe, is it?"

"It sure is, why? Something against Phoebes?"

"4B. I've been calling you 4B in my head all night."

She leaned against the wall while waiting for the elevator. I stared at the deep well at the base of her neck—the veins under her jaw were protruding as she smiled. "Never thought about that. Well, that's the universe telling you that you knew me all along." After we emerged onto the fifteenth floor, she stopped me just before her door. "I'm kidding. I don't believe in that universe nonsense. It's just a stupid coincidence, like everything else in life. At least, I think that sometimes. It changes—it depends on the day. Ask me again tomorrow."

We walked into the roomy, modern condo with a sleek, shimmering kitchen. Phoebe pointed to a large glass table in the dining room and headed down the hallway. "Put the beer and crap there. I'll be right back. I'm going to change and get you some clothes." With a grandiose, sweeping motion, she pulled off her wig. After placing it on the bedroom doorknob, she shook her head while yanking pins out of her short blonde hair. "Ta-da, the real me. I'll be right back. Make yourself at home."

I took a slow walk around the apartment to catch a view of the Boston College campus outside the oversized windows of the main room.

"Here, get out of those wet pants and that miserable shirt," Phoebe said with her head extended into the doorway. She tossed me a pair of sweatpants along with an old blue Steve's Ice Cream t-shirt.

"I can't put this on," I said after examining the gray sweatpants with LOVE written on the ass in pink letters.

"Do you need to hide in the bathroom to put them on? I won't look. I swear." She lit up the blunt, inhaled and opened her mouth wide to let out a watermelon-sized puff of smoke.

"I'm not going to walk around with LOVE on my ass." I hesitantly took off my shirt, hoping I didn't look like an arrival from Auschwitz. "Look at these sweats. LOVE looks good on you, not on me."

"Oh, don't be a pussy, 3B. I know what it says. If I can wear them, you can wear them. No one's going to see you. And you can tell your friends you got in my pants tonight." She took another hit from the blunt.

I unbuttoned my heavy, wet jeans.

"Wait. You know what? You should take a shower before you change. Otherwise, you'll get pneumonia. Go take a shower, get all nice and clean for me. After that, I have a surprise for you. You want a cupcake?" Phoebe took a sip from the Heineken. "Go shower," she added with her finger pointed to the bathroom. "Then I'm going to rock your world, and change your life."

She stood before me in tight, royal blue gym shorts and a baggy BYU t-shirt. The nipples of her petite breasts pointed from the edges of the B and U. I took a step before hesitating. She was going to rock my world, and change my life?

I was sure she said fucking was off the table. Maybe she meant on the floor. So much for friends. Holding the sweatpants hanging over my shoulder, I stuffed my hands in my pants so she couldn't see I was getting hard. How quickly things had changed. When I sat down to eat with Mon, I never would have imagined that my night would end with sex. I wasn't sure I was prepared but thought, *Bud Ready When You Are*. Be a Bud man.

Phoebe and I remained in the middle of the apartment, a few inches from each other. I briefly imagined her eyes wide and my cock in her mouth.

She stared at me smiling stupidly back at her. "C'mon now 3B, get going. You know I'm not going to wait for you all night."

Thirty-One

I was all hyped up with anticipation of the unknown as I scrubbed with two different bottles of men's body wash, resting upside down next to a razor on Phoebe's toiletry shelves. My skin was scraped raw and my balls were so shiny, I could have hung them on a Christmas tree. It was time to get back in the game. But after taking a long look at the water cascading onto my bony, naked body, I couldn't help but laugh at my own grand delusions. C'mon now. Who was going to fuck that?

My wild porn fantasies had run ridiculously amok. I was obviously spending too much time rubbing my third eye blind while watching Jenna Jameson DVDs to realize women just don't rock the fuck out of Gumby with a penis. Phoebe didn't invite me up to her apartment because I was the hot muscular pizza boy who was going to give her a large pepperoni and extra cheese. I was there because she needed someone around to help her kill the night.

Once I realized the joke was on me once again, my cock withered like a cabbage roll left in the sun.

I eventually emerged from the bathroom, dressed in her silly sweat-pants, chastened and more than a little bit embarrassed by my fantastic Phoebe fuck-me fantasia. She was holding a beer while giggling with her pale legs up on the edge of a chair—knees tucked under her chin.

"Wow, were you building a pyramid in there?"

I noticed a thick beige pouch on the far side of the dining table. One of the unusually high, futuristic chairs—seemingly built for a replicant—was placed a foot or two away from the table's edge.

Phoebe walked directly past me on her way into the bedroom. "You look like Tarzan on crack with that hair." She tapped me on the ass while adding, "Love."

"Sit down there. Time to rock the boat, and change your life. Let me get something."

Now even more clueless than usual, I quietly wondered what the hell I had gotten myself into. "Hey, Phoebe, are we having a prayer meeting?"

"I don't think so. Jesus wasn't so big on grooming either. Relax, man, and I'll be right there," she shouted.

Within seconds, Phoebe's breath was on my neck and her hands on my shoulders. She ran her fingers through my wet locks. I couldn't help but turn longingly.

"Don't, no, or you are going to knock the towel off your shoulders. So, are you ready to cut off all this Motley Crue hair?" She reached around my chin to place a duel-sided cosmetics mirror on the table. "I don't know how you go out with this." Her long, delicate fingers carefully pried opened the pouch revealing two scissors, combs, and a small electric razor.

When I jerked my body defiantly, she firmly grabbed my biceps.

"Relax. I'm not Sweeney Todd. I want to bring you into the twenty-first century, nature boy. You have such a sweet face. Stop hiding it from the world."

"No, Phoebe, don't be ridiculous. You are high, you are drunk, and be honest, you don't have a clue how to cut hair. You've got to be kidding, I thought..." My hopes had gone from blowjob to a blow dry in a matter of minutes.

"Sit up. Stop laughing to yourself, and complaining. This hair isn't funny." Phoebe held the mirror inches from my face. "You look like you stuck your finger into an electric socket."

"Hey, I know you intend well, Phoebe. If you want in the future, maybe I'll go with you to some kind of salon, but you are not cutting my hair," I said, stepping away. She ran into her bedroom again only to quickly reemerge while holding a piece of paper over her head.

"Here look. I'm licensed. It was another life, but this is who I used to be. Trust me. I can cut your hair."

I glanced at the paper. "Phoebe, I don't know you."

"Then get to know me," she said, her face dimming. "I'm being honest with you. Look. State of California Board of Barbering and Cosmetology License. Go ahead, check the license."

She pushed the paper to my chest so I examined it like someone scrutinizing a surgeon's medical degrees before brain surgery.

"But you are stoned and…"

"Look, there's the joint. Almost the full thing right there on the table. Hardly enough to even begin a buzz for me."

The blunt was placed neatly on a glass saucer next to a carton of Marlboros. I couldn't imagine Phoebe cutting a bologna sandwich, let alone my hair, but I knew she was right. My curls had become an unruly fucking mess—I was just too lazy to do something about them.

"C'mon, let me cut your hair, please? You're going to look so great. I swear. Sit down. Worst case scenario, you'll look like Emo Phillips, and then go out and do standup."

After I relented while laughing, she whispered in my ear. "Once we're done, though, I'm going to crush that joint and finish those beers. You are going to drink with me, right?"

I was still processing another limp dick night and the prospect of short hair. "One thing at a time Phoebe, please."

"Relax. Just close your eyes. Put yourself in my hands patient 3B. C'mon now. It's time to take a look and say one final goodbye to this guy."

When I heard the first snip at the very base of my neck, all tension gave way. Trust. I knew her all of two hours, but I was going to give it a try.

"Tell me, you don't smoke, and you don't seem too keen on drinking, what do you do for fun? Anything?" she asked.

I shrugged after staring out the large window at the far end of the palatial condo.

"My life has not been much fun recently. I kind of forgot what it's like, and I'm not so sure I'm meant to have it."

"Oh Lord, you grew up Catholic, didn't you? So damn dramatic. You want me to sing 'Ave Maria' for you? That's a real crucified diva attitude. You poor, poor baby." She snorted out a laugh while clipping away with enthusiasm. I could feel locks of hair fall onto my shoulders, and into my lap.

"This time, I really am going to smoke. You don't mind, do you? I'll turn the air conditioner on," Phoebe said before running to her purse and pulling out a cigarette from a crinkled pack. After lighting up, she took an extended, satisfied drag.

"Be honest. You must have some things you enjoy. I love to smoke my ass off. Those are the little pleasures, 3B. We all have them."

"I enjoyed being with my girlfriend. We had a lot of fun, and then we didn't. Once we moved in together, the fun just seemed to end. At first, we were good together. Then something happened, and suddenly we weren't." It felt like Phoebe was cutting big chunks of hair in rapid succession. I wondered if her only experience was barbering in the Ozarks.

"Stop trembling. I know what I'm doing. And you know what? I also know sometimes some people are good together, but that doesn't mean they belong together. I'm assuming when you're talking about you two having fun, you're talking about sex. Right? You moved in together, and there went the fun and the danger. Sounds predictable." She was talking slowly, as if underwater. When I glanced back to her, she kept flicking cigarette ashes into a Star Wars glass on the table.

"It wasn't just the sex." Phoebe sounded so reductive to me.

"Okay then, what else did you like?"

"I liked a lot. Jessie was the kind of person I always wanted to be with when I was in college, but when I finally got what I wanted, I didn't want it anymore. Everything kind of went wrong the longer we were together. We didn't have fun, and no, we didn't have much sex." I immediately flinched. Sex was not a topic to discuss with someone I still wanted to fuck.

Phoebe embraced it, though, and pushed further. "You know, you ever wonder, especially at our age—and I'm a just little older than you—that maybe sex should be just a recreational sport? When we convince ourselves that sex should be something more, that's when we get into trouble. We are trained to believe sex is better when you're in love, so we start thinking we are in love. Could that be what happened?

"I'm just asking because it happened to me. My mother told me, 'Phoebe, when you are in love, sex is so special. It's sacred.' It would be soo transcendent. Hallelujah." I could still feel the heat of the cigarette ash when she stepped a few feet away to admire her work. "My mom told me it was all so true, especially for women. We need to be in love. So I fell in love with a guy, and guess what?" The question hung in the air.

"I said guess what?" she insisted.

Our eyes met. "The sex was the same?"

"I wish," she huffed. "No, it sucked. He was really nice, but he treated me differently once we moved in together. I kept waiting for the special to come. Maybe he was the wrong guy, but sex always seems lot better without love. Honestly, I think we are conditioned by society to settle down, you know?

"Who knows? Maybe I'm wrong. You can ask other girls. I think some girls need to look deeply into guys' eyes and feel that connection that says you are in love. Maybe it's just me, but I don't need it and don't actually want it. I like to see and feel different bodies next to my skin and different dicks inside me."

I abruptly stood while brushing over four years of hair off my body. There were small piles of curls scattered across the floor. "Well, okay, Phoebe, you know, I'm thinking I'm not quite the right guy you should be telling this to." I was getting hard again.

"Oh stop, you have heard a girl say dick before. I said sex was off the table before, not sex talk. You're not one of those lame guys who can't differentiate between the two, are you? I took you for a smart one. It's just talk. If I am making you uncomfortable, I'll stop."

I definitely wanted to hear more of her dick talk. In fact, I agreed with everything she was saying. I used to eat out Jessie and wonder if hers was the last pussy I was ever going to see over the next fifty years. I certainly knew she was thinking there had to be more cock. It was depressing.

A thick cloud of suffocating smoke hovered throughout the room. The shitty electric fan in my bedroom offered more circulation than the purring air conditioner. The smoke alarm repeatedly shrieked until Phoebe batted it off the wall with a broom.

"I hate that thing. Now sit down 3B—the artist is still working. Let me ask you, did any adult in your lifetime ever tell you sex with different girls is the way to go? Tell me why not? The stories our parents and teachers tell us are just some fairy tales to keep us normal. You know what? I'm not so sure I want to be all that normal."

And there I was, desperately searching for just a tiny bit of normality in my life.

"Phoebe, I totally support all of what you're saying, but you know what?" I said.

She didn't answer.

"I said you know what?" I couldn't resist echoing her.

"What? I'll ask what? What?" She snapped with exaggerated indignation.

"Fuck normal life for your sake, but I would definitely like a very normal haircut. I wanna go home with my ears."

She tossed the scissors on the table. "You're getting a better than normal haircut, so don't be a bitch. What the hell?" Her eyes were on fire as she laughed and yanked my earlobe. "I'm not giving you an Abbie Normal 'do. So, no more complaining.

"You're making me lose my train of thought. Maybe you and your girlfriend were great and in love, but I hear you telling me something different. Aren't you?

I had no idea how she was translating my words.

"What I'm saying is I liked dating. But when we were living together, all I wanted to be was alone. I've been figuring this out for months with my psychiatrist. I really have. I'm not so sure I belong with anyone. Is it so bad to want to be alone?"

"That's what I needed to hear. I'm going to ask you an honest question. You don't have to answer if you don't want because it's really personal, but that need to be alone thing makes it clear to me. You okay with me asking?" Phoebe picked up the scissors again, along with the electric razor. She began chopping and shaving with fierce determination. I figured I'd end up looking like Travis Bickle after he was shot in the head.

"I think you are confirming what I already know. I see you in me. Honestly, what's your deal?" she said.

"What do you mean?" Of course, I realized she knew the truth.

"I mean I'm going to be blunt. I see you. I know. I've always known when I used to see you with your girlfriend. Are you bulimic or anorexic? You were really skinny when I used to meet you. You weigh more now, but you're still real thin."

"I know I'm thin, but what makes you think…" I slumped in the chair, uncomfortable at being outed.

"Because I've been anorexic and bulimic. Still am, sometimes. You had to realize it. Right? Look at me. I hardly have an ass and no tits. I saw you checking out my legs. They're nothing. Life ain't fair, is it? I don't think I'll ever, ever shake my problems completely." She let out a defeated sigh.

"I'm actually surprised you are here. I know how hard it is to be with people, especially people you don't know. You don't have to hide with me. You know how they say gay people have radar for people who are gay? They call it gaydar. I think people with eating problems have the same exact thing. Anorexics, bulimics. They know who's in the sorority. Or fraternity. Whatever.

"I know a heck of a lot of girls who say, 'I'm not anorexic, I'm just bulimic.'" She laughed while squatting next to me. "As if there's a difference. It's all about control. But you, I knew you were dealing. I actually wanted to reach out when I saw you one night, but I knew how pissed off I'd be if someone confronted me out of the blue. It's scary, though, to see someone else going through it."

The sadness in Phoebe's voice was much too familiar. I wanted to hold her. Finally, someone who understood. Someone who didn't need a morass of lies as an explanation to hide the truth.

"I'm anorexic, Phoebe. Like two or three years. Who really knows how long? It's a struggle. I'm trying to deal with it, and I ate tonight. I'm just not totally used to it yet. And I'm certainly not used to telling someone."

"You okay? You able to manage? Now I'm really glad you didn't go home to think about it all night."

"I'm better this minute."

I was. Talking to her somehow made me feel momentarily whole.

"Good. You have to fight it. That's what I tell myself every day. And sometimes, I can't. And, of course, I don't go around telling anyone either. I'm telling you. I guess I trust you. But we aren't freaks. You have to realize that.

"You know that girl on the train? The one you thought was hot?" She finally stopped cutting. I waited for her to continue, but she pushed me between the shoulder blades instead.

"She wasn't hot. C'mon you need to get your eyes checked. That girl obviously has a problem. That's not funny, and I shouldn't be laughing. But you knew, though, just by looking at the bones on her chest popping out. That's why you were attracted to her. You had something in common."

When I turned my head around to acknowledge her, she dolefully stared at me with the cigarette still burning between her lips.

"Don't look at me. Let me finish—you're gonna love it. Jeez, I'm dying of thirst. You want something to drink?" She quietly escaped into the kitchen.

"Can I ask you an honest question for a change?" I shouted to her.

"I've got nothing to hide."

"I saw you eat a Hostess cupcake like a python. And one of those packages of Slim Jims is gone. Do you eat normally now?" Within seconds, Phoebe charged back into the room. I watched her slide to a halt, inches from the table.

"Here's a Diet Coke, and here's my deal." She slapped a prescription bottle and two packages of Ex-Lax on the table. "Diuretics in that bottle. Can't live without them. I pay a friend for the prescriptions. Totally illegal. Unfortunately, I can go through an entire box of Ex-Lax in one day.

"I can be a mess, man. I mean a real mess. You're right, you don't really know me yet. You probably don't want to."

"Stop, don't say that, I do," I said.

"I know what you're thinking, though. Yeah, I spend a lot of time in the bathroom. It's gross, I know. Definitely not sexy. No guy ever wants to know about it. I know those pills are bad for me. But it sure feels good. It feels really good. And I'm going to warn you. It's just like crack. I just can't stop. It's easier, though. I know that for sure. I was bulimic for years. That really ruined my teeth. They were super expensive to fix." She traced my right ear with the electric razor while exhaling again, this time more emphatically.

"I'll tell you, it's just easier to let it come out the other way."

Phoebe stepped before me with her chest pumped and shoulders at attention. "All done. Look in the mirror. Ready to see the new you? If I may say so myself, I did a marvelous, brilliant, fantastic job, and you look, well, take a look at this new guy."

I took a quick, hesitant peek, only to see my five-year-old self, staring back. My hair was neatly combed straight with a clean part on the left and the sides trimmed short.

"Sooo?" Phoebe said while holding the broom like a guitar.

"I honestly don't recognize myself. This is how I used to cut my hair before…" I just couldn't admit that it was exactly how I looked before becoming a chubby teenager. My head felt so light—weightless.

"I will clean up. I can't believe all that hair came from me. Thank you, really. I owe you," I said, relieved. She took the towel off my shoulders before gently wiping the back of my neck and ears.

"You got a lifetime to pay me back. Hey, did I tell you every time I used to see you, I would think `that guy needs a haircut.' You just needed someone to tell you how nice you could look. You always looked like you just didn't care."

After scooping up large clumps of hair with my hands, I went to the kitchen to retrieve a garbage can. When Phoebe knelt before me, I swept the last remaining strands into the pan.

"Can I toss these in there please," I said after grabbing the diuretic bottle and boxes of Ex-Lax off the table.

Placing her hands on mine, she said, "Thanks, but you know damn well we can't save each other. That's like me putting a piece of cake before you and saying, `Eat.' If you throw them out, I have pills in the cabinets. I'll just go out, and get even more tomorrow. You should know that. Let's go inside and sit together. Maybe watch some television."

I spied her as she walked to the front room with Heineken bottle and blunt in hand. She tumbled onto an oversized brown couch and burned a quarter inch off the blunt with her head tilted back. With eyebrows dancing, she blew smoke at me. "My present to you," she whispered.

We sat together, her calves on my lap. "You okay like this?" she said while alternating between drinks from the beer and drags of the blunt. Any desire I had for her had long dissipated. It felt like I was sitting with my damaged sister.

"Phoebe, your license is from California, your shirt says BYU, your accent is definitely not Boston. Where you from?" She ignored me and turned on the television. After flipping through channels, she ultimately settled on a repeat of *Cheers*.

"How appropriate for us. I don't think I'd like to be anywhere everyone knows my name. There definitely are no cheers in Boston, the least friendly city I've been to. You really want to know about me? I'm from everywhere. I've moved around my whole life. Lived in L.A., Vegas— really love Vegas—Manhattan, Utah. Met my boring boyfriend there."

Pulling at the bottom of her t-shirt, Phoebe added, "This was his. It's like ten-years old. I still travel a lot, but I was born in Indiana. My mother drove me all around the country looking for a man. You believe that? We were the real Jack Kerouacs of the world. My mom ended up marrying an animal, a dirty scumbag. I can't begin to tell you about that. Maybe in our next lives. I left when I could for pure survival. And I ended up exploring. Everything."

On the verge of a deep sleep, she quietly asked if I could get her a fresh beer and the remaining package of cupcakes. When I returned, she was blowing smoke out the open window.

"Hey, you ever think we could take a timeout from our lives?" Phoebe whispered without looking at me.

"What do you mean? Timeout? A vacation?"

"No, I mean stop. Literally, stop time. I don't know about you, but my life's just hurtling by so fast, and I have nothing to show for it. No real family, no friends, nothing around me. Things just seem to pass on by. Sometimes, I just want to stop time, and re-arrange some things.

"Change the past and rework how I got here, and then move forward again. It's a fantasy, I know. Don't you wish there was a window to step through so you can see your life from the outside like looking into a dollhouse? That way you could move the pieces around into proper order."

I couldn't figure out if she was serious or taking off on some weed-fueled philosophical reverie that would be quickly forgotten in the morning.

Before I could reply, she continued. "You know what? I'm glad we connected. Somehow, I think we are connected. I always thought that when I saw you. There's something bigger going on. I have to tell you, you're probably wondering why I invited you into my place and said no sex. Then I told you sex should be a sport with no ties. It doesn't make sense, I know, but here it does. You're a nice guy. It's great to meet someone who listens."

She pulled a rubber band out of her shorts to tie the back of her hair up before collapsing on the couch again. "In a different world, it would be great if you and me could, I don't know, maybe who knows? It's kind of silly—the things we think about. But we both know we'd be a landmine waiting to be stepped on. That's so sad—the whole world is sad. The reason I asked you here..."

"No worries, I get it, it's fine. I understand," I said. "I know exactly what you mean. People like us don't belong together. It's just not healthy. We'd end up self-immolating together. It'd be way too intense."

Phoebe finished the beer without a breath. After a moment's thought, she reached for the cupcakes I'd left on the small magazine table next to the couch.

"Maybe we can be friends?" I said as she staggered into her bedroom.

I was leaning out the window to inhale the cool night air when she returned with two pillows.

"Here, let's sleep on the couch. It's safer," she said, handing me one of the large, fluffy pillows in a black, soft cotton case. "We are who we are. Friends, whatever. We don't need to label it. Who knows what's going to happen? All I know is I'm really happy right now. And you know what? That's mighty okay. That's all I can ask out of life."

Her eyes were red and very glassy. I couldn't tell if she was stoned out of her gourd or crying.

Thirty-Two

"**Y**our phone. Pick up your phone. It's been ringing over and over."

I was awoken by Phoebe's voice—she stood over me while gently tapping my shoulder. "You better check your phone."

"When did it start ringing?" I was still on the couch, now bathed in a morning sunlight foreign to me. Phoebe was holding a black mug with 'A Giant Cup of I'm the Fucking Boss' imprinted in white letters on the front as a warm breeze rushed in through the fully open windows.

"It went off like four times. I called to you, but you were dead out. At least, one of us slept well."

I sat up like a battle-scarred boxer rising off the canvas and searched the room for a clock.

"It's early, just after 8:30. For some reason, you don't remind me of a morning person. I hate mornings, but lookie here, here I am." Phoebe took a drink after blowing into the oversized mug. "You drink coffee?"

My eyes were still dazed as I tried to recall the previous night. It seemed like Phoebe was part of some unsettling dream. "Definitely, no coffee, thanks. Wait, I slept here last night?"

"It was that memorable, huh?" Phoebe smiled. "Yep, you actually slept in someone else's apartment, as tough as that might be to believe." She yanked up her denim shorts from the belt loops before sitting next to me.

Dressed in only a white, ribbed wife beater and those very short shorts, she looked like a fragment of the girl I met the night before— more than a bit waifish with shaggy, still damp hair.

"There's orange juice in the frig if you want. No Diet Coke before noon for you. It's going to be near a hundred today. Freakish weather. I'm already sweating my ass off, but I love the heat, don't you?" she said as I poured juice into a glass. "You want a pair of shorts? I have a pair that says HATE on the ass if you want."

"Jesus, I need a minute to remember all that last night. It doesn't seem real." A quick brush through my short hair confirmed my new reality.

"You have couch head, but yeah, the hair is all gone with the wind, Scarlett," Phoebe said, after rimming her fingers over my ear. My mouth was so dry that it felt like I slept face down on the beach.

"You better check your messages to see who called. After that, we'll see what we do. I have a few things I have to get done this morning."

I listened to Mon's long, slightly incoherent apology about the night before—something about business and a whole lot of "I'm sorry and embarrassed." It was obviously pure bullshit, but I was coming to realize that people used voicemail to conveniently avoid the truth or confrontation. Phoebe pulled a thick binder from the top of a glass accent shelf and placed it next to a full backpack. She slid onto an oddly designed white fabric chair near the window to bake in the sun.

After trying to decipher a long patch of static and clicks, I was about to close the phone when David's faint voice appeared. "Mike, I'm sorry I missed you. I know it's probably too early for you, but I figured I'd leave you a message. Happy birthday, brother. I'll make it up to you, big time. Just wanted to say hi, and let you know I'm thinking of you. Have fun today. Go out and get laid. Please remember life is really short, so enjoy yourself. Make something happen. Talk to you."

I put the phone away while still trying to get my bearings. Go get laid? Just who did he think I was going to fuck? I hadn't seen my brother in months—he had no idea what was going on—but he was talking like someone was going to casually walk into my life and hop on my cock.

We were so out of touch with each other—it felt like the air had been let out of the balloon. Throughout his absence, I couldn't help but wonder what was actually happening with Mon's and David's relationship. They had been separated since February, so I figured he could have been hanging out on some remote island beach while writing in a cabana with a bunch of Clapton's geriatric G-stringed groupies checking his punctuation. Mon seemed to be traveling all the time, increasingly frazzled and drinking more and more wine every time I saw her. There had to be a secret about their marriage I didn't know. Of all the people in the world, they were the last ones I took for shining examples of celibacy. Something had to be going on.

And, of course, I realized I probably would be the last person to find out.

After jamming the phone in my black bag, I walked to the window to take hold of the view spanning the broad clusters of trees beyond Boston College in Chestnut Hill. The intermittent traffic quietly streamed down Commonwealth Avenue, past a stalled trolley with its doors open.

"Anyone important?" Phoebe popped out of the chair to hover next to me.

"I need to be back at my place at ten. I almost forgot. I'm sorry. I'll just call a cab."

"Oh, stop with the nonsense. I can drive you home. I actually want to visit my old neighbor. Remember the old, bearded guy who lived next to you? He would peek out the door all the time. He was actually a sweetheart. I used to buy him groceries.

"A horny old dude, and a flirt, but I love getting a rise out those guys. Gotta keep their blood flowing. I know he would welcome a visit. I've also got something else to do. C'mon inside, let's eat something first. You haven't eaten anything since you've been here. You should shower before you leave. Wash last night away."

Phoebe marched me into the kitchen by the elbow, and after pouring another cup of coffee, she pulled a gallon of milk out of the refrigerator. When she splashed some milk into a glass, the steam from her coffee clouded her face.

"Drink the milk, you have to build strong bones with those eight essential vitamins. Breakfast is the most important meal of the day. What other clichés have you heard over the years?" With a quick leap, she propped herself next to the toaster on the counter. Her legs dangled before me. "Seriously, you have to eat something, Michael. When have you last eaten?"

I began telling her about the sushi and my night at Mon's when it registered. "Wait, wait, did you just call me Michael?"

"Yeah, that's your name, right, 3B?" A crooked smile emerged as she coyly fluttered her eyelashes before breaking out into a throaty laugh.

I was sure I had never told her my name. "What? How did you know that? And why did you call me 3B all night then?"

"Oh please, man. I was just playing with you. I was also high all last night. I was high before I met you yesterday. In fact, I was really pretty high on the train. I'm surprised you didn't even recognize it. I can't be sober all the time. It gets exhausting being the same person every minute, doesn't it? Don't you get tired just being you all your life?"

After replaying our night together a few times, I could not figure out how she arrived at Michael. "This is creepy, Phoebe, how did you come up with Michael? I didn't tell you."

"Not last night, correct, 3B. You told me your name a few years ago when we met each other on the way out of the building. Go back in your head. I see you thinking now about things. You and your girl-friend were having a party. You remember it?

"To be honest, when I met you that night, I thought you were really high. I always figured you smoked. When I used to see you, you seemed kind of out of it with a hazy, sad look and all that crazy hair.

"We were heading out that night, and we met on the stairs. I told you my name, which you obviously didn't remember. Then we walked together up to 7-Eleven together. You said to me you were getting away from the party you were having. You needed to get some air but you looked spooked like you saw a ghost. It was a crazy cold night—it's always cold, but not like that. Before you walked into 7-Eleven, you told me your name—Michael.

"Yesterday, I was having fun with you. You know really, 3B, Michael, it doesn't change anything. You are who you are, whatever I call you."

She fumbled through a mess of boxes in the cabinets with nervous energy. "I have Fruit Loops, Count Chocula—my favorite—and Captain Crunch. You want some Lucky Charms? You know I used to think if I ate that Lucky Charms crap, my life would turn out great. Who would've guessed it doesn't work, and just gives you diabetes?"

I was amused by her easy smile and nonchalance, both reminding me of Jessie when we first met. She took a handful from the box of

Fruit Loops, her legs freely swinging back and forth.

"If you want to eat healthy, you have to sleep over another girl's house." Phoebe eyed me while carefully placing the individual multi-colored sugar rings in her mouth like they were oysters. Her new, relaxed demeanor was as different as her appearance—gone was the hot-wired, scattered girl in the wig I met on the T the night before.

"Phoebe, how much of last night do you remember? If you were high all day, then you were high when you cut my hair, and after that."

She finished the Fruit Loops, handed over a bowl and put the box of Captain Crunch before me. "Guilty on all counts, but I still did a great job on your hair. I remember everything and, honestly, the idea of being friends like we talked about is kinda cute. It really is, but I'm a shitty friend. I'm just not around enough to be a good one."

I took the bowl to a stool near the table and waited patiently for her to follow.

"You can't just sit there with an empty bowl. You need this." Phoebe vaulted off the counter and tossed the box of cereal through her legs like a Harlem Globetrotter.

"How about that trick? I have plenty more. And how 'bout some milk." She glided across the floor before gracefully sliding onto the stool next to me. After a deep breath, she placed the plastic gallon near my arm.

"Let me translate what you are saying here," I said. "You think friends have to hang out all the time? I've had shitty friends I spent a lot of time with, but there were some good friends I hardly saw."

Her smile disappeared as she shrugged. "I don't know about that, but, well, let me tell ya, there's one thing I know for sure we can do together. I want you to come with me to an eating disorder meeting I go to at Wellesley Memorial Hospital." With one squinted eye gauging me, she silently poured Captain Crunch into the bowl.

"I'm a shitty group therapy member too because I pop in and out, but I'd like you to come with me. What I said last night I meant. I'd like to be friends, I just don't know if I can."

I genuinely enjoyed being around Phoebe and definitely needed another person in my life. And, at that point, I was happy to sit in therapy all day. It seemed like a win-win.

"Yeah, yeah, no worries, I'll go. Tell me when it is. I'll work my other doctors around it. Could be good. You know, I have more doctors than friends."

"Brilliant Watson, brilliant. Guess that wasn't so hard, was it? You have to meet your friend soon, right? And I have to get out of here. Got work to do," she said before drowning the cereal in milk.

"You eat that. We gotta make ourselves strong," she said while slipping away towards the bathroom. "That's what we tell ourselves right? Hey, it's so hot, I'm going to take another quick shower. You better take one too." Phoebe closed the door, leaving a small gap for her mouth. "Let me ask you, do you believe we are what we eat? Imagine how pathetic that would be."

. . . .

"This is the first stop, okay? Just one more but I'll get you back by ten, I swear," Phoebe said as she parked her Volvo in front of a large, ornate house on the perimeter of Boston College. She reached into the backseat for the bulky backpack and binder and tapped me on the knee. "You fine here for a few minutes? Take in the sun—time to get you tan."

She flicked her burning cigarette into the street before skipping down the front path through a wall of bushes. While waiting on the porch in her bright red Converses, Phoebe waved back to the car. She was fanning her face with mock exhaustion when a balding man in a sportscoat finally opened the door to let her in.

I inspected the glove compartment for something to read and found a registration card beneath an owner's manual. Her name was indeed Phoebe—Phoebe Stubb. It was a relief to know she wasn't lying. I just wasn't sure what was real anymore. As a student passed in the middle of the street on a skateboard, I guiltily replaced the registration. It felt like I was inspecting someone's medicine cabinet for prescriptions.

With the morning sun intensifying, sweat began bleeding through the Santarpio's Pizza t-shirt Phoebe had given me. I pulled the envelopes out from Mon's bag to count the travelers checks and inspect the bank account information—I carefully added up $5,000 in checks.

Inside the second envelope were multiple papers clipped together and a post-it note with Mon's handwriting: "Sign and date. Return to Robert Gibson at Bank of America on Harvard Ave." Pink stickers marked the signature lines at the bottom of each page. The last page had my name, an account number, and the account total. A drop of sweat fell from my nose, staining the type. I was staring at $10,000.

"See, it wasn't that long. One more stop. I should have left the keys with you so you could listen to music." Phoebe tossed her now empty backpack beneath her seat, and then placed an overstuffed bright orange pack into the back before turning the engine over.

"Hey you, alright? It's hot, but you look like you are going to pass out. You should have eaten more than the cereal. I'm not going to say anything, though. I think I have some water and tissues in the trunk."

She sprang out of the car again to open the trunk, allowing me time to surreptitiously return the bank envelope and checks into Mon's leather bag. When Phoebe quickly reemerged with a bottle of Aquafina and two boxes of tissues, I felt a momentary jolt of adrenalin. I had fifteen fucking thousand dollars—enough to jump-start a new life.

"Drink the water. You're shaking. You know the last thing I need is you passing out on me. Skinny people aren't supposed to sweat. You look like you did last night after the rain." Phoebe was driving recklessly while gleefully tossing tissues into my face. When she turned up the sound system, Stevie Nicks' "Landslide" vibrated through the speakers, and out the windows.

"You like this song?" I said.

Phoebe let go of the wheel to weave her hands before her eyes. "Stevie Nicks is my hero, a goddess. Find me a woman who doesn't like Stevie Nicks, and I guarantee you find someone who is not worth knowing."

After the short ten-minute drive, dodging cars and switching lanes, we parked right in front of my apartment building. Phoebe pulled out a pen out of the glove compartment.

"Give me your arm," She said, latching onto my left wrist. "Here's my number. I know where you live, so I might just pop in from time to time. I hate calling, but you can call me anytime." She wiped the inside of my forearm with a napkin before writing. The ink smeared almost immediately. After finishing with a flourish, she cautiously fingered the pink scar from the scissors gash.

"This is not what I think it is, is it?"

"Does anyone try to commit suicide by cutting the middle of their forearm? You know, you could have just put your number in my phone," I said, yanking the arm away and handing her my cell.

"And what fun would that be? And to answer your question, yeah, I've seen people do some really strange things. Really strange. I'm sure I wasn't the first person to ask that."

Actually, very few people had seen the scar because I conscientiously avoided wearing short sleeves.

"I stabbed myself with scissors," I said with one foot out of the car.

"Oh, yeah sure, see now that's not strange at all," Phoebe shot back on her way to the front of the hood. "You'll have to tell me that story someday. Why do I think it had something to do with food?"

I laughed as we walked together towards the building entrance. She awkwardly carried the bulky orange backpack that nearly tipped her backward.

A car horn forced us both to turn.

"Michael, I'm over here. C'mere." It was Mon, in white jeans, standing next to David's black BMW.

Phoebe slowly stepped backwards to the building. "Soo, wow, Mr. 3B, that's the really hot friend you are meeting? Bravo you. Who knew? That is one nice rebound."

"Sooo, that's the sister-in-law I am meeting," I replied, shaking my head.

"Well, hello to the sister-in-law," Phoebe said in a sing-song voice. She waved to Mon while walking into the apartment lobby. "She is still super hot. Wish I looked like that with those legs. "Hey, I'll let you know when our meeting is, alright?"

As I walked away, she sprinted back and moved in close enough for me to feel the heat of her body. "Listen to me. You don't belong here. 4B says get out of 3B before you die in it. You hear me? I'll talk to you."

"Hey, Samson, let's go. Get in the car," Mon's voice echoed down the street.

When I climbed into the BMW with the black bag in tow, Mon adjusted her sunglasses before touching my chin with her index finger. "I don't believe it. When did this happen? I've been telling you for months to cut your hair, and now look at you. Don't tell me you are just getting in from last night. Who's the pretty chica with those short shorts? What happened last night after you went home? I'm guessing you didn't go home at all. Good for you, lucky man."

After a long pause and a mischievous grin, she added, "You got my message, correct?"

"It's definitely not what you are thinking. And yeah, I got the message, but forget about it. Business, I understand. Mon, you don't need to explain, really. Things happen."

She abruptly drove away past the fire station and Dunkin' Donuts towards Storrow Drive. "You look so cute with short hair. You realize I've never seen you without the Kenny G curls. Michael, I'm so sorry about last night." Mon was speeding like a NASCAR driver—passing cars and plowing through yellow lights. I held onto the bottom of the seat as I checked myself in the side view mirror. Within hours, my old look had been downgraded from Peter Frampton to Kenny G—the next level of shame was Weird Al Yankovic.

The short hair was definitely staying.

"Mon, I said forget about the end of last night. I still had a good time." I had no intention of questioning her story. I once wanted to understand everything, but I was discovering that the more you search for answers and think you're reaching the light, the more you realize you are just uncovering a deeper, darker well of questions.

"Mon, I'm not going to say anything more about what you gave me. I don't know what to say." I just wasn't going to argue with her about the money anymore either. I was exhausted by micromanaging the world. If they wanted to give me $15,000, fuck it. Thank. You. Very. Much.

"Where the heck are we going?" Mon was doing eighty with one hand brushing hair out of her face as she navigated her way around Kenmore Square. We pulled off Storrow to head down Massachusetts

Avenue by Symphony Hall towards Huntington Avenue.

"We are going to where I hope you will be living if you like it."

After Mon turned onto cramped Westland Avenue, a minivan miraculously pulled away from the curb. She maneuvered past two double-parked cars, and we slid headfirst into the space.

"How you like that for serendipity? It might be an Annie Hall park, but it will do for now. Leave that bag in the car, and come with me."

She walked with long, confident strides in heels down the street—sunglasses on top of her head. I lagged behind while watching her talking nervously into the phone. After getting buzzed into the building, we marched up the stairs together. Mon hugged a tall, magnificently chiseled man with curly hair and a neatly trimmed goatee. He said something in her ear while smiling flirtatiously before heading down the spiraling staircase. She threw the door open to a large, sparsely furnished apartment.

"You like it? It's available September 15th, and you can afford it. Miguel is a friend. You'd love him, but he's going away for a year. You can go month to month here if you want. See if you like it. Or you can sign a lease. Whatever you want to do."

Sitting down at the neatly decorated kitchen table with a bowl of apples on a placemat, I couldn't help but wonder if Phoebe and Monique were working together in some kind of secret sisterhood society.

Sunshine flooded the airy room as I watched Mon repeatedly fan herself by the wall adorned with a Basquiat print. "Jesus, it's only June but I'm soaking wet. I've had enough already," she said with a cockeyed grin.

"You didn't pay anything for this right?" I strained to be heard over a car alarm wailing from the street and Train's "Drops of Jupiter" blaring from across the hall.

"No, this is your business. You want to do things yourself? Now you can. You're on your own to make the arrangements. I'll give you the information." There were deep rings around Mon's eyes—it was clear that she had not slept.

"Monique, thank you. I'm saying it so often, I should have just printed it on my forehead."

"Not me, thank Richie when he gets back from San Francisco next week. It's great his divorce is finally settled. It turns out he found this place through one of his clients who knows Miguel.

It's a small, inexplicable world sometimes. Just open your arms, and things fall into them." She walked to the refrigerator for two bottles of water. After pressing one to her forehead, she sat next to me.

"Drink or you'll get dehydrated. I need to get used to this new you. Take a look around. It's not complicated and, as they say on the *Price is Right*, 'this could be yours.'

If it's fine, let's get out of here before we melt into water puddles like the wicked witch. Jesus, new haircut, new place, new girl, maybe?" she said. "The wheel's turning, Michael. Time to grab it, and go forward. Your days of driving like Thelma and Louise are over."

Thirty-Three

The hallway outside the eating disorder meeting at Wellesley Memorial Hospital had a dank, musty smell and dismal lighting—it seemed as if I was sitting in an Ed Wood film. I had just spoken with Richie who was stuck in Chicago's O'Hare Airport after his plane from San Francisco was diverted. I insisted on picking him up at Logan Airport when he arrived because I knew a long drive would serve as the perfect post-meeting brain cleanser.

Young women slowly filtered into the small room one by one, a few eyeing me as if on high alert for a potential rapist. The bench was extremely uncomfortable with deep knife gashes in the worn, varnished slats. Every time the hallway door opened, I anticipated seeing Phoebe enter. As the six o'clock meeting approached, the likelihood of her showing up seemed appropriately slim, though.

During our phone conversations during the week, Phoebe emphasized how much the meetings would help me and how it important it would be to have someone there to support her. When I told her that we could go together in my car, she politely said she didn't want to put me out, even though her condominium was directly on the way to the hospital. It was a football field-sized red flag, but I remained hopeful I would see her again.

While staring at the old, hallway clock, I called Phoebe one more time as each suspicious woman walked past me into the meeting. After a quick half-ring, a repetitive busy signal blared into my ear. I peeked into the room at the women gathered around a table. A middle-aged Latina woman in a maroon sweater made eye contact with me. She squinted before nervously saying something to the young girl next to her.

Within minutes, a tall, stately woman with tumbles of brown hair and a slight scar above her left eyebrow emerged from the room. She held a thin binder by her chest.

"Sir, hello. Can I help you?" she said, fingering her glasses up the bridge of her nose. No one had ever called me sir before.

"I'm just waiting for a friend. She wanted me to come with her to the group tonight. She's supposed to be meeting me here. At least I think she is. I thought I might come and see what it's about. I uh, have…" I hesitated, realizing you don't randomly tell people you have anorexia before you even offer up your name.

"I'm not sure what I was thinking. She's not showing. I can just go. No worries."

The women put her hand out as I stood up to leave. "Hello, I should introduce myself, I'm Joan Bree. I'm part of the eating disorder unit at the hospital. I run the meetings. Can I ask who your friend is? You can sit down again. Do you mind if I join you?"

I waved toward the long, empty bench. She calmly sat down with hands clasped in her lap. "I'm waiting for Phoebe Stubb. She said she comes here every so often. I don't know, maybe she's late," I said. Dr. Bree massaged her temples while nodding deliberately.

"Phoebe, okay, now that's interesting," she said while straightening her glasses once more. "To be honest, we haven't seen Phoebe here in quite a while. When she did come, it was sporadic. I'm somewhat surprised to hear this, but with Phoebe, you never know." I laughed to myself while sliding further down the bench, once again felled by false hope.

"So, you are saying she is not a regular. Okay, look at that. She did tell me she pops in and out, but she seemed pretty enthused about it when I talked to her." I shook my head and offered a sheepish smile. "It's alright. Mixed signals. I'm sorry to bother you. I'll have to talk with her."

Dr. Bree looked at me with serene, compassionate concern. "I don't mean to be intrusive at all, but if she asked you to come for help, it would be for a reason. Do you mind if I ask, and I know this is delicate, but did you come for help with an eating disorder? Excuse me, I didn't get your name."

"It's Michael. And yup, yup, the sad truth is I deal with a lot of issues. I do have a doctor I'm seeing for my eating problems, so I just thought I'd come to check this out and hang with Phoebe. You know, support. But I'm okay, I really am." It was embarrassing to have to admit to my lifelong confusion, but there was no point in lying when the illness had to be self-evident.

She stood slowly with her index finger in the air as if she was paging a waiter. "Stay here momentarily, Michael. Let me tell everyone we will start in a few minutes. I'll be back in a jiffy."

I smiled at the sound of the word jiffy. Only months before I probably would have been free associating peanut butter brands in my head.

Dr. Bree returned to sit stiffly next to me on the bench once more. "Well, Michael, honestly again, I'm a bit surprised Phoebe told you to come because I'm sure she knew this is a women's only meeting. Maybe it slipped her mind."

I felt even more ridiculous and immediately looked for the nearest door. It seemed like I was always searching for an escape hatch. "No wonder everyone was staring at me. I'm sorry I intruded on their space. I was wondering why there were no men anywhere in sight. I guess then there are no meetings with men and women at all here. You never mix them?"

"Unfortunately, not. When we started this group, we had a couple of men I wanted to integrate until I brought up the idea with all the women. They just were not agreeable and uncomfortable. They voted and decided to keep it exclusively women. I think you can understand, especially with the issues they deal with.

"They are very personal and, as you must know if you are seeing a doctor, they need to very open for this to work. Things that come up might be sensitive in nature regarding their bodies and sexuality. It's important for them to have a safe environment." Dr. Bree shook her hand at me, seemingly flustered. "Not that you, as a man, is some kind of threat, please understand that."

I silently nodded. Of course, I was an outsider who didn't belong.

"Well, it's no problem. I don't think I'd want any of the women to hear my crazy problems and fantasies, so I definitely get it. I completely understand."

She quickly responded with a reassuring smile. "You know I'm not sure if you'd be interested, but I do hold a men's meeting here on Thursday evenings. There are only four men right now. It's so hard to get men to share and be open about this subject. Especially in our culture, which is, let's just say, not very hospitable to men's struggle with this. I'm sure I don't have to tell you.

"That's why I'd encourage you to think about it, and please come. I know the guys would love to have another person join the group. The meetings help. It's a different dynamic than individual therapy. You realize you are not alone. The bonding is also important." She reached into the pocket of her slacks, pulled out a card and slid a pen out of the binder.

"Here's my card. I'll write down the day, time, and room number of the next meeting on the back. If you have any questions, please call. I'm here at the hospital every weekday. If you can create the time, a meeting once a week will certainly help you. The more help the better, right?"

I took the card and shook her hand. My first thought was that another doctor's voice might lead to confusion, but the opportunity to sit down with other men who could understand the daily grind of denial was undeniably appealing.

I was actually looking forward to telling my story more often. Owning up to my life with Dr. Hampton was freeing, and it was even more liberating exploring my feelings with Phoebe. There was no shame and no blame. I could just let things go.

"I'll have to check if I can make it, but maybe I'll see you, Doctor Bree. First, I have to find out what happened to Phoebe." I tried to hide my disappointment. Of course, I wanted to believe I was there for more therapy, but my sole motivation was always Phoebe.

Dr. Bree stepped away with her index finger in front of her face. "Before I get back to the meeting, I will tell you this. A few of the women here tonight were originally brought to us by Phoebe when she first started. I personally know one woman who was recommended by her a while back.

"Phoebe hardly shows up, but she has been very proactive in getting people to come to the meetings. You can ask her. Maybe she just couldn't make it tonight but still wanted you to be here and meet me. Perhaps she was pointing you in the right direction. She wants to help."

With an arched eyebrow, she smiled again, "You never know. What I definitely do know is Phoebe has a good heart, and always means well. Okay, I hope you come next week. It was a pleasure meeting you."

. . . .

Richie walked right past me with searching eyes as I waved to him amid a stream of passengers exiting at the arrival gate. "Rich, hey, what do I need a sign with your name on it?"

He turned, startled, before offering a triple take. "Brother, oh man, oh man, look at you. When did Slash turn into Opie? I would never recognize you this way."

"And that's probably the best news I've heard all week," I said, rolling my eyes.

He collapsed the handle on his luggage and picked it up as if it was a pillow. "Did Monique take you to one of her friends on Newbury?"

"Nah, I had this done on my own. Actually, I had it done to me." We headed to the garage through a steady mix of rain and hail as thunder rumbled through the night. Richie placed the business and sports sections of *USA Today* over his head while jogging.

"Let me guess, by the girl Monique told me about when I talked to her the other day. She said she saw you with her," he squinted and laughed.

I grabbed his backpack to appear helpful and tried to keep up with his strides. The backpack was so heavy that I considered balancing it on my head like a woman in *National Geographic*.

"What are you smuggling cocaine? Jesus, this is a load." I placed my arms through the straps to carry it on my back.

"Wish it was cocaine. That's paperwork from a failed marriage. Stay single, Mike. The love you make is never equal to what love takes. Your life will be easier. Trust me, there will be no lawyers to bend you over."

He tossed the soaked newspaper pages into two different trash cans. We were running through puddles while dodging cars spitting water. The hail was the size of golf balls. "Jeez, I can't take all this rain and sick weather. When did Boston turn to Seattle? The entry was miserable." Richie was brushing the water from his carefully buzzed hair while he talked. "No more talk about the divorce—tell me about the girl."

"There's not much to tell. I don't know who she is, really. She was an old neighbor I met, but it looks like it might have been a one nighter. Don't take that the wrong way. Nothing happened."

"A one-night haircut okay, yeah sure. Those things only happen in your world. Did she give you a one-night wax, too?"

"I'm telling ya, it wasn't like that." The raindrops were blinding me when we got to the garage stairs and made our way up toward my Corolla.

"That's definitely too bad. Gotta change that soon, my friend. Celibacy makes you stupid."

Upon finally arriving at the car, Richie pressed his face against the passenger window. "I'm impressed. You cleaned the mess up. I can actually see the seat. Nothing but a book in there. Now that's improvement. At least you listen to some things I say." He picked up my journal with his claw of a hand and sat next to me. "You still writing this? Damn, this is thick with chicken scratch," he said, flipping through the pages.

"That's volume two. I'm about to start another." We slowly made our way throughout the winding, narrow garage exit. "I've been writing every day, like all day in my free time."

Richie split it open and spoke a bad British accent. "To eat or not to eat, that is the question."

I grabbed the journal and threw it in the back seat while swerving into the left lane. "Get the fuck out of here. Be real, Richie, you don't even know what play the real quote is from." He turned on the CD player after draining the last drops from a bottle of water he had stashed in his bag. Morphine's "Sharks" blared out of the speakers.

"That was the full extent of Shakespeare I know. I'm completely out of quotes and definitely could not tell you what play. I'm gonna guess *Polio and Juliet*. That was his last one—I know that." He smiled genially while wiping beads of water from his eyebrows. "You need to keep writing, Mike. Maybe, that's what you are meant to do."

"I think I'm meant to sit in traffic for an hour with you," I said as we crawled to the end of a dense bottleneck on an access road extending from the Ted Williams Tunnel back to East Boston.

Richie turned on the defroster while leaning into the windshield to get a closer look at the stuttering windshield wipers.

"Hey Mike, I've got some news for you. It wasn't all bad out there. Believe it or not, but I'm going back to Los Angeles. I did some multitasking with the help of Monique's contacts. It looks like sometime early next year, I'm going to give the L.A. thing another try. I'm out of place in Boston. I realize it was a pitstop on the journey. It takes a particular kind of person to live here. And I'm just not that guy."

"So, that's that? I won't see you anymore either?" My life seemed to be turning into one long period of attrition. "Who am I left with?"

"It's gonna be next year, brother. Relax. We have plenty of time to work and hang out together now. In fact, I have tickets to the Yankees series in two weeks. You're coming with me. Third base boxes. Now, don't worry about the future. And you better believe I'm going to get you out to L.A. First to visit, sit in the sun, meet some hot mamacitas. There's so many, if you throw a stone in any direction, you can hit one. I'm telling you, there's a lot to look forward to."

I forced a smile and said, "Guess so. Who knows where we'll be in a year?" It didn't sound too convincing even to me. I was sure I was going to be stuck inside of Boston, weathering another brutal winter again.

Richie pulled out his wallet as we crept toward the tunnel. "How much is the toll," he mumbled to himself. "So how you been? You feeling okay? Are we on the path to running serious miles?"

A Mercedes and a new Excel tried to cut me off. "I'm hoping to be running by the fall, but I'm not ready yet. I'm kinda scared my body can't take it. Get this, though. I'm thinking of joining a men's therapy group. Add that to the stuff I'm doing already. My brain will be so analyzed, I can donate it to science."

"Since when?" Richie raised his hand for a high five.

"Since like three hours ago. I think I'm getting…I don't know, but believe it or not, I ate sushi with Mon for my birthday while you were gone. I was surprisingly alright. Well, kind of alright with it." I waved away the twenty-dollar bill Richie held before me. I felt flush with cash.

"You ate sushi? You went from smoothie to sushi since we started. That's crazy fast and great. See, and you are not freaking out."

I immediately got defensive. The way he was talking made me think that it was all too quick an adjustment and I needed to put the training wheels on again. "You saying that's bad? You think I should be worried? Do I look fat?"

The tunnel provided a respite from the downpour. "Mike! Don't you twist it now. Don't you dare. I'm saying you are putting the same kind of focus into getting better and running again as you did to destroy yourself, just like I said you would the first day I met you. You remember that afternoon? Everything you are telling me is positive. Completely, one hundred percent, totally positive."

I was left to wonder why I wasn't more concerned with my relative lack of concern over eating. Of course, I was still getting fidgety. Every day, I thought the anxiety might never go away, but I was managing to live and breathe. Yes, I could breathe without feeling like I was drowning.

"Mike, you here with me?" Richie tapped his hand on the dashboard, causing the CD to skip. "You know about your birthday. I'm sorry I missed it, but your present is coming. I ordered it. I just waited until I was back here so I could give it to you personally. It's on its way."

I laughed audibly while switching the radio on to sports talk, WEEI. I knew Richie hadn't ordered a fucking thing.

"Rich forget about the present. I think I got enough presents to last a lifetime. We all need a Monique in our lives." We curved around the Fleet Center towards the entrance of Storrow Drive as the traffic opened up and the rain began to dissipate.

"That's the one thing I will agree with you. Your brother is one lucky guy," Richie said.

"But I guarantee you, Monique didn't get what I'm getting you. I know that." A van sped past us through the flooded lanes, dumping waves of water onto the windshield. I had a flash vision of an oncoming car hopping the barrier and sending us up into flames.

I exited Storrow as quickly as I could onto Western Avenue. Richie shut the radio off after I drove into the 7-Eleven parking lot near Harvard Stadium.

"Alright, Mike, get this. How about this? Rob Deer, Catfish Hunter, and Tim Salmon. You like them? You ever have deer meat? You had sushi, so imagine how many kinds of fish you can eat. I love catfish. That's number 27 on the menu."

I stood next to the garbage can filled with Big Gulp cups and broke out laughing. The misty rain had all but disappeared, but hail still bounced off passing car windshields.

"You are kidding me? You mean for my All Food Baseball All-Star Team? I thought you told me to forget that," I said. We walked through the doors past a hunched woman with groceries in black garbage bag stuck in a laundry cart. A fierce wind blew the door open again. It shut behind me like a trap snapping.

"Yeah, yeah, I know, "Richie said, his face flushing. "But once I started reading the damn thing, I couldn't stop thinking. You know me and baseball. I was even coming up with names on the plane. Your list is somewhere in the glove compartment of my car. It's a lot of fun. I scribble names down in my spare time. Dusty Baker—there's a twist for you.

"Mike, I have to tell ya, you are a really bad, bad influence, but after all this time, I think you are either rubbing off on me or I already had a little bit of you in me already. Life is crazy, brother. For some reason, all the things we know we shouldn't be doing, we end up doing anyway."

Richie picked a pack of Twinkies off the Hostess display and led me to the refrigerator filled with six-packs of beer. "I mean really, look at this place. 7-11. I bet the original stores were open between seven and eleven. Now it's 24 hours, seven days a week." He handed me the Twinkies before yanking a six of Sam Adams out of the refrigerator.

"Everything in this place will kill ya, but for some reason, we just can't stay out it. C'mon, I'll split those sugar coma sticks with you on the way home while we figure out how to get ya out to L.A. with me."

Part Five

You're Gonna Make Me Lonesome When You Go

Thirty-Four

The Red Sox were losing to the Angels after a long Wally Joyner home run on another oppressively hot night at Fenway. Unfortunately, I was stuck in my apartment watching the game on television with a wobbling electric fan on the bookshelf providing the soundtrack. When Tim Salmon grounded into a double play, my cell rang, punctuating the end of the inning.

"Mike, are you home?"

"Richie, I was just thinking of you. Some kind of synchronicity going on—Tim Salmon just hit. I'm watching the game here."

"Great, glad to hear it. Stay where you are, and don't go out." There were random shouts and music in the background.

"I'm not going anywhere. You coming over?"

"No, no, but just stay in—keep watching the game. I'm sending you a pizza."

I had already eaten, and the last thing on my mind was more food.

"Rich, you have to give me advance notice if you want to order me pizza. Since when are you in the food ordering business?"

"Mike, go watch the game and enjoy the pizza. So many questions, man. I gotta go, okay? I'm in a hurry. Talk to you later. Hope the pizza tastes good."

I hung up, wondering if Monique put Richie up to the nighttime food delivery. A pizza just didn't sound like him. After a quick shower, I peeked out the window to look for a delivery car, but the street was empty except for a group of students playing acoustic guitar on the staircase down the block. Forty-five minutes passed before Troy Percival struck out Jason Varitek to end the game. Relieved that I wouldn't have to feed the neighborhood rats another full pie, I dialed Richie back. Before I could finish his number, though, there was a timid knock at the door.

I grabbed a five-dollar bill for a tip and opened the door to see a radiant, almond skinned, Filipino woman in a skin-tight white tank top and white shorts. I was sure it was the same full- lipped goddess who Richie and I saw on the T ride home a few months before. I squinted without saying a word as she stood bored, holding a clutch on my doormat. It didn't take long to realize that she had some American blood and was slightly more weathered than the T girl.

"You Michael?" she said through a tight smile. I knew I had to immediately call Richie so he could take his pizza back. It was way too spicy for me.

The woman walked confidently through the door. "Are you going to let me in?" she said before looking around the apartment.

I raised my hand to object, but she moved towards the main table anyway. "Relax, stop looking like you're constipated. You have a good friend who wants you to be happy. Can I sit? I'm here with you for the entire night, baby."

I pulled the chair away from the table while still fumbling with the phone. She sat down and crossed her legs. Her deeply tan calves were spectacular. "Can you stay right here for a moment while I make a call in the other room? Don't you run anywhere," I said, pointing two fingers at her feet.

"And why would I want to run, baby? This place is obviously so comfy–I'm going to make myself right at home."

I closed the door behind me to call Richie. He picked up after the first ring.

"Did the pizza arrive?"

"Richie, are you fucking crazy? I'm sending her back to where she came. Is she the magic hooker I've always heard about in the movies? What do you think? I'm going to fuck her, and instantly get better tomorrow?"

There was a cackle in his laugh. "Mike, you are so predictable. It's not about healing you. She's not some exotic medicine woman. It's about getting laid and having some fun. This isn't about your eating. Stop associating everything with that. This is about having woman's body next to yours. Getting the old dipstick wet. Nothing more. Tomorrow, she'll be gone, your balls will be drained, and you can go back to being miserable if you want."

I marched around by the baseboards while looking for a secret escape vent. Richie slurred his words as he continued.

"You can't tell me this is not what you want. I know you do, and if you didn't, I would be really worried. Nobody goes like two years without getting laid. So spend the night with beauty instead of ugliness for a change. If you have a lousy time, you can hate me tomorrow for forcing her on you. I'm going have fun tonight, and so will you. You can write about it in that journal. You can't have any stories if you don't live. And I know she will be worth writing about. See ya tomorrow at the gym, Mike."

I looked into the phone, desperately hoping to postpone the inevitable. The apartment was silent except for the sound of the escort's fingernails rhythmically tapping the table. She was looking through the spines of my books as I joined her again.

"Hey, there pissed-off Michael, some setup you got here. Who is your interior designer, a prison warden?" She pulled out a chair. "Sit down angry boy and talk to the magic, definitely not a hooker. Tell me what are you so upset about. Why are you yelling into the phone? You do realize you were not in some kind of cone of silence in there. Voices tend to echo, especially without furniture."

I slid into the chair unsteadily, making sure our arms didn't touch. "I don't know, this isn't right."

"Tell me what's not right." There was a small mole under her right eye—a tiny blemish in an otherwise flawless face.

"Sex, you, me, I mean," I said hesitantly, unsure about what was wrong. "Richie paid you."

"And you find that morally objectionable," she said while leaning back, her elbows on the table. "Who are you Holden Caulfield?"

I laughed nervously, fully realizing that I was just scared and pretty sure I would last about thirty seconds inside of her. "You read *Catcher in the Rye*?" I tried to deflect my panic.

"My twelve-year-old niece has read *Catcher in the Rye*. Who hasn't?

What is it with all you silly, young Boston guys with an Asian fetish? You think I'm a just-off-the-boat Filipino fuck bunny? It's Michael, right? Well, Michael, just so you know, I was born on the lower east side of Manhattan, and this is my business. My business gets better if you have fun. People can be so judgmental about this. Are you judgmental? I hope not. I bet there's fun behind those baby blues."

I was suddenly overwhelmed by some strange paranoia. I knew there just had to be someone hovering outside on the window ledge: Monique, Jessie, Phoebe, my mom, all-seeing, roving-eye Jesus from my childhood bedroom. It seemed surreal. Ms. Definitely Not-a-Fuck Bunny thought I was judgmental? Hell, no one would be judging my magical hooker. This was going to be my trial.

"You have water, Coke, whatever, to drink, Michael? Just for now," she said softly in my ear. I hopped up like a servant to fetch something. She shouted after me, "Why don't you relax and have a good time? Time to loosen up—take the stick out of your ass. Or I can put one in if you're into that."

My hands were trembling as I handed over two glasses of water. "You know Frankie Goes to Hollywood? Remember them? When they sang 'relax, don't do it.' You know that's the only part of the song I heard. That's what I have in my head. I honestly wasn't trying to be a jerk."

She laughed and slapped me on the ass. "Well, baby, you shouldn't yell at your friend for merely wanting to open your ears to the rest of a disco song. That Richie is one generous guy—a damn great tipper. Let's be real. If you want to just sit in the room over there and watch *The Simpsons* or talk Frankie Goes to Hollywood all night, I'm good with it.

"If you want to chat like a lot of guys do when they need to unload their problems, that's fine also. I'm a good listener."

"I have a shrink already," I grinned like a Muppet, now breathing a little easier.

"Yeah, well I charge more, and I doubt she can do for you what I can. Be honest, Michael, your friend wants you to be happy for a reason, and it's just sex. You like sex, don't you?" She ostentatiously leaned forward, her full cleavage on display, to place her phone and clutch on the table.

"When your friend first contacted me, he said my picture on the website would remind you of someone. So then why not think of me as your fantasy come to life. We can't live in reality all the time."

"You remind me of someone who reminded me of someone," I said while staring at the smooth curve of her neck.

"And that's even better, a double fantasy. What's hotter? You know, I'm looking around this place—and to be honest, it's been a long, long time since I've seen this kind of, what should we call it, maybe chic monastery vibe."

She stood to kick off her sandals. "I was told to dress down or you would have gotten heels and a lot more. Mr. Michael, tell me, just for fun, when is the last time you got laid?"

"Okay now, well, you're direct, aren't you? Uh, to be honest, I don't remember," I said, suddenly feeling small.

"Why?" she replied after strolling through the kitchen and popping her head out the window.

"I've been busy." I was fully aware of how ridiculous it sounded. "Not busy making money, but busy. I had other priorities and problems."

Leisurely gliding into the main room, she craned her neck around to look at me before raising her hands. "Nothing in here but a stereo system. You know you have a scenic alley back there to commit a murder." She seemed to soften while standing with hands on hips. "I'm just messing with you, Michael. I'm sure you're moving to a better place, but you ever think that maybe part of your problem was having a woman wasn't a priority? Hey, what do you have to really drink in here?"

"You mean other than water?" I considered making her a smoothie to kill fifteen minutes.

"Yes, of course, alcohol to get your motor running. You have a twenty, Michael?"

"You leaving already? You want a tip?"

"You are cute with the jokes. You wouldn't tip the Dominos guy twenty bucks. No, I'm with you until daybreak, so get used to me. Come, let's go get some Jack Daniels. I saw a big liquor store on the corner of the main intersection."

She reached her hand back as I scrambled for my wallet. After a quick walk down the street in the soupy humidity past an ogling, middle-aged man using boxer shorts as a doo-rag outside of Rinse Lombardi's Laundromat, we returned with a six-pack of Molson's and a bottle of Jack.

"By the way Michael, I'm Duran," she said, pouring each one of us shots in tall glasses.

"Duran as in 'Hungry Like the Wolf' Duran?"

"Duran as in 'Rio,' but yeah," she replied before knocking the shot back. She handed me the glass after pouring herself another and touching my chin, "Uppity up."

I hesitated but quickly submitted. The whiskey burned my throat. I could have sworn I saw fumes coming out of my eyes. After Duran drained another drink, she poured me nearly a quarter of a glass and pulled her shirt over her head with both hands. I'd never seen such large, dark brown areolas and muscular abs. She didn't have a trace of fat. I wanted to know her dieting secrets.

"Let's go inside, bring the bottle," Duran ordered. As I opened the door to the bedroom, she pulled me back by the sleeve of my shirt.

"Are you kidding me? What is that doing in here? I expected a futon or a cot. Damn, you have Elvis's bed in CBGB's toilet stall. You just redeemed yourself here, Mikey."

The alcohol had stunned me, but I took another shot as Duran wiggled out of her shorts. She stood before me in a black G-string— across her lower abdomen was a large tattoo of a thick blue and red snake crawling from pelvic bone to pelvic bone, tail pointing down to her pussy. With a small leap, she fell onto the bed, ass first.

"Get undressed," Duran whispered while bouncing up and down playfully. "I love these silk sheets. This is impressive. Did your friend buy you this set-up, too?"

I took one more small sip from the bottle as the floor moved beneath me. "What's your real name? I know it's definitely not Duran." I was hoping to strip away a bit of the escort façade, and maybe get to who the hell she really was beneath the makeup. I mean who has sex with a Duran? It's kind of like fucking A Flock of Seagulls.

"Who do you want me to be?" She crawled under the sheets, a pillow under her back.

"C'mon, give me something," I was suddenly emboldened.

"You take your shirt off, and I'll tell you. You give me something. We have all night, so this might as well be fun." I hesitated because I was afraid she might be horrified like those ashen-faced, voyeuristic gargoyles repulsed by the first sight of Elephant Man in David Lynch's movie.

"Want to know my name, the shirt has to go. You don't swim in the pool with your shirt and you certainly don't..."

I placed the bottle on the bureau before throwing my t-shirt on the bed.

"Well, well, you definitely need to eat a few double cheeseburgers, but that wasn't so hard, was it?" Duran jumped out of the bed to walk around the perimeter of the room with the confidence of someone who knows all eyes follow. She had deep dimples at the top of her ass and hair falling to the lowest point in the arc of her bronzed back.

"There's nothing in here but a television, books, and a computer," she said while inspecting the room and tapping the IBM monitor. After taking a glimpse outside of the window, she reached behind the closet door. I covered my face as Duran yanked away the hidden Jon Bon Jovi cardboard poster. She rested it against the television on the bookcase.

"What the what? Are you a closet '80s teenage girl?" she was giggling while she made her way towards me. "What's that about? Are you into guys?" I shook my head as Jon Bon Jovi's eyes glowed and wandered towards Duran taking one final drink from the bottle. He winked at me when she added, "Yes, now we're ready to party."

The room quickly tilted.

"The poster, that was my girlfriend's. This is going to sound crazy, but that's the last thing I have of hers," I impulsively blurted out while Bon Jovi gave me the finger. The communal hum of air conditioners running throughout the neighborhood hypnotized me into a lovely, hazy trance.

Duran stood before me, brushing her breasts against my chest.

"Aha, that's what this is all about. The apartment, this whole scared schoolboy act is some kind of penance for you, and your friend is trying to make you forget her."

The fan shook, sputtered and died on the bookcase. I took it as a sign of things to come. Beads of sweat had formed on Duran's cheeks. I could feel her breath on my neck.

She gently placed both hands on my hips. "Well, it's time to forgive and forget." Her fingers nimbly unbuttoned my drooping pants just before she playfully yanked them down along with my underwear.

"Now, that's what we're talking about," she said with a step back to examine.

My first instinct was to cover up, but the embarrassment of hiding behind a paper plate during my initial meeting with Jessie flooded back. I firmly resisted and stood shoulders straight without flinching. Maybe it was the Jack speaking to me in a language I didn't recognize.

Duran hovered behind me and ran her hands over my chest while kissing my shoulders. "We could have done this slowly, but something tells me you need to be pushed off the cliff." She squatted to gently brush the inside of my legs while running some fingers through my ass.

I turned to face her. She kissed me, her thin, firm tongue slipping into my mouth. I thought it was against the rules, but she grabbed my shoulders. "It's fine, not a problem, remember, relax." After pushing me to the bed, she went to her clutch for a condom.

"I'm not going to last very long," I said while on my back. Duran placed the condom in her mouth and slowly absorbed my cock. She looked up to take a breath. "No worries about coming fast, baby, we have all night and more than one pop."

I carefully watched her securing the condom at the base of my shaft. Afraid I was going to explode in her hand, I said, "More than one pop? Who are you, Orville Redenbacher?"

"Michael, focus now," she said, pointing to the pearl piercing in her belly button. "This is the snack."

As Duran casually knelt spread-legged over me, the hip-to-hip snake did the electric slide down her thigh. I followed it go off the bed, up the walls, and out the window while she dangled her nipples over my cock for a few minutes. Finally, she gracefully slipped to her back so she could put me inside of her.

I thought I'd have some kind of celestial revelation or blow a load through her skull, but I felt nothing. Five minutes in, I thought she had secretly injected my cock with Novocain. I wildly rammed away like a bunny on a speedball while staring down at Duran fake screaming as if I'd suddenly grown a redwood, and was poking her eye out.

I quickly pulled out. "Whoa, whoa, I'm never going to come if you are going to go all Meg Ryan on me. I thought I'd put the tip in, and be long gone, but I don't feel a thing. It sure doesn't help if you fake like that. My dick just ain't that big to get that kind of crazy fucking yelling."

She looked at me, bug-eyed confused. "You don't want me to moan? I won't moan, but I like to moan."

Suddenly alarmed, I quickly rolled to her side. "No, no, no, please don't say that word. You can scream, yell 'ooh yes, yes, yes,' or 'fuck me harder, baby,' anything, but don't say 'moan.'" Monique's face flashed on the ceiling. I was forced me to cover my eyes with both hands.

"What? What the fuck are you doing?" Duran said. "You don't want me to say…"

"No moan. Taboo word. Can't hear it."

"You gotta learn nothing is taboo, baby." Duran's face was glistening, her makeup smearing. It made me want her more. She pulled me on top of her like yanking a rag doll, grabbed my cock and stuffed it back in as if connecting a Lego. "I won't scream, and I won't say that word, but for this to be pleasurable, Michael, you have to know you are not putting a loaf of Italian bread in the oven. What precisely are you doing?"

"Am I going too fast?"

"Too fast? Of course, not. No, you're fucking like you are on morphine, in slow motion. Do you even remember how to fuck? Use your hips, for God's sake."

And I thought I was wearing her out by going like a piston. "You want me to go harder?" I said before looking over my shoulder to check for hidden cameras or witnesses.

"Baby, look at me."

I turned back to Duran. She slapped me across the face, sending me cross-eyed. The stinging pain in my cheeks felt so good that I wanted her to do it again.

"What the hell was that for?" It was like getting smacked out of a dream.

"Fuck me like you mean it. I don't break, and I won't fake if you actually fuck me."

I laughed out loud while trying to pound her like I was mining for gold. Duran's breasts were bouncing sideways as her hips slapped against mine. She could have snapped me in half with her thighs. I was sure she had dildos bigger than my entire body. Beads of sweat fell off of my chin, into her cleavage. I was fucking a woman with the absolute perfect body—it was straight out of my wildest, most impossibly grand fantasies—and, of course, I still didn't feel a god-damn thing. After a half-hour inside her, I was completely exhausted.

We took a water break before Duran got on top to slow grind. We then attempted it on our knees on the floor and awkwardly against the bureau. Still nada, not even a tingle. I could have been fucking a block of ice. After she blew me with a finger so far up my ass, it nearly punctured a kidney, I put a stop to the futility. I wasn't going to come.

Duran grabbed a towel to wipe her inner thighs. She threw it at me as I lay in bed, breathless—every muscle in my body hurt. Even my eyelids ached.

"Michael, you are still hard. Did you take a pill or something? You've been hard for like an hour."

"It's called desperation," I said, shaking my head. "They should bottle it."

She sat on my stomach while leaning back against my thighs. "You definitely need more meat on you. You are not a good body pillow. I don't know what your deal is, but are you trying not to come for some reason? It's okay to just let it go. Like I said before, we can do this as many times as you want."

"I don't know. I'm lost. You are so hot and really gorgeous, I mean it. It has nothing to do with you. It's all me." I thought I was letting her down—another mission impossible.

Duran pinned back my shoulders with her ass on my chest. She leaned in, breasts hanging in my face. "Michael, it's not your Johnson. It's your head. Who do I remind you of? Let's go back to that? Get lost in her. Who did you always want to fuck, but couldn't? Don't think about what you have here. Me? I think I'm kind of invisible. This," she slapped her ass. "Doesn't seem to be doing anything. Think about what you never had, and always wanted." I stared at the sweat beneath her breasts as she lingered over me.

"Close your eyes, and concentrate on who you really want."

I thought of Christina slowly tracing my lips after we kissed. I could hear her saying, "That was sweet, really sweet."

What I wanted was a ridiculous adolescent fantasy.

"Duran, hey, you like ice cream by any chance? I smiled with an insistent nod. "Please tell me you like ice cream."

"What?" She slid down to my knees.

"I just need you to tell me you like ice cream." I jumped out of bed. She looked at me like she was confronting someone who had just escaped an insane asylum.

"Do you like to eat ice cream?"

"Of course," she said. "Who doesn't? Are you thinking what I think you are thinking, baby? Everybody has their thing, so indulge it."

I knew that I could never replicate the surreal intensity of what happened years before, after Christina and I fumbled towards an ecstasy I could only find in my hand. But I thought if I just yielded control to Duran, I'd be free to experience something liberating—maybe transformative.

Or maybe she could just make me fucking come.

"Wait here. I'll be right back," I said before running into the kitchen and digging out an old, frozen-solid pint of Haagen Dazs chocolate ice cream David always kept in my freezer. After letting it defrost for a minute in the microwave, I grabbed all of the towels out of the bottom of the bathroom closet. Duran covered the silk sheets with the towels I tossed to her.

"Let me have the ice cream, honey. I'm hungry. Are you hungry?"

"Never, but let's find out," I said. Duran pressed the pint container against her nipples as she scooped out a dollop of ice cream with a spoon. I fell on the towels while watching her swallow with satisfaction. I didn't even have to tell her what I wanted. She must have done a variation of it many times before. Placing another healthy chunk of ice cream in her mouth, she grabbed my hand and pulled me to her. "C'mere" she mumbled with her mouth full. I stopped momentarily. It was ultimately impossible to resist, though.

When she kissed me, the chocolate ice cream spilled out of her mouth into mine. The taste was ridiculously rich and sweet—I had completely forgotten how much I loved it. Duran took yet another mouthful and let it ooze between my lips as we kissed again. I was completely out of my mind, lapping up chocolate and saliva like a golden retriever. With a chocolate stained mouth, Duran inhaled my cock again. Ice cream spilled down to my thighs as her head slowly descended and ascended over and over again.

Imagining myself deep inside Christina in the back of my car, with both Jesus and Saint Anthony applauding, I came in colors. Repeatedly.

I sat up, delirious, after five limp-limbed minutes to see Duran still eating ice cream from the pint. She wiped her mouth with a towel, "You okay?"

I was laughing with delight, and flicking the sweat off of my eyelids. "Yeah, of course, I'm alright. That was fucking fantastic." She leisurely licked the spoon while sweeping chocolate off of my stomach with her fingers.

"You didn't come," she shrugged.

"Of course, I came. Are you kidding?"

Duran placed the ice cream pint on the floor. "You may have come, but you didn't come if you know what I mean. Look." She pulled the empty condom off.

"That's impossible. I had to come in buckets. I've never come like that."

She blew the rubber up into a balloon and released it into the air. It sputtered like a wounded butterfly onto my chest. "Nothing. That's okay. Something obviously happened. I think they heard you in Omaha, Nebraska. You want some ice cream?"

I slid down next to her at the edge of the bed to take a closer look.

And yes, I was still hard.

"C'mon, you have to be kidding. That's impossible. Where the fuck is it all? I felt like a super soaker."

"It wants to escape, but I guess it can't. You are ready to go again," Duran said, gripping my cock once more. She shook it like a joystick while talking to the head. "Come out, come out, wherever you are."

I massaged my temples in frustration.

"Mr. Freeze, let them free," she said, playfully dipping my shaft down.

When she leaned over to take a closer look, my legs trembled as my balls rose up my ass. I yanked Duran by the shoulder away from the eruption of a moonbeam of come. It splattered all over Jon Bon Jovi's face until he was completely unrecognizable.

Duran burst into laughter while I lay on my back, depleted. It felt like I'd just unloaded half my body weight. "Mother of God, damn. You just gave Bon Jovi the facial of his lifetime," she said. "That is an Olympic amount of come. The plumbing must have been really stopped up.

"That is also probably one of the gayest things I've ever seen. You definitely have to throw that poster out now. You covered his entire smirky face. Go drink some milk to replenish. My God, that was the stuff of Star Wars."

A warm wind blew into the room, sending the poster teetering forward. I snatched the come stained edges before the whole thing fell splat on the floor. Duran stepped far away with a towel wrapped around her breasts.

"Oh, sweet Jesus, his chin is dripping come," she said, bent over with legs crossed while still laughing. "Can you throw it out the window into the alley?" I tip-toed to the window with the poster in hand like I was avoiding a nuclear waste spill.

"It's just an empty alley in Boston. Someone will think it's a fine art project or something. Jizz Jovi," Duran giggled. "Go ahead now and toss it, and let's eat something. I'm starving. Ice cream is never enough." She pushed the window frame to the top. "Fold it a bit, and then throw on three. You know I thought this night was going to be a disaster, but this takes the cake."

After she counted down, the cardboard poster flew out the window. It fell rapidly before riding a gust of wind and rocking back and forth like a pendulum. Finally, the poster came to a silent rest on a dirty Boston Market bag. Whiteface Jon Bon Jovi smiled beatifically at the stars.

Duran moved in next to me with the bottle of Jack. I stood, totally naked, at the window and, for that one single moment, I just didn't give a fuck.

"I'm going to take a hot shower. There is running water, right? Go order a pizza, Chinese or whatever delivers at this time. We have to get some food in us, so you are ready for the next round," Duran said over her shoulder.

I was still tasting the sweet chocolate on my lips. "You mean we are going to do all this again? Really?"

She flipped the back of the towel to expose her ass. "You don't want more? If you are up to it, we can go as many times as you can stand tonight. And you won't need ice cream this time. You need a few new fantasies in your head. Trust me, that I can do. As far as I'm concerned, we've only just begun."

Thirty-Five

Whated the decidedly R-rated version of my Duran
story to Dr. Hampton, he stoically sat while nodding his head and
writing. By the way he reacted, I thought he was making notes to
remind himself to pick up Klondike bars on the way home. He just
grinned and said calmly, "Well that's not the way I would have gone,
but if it helped you get in touch with a side of yourself that was long
dormant, okay." Very rational, unperturbed, and nonjudgmental.

It shocked me.

I explained that I understood he probably didn't approve of me
fucking an escort, but I was completely fine with it because everything
in life besides memory is a short-term rental.

He smiled, bemused. "Is that you speaking or The Dude from *The
Big Lebowski* after he got his bowling shoes? Michael, you don't have to
rationalize it to me at all. Are you trying to rationalize it to yourself? It
happened, and apparently, you enjoyed it. Don't make it what it's not.

"The plus side is you were strong enough to have sex multiple times.
When you walked into my office, not only were you not thinking
about sex, but you were physically incapable of it. The key thing is
for you to keep eating and get stronger. You are on the upward tra-
jectory—Dr. Rigatta tells me the numbers on your recent bloodwork
are great. If you stay strong, it will be reflected in all aspects of your
life, as you just saw."

Of course, I had to admit to him that the accidental taste of Duran
had turned me into a walking hard-on. I was masturbating all day,
milking my cock like I was gunning for a medal at the county state
fair. I jerked off to soccer moms wearing plaid bikinis in J. C. Penney
circulars and to Katie Couric talking about decapitations in Iraq on
The Today Show.

I even rubbed a couple out to pictures of Monica Lewinsky in *The Boston Herald* while remembering Duran's magnificent asshole as she lay spread eagle in the middle of the bed at three in the morning.

It didn't end. Faces, bodies, and fantasies all blurred together to create a rush of desire I wasn't sure I could repress. And honestly, I didn't want to anymore. I just did not know how to articulate these irrational urges and frightening lack of inhibition to Dr. Hampton. When I admitted all my weaknesses, he once again was calm and much too reasonable—even slightly amused.

What the hell was wrong with him? Where was the admonishment about indulgence and self-respect I expected?

"It's all very healthy, Michael. Your libido has been liberated. There is nothing wrong with these feelings. What's wrong is thinking they are wrong. It will all translate into you making real connections—sexual and emotional—with women over time."

As I churned and churned over my sexual obsessions with Dr. Hampton, I also diligently attended meetings with Dr. Bree. I did more listening than talking through the first five weeks at group therapy. During our sixth meeting, she made the mistake of asking me to share some of the things I'd done to break out of my comfort zone and create genuine change in my life. It sounded like the typical Pablum pop culture question that leads to some sketchy epiphany people applaud themselves for on afternoon talk shows.

She peered over her glasses hanging by a chain. "Be an open book, total honesty is a must and valuable if you are going to contribute to the group." I knew stories about eating with Richie and Monique or my religious devotion to exercise would put the guys into a narcoleptic stupor, so I offered the G-rated, no chocolate, no blowjob, no shooting come version of my first sexual escapade of the new millennium. I did manage to get in a vivid description of Duran's spectacular snake tattoo. You know, I still think about that today.

And my mostly vanilla sex story got the kind of stony, concerned voice of disapproval I was looking for. Dr. Bree analyzed the other three members' reactions and said, "I guess it's good you got that out of your system. Hopefully, now you can move on to a more organic relationship-oriented sexual experience you might feel more comfortable with. I certainly hope you got an STD test recently. And of course, I know you know women shouldn't serve solely as a vehicle for your pleasure, but let's focus on your feelings and what precisely it meant to you." Yes, yes, that was the appropriate rap on the knuckles with a ruler I thought I deserved.

Even though a young engineer binge-eater kept cornering me after each meeting to get the name of the website Richie used to contact Duran, after that meeting I assiduously avoided all sex talk to focus on nothing but food minutiae. It clearly wasn't the forum for libidinous longings, and I didn't want to come off like a locker room douchebag.

I used the group to learn more about the associations, familiar triggers, and common behaviors among us. The patterns were eerily familiar, and the meetings with Dr. Bree—a bit schoolmarmish but thoughtful, kind, and always easy with a smile—became very meaningful. The structure and camaraderie of the group helped get me through the long, languorous days of July and August.

And as it does in every sun-starved city, the summer seemed to slip away right after Mon and I watched the Fourth of July fireworks on the Esplanade from the roof of her condo. I spent my days finding little thrills in the smallest of things: going on quiet book shopping safaris through Harvard Square and watching as many baseball games as possible at Fenway with Richie.

When he didn't have time to take in a full game, I went to a movie at the Nickelodeon Theaters nearby before meeting him on Lansdowne Street after he got off work. We'd wait until the end of the seventh inning when Fenway opened its gates to let straggling fans in for free, and then maneuver directly behind the third base dugout. I could hear the players chirping with the umpires as we stared at the stars over the Prudential building. It was as close to some kind of heaven as I'll probably ever find.

Mon spent most of the summer in Manhattan. Every few weeks or so, she took time away to come home and have dinner with me. I was sure she was setting the groundwork for a move once David got back. Of course, I missed my brother dearly and awaited his return. Our often awkward and rushed telephone conversations sadly never served to bring us closer—they just compounded his absence. Every day, I lamented his transformation into just another ghost in my life.

Like Phoebe.

Yes, she simply vanished without a word. Her phone was disconnected, and every time I visited her condo, Russ, the doorman, casually told me he hadn't seen her. I made one final Hail Mary stop on a cruelly humid afternoon at the end of July that reminded of the last day I saw her.

Russ looked at me with the grim, exhausted face of someone trying to comfort a smitten ex-boyfriend. "Phoebe's gone, son. Moved out. Have no idea. They took her stuff away during the night weeks ago."

Of course, I knew I'd never see Phoebe again, so I tried to compartmentalize my brief memory of her. It was tough, though. She was just a snap of the fingers in my life, yet I missed her.

I'd successfully blocked Phoebe out of my mind until her name came up during the night Ichiro and the Seattle Mariners played at Fenway in late August. It was the game Richie and I bought tickets for during that dank day back in March. Ichiro turned out to be the superstar that everyone had predicted he'd become, and I have to admit, watching his sleek athleticism as he ran around the bases was a well-needed reminder that there was still more than a little grace in this world.

During a pitching change in the bottom of the ninth inning, I asked Richie what happened to Amanda. He was eating a large mustard-soaked Fenway Frank with his eyes on a platinum blonde flirting with a sweating Chipwich vendor. "I'm telling you, Amanda is more your territory," he said after Jose Offerman slapped a single to left.

"She deserves someone smarter than me. Amanda was talking about violations of the Geneva Convention, and things like that. She wanted to discuss books I never read. *The Color Purple*. Why would I read *The Color Purple*? Seriously. Michael, you know I have a finite world of knowledge. She's a great person, but we're a bad match. She was way of out of my intellectual league."

It sounded so silly to me—more in line with something I would say. "Stop, c'mon, Rich. Hot girl, hot guy. Seems like a perfect match. You could probably figure it out if you really wanted to. What happened to the self-confidence you told me I needed?"

"It's not about self-confidence. It's about self-awareness. I know who I am. And I know I'm not good enough for Amanda. She deserves better. You're going to work with her. Maybe, it's time for you two now."

After Manny Ramirez hit into a double play and Trot Nixon struck out, we made our way towards a crowded Beacon Street, filled with screaming kids. When we passed the office of the shrink, who years before had asked me if I had stopped menstruating, Richie requested to see my phone. I couldn't help but laugh at the quaint memory as I handed it over. "What's so funny? I'm going to give you Amanda's number."

He locked her name and number in and shuffled through my contacts. "I'm going to delete Jessie for your sake," he said with a shake of his head. "I know this is nosy, but I'm disappointed you don't have that Duran's number in your phone for future reference."

"Since you called her, and she was your idea, I'm sure I could find her if in great need," I laughed.

He tossed me back the phone. "Mike, I'm going to just say one thing and nothing more about that. Understand, I tracked her down and made the call, but that wasn't my idea. Just so we make that clear."

"What? You are definitely kidding here," I said while walking in the street as cars sped by late-night joggers running past us. "Whose idea was it then? You telling me it was David's? Get outta here."

"I'm just saying it wasn't my idea. I was the facilitator for your birthday. That's all I'm saying. You're never going to know who was the brains behind it." He twisted his fingers near his lips, pretending to throw away a key.

"You're not telling me it was Monique. That's impossible, not a chance." The thought had never crossed my mind.

"I'm not saying what I'm not saying," he replied with his arms in the air.

We meandered past Wok This Way, the Chinese restaurant transformed into a rock club, just on the outskirts of Coolidge Corner.

Richie smiled as two girls in motorcycle jackets and Tina Turner heels stared him down. "So, who's that Phoebe in your phone? You think I missed that? I can be a gossipy housewife with the best of them. She new? You skipping over something? I see nothing else but guys in your contacts. Just one Phoebe."

Just hearing her name again made me uneasy.

"Phoebe is the girl who cut my hair."

"The cute girl Monique told me about? I thought you were going out with her."

"No, you don't listen. I never went out with her," I said as we turned onto Harvard Avenue. "Remember, I spent one night with her. It doesn't matter because she disappeared. Poof. I have no idea where she is."

"Brother, brother, please. I'm going to be cool about this because I know everything for you is associated with your dad, but people normally just don't disappear. You call her?"

"Many times. It's disconnected. She's gone, and I don't know why."

He faced me while slowly walking backward. "She'll return. There's always a why. Unlike you, I believe there's a reason for everything in life. She'll be back, and she may leave again, and then come back. You didn't know her well, right? I'll bet you five dollars she returns with a reason. There are always reasons."

Bemused by his surety, I shook his hand amid a group of Chinese tourists in front of Brookline Booksmith. They must have never gotten the memo saying the only thing to see in Brookline is Conan O'Brien's parents. Richie snapped a photo for a young couple before pointing over my shoulder. "You know that guy? He's calling your name and waving."

I could barely hear him over a gray-bearded black man on the corner hacking away at a guitar while singing "I Can't Be Satisfied."

"What are you talking about?"

"That guy across the street." Richie squared me up and pointed again.

I filtered out a gaggle of women heading to a café only to see Les in a dark blue sportscoat. He was shouting with his hand in the air. "Hey Michael, Michael." I stood like an Indian totem pole as I watched him wave in front of The Coolidge Corner Theater. While cars briskly passed on Harvard Ave., a flood of people exiting the Booksmith pushed me out of their way.

Richie quietly moved closer. "Mike, who the hell is that? He looks really happy to see you."

Les continued to call my name under the brightly lit Coolidge marquee with *Jules and Jim* and *My Life to Live* in bold black letters. "It's Les, Richie," I said, still motionless.

"Who's Les?"

"Jessie's Les."

"You are kidding me? I thought they were long gone. Damn," Richie snorted, his face all twisted. I realized Phoebe wasn't hallucinating when she thought she saw Jessie at Bread and Circus—she just denied the truth after it slipped out of her mouth to protect my feelings.

I offered a weak wave from my waist toward Les. "Tell me, Rich, how would it look if I started running like Ichiro?"

"Like a pussy. A really big pussy. Go over and say hello," he commanded.

I switched to a high, confident salute before searching the crowded block for Jessie, but she was nowhere to be found.

"Richie, are you coming with me?"

He quickly marched across the street toward Les, and I followed, dodging cars and hoping one would flatten me like a cartoon character before I made it to the other side.

Les was smoking a cigarette with a CVS bag held to his chest. His skin was unusually pallid, and his hair, seemingly cut with a butcher's knife, had streaks of blonde. He enthusiastically smiled with his hand extended like he had stumbled upon Bob Dylan. We shook, his left hand on my shoulder—the cigarette quietly burning in his mouth.

"Look at you—I knew it was you. The hair is gone, and you are positively healthy looking. You look great. Jessie's going to be so happy."

"Les, this is my friend, Richie," I pointed to Rich rocking back and forth on his heels next to me. Les's hand looked like a baby lamb chop in Richie's massive clasp. An old couple smiled at us. No doubt, they thought it was a long, lost reunion among friends.

"That's some shake," Les said. "Don't tell me, you're the guy getting Mike to eat. I'm going to say you are a personal trainer."

Richie glanced at me conspiratorially.

"That he is. He's the Yoda to the Darth Vader in my head. He's also my friend," I affirmed confidently. "Les, what are you doing back in town? You visiting?" Of course, I was already resigned to the idea that they had never left.

He burned the cigarette down to the filter and dropped the butt, killing it with a quick step. "No, no, we moved back a few months ago. Yeah, Jessie and I spent some time at my aunt's house in North Carolina, but we always intended to return. I love this city. Such atmosphere.

"Jess got a great job in the Harvard offices, and I applied to go back to school last year to finish my master's. I'm teaching at the same time. We came back for the spring semester. I guess we've been back since March or April. Time goes so fast, who can tell?

"So tell me, what have you been up to, Michael, besides getting your hair cut and doing this?" He motioned towards my waist. "You must have gained like twenty or twenty-five pounds. Maybe more?"

I cringed, refusing to acknowledge him. Of course, I was pleased I did not look emaciated, but somewhere deep inside it felt like he was twisting the knife with a vengeance.

"Like I said, Jessie would be so happy," he said, ignoring my obvious dismay. "Wait until she sees you. You still living at the old place?"

"No, I'm moving in a few weeks. I obviously needed to get other things in order first." I breathed very slowly and quietly, just as Dr. Hampton had taught me.

He smiled sweetly like nothing had happened and we were still sitting on his porch listening to music on a Sunday afternoon. I gazed off into the distance. All I could think about was how I could delicately phrase, "So what did it feel like to lie to my face while fucking my girlfriend in my bed, and then making off like Bonnie and Clyde?"

Of course, I said nothing.

"That's great. We all need a changing of the guard every once in a while," Les said before lighting up another Marlboro. He nodded at Richie while stabbing at me with the burning cigarette between his fingers. "Big changes with this guy. This guy, he's a good man, and I'm happy for him. We had a lot of fun times together."

Richie tapped me on the shoulder as he departed. "Mike, I'm going to get some ice cream." He shook Les's hand one more time and flipped the hood of his sweatshirt over his head. "Nice to meet you."

After Richie cleared the area, Les let out a long stream of smoke. "You know Michael, I hope there's no hard feelings between us. In fact, I'm really hoping we can be friends. I'm sure Jessie would love to see you again now. She was always worried about you.

"She even said she thought we'd run into you. And man, would she be surprised. Look at you, night and day. It looks like it all worked out for the best. You look happy. We're happy. Sometimes life works in funny ways. Simple twists of fate."

Richie was pantomiming taking deep breaths—his hands rising and falling—outside the ice cream shop. To my own astonishment, I looked Les directly in the eye. "Yeah, you are right. It's funny how life works out. We all need to make peace with ourselves. If that's how you want to see it, I couldn't agree more." There was no way I was going to play the bitter, scorned man. "I guess everything always works out for the best."

That last part was complete bullshit, but it sure seemed perfect for the Up With People fog of faux gratitude we were lost in. I also figured it would be just the right line to punctuate my goodbye.

For some strange reason, though, I couldn't just walk away. I was compelled to find out where Les was finishing his degree. He was at least eight to ten years older than me, and he hadn't been to school in over a decade. I never thought he'd want to go back.

"So, where'd you end up going for the degree?" The movie crowd finally broke—dozens of people swarmed around us.

Les let the cigarette burn in his hand while spying a group of under-grads. "I'm at Northeastern. It's tough juggling the classes and teaching, but I love it. Learning something new every day, just absorbing things. The paper grading is brutal, though."

I staggered backward into a man talking about the genius of Truffaut. "You are shitting me. You are at Northeastern?"

He nodded his head with a smirk. "Yeah, why?"

"Uh, nothing, I just, I know, well, I know someone who teaches there." I scrambled to answer coherently. "Amanda Crosetti. She's Richie's neighbor."

Les hit his head with the palm of his hand. "You're kidding? Amanda, she's so smart. I love her. I talk to her all the time. She's a Melville scholar. You guys must really get along. We need to all get together some night. I'll invite her, and you and your friend over there can come to our place some night for some wine.

"We can have a big party. We live now in this great place by NU on Westland Ave., behind Symphony Hall. A big two-bedroom. I couldn't believe it when we snagged it. So where was it you say you are moving to?" he said, the cigarette hanging from his lower lip.

A poster for a Somerville Reggae Festival taped to the corner of the coffee shop window caught my eye. "I'm moving to Davis Square in Somerville." My stomach collapsed while I began counting down the seconds for the cement to give way so the earth could swallow me.

"We haven't been to that side of town since we've been back. You'll have to give us the address so we can visit. Jessie would love it." Les flipped the cigarette butt under a car tire.

"Mike, I'm disappointed Jessie isn't here to see you," he said as I tentatively walked away. "I know she would have been surprised, but this heat is too much for her. We had to put air conditioning in the apartment."

As we shook hands for one last time, I hesitated. Jessie had always loved to walk around the city on summer nights. Something must have been wrong. "I don't get it. Why is the heat too much for Jess? She okay?"

He tapped his head again. "Oh shit, I forgot the most important part. Jessie's pregnant, Mike. Get this, twins. You should see her." He extended his hand well beyond his stomach. "Jessie is huge. I mean really big these days, but she's so, so beautiful. It's amazing."

Thirty-Six

"**S**o what are you going to now? Monique had been quietly tapping her thumb against the back of the chair at the main table of my apartment for over forty minutes after arriving from the gym. She kept repeating the same question over and over while I was wildly swinging a baseball bat in the bedroom. Hacking away with my black Louisville Slugger like Junior Griffey on crack was always a great stress reliever for me. For months, I'd fantasized about smashing the television to pieces, and now I finally had an excuse to do it.

"Mon, if you ask that again, some brilliant idea is not going to just pop into my head," I shouted. "Like I said, I didn't sleep last night and thought of every single scenario. They all lead nowhere. I need to be out of this place in two weeks and start a job search from scratch. I can't teach. School starts in a week or so. Who's going to hire me now? How many times can we go over this? I don't want to fucking go back to the record store."

Mon's sharply etched face looked gaunt without makeup and her hair back in a ponytail. With each slow shake of her head in resignation, Monique still displayed a different shade of loveliness, but she had been transformed into a pale shadow of the woman I'd known. It was obvious she hadn't seen the sun all summer. Somehow, my cheeks had more color.

"Michael, just don't make a rash decision out of anger. It's always the wrong one," she said, pacing the floor with hands in the pockets of her hoodie.

"I can't make a rash decision because I'm out of options. There are no decisions to make here. I don't know what to do."

"Stop with that—there are always options."

"You realize walking around the apartment doesn't help, Mon.

You're going to get dizzy if you keep walking in circles. I did it all night and got a big fat zero. Les and Jessie fucked me over once, and now they both are finding new, imaginative ways to do it again. Tell me, what are the odds?"

I picked a stray pen off the table and violently whipped it across the room. It fractured into pieces. "Imagine what it would have been like if I didn't know and blindly walked into an English department meeting. Les could have been eating a donut or talking to Amanda about his twins. Unfuckingbelievble. And now I need to delete Amanda's number from my phone. She's a co-conspirator. Insane, but I was even thinking about asking her out sometime. I must be delusional."

"Michael, don't you dare throw one more thing." With one quick motion, Monique swept everything off the table onto the floor. "Are you really crazy? That pen could have hurt me. This is not a baseball field. This is real life. Get your head in this game. Deal with it. There is no great plan against you. You and all your enemy conspirators. Believe it or not, you're not Julius Caesar. Shit happens. What about Dr. Hampton? Maybe he can help you? When do you talk to him?"

"I don't—you must realize it's August. What shrink works during August? He's been off for three weeks. He's probably in the Hamptons where he belongs, and he's not some magical wizard who can make Les disappear."

Students were yelling on the street below where Def Leppard's "Pour Some Sugar on Me" powered from a boombox. Mon shouted, "Do you have his emergency number?"

"Yes, of course. But this is no emergency. What am I going to say, 'Hello Dr. Hampton, I just can't manage to get my ex-best friend's dick out of my ass?'"

"And your group doctor? What about her?" Mon completely ignored my words.

"August, it's August. They all take the same plane out of town together. There's some young doctor filling in to lead the group. I can't believe it. She's this incredibly hot Indian woman—must be an intern or something—and the guys just sit there all google-eyed, no doubt dreaming about licking curry off her breasts. They all have hard-ons, and are suddenly happy-go-lucky, talking about how fucking good life is."

Monique angrily shut the windows to muffle the music. "The doctor is on vacation would have been fine. I didn't need the rest, thank you. Leave your imagination out of this." After a moment's silence, she rushed towards me with eyes wide and placed a hand on my shoulder.

"Michael, I know. I got it. Just take a break. Everyone's on vacation, right? So, you go, too. Take a week or two away, and think about it. Use that ticket I gave you to sit on a beach or relax at some hotel pool. You'll come up with something. Time away. It's perfect. You come back refreshed and…"

"And what?" I stuck my head in the refrigerator for five minutes to cool off before pulling out two bottles of water.

"And what what?" Mon said, exasperated. "There doesn't have to be a what here. I think that's the idea. Take a time out from life, and you can think clearly about it. It can't hurt. What's the harm? You've got nothing to lose. Go to Vegas or see the Grand Canyon."

"My life just turned into a big fucking hole, Mon. I'm not going to a place that reminds me it can only get bigger."

"I vote for vacation. Spend the night here to think of where you want to go. Just pack a few things. I'll drive you to the airport this week. Tomorrow even." Mon was now sitting at the table again with her forehead in both hands.

"For the first time, I'm going to tell you as politely as possible, you are giving me shitty advice." I laughed as Mon snatched a bottle of water from my hand. Rage Against the Machine's "Pocket Full of Shells" suddenly blasted from the sidewalks. Zack de La Rocha's angry, staccato flow was punctuated by three knocks at the door. Not expecting company, I eyed Mon cautiously. When she shrugged at me, I had a faint, fleeting hope that another hot pizza might have arrived to brighten my day.

I yanked the door open to see a beaming Phoebe, dressed in a demure, navy-blue blouse and crisp jeans. Apparently, all the dead were magically coming back to life.

"Remember me?" she said, smiling broadly and stepping in from the hallway. "Can I come in and talk? Pretty please."

Mon craned her head around to face us.

"Hello, sister-in-law," Phoebe confidently said with a wave.

"It's Monique," Mon replied with a quick smile. I retreated as Phoebe extended her hand.

"Oh God, I love that name, it's so beautiful. I'm Phoebe. You mind if I say you are so pretty," she said, bowing slightly. "I always try to admire the pretty in the world."

"So are you, Phoebe, thank you." Mon abruptly stood and nestled her bag beneath her elbow. "I'm just leaving. Michael, I want you to think about what we talked about. I will drive you to the airport." A warm wind blew through the kitchen window, rattling the wooden frame.

Monique quietly walked out of the room after gently touching Phoebe's arm. When the door closed, Phoebe turned to me. "Where are you going?"

"Nowhere. I have no idea—ignore what she said. It's nonsense. Phoebe, this is a weird time for me. Please tell me what you are doing here. Where the heck have you been?"

She dropped into the chair that Mon had been warning all morning. This was Phoebe 3.0, so very different than the flirty enigma I'd met on the train and the Stevie Nicks-loving, go-get-'em girl who drove me home. Her tan cheeks were fuller. Those eyes—still so blue—were clear, and she filled out her jeans. The surfer, bleached blonde hair had been dyed a regal auburn.

"Michael, that's a really fair question, and I know I was unfair to you. Honestly, though, I'm disappointed you are still here. I took a shot to see if I could find you. So now what a surprise. Look at this—I'm here. I know I left you hanging but..." She paused while frantically pulling her hair back. Her biceps were developing defined muscles.

"But you've been in rehab," I said, simply confirming what was self-evident.

Her smile softened my anger. "Yeah, I'm clean. Of everything, and I've been in an eating disorder clinic to get healthy. I had to, actually. I really didn't have a choice. I didn't have a choice because I made a lot of bad choices—what else is new, you know? We do what we do to survive. And everything came back to bite me in the ass, as it always does. So, I had to go. But I'm now glad it all happened."

There were so many questions I needed to ask, but I didn't know her well enough to deserve any answers. Whatever she had been doing to maintain that high-rise condo lifestyle really didn't matter. Nothing mattered at that point. I was just too happy to see her to care.

"I barely recognized you. It's you, but so different," I said.

I slid into a chair next to her as she readjusted and sat on one bent leg. When she angled towards me, there was a new tattoo on the side of her neck with the word "Love" above a skull with hearts for eyes. I quickly remembered the sweatpants she forced me to wear. At the bottom of the skull's jawbone was the name Myles in stylized script.

"I'm sorry I left you hanging, and I know it's crazy to pop back into your life like this."

I found her understatement strangely entertaining. "Somehow, I should have expected you. You're not the only one who's back. I'm getting used to it these days."

"No, no, please now, don't tell me. The girlfriend?" she said, squinting.

"Phoebe, who is Myles?"

"You first. Is she back?" She tenderly touched my arm. "You don't need to tell me—I know she is. It's stamped on your face. She wasn't here, was she?"

"No, of course not. Please. Now that's nuts. What would she do here?"

"Aha, now that's why you are going?" Her quick omniscience—reminiscent of the night we met—was unnerving. She just seemed to know exactly what I was thinking.

"Phoebe, can you tell me who is Myles?" I asked as she mindlessly spun the bottle of water Mon had left on the table, and watched it point towards me.

"Myles is why I'm here. I want to invite you to my wedding. Michael, I'm getting married next month. You know, I want you to be there."

"You want me where? Your wedding? Oh stop, how long have you known this guy? C'mon, Phoebe." I laughed indignantly, disregarding how cruel it sounded.

"I met him in rehab, and I'm in love."

I stared directly into her eyes. I thought for sure she would break into a smile and say it was some sort of silly joke. "Stop. Love? Wait, what did you tell me about love the night we met? Are you in love or do you think you are in love?" I was trying not to sound bitter and failing miserably.

As she shook her head and smiled, all I could see was Les with his hand pretending to measure Jessie's enormous waist. The words, "She's so, so beautiful" echoed in my head.

Phoebe didn't flinch. "Well, thanks for the congratulations. I get your reaction, though, and I know you are right. That night I told you a lot of things. Some were real for me, but some didn't make all that much sense."

"Well, they sure made perfect sense to me." I fired back, crisply enunciating the words.

"Michael, I can understand that. And what I said may ring true to me at another point in my life, too. We hear what we want to hear. Listen to me now, though. I'm happy. Yeah, I'm happy. Doesn't that count for something? Today, I'm saying it completely sober. I'm happy, and I want you at my wedding. Is that too much to ask? I know this is completely out of the blue. It probably seems crazy to you, but it's important to me. I want you there."

Her fragile voice betrayed the determination in her eyes. I instantly regretted my selfishness. "You know Phoebe, I'm so fucked up. I'm sorry I didn't mean…"

"To be an asshole. I know you are not, even though you always think you are. That's what we do. It's our thing. We hate ourselves and alienate people we care about. You're obviously going through whatever you are going through. So please tell me about your girlfriend and what's what."

She snuck into the kitchen only to immediately return with an apple. "I quit junk—no more Slim Jims—and I eat a lot of fruit now. You believe that? I love Delicious apples. The new me. Scary, ain't it?

"Okay now, girlfriend. What happened? C'mon." She held my shoulders while squatting next to me.

I proceeded to tell her about how all of my plans had all been wiped away by the tsunami of coincidences. The past flooding out the future. Phoebe meandered over to sit on the boxes of books in the corner of the room.

"Now, you are going away to start over with a blank slate, right?" she said.

"What? No. Monique was talking about me taking a vacation or a trip to clear my head out and think things over." Recounting the idea only made it seem more preposterous.

Phoebe laughed with her mouth open before offering pitying shakes of her head. "Oh, you stop. You know that is no plan. That's a tourniquet while you bleed out. You are going on vacation? That's totally ridiculous. What are you going to do smear Bain De Soleil on your skin while you sit by yourself, looking at sad, lonely, drunk girls at some hotel pool? Tell me, what the heck will you be coming back to? "What are you thinking here? You're smarter than that, I know."

She tossed the apple core into the garbage while giving me the stink eye, "You said, c'mon, Phoebe. Well, c'mon, Michael. Be real."

"So...I'm supposed to do what?" I batted the lukewarm bottle of water against my forehead until it hurt.

"You start over, that's what you do," Phoebe said, shrugging as if I asked her to add two plus two. "Do you need money? I can lend you money. I can give you money. Lots."

"I don't need money. I'm fine for a while. That's not my problem."

"Then just go. There's nothing here for you. There's nothing but miles of bad memories in Boston for you. Boston is your past, and where you were. You don't know how much better you look than the night I saw you. And you didn't even need rehab. Both of us, we're getting better. That's our way out. I refuse to go backward. You have to refuse also."

"Phoebe, you're coming in here without notice like a tornado. I don't even know what's up or down." She was bringing an unforeseen light into my life, but I desperately needed to hold onto the comforting darkness.

"No, I'm definitely not. Wow. Now that's really unfair. Tornadoes destroy. That's not what I'm doing. I want to help. Why can't you leave? Tell me. What is so important here? I think it's because this is what you know."

"I have my family here."

"Your family will always be with you."

"But they're all I have." The thought made my legs weak.

"And that's what you are going to settle for? Your family will be supportive no matter where you go. Even my own apeshit mother is still supportive of me. There are people out in the world for you to meet. Women to…" She stopped and pointed to her neck. "Love."

Tattoo philosophy was not going to flip the switch. "But my doctors are here." I had an entire list of things I couldn't live without.

"I know what you are doing, Michael." Phoebe firmly grasped my forearm and tugged me towards her. "You know there are doctors everywhere. Ask your doctor for a recommendation. He can talk to your new doctor and email your medical records. We are not in the Stone Age. We survived stupid Y2K, remember?"

"And what about my books?" I said, pointing to the boxes. I was unable to take the leap of faith with her.

"You're getting really ridiculous now." She was laughing uproariously and falling back on her heels. "I will buy all your books to put them in storage. Donate them to the Brighton Library. Give a piece of yourself to something bigger. Just take your two favorite books, and get on a plane and start over, Michael. I'm telling you, you will be miserable if you stay in this town.

"This is the place you identify with your illness. I learned that in rehab, and believe it. Myles and I are moving to Toronto. It's a beautiful city with no ugly Americans. It can't get more perfect. I'll deal with the cold. I have no idea if it'll work. But I told you I've been exploring my whole life, and you know what? I'm going to keep doing it."

Her voice deepened and suddenly turned troubled as she pushed the hair off the back of her neck. "I have to tell you, honestly, every day is still a struggle for me, Michael, and I know it is for you too. I can see it in your eyes, but that doesn't mean we can't find something meaningful within that struggle. I learned that in rehab too. That, I know is real. It's not just talk.

"Come here. Where's your phone? Give it to me."

Everything Phoebe said seemed to make sense because nothing else did. Did it ever? Her plan was reckless and mercurial, but the more I thought about it, the more I was inexorably drawn to her brave new frontier mentality. It was so far beyond the realm of my reasoning.

"Here you go—here's my number," she said while carefully pecking into my phone. "It won't be disconnected this time, I swear. You know, actually, I was hoping I'd come back and see that you never washed your arm with my number on it." Phoebe's wink weakened my legs.

"Seriously, this time yes, we can be real friends," she added. "I'm getting married. And that's a good thing, but I need a good friend, too. I'm not disappearing. You would love Myles. He's a great guy. He just lets me be me. That's all I ever wanted.

"I gotta tell you, I think a lot about some of the things we talked about the night we spent together. Bottom line, you understand me, and I understand you. If one of us is ever in danger of backsliding, we can call each other. We have our own Batphone for help. More importantly, I just want to be able to talk to someone who gets it. It helps us both. I'm looking forward to starting something new, and of course, I know things might get messy. I'm not scared of that. We can't live scared all the time."

She exhaled before delicately touching the corners of her eyes. "Now please, you know I'm not going to start sounding like Oprah. I honestly never got her. Enough with the advice, for God's sake. But maybe that's why I'm not a millionaire, I guess. She makes it look like she's in control. There's some genius to that, no doubt. I don't have the answers. You know, sometimes Michael, I think maybe we're the questions."

I sat down again, now dizzy, and watched Phoebe quietly slip into the front room to open the window and take a deep breath. "It already is beginning to feel like Fall," she said. "You can feel it in the air. There's something about the end of August that always makes me sad. But I'm not going to be sad. I just will not."

Finally, she strolled back to me and handed over the phone, her fingers lingering on my palm. "I'm going to expect a call after you arrive. In a few months, you can tell me all about the hot babes you better be dating. That sound fair? We have a deal?" With hand extended, she said, "To a new start?"

I couldn't imagine telling Monique, David, Richie, and Dr. Hampton that I was just packing up and leaving, but I clasped her hand anyway. "What do I have to lose?" I replied, skeptically echoing Monique's words.

"Books?" Phoebe smiled before quickly hugging me. "I really just came to invite you to the wedding, so I'm not going to stay this afternoon. I actually thought we could catch up on the last months before Myles and I moved, but I'm just going to go, and let you be. We can talk on the phone later. No thought and no reservations now for you. You have to go."

I was still considering the logistics in my head. There was no blueprint for this. No heading to AAA for tips. "Phoebe, it sounds nice and something out of a movie, but honestly, where am I going to go?"

"That's the damn voice of no that we've been battling for years, am I right?" she said defiantly. "There's nothing Hollywood about it. It's actually the most pragmatic option you have. Are you going to stay or come back to this?" she added while twirling around the apartment floor like Julie Andrews on the hills in *The Sound of Music*.

"I'm sorry, that's not an option. Go wherever you want. When do we ever have that kind of freedom? It's really now or never, and never is the one thing you have told yourself—I have told myself—over and over again. And look where that got us."

Nowhere. I knew the answer was nowhere.

"Hey, I'm out of here," she whispered after hugging me once more and touching my chin with her fingertips.

I stood dazed in the middle of the room as she pivoted away. "Wait, Phoebe, what about your wedding? I thought you came to invite me. I can't go if I leave."

Standing with her chest out, shoulders back and one foot in the doorway, she said, "You'll be there, wherever you are. Remember, we are connected. I know you remember what I told you that night. I'll talk to you, 3B." She tapped the sign plate on my door. "Repeat after me. No to the no. That's the only way you and I will survive this shitty world. I'll talk to you soon."

I watched her wave a hand over her head as she walked away, leaving the door wide open.

Thirty-Seven

After hours debating whether to stay and grit my teeth through another winter or finally put Boston in my rear-view mirror, I found an old photo Patty took of Jessie, Les, and me standing together around a group of Jack O' Lanterns outside of Faneuil Hall. It was frayed and folded in half, beneath an unopened package of tube socks in the bottom drawer.

We all seemed so happy together. And maybe we were at that split second—I don't know. Or maybe it was just another picture capturing the false truths we create with awkward poses and forced smiles. Honestly, I have never trusted photographs. Let's face it, they only reflect the faces we temporarily show to the world. We decide to preserve the memories that comfort us. The moments after the cameras click usually tell the actual stories we end up carrying around throughout our lives.

I sat silently, inspecting every minute detail of that split second of time. Les's hand casually cradled Jessie's small waist—his index finger circling through her belt loop as she leaned into his chest, her lipstick slightly awry. They were both laughing, playfully. I was somewhat out of focus, standing just off center with pinched eyes gazing into the distance.

The worn photo shook in my trembling hand. All of the paralyzing emptiness associated with those days overwhelmed me once more.

I welled up upon seeing the truth—my story. After years of searching in the in the mirror for imaginary fat, I finally recognized what had mysteriously eluded me during my time with Jessie. My image in the photo was terrifying: a sad, skeletal kid with long, straggling hair covering deep wells under each side of his jaw. The wrist hanging over Les's shoulder was as thin as a knitting needle. This was the Michael I refused to see. The Michael I simply could not acknowledge.

I remembered how I arrived home from Downtown Crossing that night, struggling to make it to the apartment building foyer. Jess scooted up the stairs with a pumpkin under her arm. When she vanished, I contemplated the long walk up three flights.

It seemed beyond daunting—like climbing the Himalayas. I was unsure if I could make it inside our doorway. It was a familiar fear: each step just might be my last. There was no guarantee I would ascend one more floor without collapsing. It took all my strength to make it up one flight, weighed down by Filene's bags and years of denial. I was forced to sit on the stairs and recharge a completely depleted battery before I stumbled into the apartment.

Yes, looking at that picture—the only one Jessie left behind—reminded me that I had played Russian roulette for years and somehow survived. I knew if I gambled against the odds again, the next chamber would be loaded.

The fear of getting sucked back into that vortex of despair was far more tyrannical than the anxiety I had about stepping off of a plane in a strange place. I had no idea what awaited me on the other side of my new journey. I definitely knew what it would mean to fall helplessly into Les's and Jessie's orbit once more.

And I was sure it would kill me.

I decided to trust the one voice in my head that made sense: Phoebe's.

After leaving a long, detailed message on Dr. Hampton's voicemail, I didn't hear back from him until late afternoon. I'd already called Kathy Myers at Northeastern to tell her I was declining the teaching position after I apologized to Miguel for backing out of the apartment on such short notice. Both of them were unusually sympathetic. Myers invited me to teach if I decided to return someday, and Miguel refused to cash my check because he already had a friend lined up to move in immediately. It was a rare alignment of goodwill to brighten my spirits.

Dr. Hampton, though, was unusually dour when he called back. He quickly cut to the chase in a steely, terse tone. "Michael, if I understand what you said correctly, I have to say I'm more than a bit surprised by this sudden decision. You must realize, as your therapist, I really can't approve of this. I can't stop you, but I will let you know I think you are making a mistake.

"You have your entire medical infrastructure here, and you still have a lot of work to do. You have made such great strides over the past months. Now you are making a decision that will jeopardize your progress. This seems rash. Michael, it doesn't sound like you."

I muted *Wheel of Fortune* on the television and tried to summon the words I had rehearsed in anticipation of this reaction. I was not going to waver. It was time to calmly express my decision.

"Dr. Hampton, I don't expect you to understand, but you always told me to take charge of my life and make decisions. We talked about how I try to control my eating because my world seemed out of control, and here I am taking the reins in a constructive way. I'm taking a step forward into the unknown. I don't see that as a bad thing."

"Michael, this isn't about good and bad—try to stop thinking in those terms. This is about being smart and doing what is best for your health. Staying with your program that has served you so successfully so far. Have you talked to your brother and sister-in-law yet?"

"I wanted to speak you first. I'm honestly really not looking for your approval. I knew you wouldn't like it. Please don't take that disrespect-fully. Somewhere along the way, though, I have to throw the crutches away and walk, don't I? I'm never going to be fully healed. I'm always going to be in the process of healing. Every day is going to be a struggle, right? Maybe there will come a time when it gets easier, but I know I'm always going to be looking at that shadow hovering in the mirror."

Rain began pounding the window as the late afternoon sun disap-peared and winds kicked up. September was making its presence felt with authority. "I love working with you and Dr. Rigatta, but now I'm hoping you both can help me find other doctors. Someplace far away from here. I just don't want to be here anymore. You have to understand that.

"I'm not saying a change of scenery is going to magically make things better. You and I both know those kinds of easy answers are bullshit for self-help books. Boston is the city where my life unraveled. There has to be someplace else out there for me."

There was a long, frustrating pause before he spoke again. "Of course,

I will help you find a new doctor, and I'm sure Dr. Rigatta will be of help also. Michael, I am always here for you. Yes, there are many good doctors everywhere, so that's not my primary concern.

"I'm worried about you on your own, knowing no one and having no support. I'm worried about you not eating and falling into old habits. Even with a new doctor, you will be starting the process all over again."

Everything he was saying made complete sense. It was what I thought about throughout the night and morning, but I needed to remain steadfast. I genuinely believed I was finally strong enough to move on.

"I need to find out on my own if I can survive. I know I can't fail. If I fail, I'm going to die. And one of the first things I told you was, I will not kill myself. I know it's going to be a fight every day, but I have to shake little Michael off my back. He needs to fall away. That's what we've been working towards. Now's the time—it has to be. Les and Jessie are having babies, and I'm still struggling to come to terms with eating solid food. What does that say about me?"

I was yelling into the phone while watching the rain intensify outside the window. It shook the screens—little puddles of water were forming near the moldings.

"I understand what you are saying, Michael, but I want you to be cognizant of the pattern you are repeating. You see that, don't you? You know you can't run away from your problems. And you certainly know you can't run from your past."

I hustled around the apartment to shut each window one by one. The incessant noise of the street suddenly disappeared as if someone pulled out a radio plug.

"I do know what you are talking about. I've been over it time and time again. I don't see it like I'm running away from my problems. Maybe I'm running to something. Maybe my dad was running to something, too. I don't know. I forgive him, wherever he is.

"You've been telling me to forgive myself. I think I need to forgive him, too. I was almost an adult when he disappeared. He left me with everything. I guess he took care of me. I don't know if he needed to find something he didn't have. I'm thinking maybe he needed to be released from his pain. Who knows? We just don't. Dr. Hampton, I'm not him. I'm not, and I'm not closing that circle by leaving. I'm just not.

"Everything you helped me with was about trusting myself, and now you're telling me not to do just that. Well, let's see what I'm capable of. As I said, failure is not an option."

The rain let up, but gusts of wind jolted the windows. For a moment, I thought they'd give way.

"Certainly, Michael, as you said, you don't need my approval, but I do want you to speak to your family and then get back to me. I'm returning to my office in two weeks. Don't we have an appointment?"

"I'll talk to Monique, but I'm going to tell her I'm leaving. I can't just linger in limbo here. I can't." Two weeks were much too long to sit around to let doubt creep in. "It may be impetuous. I get that, still, this is what I need to do. I will call you back later, I swear."

After repeatedly apologizing to Dr. Hampton for ruining his vacation, I immediately called Mon. Of course, she didn't pick up. It seemed like no one answered phones anymore. We were beginning to live life once removed and filtered by machines.

I wasn't hungry, yet I still downed a three egg-white omelet in seconds. If I was begging to be released, I also needed to prove that I would not be eaten alive in the wild.

Two hours later, Mon called. "Michael, I'm sorry I didn't ring you this morning. Are you going away like we talked about? You need a ride to the airport? Where'd you decide to go?" I heard the shuffling of papers and muted jazz in the background.

"No, Mon, hey, well, how can I put this? Maybe I can come over and explain it to you. I'm going away, but away away. I'm leaving. You know a vacation is a ridiculous idea. I'm sorry, but it is. I've had it living here, so I'm going away for good. I'm moving to sunshine. I've got no job or place here to live. Why don't I have no job or place to live where it's warm and there's beaches. I'll get a job. I can do things. Let's face it, I just need to get the fuck out of Boston."

I sat on the floor and collected dust bunnies for five minutes while listening to Mon's music through the phone before she finally spoke after the be-bop abruptly stopped.

"I'm sorry, but what are you talking about? Did you lose your mind? Michael, stop now. You said you're leaving when? No."

I was perched on the bed in silence—my hands were shaking uncontrollably. Confronting Dr. Hampton was easy, but each one of Mon's words wounded. "Monique, please don't be mad. I need you on my side. And I need you to trust me."

"Michael, is this the girl Phoebe's idea? Is she going with you? You want me to trust you. Well, where are you going? With a girl?"

"No, it's something we talked about, but I decided. And no, of course, she's not coming with me. She's getting married."

"She's what? What? What are you talking about? Michael, please tell me what is going on because I'm lost."

"I said it already. I'm leaving."

"What, on a jet plane? Are you now John Denver? Are you fucking kidding me?"

"Mon, please no, don't be mad. C'mon. This is not how I wanted you to react. My mom used to listen to John Denver, so I have no idea what that means. He died in a plane crash, right?"

"I'm not your mom, Michael, and I'm not mad. I need you to tell me with a straight face you know what you're doing."

"Okay, I will if you calm down. I'm going to go to the airport, choose a city and get on a plane. That simple. Day after tomorrow. Is that easy enough to understand? It may sound crazy, but I think staying here is crazier. I've lived crazy. My whole life has been one crazy fuck up. What's the point of doing the same thing?"

As I waited for Monique to answer, a teenager in blue boxer shorts with a guitar held to his bare chest began playing Hole's "Doll Parts" in the apartment across the back alley. Every time he finished picking a string or bashing a chord, he raised his arm in triumph.

"When did you say you were leaving?" Mon said.

"Day after tomorrow." A pasty-faced girl, decked out in horn-rimmed glasses and a brown fedora carefully propped on the back of her head, joined the guitarist in the cramped room. She sang violently out of tune over the waves of feedback. This was my appropriate, atonal Allston sendoff.

"No Michael."

"Yes Monique, I'm doing this."

"No, I mean, no you can't. You don't understand. You can't leave the day after tomorrow."

The girl across the way started chanting like an unhinged Kate Bush on steroids while another young woman with cotton candy-colored hair hit a snare drum with one drumstick.

I yelled over the din. "Yes, Mon, what's the problem? I thought you'd support me."

"I'm sorry. I really am. Michael, I'm sorry about all this. Listen, let me call you back. Give me five minutes."

The phone clicked, leaving me alone with the sonic youths.

I was trying to decipher the girl's endless freeform lyrics when the phone rang again.

"Monique, where'd you go?"

"Michael, it's me." David's voice stunned me.

"David, where you been? What's going on?" I ran into the hallway and sat in the stairwell to get away from the clatter. "Where's Monique. Where are you?"

"Mike, you have to listen to me. You can't go anywhere the day after tomorrow." His words were deliberate and faint.

"Wait, you know? David answer my question. Where are you? I can't wait until you get back. I can't put my life on hold while you are away doing your thing. You just left, and now you expect me to just sit around. I want to get on with my life. I have no idea when you are coming back."

"Meet me at our place on Friday. That gives you four days. You can wait that long."

"Meet you? David, you are here? No, no, wait. What? You're kidding me." My heart fluttered as I lost my balance and nearly slid down the steps.

"No, I'm not Michael. I'm in New York, but I'm asking you to be at our place on Friday."

I just couldn't believe what I was hearing as I held the phone between my legs to think. My defiance and defensiveness immediately wilted.

"David, I'll come to New York. I can be there tomorrow."

"Mike, will you for once please listen to me, please. Just once." He spoke so timidly, almost begging. "I'm coming to you."

I realized David might have had some secret, baffling agenda. I desperately wanted to see him, but in my heart, I felt as if he was hell-bent on trying to thwart my escape. "David, you are not coming here to prevent me from going, are you? This is my choice. You didn't come back to stop me because..."

"Brother, brother, I'm not, I swear. In fact, I think you are doing the right thing. Go. You should leave and start over. There's a life out there for you to live. What I'm saying is, you can't leave the day after tomorrow. Mon is coming here.

"She's headed to the airport now. And I will see you on Friday. Can you handle that? That'll give you a few days to get all the things in order I'm sure you haven't done. Get rid of your car. I know you haven't sold that yet. Do whatever you have to do. Michael, I wish this could be easier, but it never is. Before I hang up, I need you to tell me you will be there on Friday."

Suddenly feeling overwhelmed, like I was hurtling through space, I ran down the stairs onto the rain-stained street. A bald man in a white BVD shirt was leaning out a window in the building across the way. He raised his fist with fury while shouting, "Will you shut the fuck up. All that fucking noise. Enough. This isn't a fucking garage. It's a neighborhood." The primitive cacophony just continued unabated.

"David, I don't know what's going on," I shouted into the phone over the din. "But I'll see you at your place. I can't believe this, and can't wait to see you."

Thirty-Eight

"**M**ike, you ready? I'll be over in ten minutes." When Richie called, I was sitting on the curb after pulling a $100 ticket for parking a vehicle without a license plate off the windshield of my car. The driver from the children's charity that I donated the car to failed to show before the parking patrol did its rounds, so I was stuck with an apropos parting gift from the city of Boston.

"I'm just out here getting a tan. You realize I can still grab a cab. I just have a small bag." There was a distinct New England Fall chill in the soft breeze as the brilliant morning sun peeked over the building tops.

"No worries, I'm definitely coming with you." Richie had volunteered to drive me to David's after spending the previous two days helping me drop off fifteen cartons of books at the Brighton and Newton libraries. At least part of Phoebe's ad hoc plan had already come to fruition.

I spent most of the week's hours down at the gym, probing Richie for information. During the evenings, we had long, meandering conversations over anxious dinners while watching the Sox, ESPN, and CNN at his place. Some nights we ended up bullshitting until well after midnight. Rich talked a lot throughout our chats, but he said very little.

All of my questions about David were either ignored or deflected. He just kept asking me to postpone my move a few months so we could go to Los Angeles together. I reminded him that David had always said L.A. was the place the human spirit went to choke on John Bonham's vomit. He laughed wistfully with a faraway look. "Your brother always makes me laugh with nonsense like that."

It was the only brief moment during the entire week when I saw Richie smile.

"Let's do it. I packed what I'm taking—you realize I'm leaving a lot of stuff behind. I'm gifting you the bed," I said into the phone while walking up the block to 7-Eleven for a Big Gulp and a last goodbye to my Indian friend. My plan was to spend the day with David so I could hear him out. I knew that despite his encouraging words on the phone, he was probably going to try to convince me to stay.

I couldn't help but think his return was some kind of grand manipulation—his way of saying I was fucking up again and needed to listen to his older brother common sense. There was no way he was going to stop me from moving on, though.

It took a while, but Richie finally picked me up in front of the liquor store I'd gone to with Duran, and we were on Storrow Drive in minutes. He was pensive—his eyes lasered on the road—as we breezed through traffic and into Back Bay. I placed a five-dollar bill in the cup holder while he carefully jockeyed around buses and speeding cars.

"That's the money I owe you. I forgot to tell you. You know that girl I told you about? Well, sure as shit, she reappeared just as you said. You won the bet. And I'm kinda glad you did." He barely acknowledged me with a few nods.

"Rich, is my All Food Baseball All-Star list still in here like you told me?" I said before fishing my hand around the driver's manual and envelopes in the glove compartment. "I'm going to add Herb Hash. He's a jackpot. Look him up. Played for the Red Sox in like 1941. That's gotta be double points."

Richie was gripping the wheel with white knuckles while maneuvering down Beacon Street through surprisingly light traffic. I pulled the torn, yellow lined piece of paper with the long list of names from the morass of maps. My shaky script handwriting contrasted with Richie's block print and curlicue punctuation.

"Mike, you can keep that now. Hold onto it as a reminder of where you started and where you are never going back to," he said through gritted teeth. We slowly circled around the block three times while looking for a place to park.

Now clearly irritated, Richie aggressively pulled into a space without even checking for the curb. I peered out the window at the front tire perilously close to a hydrant. "You're going to get a ticket. Let's

keep looking. Something will open up. I think that guy's going out."
I pointed to a red Camry at the far end of the block. He ignored
me while popping his seatbelt after snapping the emergency brake
to attention.

"Let's go. I'll come down and move it. I don't care," Richie said as
he took out his phone to call Monique with one eye on me.

"Mike before we head up, I think I need to tell you."

"Let's just go up." I was antsy with anticipation, so I brushed him
off with a wave.

"No," he insisted with uncommon brusqueness. "Before we go, just
understand I'm sorry. I want you to know from my heart, I should
have told you, and it was wrong." He refused to look at me as his
voice broke. Richie's thin veneer of strength and cool cracked once
our eyes finally met.

"Rich what? Told me what? What the fuck is going on? What's been
happening while I waited like a fool this week? Is David even here?
He's not, right?" After leaping out of the car, I started sprinting down
the street. "What are you not telling me?" I shouted over my shoulder
just before arriving at the doorway and rushing through the open
security door.

As I hammered at the elevator button, Richie finally caught up to
me. He placed his hands on the elevator door. "Please listen, wait.
I…I couldn't tell you. It was wrong, I know. You have to understand."

"Understand what?" The bag on my shoulder felt like a dead weight.
I aggressively pushed him out of the way so I could bolt up the stairs
two at a time. When I got to the fourth floor, Mon was standing in
the doorway with wilted chestnut eyes.

"Monique, where is David?" She reached out to me as I brushed past
her into the apartment. "Will someone please tell me what the fuck is
going on?" There were prescription bottles on the dining room table
and an electronic blood pressure monitor in the corner of the room.

"Michael, please," Mon said softly. She reached to me after I dropped
my bag on the floor.

"Please what, Mon? Where's David?"

"You have to understand this is definitely not the way we wanted.

We were going..." She covered her mouth with her fingers. My thighs spasmed and nearly gave way while I searched the apartment. Out of the corner of my eyes, I saw David entering from the bedroom. A bulky, gray-haired woman trailed with her hand on his back. "I'm here Michael. I'm here."

Mon grabbed my wrist as I staggered back. David walked slowly with one deliberate step in front of the other. He was drained of color— a San Francisco Giants cap over his bald scalp. His cheekbones were ashen, the sides of his temples concave.

I hesitated, momentarily unsure if this was just another fasting hallucination I was bound to sweat my way through. "Michael, it's going to be okay," David said haltingly.

Unable to move, I looked to Mon once more. One small tear fell off of her chin.

"Oh, fuck me, no, no, no," I rushed down the hallway and swallowed David in my arms. His shoulders were so frail that I was afraid he would crack if I squeezed him too hard. "David, no, this isn't happening." I could feel his hands grasp onto my shoulder blades before he straightened himself up. Monique ran to his side, next to the nurse holding his back.

"I need you to be strong, Michael," David whispered, his warm breath on my neck. "I didn't want you to have to find out this way. I was coming home next month..."

I thought I was staring directly into my own broken, rawboned face. The face that had glared back at me in the bathroom mirror throughout my years with Jessie. The face I'd tried to achieve by starving part of my life away.

David clenched the back of my neck before pulling me toward him. The deep lines around his eyes mapped out months of agony. "Michael, I'm sorry, but I couldn't tell you. We couldn't tell you. This is not how I planned for you to find out, but I couldn't let you leave. We kept this out of your sight..."

My left eye went numb momentarily while I tried to steady my breathing.

I turned to Mon and let out the silent scream in my head. "You lied to me all this time? How could you? You mean, all these months were one long lie? Monique, I trusted you. What the fuck is wrong with you?"

Out of the corner of my eye, I saw Richie recede quietly to the end of the hallway. "And you knew too? You knew as you drove me here. You let me talk like a fucking idiot about baseball players' names? And the last few days? What were you thinking?"

I stepped back warily from my brother, still unable to face him. "I could have helped you. I could have done something, been there for you, David. You kept me out for what? How could you all keep this away from me? Why wasn't I told? I could have done something for you."

"Michael, you have to know I wanted to tell you but..." Monique said, slowly approaching me with her hand up defensively.

"But what?" I shouted. I could feel Richie's thick hand on my back as David yanked me by the arm. He almost fell forward.

"Stop it, Michael, stop it. Don't you yell at her. That's enough. You have every right to be angry, but if you are going to be angry, it's me you can yell at. It was me, all me. I told them not to tell you. I made them swear not to tell you. They wanted to from the very beginning when I was diagnosed, but I didn't think you'd survive. Go ahead get angry, just don't take it out on them."

David walked to a stool in the kitchen where he sat, bracing himself with the counter. The nurse guided him, but he raised his hand to her.

"I'm fine," he said with a dim smile. She disappeared into the living room while David pointed me to the stool next to him. I struggled to look at him—unrecognizably sapped of life and a mere outline of the brother I loved. He wrapped his right hand, scarred with IV marks, around my forearm.

"We didn't tell you to protect you, Michael. Listen to me," David demanded. Monique walked behind him to tenderly touch his back.

"I said listen, Michael." I was forced to look directly into his eyes, terrified by my own rage and confusion. "I made a decision when I was diagnosed because I was afraid of losing you. I really was. There was so much happening to you at once. You were so fragile. I really didn't think you could take it. I couldn't let you bear witness to this...

"To this slow massacre." He waved his hand down the length of his body. "Mike, I was so scared for you. You were slipping away from us right before our eyes. The night you cut yourself, you stepped on the scale that night and closed your eyes. Remember that?

"You were ninety pounds. Ninety, and you were refusing to face it. You were so intoxicated by your own emaciation, and willing your annihilation. I saw you lost in a spiral. You have to understand—I couldn't let you fall away. I just couldn't, please, please understand.

"Dr. Graynor wanted to hospitalize you. She intended to put a tube in your nose. They wanted to force feed you because you kept saying no. You were refusing to come to terms with your life at the time. All you said was no. But I told her I knew who you really were, and I knew you would respond if we got the support all around you. And you did. You pushed back.

"Just as you were beginning to...I don't know what it was. Wake up? You began putting some food in your mouth—the light came on again—and that's when I found out what was happening with me.

"Those headaches I had that you kept thinking you were responsible for. You kept blaming yourself, thinking you were the reason behind it all.

"You weren't the cause. Please, please stop blaming yourself, Mike." He squeezed my arm tightly and slowly managed another faint smile. "There are things in life so much bigger than us that we just aren't responsible for. The one thing we can't do is self-destruct.

"The day I lied to you about leaving broke my heart. You know I would never hurt you, but I just couldn't allow you to live every day in the shadow of death with what you were going through.

"I, we, Mon, Richie, we needed you to believe in hope and life—your life. I needed you to focus on you without any thoughts about what was happening to me. And I just couldn't allow you to see the shit I was going through. I wanted to protect you from the shit. It's all so very ugly.

"I wanted you to visualize health and strength, not come to a hospital surrounded by small reminders of the slow everyday decay. You have to realize that I needed you to be healthy. To recognize you deserved to be working out with Richie and eating with Mon. You had to keep going forward.

"That's all I ever wanted. So, am I sorry I lied to you and maintained such an elaborate, what? Story? Call it whatever you want.

"Of course, I'm sorry, and I will be to the end. But I needed you to get to right here today. We couldn't risk losing you, too." David drank a glass of water slowly, as if it was a life source before reasserting himself on the stool. The bones in his hand were like wires.

"Do you understand why? And understand that now everything's in front of you. I'm looking at you, and you look like yourself again before the world went dark. I know you still have ways to go, but I've been keeping up. All the time I was in New York dealing at Sloan Kettering, I was keeping tabs on you. Dr. Rigatta is wonderful—she kept us updated."

As I walked hesitantly to the large bay windows, the sun reflected off the Charles River, where crew teams streamed behind narrow shells filled with coaches barking out encouragement through a megaphone.

No one spoke for a couple of minutes—they felt like two lifetimes. Richie sat quietly on the couch across from the nurse. I could see Mon walking towards me as I leaned my head against the window while trying to absorb the enormity of David's words. It was impossible to imagine an existence without him. He was the only constant throughout my life, which now seemed carved in half. No books or doctors ever prepared me for this. What possibly can? They can teach you how to analyze your feelings and order the chaos in your head, but there are no life instructions for making sense out of the incomprehensible. I balanced myself with one hand against the warm windowpane.

Monique carefully drew closer, but it was impossible to look at her with my tantrum still reverberating in my head. I had irrationally lashed out at the one person who I owed the most to. I would not have been in the room without her. She helped save my life, and now I needed her in my world in order to go on. Anything else was inconceivable.

"Mon, I'm so sorry I never meant to yell like that. I don't know where that came from. You are the last person to deserve it."

She hugged me as I stood depleted and ashamed. "Please don't. I'm the one who should be apologizing. I never meant to deceive you, Michael. It was wrong."

"There is no right or wrong here. Neither one of you needs to apologize. This is life," David said from across the room while motioning to the nurse to bring him the prescription bottle from the table to him. "Time for a horse pill, Maria."

Walking with a slight limp, the stolid woman poured two glasses of water and rushed to his side as Mon followed. I timidly trailed, afraid to ask the questions I didn't want answers to.

"Excuse me. I'll be right back," Richie whispered before hopping stealthily towards the door. "I'm going to see if my car is still there." I stifled a nervous, involuntary giggle at his innocent but seemingly inappropriate exit.

"Where did he park?" David said while swallowing the pill with water.

"I'm sorry, I don't know why I laughed. Fuck."

"Mike, please. Take a breath, just relax just for a second. We are all still here. I'm still here. Look at me, deep breath and tell me was it a handicap or..."

"Why are you asking this? What? I don't know, a hydrant," I answered solemnly.

David exhaled with mock disgust and laughed. "In this city? Forget it, he's fucked."

I was taken aback by his glib nonchalance. "I don't believe you. How can you be like that? You are acting as if nothing is happening like life just goes on. It doesn't. David, I mean, what are you thinking? Listen, please, I feel so in the dark. I don't know what to say here, but I need to know...I mean, I don't know how to say it, but how..." He cut me off before I could finish.

"Go ahead ask it. It's okay. Honestly. We don't know. At this point, it could be weeks, months, days. One day it feels like I'm going gangbusters, and the next," he sighed.

"We tried everything, Michael." Mon poured herself a cup of coffee before wiping her nose with a tissue. "He's got the best doctors, and they don't have answers now. No one has answers. Things were going well for a while. We had hope and then..."

"I got worse," David interjected. "We even tried alternative treatments back in early summer. Remember all the craziness around your birthday with Mon. Well, things went sideways when I got desperate and listened to bad advice from people I shouldn't have listened to.

"You ask how I can be like life just goes on? Because it just does, Mike. How am I supposed to act? You want drama? Is that what you want? What is that going to do? Thing is, I've come to terms with it. There's no sugarcoating this. There are no miracles or happy ending here.

"We want to believe there are alternatives to inevitability. I tried that. We tried everything. Anything to keep us both dreaming. What we have is this right here," he said, winding down while pointing to the table. "This moment. So how you want me to act?"

David reached across the counter to slide a bowl with chunks of cantaloupe and honeydew melon towards me. He walked ever so gingerly to the refrigerator, pulled out a gallon of milk and poured some into a glass.

"Drink this milk and eat some of the melon. I know you can do that."

"No ticket, nothing, a minor miracle," Richie said before he picked up my bag after walking back into the room.

"There's your miracle," David said, nudging the glass to me.

"Mike, what do you want me to do with your bag? You want it back in the car?" Richie asked.

I shrugged—the question seemed irrelevant at that point. "Forget it. Just leave it here. I'm not going anywhere."

"Why not?" David said with the life returning to his eyes.

"Why not? What do you mean why not? I'm staying to help you. How can I go anywhere? I'll find a place. Can I stay here for a while? I'll do whatever." I watched Maria shut off an electronic monitor in the bedroom.

"Michael, you can stay as long as you want," Mon said from a stool near the toaster.

"Of course, you can stay here, but for what reason? Why?" David added with palm open to suggestions. "It's senseless. You were leaving, weren't you? What I said on the phone, I meant. You need to turn the page. This, all this, is exactly what you need distance from." He picked up the prescription bottle sitting on the table and raised it over his head for emphasis. "You need to remove yourself from all that this represents. No association with this. Now eat the cantaloupe."

"David," Monique said. "He can stay."

I finally ate two pieces of melon, evoking a smile from my brother. "You know how long I've been waiting to see that? Life's small wonders." He touched my forearm and tossed a few chunks of honeydew in his mouth. "Michael, you have a decision to make, and in my mind, it's not a hard one.

"You can stay, but tell me, what are you going to do? Set up a vigil here? You going to do stations of the cross every night? Light candles? Be honest, are you staying for me because if you are, don't. That's insanity. If you are staying because you might not be ready to leave, that's fine. I get that. You'll be on your own, that won't be easy. No beginnings are."

"Stop David. It's not that. I'll be fine on my own. I'm not a child. I told you. I want to help you."

"Help me what, Mike? Help me what? You do know what that answer is, right? I love you, and I know your heart is in the right place, but I need to know your head is. Being around all this all day, every day, is not healthy. It's just not—even you can acknowledge that."

He carefully placed the glass of milk in my hand while imploring me with his eyes to drink. I immediately knocked it back.

"Listen, Monique talked with Dr. Hampton yesterday." David continued to pat me on the back. "He said he knows an entire network of excellent doctors. He is definitely willing to help. You just have to tell us where you end up.

"And you have to, have to, be in therapy. You hear me? You need to continue the work. Mike, look at me for a second." My face was burning when I turned to David as he pointed to his chest. "We know how this story ends. It's yours I care about now. Go and do the goddamn work in therapy that's going to allow you to flourish far, far away from here. You hate it here, with good reason. Live life on your terms for once."

"David, I don't want to hear this," I said after retreating to the corner near the bathroom.

"You don't want to, but you need to. I don't want you to remember me this way, Mike. And I sure don't want you to remember what you would see if you stay.

"You know what I want you to remember? Remember us playing catch when you were nine in the field behind the high school. You were already burning holes in my glove. It was just me and you, and it seemed like there was no outside world. You need to hold onto that. Remember the night we saw Erykah Badu. What was it? Months before Jessie left?

"We were together on the dance floor. Remember how the music just seemed to connect everyone in the club? The room felt like it was elevating. We were shoulder to shoulder, and the universe was just right that night as if everything was aligned. We laughed in the car all the way home. You remember? Even in your darkest, worst days, you found happiness that night. Hold onto that because that always going to be you and me together, Mike. That's what you need to remember, understand? Not this horror show."

Monique disappeared into the bedroom, quietly closing the door while David sank into the couch and placed his feet on the table. I decided to make my presence felt again and slowly wandered back towards Richie by the front hallway.

"Do me a favor, spend the night here," David said, breathing easily with a smile. "You can think about it. We're all going to have dinner together. Richie, I know you have to get to work. You're coming back, right?"

"I'm cooking—you know it." Richie tapped David on the shoulder and walked past me on his way out after casually punching my chest. "See ya later, brother."

I could hear Monique's footsteps on the hardwood floor. Within moments, she hesitantly touched the base of my back. Forcing a weak smile, lifting tear-stained cheeks, Mon whispered, "Whatever you decide, I'm here."

I squeezed her hand before turning towards David. "I'll be right back, guys. Stay right here. Please." I shuffled out of the condo and bounded down the stairs. When I got to the street, Richie was getting into his car at the end of the block. He hesitated as I shouted his name while running furiously straight at him.

I abruptly came to a halt near the car door.

"Mike, you okay?" he said.

"Tell me, please. What can I do for him? There's got to be something. Rich, c'mon. help me here. I feel so helpless."

He yanked me out of the way of a passing minivan before placing his arm around my shoulder "Listen to him. That's what. There's nothing for you to do otherwise. He's got an army of doctors. You can't believe how hard he's battling. They both are. Monique's been by his side him since the beginning."

"I'm so worried about Mon, too—she doesn't look good. Rich, tell me why is this happening?" I bent over with my hands on my knees to prevent them from shaking.

"It's happening because it is. You know I've prayed every day since I found out, but that only helps me. You have to do whatever will get you through this. And if you listened carefully to your brother, then you know the way you deal with this is by taking care of yourself. You help him by helping yourself. That's what he's asking of you.

"Everything else is meaningless. You hear me?" Richie opened the car door. "And don't worry about Monique," he added while resting his elbow on the open window.

"She's stronger than you, me, and David put together. Mike, it's gonna be alright. I'll see you tonight. You eating dinner with your brother is going to be a big deal for him. It really is. It'll make him happy."

As I stood in the middle of the street, watching the taillights of Richie's Miata fade at the end of the block, I realized the dinner with David would not only be our first one together since I moved to Boston but also most likely the last.

Thirty-Nine

How pretty and neatly wrapped it would be if I could say that the shock and emotional fallout of that morning immediately jolted me towards enlightenment and paved the way for a great epiphany. Life doesn't work that way though, does it? And the terrifying grip of anorexia most certainly does not yield that easily.

I spent many years trying to get some distance from the guilt and shame of my darkest days in Allston. Getting over losing David? Well, I doubt I'll ever make peace with that. But I'm trying. It takes time. A lot of time. Let me tell you, though, I've come to understand one thing for sure: you must achieve genuine separation from your past before you can begin to rewrite the fiction other people believe is your reality.

Throughout the first few months after I left, Mon thought the trauma of David's death would set me back, and I'd lapse into starvation again. That simply did not happen, and I've managed to maintain my weight without letting the bottom drop out. Perhaps there's a statute of limitations on such pain and recrimination.

Okay, okay, I know that sounds like a Counting Crows song. Let's not get too romantic. The truth is, as time passed, I experienced just enough brief moments of clarity and love amid all the white noise to make life worth living once more. Yes, of course, I also firmly believed David would never have wanted me to shrug at life again, and simply give up. As we all eventually discover, the road to some kind of meaning can be a crooked, perilous path. That is if the road doesn't ultimately lead to a dead end.

I can't let you think the years after Boston were easy or anything close to what others might deem normal. There were many more stumbles to come, but the thing about stumbling is, you usually end up falling forward.

As I sit here writing today, I have to confess: I still never eat without a trace of unease and doubt. What I told Dr. Hampton on the phone was eerily prescient. The anxiety never goes away completely—the intensity just diminishes. I can say with pride, though, that I'm running again, and I've managed to find what Mon once described as the happy medium. I call it my own private comfortable level of discomfort.

I wish I could also say I eat with the kind of enthusiasm and casual assurance of Anthony Bourdain throwing back mongoose eyes and rattlesnake tails deep in the bowels of Cambodia. It sure would be nice. It just wouldn't be true. You can wait for that ending in the Lifetime movie of someone else's story.

In fact, I still scramble to make some kind of sense out of my life, but I also find small things to keep me grounded. The memories of the last moments I spent with David definitely helped carry me through many rough times, and I continue to hold them dear to my heart. Throughout the afternoon, he carefully explained how and when he found out about the brain tumor. Unfortunately, I recognized its appearance coincided precisely with Jessie leaving. Of course, I couldn't help but think there might be some weird, cosmic significance in the timing. I was worried that someday I'd find a Ken doll with a safety pin through its head on a deserted beach.

You see, I was still seized by an insistent paranoia about some grand plan of retribution at work. It was all part of the illness, which spread its powerful tentacles in so many directions. So, as David napped that Friday, I repeatedly detailed my elaborate theory of universal vengeance to Mon while we walked through the streets of Back Bay, crowded with moving vans and wandering, bright-eyed freshmen filled with big dreams.

She took off her sunglasses and looked at me with disbelief. "Now don't be silly. Please don't go down that avenue again. You're grasping to try and connect the dots, just like I did. We have to let that go. Michael, who knows? Just maybe there are no dots at all. You know in your heart it's all coincidence, and nothing more than a random overlap of events."

"Mon, I realize that's supposed to make me feel better, but isn't it a fucked-up thing? The idea that we're all just clowns running around with our pants down in a crazy, chaotic circus. That just doesn't make it all go down easy. I gotta tell you, a lot of times I think there are things going on in my life, and I just don't know what they are or why they're happening."

Mon offered a loose-limbed sweep of dismissal with her hand. Two tall young men in Boston University t-shirts waved back comically while staring at her over their shoulders. "Forget about easy," she said while taking long strides. "And answers, Michael? We know better than that."

We walked on, buoyed by an unusually warm late afternoon breeze at our backs, through the sun-soaked city streets. After well over an hour, we ended up sitting by the edge of the reflecting pool in the middle of the Christian Science Center plaza. Mon strolled to the far end of the Copley side and exuberantly shouted to me. Her slim silhouette was barely visible amid running children and kneeling tourists taking pictures of the water surface—a sheet of glass seemingly without boundaries. She aimlessly wandered, her eyes to the sky and her fingers skimming the pool's tranquil water.

"It's so beautiful here. Like an oasis. This is something so still, so lovely. It helps me feel at peace," she said as we walked away.

Richie returned in the early evening with three bags of groceries and proceeded to cook us an elaborate fish dinner. I marveled and the care and tenderness he put into deboning the fish and preparing his fresh pasta. It was like an obsessive artist at work—he seemed to do it all as an act of devotion. I wasn't sure if I had ever put that much effort into anything in my life. The four of us ate while looking out over the Charles River amid candlelight with *In a Silent Way* serenading us. It was David's favorite album—he used to play it in his bedroom when I was counting baseball cards or munching on buttered bagels while watching cartoons.

As Richie poured wine, Monique placed a small dish of wasabi on the table next to my plate and forced me to recount our night of sushi on fire. Somehow, she still found it wildly amusing. When I told the story, she gleefully wagged her tongue, imitating my desperate attempt to drink milk.

They all laughed and reminisced throughout the night like nothing was amiss. Although it was jarring to watch David struggle to eat in slow motion and walk so cautiously, seeing him smile and look at Monique with such love and adoration brought me a kind of unbridled joy I'd rarely felt before. It was brief and fleeting but so real, and something I'll never forget. I was sitting, seemingly suspended in time and somehow outside of reality, with the three people I loved so much.

After eating, I patiently listened to Richie regale us with wild stories of driving cross country with David. He recounted how he nearly got his ear cut off in a backwoods Oklahoma bar by an angry, drunk woman who thought he looked like an evil Van Gogh. He said he was surprised by the pocket knife in her cleavage, and even more shocked to find out she'd ever heard of Van Gogh. All I could focus on was my brother's uproarious laughter—the pain just seemed to drain from his face.

Mon spent part of the night describing her raucous adventures as a teenager, traveling from city to city on the trail of different punk bands. I never saw that side of her and couldn't imagine her sweating through a mosh pit or crowd surfing. She had tears of happiness running down her face while recalling doing backstage bong hits with the members of the very young Bad Brains in a small Washington D. C. club.

"One time, I woke up two mornings later with my girlfriend, poolside on the roof of a hotel in Las Vegas," she said, punctuating the story with a loud clap of her hands. "I still don't know how I got there, and to this day I don't have a clue about what must have happened in between. But let me tell you, those were the best days, Michael. It may be hard to believe, but I was a real-deal hardcore nut. And God, I genuinely loved every minute of it."

"And then when she ultimately met me, it was straight into Stankonia," David replied with a grin. He calmly eyed Mon gesticulating with both hands and flipping her hair to music only she could hear.

Monique threw a few grapes at his chest before embracing him as if she was never going to let go.

I remained quiet and still, like a young child holding onto a fading Christmas evening. David barely made it to the finale of the Letterman repeat, though, and quietly bowed out with a sigh. He hugged Richie, who glanced over his shoulder towards me as he departed.

"You call me tomorrow, wherever you are," Richie whispered.

David nodded to Monique as she blew out the candles before slipping away into the bedroom. When she disappeared, he asked me to retrieve her glass of wine. "Don't say anything," he said while the last notes of Marcus Roberts' *Blues for the New Millennium* played.

"Mike, I'm not going to push things or say much. I think you know what you need to do for yourself, and you sure as hell don't need any more advice from me. I probably gave you too much over the years. I do want you to know one thing, though. I realize you might have some lingering resentment about what happened between me and Jessie all this time. Especially that night I told her to leave you."

"David, I don't. We settled this a long time ago. Stop." If I could have put my fingers in my ears without embarrassing myself, I would have done it. Excavating the past and drawing Jessie back into our lives were the furthest things from my mind.

David was determined to finish. "I know we talked, but I also know human nature. And bottom line, I need to tell you this. She was your girlfriend. I have a lot of regrets, and I fucked up a lot, but I guess what I regret most is getting in the way there."

"I don't want to talk about it, please, c'mon. It's one thing we both need to let go. I know you did what you thought was right."

He continued with his palm out, almost begging me to pay attention. "Thing is, I don't really know if it was right to get between you two. These days, what I once was sure about, I'm not anymore. I got in the way, but Jessie was smart enough to not give a fuck about me, and move on because she had to. Monique told me Jessie's pregnant and happy today. Well, I know that's right for sure.

"What I'm trying to say, Mike, is you need to make a choice that has nothing to do with me also. I know after tonight, the urge for you is to stay. I get that, but we both know what's ahead won't be like tonight. I'm tired, and I'm just not thinking clearly. Just understand, I get up quite late in the morning. I want you to take this now." He reached into his wallet and pulled out a check.

"You gave me money. No." I was afraid to push his arm away—he appeared so small and vulnerable. My "no" seemed much too final, like my last repudiation, so I relented. Unsteady on his feet while finishing the wine, he slipped the check in my shirt pocket. I approached to help him, but he quickly snapped to attention once I touched his shoulder.

"Just take and cash it. It's for therapy. Mon will transfer you more once you settle and get a doctor." David took off his black 49ers cap to scratch his bumpy scalp before looking at the hat with a smile. Finally, he tossed it onto the dinner table.

"Mom would say never put a hat on a table. It's bad luck, remember that?" He gently squeezed my elbow. "I guess something bad is going to happen to me now."

I refused to laugh at the memory because I knew I would end up breaking down.

"So be smart. When I get up in the morning and sit down with Monique, I'm going to be thinking of you in a good, warm place. Because that's the choice you have to make. You know I love you, Michael." He kissed me on the forehead and held me with what had to be all his strength.

As he stepped away, David looked back to me. "You know what I can't get over? The one thing that I'll never live down?"

I shook my head timidly, unable to look at him.

"That my brain failed me. You believe that? Who the fuck would have ever thought that? I'll talk to you tomorrow when you land, okay? Call first thing. We'll help get things in motion for you. I still know many good people at a lot of schools. It's all going to work out. It really will."

Of course, I didn't sleep and spent most of the night collecting my thoughts in my journal while wrapped in a blanket Mon had set out on the couch. Despite the unusually balmy September weather, for some reason I was so cold that I ended up retrieving an extra comforter from the bathroom closet. I repacked my bag three times—it just never seemed right—and throughout the early morning, I watched the same CNN report on the assassination of a sect leader in Afghanistan at the top and bottom of each hour.

With sunrise still about an hour away, I took a long shower before preparing to leave. After sitting alone on the bathtub edge for minutes, I hesitantly entered the kitchen—walking quietly across the hardwood floors like a monk over rice paper.

"You weren't going to say goodbye? I see your bag packed next to the door." Mon smiled at me with arms crossed, a cup of coffee in her hand. She was fully dressed in jeans and a crisp, white t-shirt.

"No, of course not. I just didn't want to wake you."

"You think I could sleep? I was going to come watch CNN with you, but I wasn't sure you wanted company, and I can't watch the world implode. Not now. Every time I see that moron Bush, I want to throw up." She exhaled deeply while waving me towards the breakfast bar. "Sit down. You need to eat something before you go anywhere. I'll make us some eggs."

I was set on taking a long walk before eating anything. "I'm fine for now, Mon. I'm not…"

"Uh, uh, uh, no. Sit. We'll eat together. You probably noticed I need to gain some weight. I've been living on coffee and nerves for months. And you're going to be doing this every day. No one's going to be there to remind you. Did you figure out where you are going yet?"

"When I get to Logan, I'm going to choose." I sat with her hovering over me.

"Okay, I see you've carefully thought this out," Mon said after startling me by turning on all the lights.

"I may just take a few bong hits, and see which city I end up in a few days from now," I said as Mon began scrambling some eggs.

"Yeah, right. Touché. At least someone was paying attention." She was dimly smiling while rummaging through a box of pastries. The front door opened, allowing for Maria to quietly enter.

"Good morning Maria, he's fine." With a smile, Mon acknowledged the quiet, still woman. "I'll be in with you shortly." She placed her fingers under the faucet before cooling her cheeks. "She's been a godsend.

There from the beginning. We put her up at the Copley. There really are good people in the world, Michael. Never forget that."

When the bedroom door clicked closed, she continued. "So, tell me, are you sure about this? I mean really sure?"

"Someone once told me if I needed to be sure about everything, I'd probably never get out of bed in the morning. I think she was right, Mon. Turns out she was right about a lot of things."

"None of that really matters now, does it? What matters is you know how to make scrambled eggs, right?" Monique neatly filled my plate and poured a glass of milk.

"You crack eggs and scramble. I'll watch *Yan Can Cook* 'till I get it right. I'll be fine. I swear. Monique, please, there's one thing you have to tell me before I go, and it isn't about eggs or any stupid food." She ate out of the frying pan and broke a pastry in half. I watched her swallow before I continued. "How'd you do it? How are you doing it?"

She squinted after taking a small bite out of the buttery puff. "Do what?"

"Keep it together. You knew all the time we went out and I was here, but you always still seemed like you."

"I didn't keep it together. When I wasn't here, I was a wreck—especially, in the spring. When I was with you, well, I don't know how to say it, but this seemed like a different life. You didn't know, and I wasn't going to let you. I tried to forget about all David was going through, and be present with you.

"Obviously, I could never forget. I wanted to be with him, but I couldn't, so tried to put it out of my mind for the time we were together. And that became my reality. It was like living two lives. And this one kind of kept me going. I know that's strange, but it's true. I was seeing you eating and looking better every time I came back. It gave me strength."

I had long finished my eggs, so I sat quietly to watch the sun come up over Mon's shoulder. She opened a drawer of the cabinets to search for a band to tie back her hair. "Mon, give me that phone book in there. I'm going to call the taxi," I said.

"You know I'd drive you," she replied, her voice quavering.

"You are going back to bed to get some sleep. I have the number right here." There was a Yellow Cab ad on the back of the book cover. "I love talking to cranky taxi drivers in Red Sox hats. They have an endearing kind of pent-up hostility indigenous to this city."

Monique handed me two pastries she had wrapped in aluminum foil. "For the road."

"Now that definitely sounds strange." I had never left anyone behind.

"Mon, you know I'm going to miss you. I can't thank…"

"Don't do that, please. Not now. Let's just say, I'll talk to you later. Remember, no Newark," she said, wiping the corner of her small nostrils with her fingers. "Think sun."

I squeezed her hand before making the long walk down the hallway to say one last goodbye to my brother. The door was slightly ajar. Maria was sitting in the corner, watching over David sleeping quietly beneath a royal blue blanket—his thin forearms exposed. While I watched his slow, silent breathing, I knew it would have been selfish to wake him. We were at a place beyond words anyway.

I walked on to find Monique waiting by the umbrella rack and quickly embraced her while trying desperately to maintain my composure. She squared me up to hold my biceps in each hand. "You know, I never ever wanted to tell you what to do, but all I ask is for you to eat."

"I swear I will. I'm telling you, I'll do it for David."

Mon hugged me again, this time drawing me close. "No, Michael, no, not for David. You do it for you. It's gotta be for you." She touched my face with the base of her palm as the phone rang. "That's the taxi. You go. We'll be waiting for you to call."

I struggled to breathe as I sat in the back of the musty cab idling in the middle of the quiet street. "Can you head to Fenway Park?"

"Early bird," the hack said with a hearty laugh. I merely needed time to gather myself and prepare for the unknown. When we arrived on Lansdowne Street, I told him to slowly circle the stadium a few times. After the third leisurely lap, I asked if he could park in front of the Green Monster, the large looming wall in left field.

"You alright, captain? You know the meter's running, my man," the thickly bearded cabbie said in a Haitian accent.

"I'm fine now. Just saying a last goodbye—it's weird, I can't believe I'm going to miss all this. Let's go to Logan."

The main floor of the terminal was practically empty while I surveyed the flight charts after a quick stop at the ATM. If I wanted to live in Nebraska, Chicago or St. Paul, I could have left within the hour, but I knew precisely where I was going. I waited for two more hours to board the plane with nothing but my single bag and a lifetime of uncertainty.

I was seated by the window in the back of the plane, next to a deeply bronzed woman with Angie Jolie lips and blonde highlights in her sun-drenched red hair. She talked incessantly to the man across the aisle while standing to take a book from the overhead bin. As she laughed freely, I sat buckled in like John Glenn blasting into space. Every time the slightest bit of turbulence hit, I looked out the window to see if we had lost an engine or if perhaps a meteor was on the way.

Throughout the first hour of the flight, I kept adjusting the seatbelt away from my stomach while writing in my journal. A pretty, middle-aged Latina flight attendant with a magnificent smile and warm, sympathetic eyes attempted to give me a bag of peanuts as she passed my seat.

After the man on the aisle fell asleep with a black mask over his eyes, the woman next to me finished her Sprite and looked up from *The Unbearable Lightness of Being* spread out on her tray. "You realize peanuts are free, and you can breathe a little. You turn blue if you don't. Your first flight?"

I stuffed the journal in my bag, next to the two pastries Mon had given me. "Shocking you can tell I've never flown. Embarrassing, but true," I winced. "I keep thinking we are going to suddenly fall out of the sky."

She nudged my arm with her elbow. "They have pretty much perfected the technology. I'm not sure, but it might have been a few years ago. You a writer?"

"Not yet. Maybe never. My brother's a writer. He's the best—he really is. I see you reading Kundera. You like it?" I readjusted in the seat and sat back, her smile allowing me to rest.

"I'm just scanning this. Every time I visit Boston, my family sends me off with some deep book they think I should read. They think it's brain food for us Philistines." She crossed her long, tan legs, fingered her wedding ring with a large mounted diamond, and leaned in. "I have Steven King in my luggage. And who knows, maybe someday I'll read a book you write."

I laughed quietly with my head resting against the window. "The odds of that are slim and none."

She tossed her hair back with her left hand before placing the book with the magazines in the pocket of the front seat near her calves.

"Perfect then, let's say none just left town, leaving slim. Here Slim," she smiled. "Have my extra bag of peanuts. I'm Tina. It's a long flight, and we're not getting a meal for a while. I'm going to go for a walk. When I get back, I'll tell you about a book idea I have. Maybe you can write it for me. I have so many stories. We all do." She dropped the bag of peanuts in my hand and wiggled out of the seat, leaving behind traces of perfume. "Hey, you are not stuck, you know. You're free to get up. You can do what you want."

I placed the salty peanuts in my mouth one at a time while listening to Tina's hearty laugh echoing down the aisle. Finally, I released the seat belt to take a long, slow breath. When the cabin teetered, I peered out the window back towards Boston, which was long, long gone. The plane plowed through a mass of clouds dotting the sky. Everything seemed so serene and calm, even though we were making our way furiously forward.

While I stared into the emptiness and thought about David and Mon, a great white mist rolled past, as it has for years and years and years.

Acknowledgements

This book would not have been possible without the dozens of doctors, nurses, EMTs, and psychiatrists who helped keep me alive throughout my long fight with anorexia. I especially want to thank everyone who worked at St. Elizabeth's Hospital in Brighton, Massachusetts between the late 1980's and early 2000's. I spent so much time at St. E's, they probably kept a room open while waiting for my arrival.

I would also like to thank all of the many music editors I've worked with so far—every one of you made me a better writer and supported me even when the trap door of my life was falling out. A standing ovation goes to Tris Lozaw, Steve Morse, and Ed Symkus for getting me started.

A special shout out goes to Dr. Jack Salzman, the man who opened the window to the world and told me to go out and ask questions. Thank you for your brilliance and nearly 40 years of non-stop support. As I've often said to you: You turned my life around—after I met you, I went from feeling horrible and miserable to feeling miserable and horrible (they love that in the Catskills).

Of course, many thanks to my family who always supported me throughout the lean years. To my always supportive late mom and dad—my greatest regret is never sharing a meal with you during my adult life. Thanks to my brother Rich, the world's Yoda, for throwing me through the basement wall (that's truth and metaphor). To Viv, for the help and all the spinach quiches I almost ate. To Nick, for reading an early draft and your continued encouragement and friendship. To Stefan and Alex, thank you—I confess, I truly apologize for being MIA during most of your childhoods while I was in and out of hospitals. To Maryann and Fred, for an entire lifetime of support, Packers jerseys, and for always boosting me up with phone calls during every one of my hospital stays. Those calls helped me to make it through the lonely nights. Much love to both of you.

A holler to everyone in the Boston rock and roll and hip-hop communities of the 1980's and 1990's—fellow music critics, musicians, bookers, radio DJ's, and publicists. It was the music and camaraderie